"It throws *flame*," ̶ ̶ ̶ ̶ ̶ ̶ ̶obvious, the horrific.

"Little man, it burns disobedient cattle. ̶I̶t̶ ̶w̶i̶l̶l̶ ̶ ̶you. *I* will burn you. I, Carcharoth, Balrog of the Citadel. Come to me! Learn the truth."

A pause. Then Barak shouted, "Who here is brave?" It nearly started a riot but he shortly had his death chargers. The commandos sprinted single file out onto the narrow strip of stone. Behind them, assault rifles snapped viciously.

When the first to charge was nearly across, Carcharoth rose, just a little, just for an instant. A hissing roar like a thousand land gators filled the air and a great billowing shaft of fire engulfed the men of the first onslaught. Living torches tumbled one by one into the abyss; bare seconds after the charge began, the bridge again stood empty, inviting.

"Come to me," Carcharoth crooned.

They took more time readying the next assault, forming the attackers well behind the tunnel, positioning the riflemen to better advantage. Again the assault rifles crackled forth, again the attackers made the best speed they could across the bridge, this time well spaced, forcing the Cyborg to spend a burst of flame for each victim.

Carcharoth incinerated them, one and all. "I am the Balrog, flame of Udûn!"

The third group, spaced a little more tightly as they learned through bitter experience the limits of the Balrog's flame, advanced over the bridge. As before, Carcharoth let the leader get nearly across, then crisped with individual bursts. How many gone? Near a hundred now. "I am the Redeemer!" Carcharoth shouted. "Through me, the Citadel lives!"

He was crazy, but that didn't make him wrong.

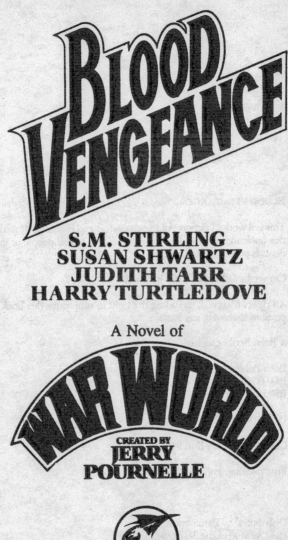

# BLOOD VENGEANCE

**S.M. STIRLING
SUSAN SHWARTZ
JUDITH TARR
HARRY TURTLEDOVE**

A Novel of

## WAR WORLD

**CREATED BY
JERRY POURNELLE**

BAEN

BLOOD VENGEANCE

Copyright © 1994 by Jerry Pournelle

A Baen Books Original

Baen Publishing Enterprises
P.O. Box 1403
Riverdale, NY 10471

ISBN: 0-671-72201-8

Cover art by Gary Ruddell

First printing, January 1994

Distributed by Paramount
1230 Avenue of the Americas
New York, NY 10020

Printed in the United States of America

# DEDICATION

To Iskander and Jim Grim and Shahrazed, Kim and T.E. Lawrence and Flashman, to John Carter, Khlit the Cossack and King of the Khyber Rifles and J.E. Flecker . . . and to all who played the Great Game and took the Golden Road to Samarkand.

To Homer and Sophocles for the grand scheme of things.

To horse thieves everywhere.

We'd also like to thank Dr. Jerry Pournelle for graciously allowing us to turn Haven upside down, John Carr for composure in the face of the revolution, and Baen Books for saying "yes."

We are obligated to James D. MacDonald, former sysop of the Science Fiction Round Table on GEnie, Martha Soukup, the current sysop, and Katherine Lawrence, topic leader, for work space and forbearance. We also gratefully acknowledge the help of many members of GEnie's Military Round Table.

Special thanks to GEnie friends and co-conspirators for their assistance and, in many cases, allowing their names to be taken in vain: Robert "Mr. Spook" Glaub; William "Sapper" Gross; John "The Hammer of God" Johnston III; Richard "Captain Kirk" Kirka; Al Nofi; Tim "Plez" Pleasant; Trent "Flamingo" Telenko; and Mark "Raven" Turnage. Thanks also to Master Sergeant Lance Bolun, U.S. Army.

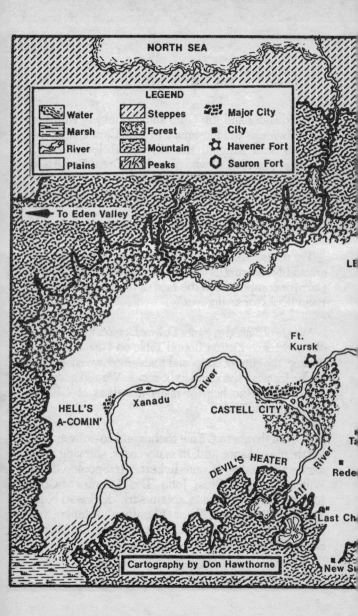

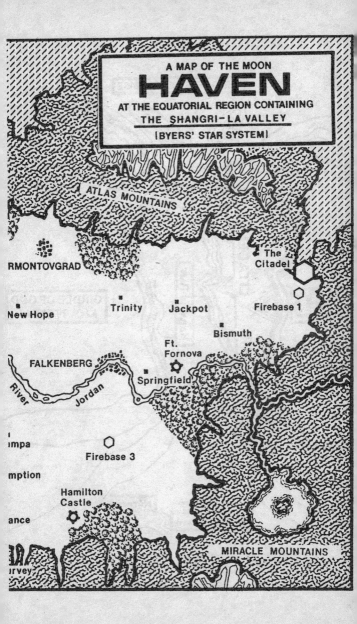

A MAP OF THE MOON
# HAVEN
AT THE EQUATORIAL REGION CONTAINING
THE SHANGRI-LA VALLEY
(BYERS' STAR SYSTEM)

ATLAS MOUNTAINS

RMONTOVGRAD

The Citadel

Trinity       Jackpot

New Hope                              Firebase 1

Bismuth

Ft. Fornova

FALKENBERG                Springfield

River       Jordan

mpa

Firebase 3

mption

Hamilton Castle

ance

MIRACLE MOUNTAINS

rvey

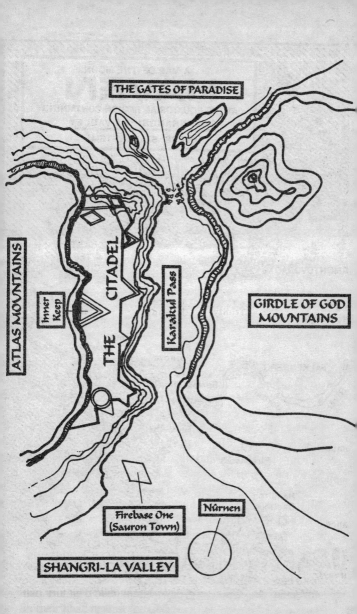

# • WHAT HAS GONE BEFORE

Under the CoDominium, under the Empire of Man—for six centuries Haven had been a place of exile, a dumping ground for the unwanted, the inconvenient, the dissident, and the criminal. There the weak died and the strong, the clever, the hardy survived; just barely, for Haven was among the harshest of all the worlds settled by man, a world described by its discoverer as a place where life had, not precisely a niche, but a loophole. The last survivors of the gene-engineered warriors of Sauron found it a haven indeed, fleeing the burning wreck of their world and the shattered chaos their attempt at conquest had made of the Empire of Man. Civilization was nearly dead among the stars, and wholly dead on Haven—destroyed in the Saurons' initial bombardment. Technology was ruthlessly suppressed, lest the Empire of Man find the last Sauron haven. A priestly caste, hidden from all but the highest ranks, tended weapons and equipment that no Soldier understood.

From the Citadel and their lesser Bases the Soldiers of Sauron began to breed their Race anew, and struggled to subdue their new home. From it they took tribute, most of all, the tribute maidens for their breeding program. The best of their children were bred back into the Soldier stock, the rest exposed on the culling grounds.

Three hundred years later, two children were rescued from the culling field of Angband Base, a brother and a sister. The sister became Judge of the Bandari; the brother, Juchi, later called the Accursed, rose to be war-captain and *khan* among the nomads. Together they cast down Angband.

Juchi is dead, but his children and his sister live. Together they have raised the valleys and the plains, nomad and farmer, Turk and Americ, Russki and Jew—united for the first time. United in Holy War against the Citadel. For three hundred and fifty years the Saurons have ruled Haven. Now is the time of . . . Blood Vengeance.

# • PROLOGUE

Truenight on Haven, three hundred and fifty years after *Dol Guldur* fell, three hundred and fifty years since the rise of the Sauron Dominion.

Truenight, beneath a vault of stars that had grown beyond the reach of any man on Haven, even were he Soldier and Cyborg. Truenight, but the earth blazed with light. Campfires spread far across the steppe, and figures leaped and capered around them, singing a song of victory.

> *"Turn around and go back down,*
> *Back the way you came—*
> *Don't you see the flash of fire*
> *Ten times brighter than the day?*
> *and—*
> *Oh, Lord, the pride of man,*
> *broken in the dust again!"*

Oh, there was pride, raised up on pikes for Haven's cattle to leer and spit at. Fifty-six light-skinned, blade-nosed heads hacked from their bodies—near two fighting Groups of Sauron Soldiers, dead at the hands of common stinking human men.

> *"Turn around and go back down,*
> *Back the way you came—*
> *Terror is on every side,*
> *And your leaders are dismayed,*
> *The mighty men we've beaten down,*
> *Your kings we scatter in the waste:*
> *and—*

> *Oh, Lord, the pride of man,*
>     *broken in the dust again!"*

No Soldier would ever stoop to call himself a king, but any one of them had strength to put human kings to shame. There was Atanamir, commander from the Citadel, staring blind into the leaping light. A hundred of the cattle had fallen before his assault rifle, half a hundred more to his naked hands, before the sheer mass of them overwhelmed him and a shrieking mob of Bandari warriors tore him limb from limb. There was Hurin whose brother Turin had been a Cyborg, experiment in twinned offspring, one superaugmented, one simple Soldier; but the Cyborg had died of lethal recessives before he reached maturity, and the Soldier was dead of a Frystaater hammer in the skull. There was Odo, there was Isengrim, there was Grima with his jaw hacked away and an expression of perfect astonishment on what was left of his face. The cattle had killed them all. And would kill every Soldier on Haven, if this war achieved its object.

> *"Turn around and go back down,*
>     *Back the way you came—*
> *Take a warning to your peoples*
>     *That the Sword of God is raised!*
> *and—*
>     *Oh, Lord, the pride of man,*
>     *broken in the dust again!"*

They fancied themselves the very Sword of God, this horde of many tens of thousands strong. They accreted like a dung-beetle's ball of filth, rolling eastward across Haven. They aimed themselves at a Citadel that, they prayed their manifold gods, was emptied, its defenders lured away to quell a false rebellion at the farthest end of the Shangri-La Valley.

They dared what no herd of cattle had ever dared. They had taken a miserable outpost manned by boys and a worn-out old Soldier, and plumed themselves on a victory won by a trick as old as Nineveh. A wagonload of Finnegan's fig brandy and muskylope oil, a judicious quantity of gunpowder, a spark—and death to the Saurons. They had fought a vicious skirmish with a herd of loyal cattle and two assault groups of ordinary Soldiers, not even a Cyborg cub to give them distinction, and they believed, some of them honestly believed, that they could conquer the heart of Sauron on Haven.

> *"Turn around and go back down,*
> *Back the way you came—*
> *See Babylon, the mighty city,*
> *Rich in treasure, wide in fame:*
> *We have brought her towers down,*
> *Made of her a pyre of flame.*
> *and—*
> *Oh, Lord, the pride of man,*
> *broken in the dust again!"*

Sigrid sat in the flicker of the firelight, with the shadows of the pikes falling long across her lifted face. Her eyes, she knew, gleamed red when the light struck them. She would have concealed them if she had cared. There was a blanket wrapped about her—she did not remember how she had come by it, nor did she need its warmth. But it was comfort, the comfort of something to hold onto in a world run out of control. Under it she clasped arms about her pregnant belly, and nudged feet against the warm breathing weight of dogs who persisted in leaning against her.

"One down," said a voice too joyous to gloat, "twenty-nine to go."

Her eyes darted to the speaker, a blocky little Bandari *meid* with a rat's nest of black hair and a face that seemed set in a permanent sulk. The blue eyes were smoky with pleasure. "You should listen," the little bitch said. *"Babylon is fallen.* And so is Old Sauron, and there's a curse on her seed. Where are our enemies, Pharaoh, Romans, Germans, Philistines, time out of mind? Ashes on the wind—as the Citadel will be."

*Cant*, thought Sigrid. *Cattle boasting.* A hundred thousand of them had just managed to deal with two units of Soldiers. Units that, if not taken by surprise—otherwise they would not have been accompanied by an alliance of loyal tribes—certainly had not expected to find such opposition as they had found.

But there were only fifty-six pikes, and fifty-six heads. Sigrid could account for two more in Soldiers blown to chopped meat and bonemeal by the explosive bombs the Bandari had, surprisingly, possessed. That left two—and she had found sign of Soldiers running light, faster than a horse could gallop, eastward—running to the Citadel.

> *"Thy holy mountain be restored—*
> *Thy favor on Thy people, Lord!"*

*Yes*, thought Sigrid. *Whose favor, and whose people?* This was an army to give even a Soldier pause, but it had done nothing yet. It would break on the rock of the Citadel, break and fall. She had no faith, not she who was Soldier and Cyborg and Breedmaster's daughter, but she believed in clean reason—and reason said that the Citadel would win.

The Bandari woman was gone. She knew what Sigrid was: she babbled it all over the army. No one believed her. That was Sigrid's protection. And maybe Sigrid was arrogant and should die as these Soldiers had died, fighting to the last drop of the blood and the last molecule of breath. But being female and Cyborg both, and pregnant by no less than a Bandari of the Founder's line, she had other—and perhaps greater—priorities.

She would endure. And so, she swore to herself in the smoke and the firelight and the near-sexual reek of blood and battle, would the Race and the Citadel in which it was bred.

Battlemaster Carcharoth stood in the doorway, waiting for Titus to notice him. The Breedmaster took a few seconds to finish scribbling a note before he looked up.

Among Cyborgs, that was studied rudeness. Carcharoth felt his body chemistry surge toward anger, suppressed it without conscious thought. He could allow himself no weaknesses, not when facing one of his own kind. Titus' voice was friendly enough when he deigned to speak: "Here, sit down. Will you take tea?" At Carcharoth's nod, the Breedmaster poured from an elegant silver samovar: tribute from the New Soviet Men in the distant west of the Shangri-La Valley. Carcharoth sipped the tea with care, not because it was hot but to see if he could taste any lurking wrongness. Poison had its occasional place in the power games the elite of the Citadel played among themselves. He tasted nothing out of the ordinary, nor did his stomach twist when he swallowed. *Sometimes tea is just tea*, he thought.

Titus poured himself a glass, too, then returned to his own seat. When Carcharoth looked at him, he saw his daughter Sigrid. She had the looks too: pale hair; ice-blue eyes; long, narrow-chinned face with thrusting cheekbones. Sigrid was . . . a problem. Carcharoth didn't care to be reminded of problems that weren't immediately urgent. He had enough that were. The samovar set off uneasy association patterns in his brain: it called to mind the rebellion the New Soviet Men had raised against the Citadel along with their usual rivals, the Sons of Liberty.

Which led to business: "The Threat Analysis Computer did not predict an outbreak of revolt in the West for some time to come."

"I know that only too well," Titus answered. "Our technicians are examining the TAC for programming glitches, data retrieval failures, and even hardware problems. Should the latter prove to be the case—"

He spread his hands. The Threat Analysis Computer had come from Old Sauron, the murdered Homeworld, aboard the *Dol Guldur* three hundred and fifty T-years before. Technicians might be able to spot what had gone wrong with it, but the technology for repairs simply didn't exist on Haven; one of the smaller models from the outlying

Bases wouldn't have the database to be useful. Titus seemed calm enough contemplating the breakdown of the TAC, but then Titus was Breedmaster, used to working with the statistical uncertainties of genetics. For a Cyborg, he had an unusually flexible mind.

Carcharoth's ran in more familiar Cyborg channels. When he eliminated data from consideration, he eliminated them completely. When he was right, as he was most of the time, that was an asset: it let him concentrate unhindered on the optimum solutions for threats. When he was wrong—being wrong had cost Glorund, the Battlemaster before Carcharoth, his life. He'd reckoned the woman with Juchi the Accursed just a nomad and paid for it when legend proved true and she proved to share the Soldier genes of her father/brother. Oh, Juchi's quartered corpse hung on pikes outside the city of Nûrnen, but even Juchi's life for that of a Cyborg was the worst of bargains.

"I relied heavily on the accuracy of the TAC," Carcharoth said. "Ever since the Race came to Haven, we have relied on the accuracy of the TAC. So far as I know, it never failed us—till now."

He stopped there. He did not have a name for the unease that trickled through him, that skulked round the edges of his ordered thoughts and showed its leering face whenever he least expected it. Such emotions were not supposed to mar the genetically enhanced, biomechanically augmented stability and power of his mind. Superstitious dread was the province of the steppe nomads and Haven's other human cattle, not of the Soldiers, most especially not of the Cyborg supermen who led the Soldiers. No wonder Carcharoth failed to recognize it when it gripped him. Titus said, "We all relied on the TAC's accuracy, Battlemaster. But now its potential for inaccuracy is but one more factor that will have to enter into our calculations. We can still use it, but henceforward, at least until the anomaly is detected, it will be but one tool among many. Perhaps we have counted on it too heavily up to this point. We are accurate enough calculators ourselves, not so?"

His armor of Cyborg assurance—not to put too fine a point on it, Cyborg arrogance—remained undented and undaunted. Carcharoth wished the same could have been said of his own. He'd counted on the TAC to be right, and it had been wrong. Not only were its calculations inaccurate, his were, too. Along with nature's imperative to reproduce his kind, genetic engineering had imbued two chief drives into those of the Soldiers who wore the *Totenkopf* on their collar tabs: to fight and to calculate. Having his calculations fail him was as alarming for Carcharoth as impotence or uncontrollable cowardice would have been, and argued for something badly wrong inside him.

Titus coughed. "I said, we are accurate enough calculators ourselves, not so?"

"Eh? Oh, certainly, Breedmaster." Again, an unaugmented man, even a non-Cyborg Soldier, would have known anger or alarm. All Carcharoth felt was embarrassment at having been caught woolgathering. Titus was no fool—he could detect stress even in one of his own kind. And, sure enough, Titus also hesitated before continuing. Carcharoth recognized that hesitation: *incorporating an evaluation of my revealed weakness into his own schema.* He would have raged at that had he not recognized weakness in himself. He did his best to recover: "Aside from the uprising of the New Soviet Men and the Sons of Liberty, the most urgent matters before us appear to be the Bandari-led turmoil on the northern steppe and the disappearance of the Cyborg Sigrid, your daughter. I hope the TAC was also in error when it assigned the connection between those two events a probability of sixty-one percent, plus or minus 12."

There had been a lot of talk about Sigrid in the corridors of power in the Citadel. Sigrid herself, though, had proved more partial to action than talk—like any Cyborg worth the name. "When dealing with intermediate probabilities, the chance of separating error from mere randomness becomes vanishingly small," Titus answered.

"Perhaps I was in error myself when I permitted her gestation to go forward. As with the difficulties exhibited by the TAC, however, at present we can but deal with the datum as it exists; retroactive revision is not possible."

"True enough." Yes, Carcharoth envied the Breedmaster's shell of imperturbability. He'd been armored so himself, not long before, till doubt wormed its way in. And, just as the Shangri-La Valley west of the Citadel lay open because no danger could conceivably reach it, so doubt, once it had entered his thought processes, had no trouble spreading.

"One fortunate thing," Titus said. "The Council confirmed your judgment—and that of the TAC—that the difficulties on the steppe and in the distant west of the Valley are independent of each other. Our choices would have become more complex were it otherwise."

"Indeed," Carcharoth said. The whole western end of the Shangri-La had blown up, and there were rumblings of discontent in the eastern valley as well. The Soldiers ruled as much by the terror of their reputation as actual physical might; rebellion had to be scotched, and at once.

That was what he had argued, and the Council and First Citizen had accepted it—as they almost always did. Now he was uncertain himself; a novel and alarming experience for a Cyborg. If the Breedmaster wanted to reassure him, he would accept that; at the moment, he would take all the reassurance he could find, the better to resist the worm that gnawed at him from within. If all went well—which is to say, as predicted—he might yet regain full operational capacity.

Without his quite willing it, his eyes slid to the silver samovar once more.

*I'm rid of the Saurons,* Temujin thought bitterly. *I'm supposed to be free.*

Temujin son of Toktai had been getting a lot of grief from the *Atagha tngri,* the spirits who ruled the world, just lately.

First he'd met Sigrid the Cyborg in a Nûrnenite dive. That had been bad luck. Getting drunk had been stupid, and had broken the Yasa of Chingiz *Khan* as well; if he hadn't been drunk he wouldn't have told her of the secret valley of the women warriors, and the breed of horses they kept, horses who could foal on the high steppe. She'd tortured him to get the information, but the first slip had been his.

Becoming besotted with the narrow-faced bitch was worse than bad luck and stupidity—it was the malice of some wind demon, without a doubt. He should have paid a shaman to take the curse off him with a ceremony and a sacrifice.

Going back to Nûrnen to look for her had been stupidity twice confounded. Getting drunk *again* in the same bar and blurting out his knowledge had been beyond all stupidity, and Temujin had been acquiring a healthy respect for that quality over the last T-year. That had earned him a trip to the Red Room, the interrogation chamber of the Citadel—where he learned Sigrid was the daughter of Cyborg Titus, the Breedmaster of the Saurons. It had also gotten him a position as very unwilling guide to the Sauron search party sent out to bring her back.

*I was lucky,* he thought with bitter sarcasm. Lucky that the party turned aside to deal with the advancing nomad horde; Sauron fighting skills were matched only by Sauron arrogance, and by some special favor of the *tngri* he'd lived through the battle and final slaughter of the Saurons. Then that same wind-spirit had snatched away his chance of escape and made him a prisoner once more, of the horde. Who were not charitably inclined to a plainsman found associating with Saurons and wearing a pair of their boots and carrying a purse full of Citadel-minted coins.

*Unfair!* he thought. He'd robbed the purse from a corpse not twenty minutes before the horde scouts caught him.

Now he was worse off than when he was in the hands of the men from the Citadel. They'd trusted their own bodies and senses too well to bother binding him. His present captors, being like him merely human, had roped him up like a sack bound onto a baggage cart, ever since he woke up after a high-speed trip at the end of a lariat looped to a saddle horn.

He wasn't gagged, but when he opened his mouth to speak, one of his captors backhanded him across the face. "Be still, Sauron's dog," the fellow snarled. "You will speak when we ask you questions. Oh yes, you will speak then." He laughed in gloating anticipation.

The Saurons were subtle. They'd tortured his mind with the implied torture of his body. He knew his own plainsfolk too well: subtlety was not their long suit. They'd just start slicing and crushing and burning to get what they wanted from him.

Careless of another wallop, he exclaimed, "Allah and the spirits" —unlike most nomads on the Great Northern Steppe, Temujin's folk worshipped the Eternal Blue Sky, but there was no need to emphasize the point— "you don't *need* to torture me! The Saurons forced me along with them. I'll tell you everything you want to know, down to the stink of the Assault Leader's farts. Just ask!"

The nomad who'd belted him drew back his hand for another blow, but a sharp command— *"Halt!"* —made him pause. It wasn't Turkic, it wasn't a word in the Americ dialect Temujin knew, but its meaning was unmistakable. Even so, Temujin was surprised his captor would obey a woman.

*No, a girl,* he thought, when she heeled her horse to the side of the cart where he could see her. Perhaps seventeen or a little older. And when he could see her well, his heart sank and his testicles crawled up into his belly. *"Tngri* deliver me," he muttered. "Another warrior maid!"

*And a high-ranking one, too,* he thought. She bore precious spoil, a slung Sauron assault rifle, and had more magazines stuffed under her belt. She studied Temujin as if he were a louse she was about to crack between her fingernails. Normally he didn't mind women looking at him;

he was a *khan's* son, and handsome—although the bruises and scabs probably didn't help. This woman's eyes had flaying knives and boiling oil in mind.

He looked at her, too. She was closer to pure Caucasoid than was common on the steppe: closer by blood to the Saurons than he, as a matter of fact. But she was no Soldier, or she'd have heard him muttering. Just a woman, then. Sitting a big horse as if she'd grown there; it was a good horse, too, and iron-shod. Wearing a sheepskin jacket and leather pants and boots, standard garb but cut differently from most he'd seen and of high quality. Two knives on her belt, a saber at her hip, a cased bow at her knee. She was stocky, broad in the shoulders and hips and deep-bosomed for her age, with a weathered, beak-nosed face and bright blue eyes under braided black hair. A silver chain around her neck held an ornament, peeking out from behind the assault rifle's sling: a six-point star.

"HaBandari!" Temujin exclaimed.

"You know me for what I am, eh, Saurons' slave?" she jeered in accented Turkic. Her blue eyes—unnervingly close to Sauron gray—blazed at him. "Well, you're right, by Yeweh—Shulamit bat Miriam fan Gimbutas, at your service." Her laugh told him (as if he hadn't known) that was mockery, not promise. "And I know you for what you are: another one who licks the Citadel's arse. If you weren't a waste of a good round, I'd put a bullet in your guts to watch you die."

"Knife thrusts are cheap," the driver remarked hopefully, drawing his own and touching it to the side of the cart. A shaving of wood curled away from the curved edge.

"No!" Temujin wailed. He'd done altogether too much grovelling for a chief's son lately. "They would have killed me if I hadn't guided them here—"

"Against us?" Shulamit asked softly.

Temujin knew that death walked very close. "Allah and the spirits, no!" he shouted. "Will you listen to me, you mad, vicious bitch? If you murder me before I tell you what you need to know, where is the profit you Bandari are mad for?"

"I ought to murder you just for that crack," Shulamit said. But then, to his vast relief, she started to laugh. "All right, *hotnot*, you got a point. Go ahead an' sing—but you better sing your head off."

Temujin sang and sang; he might have been a tribal bard. And from the bards, he had learned to compress a story, to say a lot in but few words. He told of leaking the secret of Katlinsvale to the Saurons—

"How'd you go and do a stupid thing like that?" Shulamit broke in.

"I was drunk," he answered shamefacedly.

"You damnfool Muslims aren't supposed to drink, so you make twice the jackasses of yourselves when you do get shikkered up," she observed. Since he wasn't about to tell the listening driver he was what Muslims called an idolater, he didn't argue. Besides, she was more or less right.

—and then how, drunk again, he'd made his second mistake in Nûrnen. Shulamit rolled her eyes in eloquent disgust when he admitted that. Through it all, he managed to keep to himself that the Sauron he kept diving into the boiling stewpot for was female. The heartless Bandari whore would only mock him the worse if he admitted that.

The omission left holes in his story: Shulamit, however heartless a whore she might be, spotted them fast enough to prove herself no fool. "Hold on there," she snapped, lifting up a hand palm-out. "You say this first Sauron you blabbed to was supposed to have gone and headed for the Katlinsvale place you were talking about?"

"That's what the two in the Red Room said." Temujin remembered everything in the Red Room most exactly. Fear will do that to a man. He had the feeling he was going to remember this conversation with Shulamit bat Miriam fan Gimbutas forever, too.

"How'd he think he was going to get away with it?" she demanded. "From what you say, those folk won't have men about. Sounds sensible of them," she added in a bitter murmur. *"Dumbkopfs."*

"Well—" Temujin knew he shouldn't pause. Pausing would make her suspicious. *More suspicious*, he amended. "The Sauron wasn't—exactly a man. Her name was Sigrid."

He didn't know what sort of reaction he'd expected from Shulamit. Surprise, yes, and he got that; her eyes widened till white showed all around the irises. But then she jumped from the saddle into the cart. She took his face in her hands, stared deep into his eyes. He thought she was going to break his neck; he could feel the trained strength in those fingers.

Instead she kissed him as a lover would, long and deep, her tongue probing, penetrating, almost raping his mouth. He was so shocked, he nearly forgot to breathe. She pulled away for a moment. Now her eyelids were half-fallen; she might have been on the point of coming. She leaned forward, kissed him again.

"What's going on?" he asked plaintively when she leaped into the saddle and galloped away. "What's going on?"

The driver guffawed. "First rape, *then* torture!" He guffawed again.

"What's going on?" Temujin said again. He got no answer. He didn't even get untied.

# • CHAPTER ONE

Barak bar Sandor fan Reenan, *kapetein* of the Bandari, supreme leader of the Pale of Settlement and the Assembled Congregations of the True Faith, pushed back the stack of papers and groaned. Now he was *kapetein*; so he had to decide if more of the treasury should be spent on schools in Tallinn Valley, or the equally urgent irrigation canals. Both were necessary to knit Tallinn and its folk into the fabric of the Pale. He had to settle the endless squabbles of the Congregations of the Edenites—the original inhabitants of Eden Valley, and after three centuries still far from universally content with Bandari rule. On top of this he had a major undeclared war to run, and the convulsions on the northern steppe had disrupted trade . . . and the folk of the Pale were the primary long-distance merchants of this world of Haven.

*Why does anyone* want *this job?* he thought bitterly. He'd done his best to avoid getting elected to it. Twenty years as *kommandant* and now *this.*

"What's got your stomach in a twist now?" his assistant asked.

"More dispatches from Hammer-of-God," the older man said. Barak was sixty T-years, Old Earth measurement—and right now he felt every one of them. For most of those years he'd been a soldier of the Pale, and the bloody necessities of that trade had seemed hard enough. Being ruler was turning out to be worse, just as he'd feared.

*You died too soon, Mordekai. You should have lived to see this day,* he thought.

The room was warm and brightly lit, even twenty hours into truenight; it was summer, and in Eden Valley that meant that water would scarcely freeze even with the sun and Cat's Eye both out of the sky. Almost tropical, compared to the high steppe.

This house was ancient, built on foundations nearly a thousand years old—back when the CoDominium still ruled Earth, at the dawn of Man's expansion into the universe. The present walls had stood when the First Empire fell and the Saurons came to Haven, in flight from the destruction of their homeworld. Perhaps the Empire still did exist, somewhere—nobody had come to tell them. Haven had been a dumping ground for the CoDominium, and a place of exile under the Empire established by the kings of Sparta. The Saurons seemed to have known what they were doing when they came here looking for a bolt-hole.

The air smelled of coal from the stove, of wax and polish and careful cleaning. He never really felt at home here; it was the smell of Mordekai's house. Old Mordekai had been *Kapetein* for most of Barak's life. All his adult life. Barak looked up to the far wall, where Piet fan Reenan's portrait rested. The sardonic almost-smile of the Founder seemed to comfort and taunt him at once; it had been drawn by Ruth, daughter of Boaz, self-proclaimed Prophet and last Edenite ruler. She had rebelled against her father's madness, and he had hung her from a cross of iron outside the city walls. Piet fan Reenan had taken her down from the cross and together they had overthrown and slain him.

*We are the Kings who die for the People.* Those had been the Founder's last words, and Barak decided you had to be *kapetein* to realize their truth. Piet's eyes were green, in the dark Frystaater face. The thick body—Frystaat was a heavy-G world, much heavier than Haven—seemed to radiate indomitable strength. Father Piet fan Reenan had lived through the Sauron attack on Haven, had led a band of refugees here to Eden and made them the People . . .

haBandari, in the new tongue. Fan Reenan's Band, in the old. Barak was one of those who believed his *anima* and those of his wives Ilona and Ruth still watched over their descendants. Frystaater, *Ivrit* and Edenite, together making up the People.

*Give me strength,* he thought and prayed. The painted smile watched him. *You died, Father Piet, but the People live.*

The thick callused fingers of one hand prodded at the letters and maps on the table. "This thing is growing like mushrooms on horseshit," he said.

His finger traced a line from the Pale, up north, around the mountains and across the Great Northern Steppe, that surrounded the Shangri-La Valley like a horizontal *C*. The Citadel—the inner fortress of the Sauron Soldiers' power—sat at the northeastern end of the Valley, above the sole pass into the great equatorial lowland. The Pale was at the far western end of the *C*, comfortably distant. Twelve thousand difficult kilometers. There were outlying Bases much closer; Quilland up at the gap where the cul-de-sac of the Pale met the Great Northern Steppe. Angband Base had been *much* closer, but had fallen half a lifetime ago. As a satellite might fly the Shangri-La was only a few hundred kilometers away, but the Afritsberg stood between, the horns of its peaks far above any breathable atmosphere. The Karakal Pass was the only entrance . . .

*The only pass until we discovered one,* he reminded himself. He traced that, too. Down the escarpment south of the Pale and over the Afritsberg mountains where they dwindled toward the sea, a narrow winding trail through deadly jungle and up to the very edge of breathable air, then down into the western Shangri-La. Another branch ran further down the escarpment, down to the sea and the mouth of the Xanadu River. Down to Khanut Base, the Saurons' ocean outpost. Fifty T-years of secret labor and incredible expense to make those roads. Hundreds of lives.

"Do we send it?" the assistant asked. He was a pushy youngster. . . .

*No, curse it, he's a grown man and a father himself,* Barak reminded himself.

"Yes," Barak grunted, shaking his head in wonder. "We send the Seven everything we can. It's fated, I think."

How long since Juchi and Chaya were exposed on the culling ground of Angband Base? More years than he had lived. The Saurons cast out their get if their accursed blood ran too weak in it—and that sin had come back to haunt them. Women sometimes took the children in. Juchi's foster mother had, and he had grown to be the chief of Dede Korkut's tribe. His twin sister Chaya had been taken by Dvora bat Lizabet on the same night, and became Judge in the Pale. Together with Badri, their mother, they had brought Angband Base down and freed the Tallinn Valley it had dominated.

Barak shivered slightly, making the sign of the horns under the table with his left hand—a habit he'd picked up fighting the plainsmen. Juchi hadn't known of his ancestry until too late; so he had killed the wandering Sauron scout Dagor . . . who was his father. He'd wed Badri . . . who, all unknowing, was his mother as well as the mother of his children Aisha and Dagor. Badri had hanged herself on the day that terrible knowledge came to light, and Juchi had put out his own eyes. Who knew where Dagor had gone? Aisha had wandered the steppes for thirty T-years, leading her blinded father. Leading him at last to the Citadel, where he died. Died, and Aisha nearly died, killing Glorund the Cyborg Battlemaster.

Barak shivered again. It was an ill thing to be caught up in the webs of fate. Aisha came back to the Pale and chaos exploded. Mordekai dying—well, he'd been an old, old man—plots uncovered. Chaya's son young Barak revealed as the son of a wandering Sauron she'd trapped and killed the night Angband fell and her husband Heber died helping to take it. Aisha and Chaya, Karl bar Edgar the *mediko*, young Barak, his lover Sannie, Kemal who was heir to

Juchi's tribe—maybe—and his blood-brother Ihsan—
they'd all gone out into the steppe north of the Pale's
ranchlands.

The Seven. Seven against the Citadel, preaching jihad
against the Saurons. A living myth, that had set men's
minds aflame.

"Seven maniacs, plus about two hundred thousand
fools."

"Sir?" Ariel asked. He was a portly man in his thirties,
plump but with hard muscle under it, and scars to show he
knew how to use it.

"Perhaps two hundred and fifty thousand. Hammer-of-
God thinks the Seven have that many now."

Hammer-of-God had been Barak's right-hand man
when he commanded the Pale's armies, for all that he was
pure Edenite peasant by birth. He'd come out of a retire-
ment that proved less pleasant in reality than prospect to
join his old friend-adversary Chaya in one last fight. One
last crusade, for God spoke to His Hammer . . . or at least
that was what Hammer-of-God Jackson thought.

The younger man shaped a soundless whistle. "That
must be nearly every *hotnot* able to walk," he said.

"There are more of them up there on the steppe than
you might think," Barak said. Most of Haven was steppe;
too high and dry and thin-aired for farming. Too thin-aired
for safe birthing, apart from the great lowland of the
Shangri-La and smaller valleys like Eden. "And everyone
hates the Saurons."

With good reason: their bloody-handed levying of tribute, and the tribute of breeding women—tribute
maidens—worst of all. Saurons bred three sons for every
daughter, and they needed females from the *cattle*, as they
called unaltered humanity, for their breeding program.
The Bandari had never paid so much as a sheep to the
Saurons—but the Bandari held Eden Valley, as well as
broad steppe lands. Others were less fortunate and had to
bend the knee to the Citadel for access to Shangri-La or
the outlying valleys staked down by Bases.

"So we'll send the Seven more help."

He traced the route, past the shoulder of the Atlas Mountains and eastward. "Step up the raids on Quilland Base, here."

That was the Saurons' westernmost outpost, since the fall of Angband. He grinned in his white beard; Quilland had thought that the Pale was doing no more than harassing because they were intimidated, or too weak. Mordekai's cunning. He'd been a careful steward. The numbers and wealth of the People had doubled in his fifty T-years of rule, and that wasn't counting Tallinn Valley or Juchi's tribe, who were tributaries now and marched to war with the Bandari. Clan fan Gimbutas, the engineers and artificers of the People, had been building weapons in secret all that time too, new and powerful weapons.

The Pale didn't have the numbers or the technology or the wealth that the Citadel did—but they were *second* in all those categories, a closer second than the Citadel dreamed. The Citadel's technology were leftovers from the ship that brought them from the wreck of Old Sauron, the *Dol Guldur*. Bandari technology was their own reinvention; they understood it and they could make more. And they didn't have the planetwide assortment of sworn enemies the Citadel did, either.

"We've taken Khanut Base," Barak went on.

That was Yohann bar Non's force; he was one of the Orphans. The Bandari had taken in the Sauron children of Angband Base and raised them as their own; they'd also been systematically rescuing infants from the culling grounds wherever Bandari merchants went. Which was all over Haven.

"Khanut was easier than we expected." The Saurons had stripped its garrison to deal with the revolt of the New Soviet Men and the Sons of Liberty in the Shangri-La, a revolt the Pale was secretly backing.

"Send another brigade—Pinkas bar Rhodevik's—up to keep Quilland occupied. Get the heavy equipment rolling toward the Seven at once. I authorize as many extra draught animals as necessary. And tell Pinkas to push out strong patrols, well-armed—all riflemen—further east. Start building a chain of supply depots; the steppe will be empty behind the Seven. When they come back, the Bases" —there were four, counting Quilland, along the arc of the Great Northern Steppe— "will give them bad trouble. If we raid and harass, we'll keep them too busy and off-balance to coordinate their actions. And Yohann took a fair number of Sauron weapons at Khanut; have fifty percent of those sent up here and passed on to Pinkas."

The Seven were leading a folk-migration, and necessarily moving slowly. Picked troops, even with a siege-train, could double or triple their speed and catch up with them.

"And get me that agent we had down in the Shangri-La," he said. "I want to know how that rebellion we fomented is coming."

The cold night wind hooted around the adobe walls of the *kapetein's* house, through the streets of the city called Strang that had once been Strong-in-the-Lord. Out beyond it, out beyond the city walls and the fertile valley fields of Eden, men were dying across half of Haven. On the northern steppes, on the shores of the Southern Ocean, soon under the terrible walls of the Citadel itself. Dying by his command, or because they were caught up in webs of power and intrigue spun out from this house over generations. He'd sent men to die before, but he'd led from the front when he was a commander.

Barak hunched his thick shoulders. Ruling was a cold thing.

*I told you so.*

The words were bitter as wormwood in Sharku's mind. Nothing hurt worse than being proved right too late to do anything about it. Sure enough, there *was* a connection between the Pale and the west of the Shangri-La Valley, whether the Threat Analysis Computer, Cyborg Rank Battlemaster Carcharoth, or anyone else back at the Citadel believed it or not. The TAC was a *tool*, not an oracle—but the Cyborgs didn't see it that way, possibly because they were too much like computers themselves. They treated its conclusions as infallible, on a level with observed fact. He'd argued against it, taken it right to the Council—but the Council was a collection of nonentities these days, half of them senile.

*We retreated to this barren world because we had no choice, and we hid because we had no alternative. And now we stagnate here. And what would First Soldier Diettinger and Lady Althene say if they knew what we had made of the Race? Soldiers. We came from the stars! Now we hide in fear of the Empire, we who made the Empire tremble. And because of our fear we have—this.*

Now two regiments of Soldiers deployed on the rolling plains waited for his commands. His commands. Regiment Leader Sharku.

It had happened suddenly. The strength of the Citadel was entrusted to Deathmaster Ghâsh, sent southwest to the ends of the Shangri-La to rescue a Firebase that ought to have been reinforced months ago at the first sign of the new barbarian activities. The Sons of Liberty and the New Soviet Men, an improbable alliance of barbarians who ought to be fighting each other. *But they aren't fighting each other, they have allied. As I predicted* . . .

"Are you afraid?" Deathmaster Ghâsh had asked when they had passed Castell City.

"No, but I am concerned. Why are these barbarian groups banded together?"

"What do we care what thoughts enter the minds of cattle?"

*We should be.* "First Soldier Diettinger did not call enemy *soldiers* 'cattle.' Only their civilians."

Ghâsh smiled mirthlessly. "That was long ago, when there were fighting men among the cattle."

"They threaten a Firebase. That has not happened in your lifetime. They have learned to ally, and learned to fight. Perhaps they are no longer cattle." A phrase from an ancient history came to mind. "Do you recall the speeches of Demosthenes of Athens?"

Ghâsh looked at Sharku, a puzzled look. "I was told you have odd thoughts. Speak."

*You hear that Phillip is in the Chersonese and you vote an expedition there. You hear that he is in Thessaly and you send another there. You march the length and breadth of Greece at his command, and you take your marching orders from him.* Which is what we are doing."

"And what would you do?"

"The key to an alliance is what one partner holds dear. In this case the city of Cobalt. Take their capital and the Sons of Liberty will come streaming home to rescue it. Cobalt is much closer than Firebase Six."

"We have our orders." Ghâsh looked thoughtful. "I have had my doubts about the Threat Analysis Computer for some time." He nodded. "Regiment Leader Sharku: take two Regiments, and capture the city of Cobalt. I will continue the expedition as ordered, but it may be that you will achieve results sooner than I will."

And now two Regiments waited his commands. Behind them the ruins of the New Soviet Men's town of—his mind hunted through its files—Beiragorod was in flames. He gritted his teeth. The enemy had set it on fire before they retreated, as they had burned all the settlements in the Soldiers' path. *Here it is not so important, but Ghâsh will have nothing behind him but desolation. A long supply line. Unless we achieve something first. More enemies ahead. Enemies. Not cattle.*

*Strike where the enemy does not expect.* "Forward!"

Almost invisible against the pale straw color of the reaped barley, the troopers moved out; teams to set up portable Gatlings, and the rifle squads leapfrogging forward, cover and advance. The savage *brrrttttt* of the Gatlings sounded; short economical bursts, since every round had to come seven hundred kilometers from the nearest Firebase, and down the Xanadu from near the Citadel to the Firebase in the first place.

Far too soon, the enemy in the earthworks ahead opened up themselves. "Bandari rifles," Sharku said.

The whole western valley had blown up. Close to a million barbarian warriors—cattle to the fools in the Citadel—were in the field; Hell's-A-Comin' had fallen to them, and many lesser posts. Even with the Khanut garrison called back from over the Escarpment, the Soldiers were having a hard time getting things under control. Despite their speed, despite their fieldcraft, Soldiers were falling. Not all that many, but . . .

Mumak, his second-in-command, nodded. *That* had been the final proof. The Bandari manufactured a breech-loading flintlock; it could fire five big elongated slugs a minute and was accurate out to a thousand meters. The Sauron assault rifles had similar range and were vastly quicker-firing, but the difference was a whole order of magnitude less than it had been back when the cattle had only smoothbore muzzle-loaders. Every advance in range decreased the Sauron advantages of quicker reflexes and better eyesight, too.

The Soldiers advanced. Their fire, and the fire of the Gatlings, began to beat down the defenders'.

"How many?" Sharku said, moving forward with the command group. They trotted not far beyond the rearmost firing line; the day was long past when even Soldiers could have easy radio communications with individual units.

"Forty thousand in this bunch, I'd say," Mumak estimated; that was a little more than the Intelligence reports, but about what you'd expect from the rate of fire. Forty thousand cattle against four thousand Soldiers was long odds—against the cattle.

Black-powder smoke was beginning to obscure the front of the enemy position; the flanks were anchored in deep wooded ravines on one side, and a tangle of hills on another, capped with one of the local feudal noble's castles—chairman of the *Kolkhoz*, in the local Russki dialect. It was from the castles that the local aristocracy, the *nomenklaturniks*, ruled the serfs.

Like any such fortress, the muzzles of brass cannon frowned from its stone-and-earthwork ramparts. He ignored them, even when they began to belch smoke and jets of reddish flame; cast-iron roundshot weren't much of a menace, and the range was over three thousand meters.

His ears warned him; the whistling screech was too high-pitched.

"Down!" he shouted.

The command-group flung themselves flat. The first shell exploded at five meters, slamming up a pancake of dust as the musket-balls inside it lashed down. The lash fell across several Soldiers as well. More shells burst, some in the air, some plowing harmlessly into the dirt first. Sharku snapped orders to continue the advance. The subordinate commanders and the men themselves thinned the firing line and moved the Gatlings on their own initiative, good tactics. Except that by dispersing the firing line they weakened the main attack, of course.

Something else fired from within the castle's courtyard. The projectile arched up over the plain. Sharku's Sauron eyes could penetrate the blur of speed to catch a long-finned cylinder in flight. Some sort of mortar . . .

*BWAAAMP.* Dirt fountained up ten times man-height. When the smoke settled a Gatling and its crew were *gone*, nothing but a crater visible.

The Soldiers ignored it, as they ignored the steady shelling. The firing rose to a crescendo along the line, then suddenly ceased over on the right. Sharku nodded and turned his eyes there, in telescope-mode. Figures in field-gray, tiny as ants, were swarming out of the woods behind the curve of the New Soviet Men's line. That was *his* little surprise; the enemy didn't appreciate just how fast a Soldier force could move on foot. This one had looped around the outer posts of the New Soviet Men's army, punched through, and outraced any word of its coming.

"Let's wrap this up," he said. "No prisoners except for interrogation."

❖    ❖    ❖

Deathmaster Ghâsh turned the dud shell over with his toe. It was a long cylinder of rough cast iron, with a lead flange around its middle. The flange was grooved, much like the lands in the barrel of a rifled firearm—but this was on the projectile, not the weapon itself.

"Ingenious," he said. "And simple to make—given the mold to cast from, any village blacksmith could run it up. The grooves will spin the projectile from a smoothbore. You did well to send for me."

"Thank you."

"I should thank you, Regiment Leader. No sooner had you moved toward Cobalt than the attacks on Firebase Six faltered. The Firebase can hold now."

Orderlies handed cups of eggbush tea and loaves of plundered black bread to the commanders. They began to demolish it with methodical speed. Not far away, Soldiers were destroying the captured weapons; bending the barrels of muskets into knots, and smashing the stocks. The piles grew, amid the iron clamor. Nobody was bothering with the enemy bodies; they could lie in their tens of thousands. The maniac laughter of stobor sounded, still cautiously distant, but getting nearer. Now and then a cannon boomed from the New Soviet castle, but the pickets around it were safely out of range. Nearer to the walls Soldier snipers kept up a steady harassing fire. As they watched, a figure pitched out of an embrasure and lay with its limp arms dangling down the wall.

Ghâsh took out a map. "You changed the route of advance."

"I sent you full reports—"

"I am not reprimanding you, Regiment Leader."

Mumak visibly relaxed. Deathmaster Ghâsh frowned slightly. "A word of advice, Regiment Leader. It is well that your troops are loyal, but perhaps they need not be quite so eager to show that to me." He looked at the map again. "So you have chosen to stay on the border between the New Soviets and the Sons of Liberty."

"Yes, Deathmaster. We threaten both Cobalt and Novy

Kiev. Why should the Sons of Liberty be the only ones to fear us—"

"We have been victors too long, Sharku," Ghâsh said. "I must admit that I would not have been concerned about which groups of cattle we fought. I think it is time we learned more of these—barbarian warriors."

Mumak grinned. It was the first time he had heard any of the Soldiers refer to the enemy other than as cattle. *Except for Sharku . . .*

Ghâsh bent to examine the projectile. "What's the performance?

"About three, four times the range of a smoothbore cannon," Sharku said. "They must have found a way to reinforce the breech; shrink on a band of red-hot wrought-iron bars, at a guess. And the shell's a lot more effective than roundshot as well as hitting further. The fuses are powder-train in drilled wood. They work, after a fashion. They have a lot of them."

Ghâsh nodded. "We found that out on the way here. The Sons of Liberty tried to stand in our path."

"As Sharku predicted," Mumak muttered.

The other regimental officers nodded silent agreement. Ghâsh nodded silently to himself. "I thank you for the warning. Well done."

A junior officer rode up. He ignored Ghâsh and ran up to Sharku. "The supply caravan, Regiment Leader. We found it."

Sharku looked up at the castle walls where the New Soviet banner flew. "Destroyed?"

"What we didn't capture."

"Good. Continue as ordered. Perhaps I'd better come with you. With your permission, Deathmaster?"

"Certainly." Ghâsh watched Sharku and the Assault Leader ride away. He also noted the looks the other officers had given Sharku. He turned Mumak. "As a favor, Deputy Regiment Leader, what are those orders?"

Mumak grinned. "Sharku says assaulting strong walls is for culling troops, not a way to win wars. Sir."

Ghâsh smiled faintly.

"So we make like we're charging them, get them to shoot up their ammunition, and stay just out of range. Doesn't work with their best, but they don't leave their best to guard these castles."

"Ingenious."

"Yes, sir, there's a lot of these castles, and Sharku said if we stop to take every damn one of them we'll never get to Cobalt. Attack them, make it look like we didn't really surround them so they try to sneak in supplies—"

"I see. As I said, ingenious. You seem to have great confidence in Regiment Leader Sharku."

"Damn right, sir! He knew these damn tribes, Valley and Pale, all of them were working together, and nobody in the Citadel knows that yet!" He pointed to the rocket. "Look at that damn thing. Right out of the Pale. Nobody in the Valley invented that."

The camp was just beyond range of the fire from the castle walls. Deathmaster Ghâsh drank his after-meal tea and turned the shell over and over as the countryside around grew darker.

"That's the clincher," Sharku said. "But there's more. Better rifles. Communications and signals. Organization. Deathmaster, the Valley and the Pale are working together."

"The Pale has always envied the Valley," Ghâsh said.

"Exactly. And how is arming the Valley going to help them?"

"Disturbing. You imply that they will—Sharku, that's impossible."

"It was impossible that the New Soviets and the Sons of Liberty would ally. It was impossible that the Pale would enter the Valley."

"Let us be clear. You believe the Citadel is threatened."

"I do. I believe this has been a ruse to draw our strength here to the south. A successful ruse."

Ghâsh stared into his empty tea cup. "The TAC knows nothing of this."

"Sir—"

"I know. We trust the future of the Race to a machine we do not understand."

Sharku sat motionless.

"Tell me more," Ghâsh said.

Sharku spoke quietly. "The Sons and the New Soviets have been at war since before the *Dol Guldur* arrived. The Citadel has encouraged this. Let the tribute cattle fight, let them cull themselves. But Deathmaster, do not the Breedmasters teach that over a long enough time a race under stress becomes stronger?"

"Strong enough to threaten the Citadel?"

"Deathmaster, there are many of them. Perhaps half a million are marching on the Citadel, and we are here."

Ghâsh stood in decision. "Ready your forces, Regiment Leader. I order you to return to the Citadel. I am under orders to rescue Firebase Six, but I see now that is more efficiently done by threatening Cobalt and Novy Kiev than a direct march. You have trained officers to think as you do, to understand these ca—these barbarian warriors?"

"Yes, sir."

"You will leave two of them to advise me. Take your Regiments and return. You'll have written orders in the morning."

# • CHAPTER TWO

Dagor son of Juchi watched Carcharoth fiddle with the nozzle of a device that looked more arcane than anything the shamans sang of. Carcharoth had to know he was there, but took no notice of him. Cyborgs, Dagor had discovered, were masters at ignoring anything not directly relevant to them.

Sick of being ignored, Dagor asked, "What is that thing?" He was picking up Americ pretty fast, but still spoke the Turkic steppe dialect most of the time.

"Flame thrower," Carcharoth answered in Americ without looking up.

"What?" Dagor fell into the Saurons' (Soldiers', he corrected himself) usual tongue. He wasn't sure he'd understood correctly. "It—throws fire?"

"Yes." Now Carcharoth did look up. He enjoyed talking about weapons. "Nozzle. Hose of drillbit gut. Two tanks in backpack: one compressed air to push out the flame, the other *ghee* and muskylope lard to make the flame. A little battery pack fires blank cartridges at the end of the nozzle to ignite the liquid."

"Really?" Dagor wasn't sure whether to believe Carcharoth or not. He'd already seen so much at the Citadel that would be flatly incredible anywhere else on Haven— miracles like electricity and refrigeration, even greater miracles like the machine shop that turned out brass cartridges for the Soldiers' assault rifles. But would even the tribal bards, notorious for tales of things that never were, have had the gall to sing of a weapon that shot fire?

Carcharoth was not a bard. He was the single most

dangerous man Dagor had ever seen, and therefore one
whose opinion carried a great deal of weight. He was altogether serious as he answered, "Yes, boy, really. Effective
range is out to about thirty meters. The tanks carry enough
propellant and fuel for about a dozen ignitions."

"Thirty meters?" Dagor scratched his head. "What good
is a weapon like that? A bow can strike at five times that—a
rifle ten times as far."

"True enough," the Battlemaster admitted. "A rifle is a
general-purpose weapon. A flame thrower has a few special functions. If an enemy is concealed inside a house and
you don't care to go in after him, you can burn it down and
either take him with it or pot him when he has to flee. If
he's down a hole or in a tunnel, you can likewise smoke
him out or make him run. And a flame thrower is a terror
weapon—watching one man burn will do more to enemy
morale than having a hundred men shot. Cooking to death
hurts, and looks as if it hurts. Exploiting this can be useful."

He spoke as a teacher would to a student who might show
promise. No one had ever taken that tone with Dagor
before. Dagor had been a little boy when his father/brother
and mother discovered the tragic web that trapped
them—and escaped that web only through grisly mutilation
and death. He still had nightmares of the blood streaming
down Juchi's face after he'd torn out his own eyes.

And ever since that dreadful day, Dagor had been an
outcast, despised for the blood he bore and mistrusted by
all he met. As if he could help that, or as if the sins of his
parents were his fault! But the tribesmen did not see it so;
to them, sin passed down from father to son like endur-
ance in horses. And when father was also brother . . .

He'd left the Tallinn Valley young. It hadn't helped. His
name and reputation ran ahead of him like fire before the
wind. He'd learned smithing, become better than average
with his Sauron speed and strength and dexterity, and normally a smith could support himself come good times or
bad. But he'd been hungry when he tried to join the Seven
in their jihad against the Citadel.

And they'd sent him away. Even his kin wanted none of him—his kin on the steppe, that is. Here at the Citadel, things seemed different. They had every reason to hate him here, being as he was the son of a man who'd worked great harm on them. But they saw him only in terms of how he could be useful to them. Inbreeding was a standard technique of the Breedmasters. Other than being intrigued at his genetic background, they didn't care about the incest that had spawned him. He'd never before known an attitude like that. He reveled in it.

As a smith, he had a feel for the way arms should look. The flame thrower didn't come up to his standards. "It's very ugly," he said, pointing.

"So what?" Carcharoth answered. "It does what it's supposed to do, and does it well. Making it pretty too would just be wasted effort."

Dagor had never known an attitude like that, either. He said, "But would not the Soldiers fight better if they admired and cherished the arms they bore?" He had to fall back into Turkic to ask the question in the way he wanted.

"They admire their weapons because those weapons are what keeps them alive," Carcharoth said. "You've picked up a lot of damnfool notions out on the steppe, do you know that? The only reason to fight a war is to win it. They don't give points for style."

"But—" Dagor thought of his own father, of Hammer-of-God, or Piet whom the Bandari revered: stylish warriors every one. Could any of them have stood against a Soldier in single combat? Well, Juchi had, but that was only because he was Sauron himself, not because he was stylish.

The ceiling speaker said, "Battlemaster Carcharoth, report to the front gates. Battlemaster Carcharoth, report to the front gates."

"Shit," Carcharoth said mildly. He set down the flame thrower nozzle, rose fluidly from the lotus position in which he'd been sitting, trotted off toward the gates. Dagor tagged along after him. Though the Battlemaster mocked style, his daunting all-around competence was a style of its own, and one to which Dagor responded. It put him in mind of Juchi: to what boy, after all, does his father not seem omnicompetent?

Just inside the gates stood the most decrepit Sauron Dagor had ever seen. Had he been a horse, the young man from the steppes would have cut his throat as a mercy. His face was all but skeletal; every bit of flesh left on the bones was stamped with the marks of ultimate exhaustion. He'd run right through the soles of his boots. Though Soldiers' blood clotted with unnatural speed, all the same his feet left bloody prints on the concrete floor.

His eyes had what the nomads called the thousand-meter stare: they peered not at his surroundings but at something far away only he could see. Then those eyes—all the more alarming for being as blue as a land gator's—registered the death's heads on Carcharoth's collar tabs. The Soldier stiffened to a painful sort of attention.

"Sir," he said in a ghastly croak. "Trooper Mewlip, sir, returning to the Citadel to report the failure of the detail assigned to capture or destroy the Cyborg Sigrid."

"What are you doing here?" Carcharoth demanded. After a moment, Dagor realized he meant, *Why aren't you dead?*

"Sir, I am reporting as ordered," Mewlip replied. "While following the course given by the nomad Temujin to the alleged Katlinsvale, the two sections led by Assault Leader Atanamir encountered the van of an extremely large party of nomads travelling in the direction of the Citadel. We attacked said van and inflicted severe damage upon it. More nomads, however, continued to press down upon us from the west and north. Outnumbered and required to be conservative of ammunition, we yielded ground while performing reconnaissance and devising a stratagem."

The Battlemaster rolled his eyes. "Atanamir may be a promising officer, but he is very young. So tell me, what brilliant piece of military trickery did he invent?"

Dagor would have attacked any man who spoke to him

so. The Soldier, however, ignored the sarcasm and answered the question: "Sir, he assumed that two sections from the Citadel would be inadequate to check the oncoming nomads. Accordingly, he and his men enlisted tribes known to be loyal to our cause, expending them to delay the arrival of the nomad horde in this vicinity."

"He could have done worse," Carcharoth admitted. "Did he have any hope of actually blunting this onslaught rather than merely delaying it?"

"Sir, he did not," Mewlip answered. "Our estimates from observation and interrogations were that the horde totaled more than forty thousand effectives and is growing every cycle by several thousand more. Atanamir's expectation was of selling himself and his men as dearly as he could. It is because he expected that there would be no other survivors that I was dispatched here under orders; without them, I assure you I would have shared my comrades' fate. But Atanamir impressed on me that the Citadel *must* be warned."

"As you say, Trooper. I do not doubt your courage, I assure you," Carcharoth said. "But the works here are built to withstand anything the steppe tribes can throw at us. That is their function, after all. So why, aside from size, did Atanamir particularly fear this nomad grouping?"

"Sir, I am directed to report to you that after the initial encounter, in which the steppe nomads were armed with their usual worthless assortment of bows, muskets, carbines, and whatnot, we encountered men armed with Bandari rifles: both Bandari, and steppe tribesmen. Blackpowder breechloaders with effective range as great as that of our own weapons and capable of fire rapid enough to prove more than a nuisance even to Soldiers."

"Bandari rifles?" the Battlemaster repeated.

"In large numbers, sir," Mewlip said. "No possible doubt; I examined captured specimens. And that stinking rifled slug, sir, does a lot more damage than the usual run of musket ball."

"Bandari rifles?" Carcharoth said yet again. The Soldier

gave him a puzzled look. So did Dagor. From what he'd
seen, the Cyborg Battlemaster did not waste time on conversational frills and did not need information repeated.
He hadn't thought Carcharoth showed so much emotion,
either. But the Cyborg looked suddenly lost, as if the world
were falling apart before his eyes.

"Sir, why is that a surprise?" Dagor asked. "You learned
from me that the Pale is involved with this movement, if
you hadn't known before."

Carcharoth didn't answer, not directly. Instead he said,
"Bandari rifles?" for the third time, then added, "The very
same as the ones the rebels are using in the west end of the
Valley. It was a feint after all . . . yet it couldn't have been
. . . yet it was. Inconsistencies . . ." His voice trailed away.

Mewlip and Dagor exchanged glances. The Battlemaster did not seem in control of the situation, not even
slightly. The Soldier said, "Sir, permission to report to the
infirmary to get my feet seen to?"

"Granted," Carcharoth said, but absently, not in the
crisp way he should have.

"Are you all right, sir?" Dagor asked as Mewlip left.

Carcharoth looked him full in the face. "No."

Chichek heard the news in the refectory. Where else?
The whole Citadel gathered in its mealrooms; sometimes a
Cyborg would sit down at meat beside a tribute maiden
and her squalling brat. These days, with Regiments of Soldiers out pacifying the west of the Shangri-La Valley, the
big chamber seemed chock full of women and children;
the remaining Soldiers in their sober field-gray were punctuation marks scattered among the bright raiment of those
with whom they lived.

Rumors had been flying for several cycles, rumors of
steppe clans on the move against the Citadel. From what
Sharku had told her, Chichek knew more about the truth
behind those rumors than most of the Soldiers' women:
even among the elite who had permanent partners, few
had spouses who were so well connected, or who loved

them enough to care to confide in them. She prided herself on the trust Sharku showed her, and did not gossip to excess. Sharku knew how to bring out such loyalty—in her, and in the men he commanded. Few had risen so high so young . . .

Besides, as long as the reports were rumor alone, she'd done her best to ignore them. She didn't want them to be true. But now there could be no possible doubt. The clans *were* coming. What Mewlip said in private when he arrived was common knowledge ten hours later.

"Can they take the Citadel?" Kortla asked anxiously. She dandled a baby boy in her lap as she ate. Kortla had to move sharply; the babe's grabs showed Sauron speed.

"Don't be foolish," Chichek answered. "You know the might of this place."

"Yes, but I also know how many of our men are gone," Kortla said.

Chichek frowned; she knew it too, and knew how Sharku had railed against it. On the bench beside her, her son Gimilzor puffed out his small chest and said, "Don't be afraid, mamma. I won't let anyone hurt you."

He spoke Americ, as he usually did, but had no trouble following the steppe tongue those women of the Citadel who came from the tribes used among themselves. Valley Americ and Russki were more common, but the women tended to make their friends among those with the same background.

She smiled fondly and ruffled the boy's hair. "My little cliff lion," she said. The other women at the table looked admiringly at Gimilzor—so young, and already a warrior spirit! No less than the men of the Citadel, the tribute maidens sprang from folk who admired strength and daring.

Erka said, "What does it matter whether or not the clans take the Citadel? They will come close enough to see us on the battlements. We are dead to them, you know; they cast us out when they grant us to the Saurons. Yet they will see us! How shall I not die of shame?"

"To go to the stronger is no shame," Chichek declared.

"No shame to us, perhaps, not for that," Erka said. "But shame for the clans at having to give us up. They hate having to turn some of their maidens over to the Saurons so the rest can use the Valley to safely bear their babes—even more, when they must for fear of the Saurons' power. And they will hate us, as reminding them of their shame."

"That's not all they'll hate us for," Kortla said. "What's the blackest thing you can call a woman out on the steppe? Both of you know the answer to that as well as I do: Sauron's whore."

"What's a whore, mamma?" Gimilzor asked.

"Nothing you need to worry about, little one," Chichek answered. All the same, she bit her lip. What the other women said was true. She hadn't thought about it in a long time, being happy with Sharku, but it was so. Suddenly all the loss and fear she'd felt when the tribute party seized her for the Citadel came flooding back."

Vindictiveness twisting her face, Erka said to Kortla, "Now Chichek the pampered pet sees the life the rest of us live here. She fears the men of the clans as we fear the men of the Citadel. Her love is here, ours still out on the plains."

"Aye, by Allah and all the spirits," Kortla answered. "I could have been happily wed—there was a boy who mooned after me, and his father was rich—but instead I was forced to submit to the embraces of a pork-eating infidel."

"And I," Erka said. "What if my lost sweetheart recognizes me? I'd throw myself off the wall, I swear I would. But Chichek waits only for her Sauron to come home."

"Don't you talk mean about my mother," Gimilzor said, understanding the tone if not content. "I'll hurt you if you do."

From a normal boy of about five T-years, the threat would have been idle. From a Soldier's son of promising genetics, it was anything but. Gimilzor might have given a grown man without genetic augmentation all he could handle.

Chichek automatically restrained him, and he yielded to his mother's touch. But she was tempted to turn him loose against Kortla and Erka. Never till now had they shown her how they resented her for being happily partnered to Sharku. Did most of the tribute maidens feel as they did, hating their men and hating the Citadel? She hadn't thought so. Now, all at once, she felt adrift, as if on the Northern Sea.

Suppose . . . suppose the Citadel fell. Madness, she knew, but this seemed a meal period made for madness. What would she do, assuming she lived through the sack? Go back to her old clan? There the other two were right: the clan would not have her. What then?

She shivered, wishing Sharku and the Regiments would return. Then all her vapors would be swept away into the land of lies where they belonged.

Erka began to keen, the old mourning cry of the steppes that Chichek had not heard since she came to the Citadel. "What shall we do?" the tribute maiden cried. "What shall we do when they come against us, the ones we might have loved, the ones who cast us forth into the beds of infidels? Allah and the spirits, what shall we do?"

Ice tingled through Chichek; the small hairs on her arms and legs tried to rise, as if she were a wild beast showing its alarm. All through the refectory, tribute maidens joined the outcry, their voices rising and falling in a ragged chorus of pain whose like had surely never been heard in the Citadel since the long-vanished days of its raising.

"Stop!" The harsh Americ command cut through the uproar as cleanly as a saber cleaving man's-flesh. Carcharoth the Battlemaster stood by the bench where he'd been eating. Though his field-gray uniform was designed not to draw the eye, the quivering outrage of his posture utterly nullified its camouflage. "Stop!" he said again, this time louder than before. "The Citadel endures. The Citadel shall always endure. Doubt it at your peril."

Had he stopped there, Chichek thought, he would have won the women back to obedience. They were used to obeying Saurons; they were especially used to obeying Cyborgs. Who, after all, dared to do otherwise?

But Carcharoth did not stop: "We shall annihilate the nomads utterly; we shall make it as if they had never been. We shall betray them as they have betrayed us, shall send them into the outer darkness, shall pound them into paste. They will be lost in the fiery flames forever, sent up in a pillar of smoke that may look toward the Citadel but shall always be blown away by the great and righteous wind of our wrath."

*Now he's gone and done it,* Chichek thought. *He's laid it on too thick.* Sure enough, the keening broke free again, louder and wilder and more desolate than before. The tribute maidens had but mourned themselves; now, they lamented the promised devastation of the clans from which they'd come. Chichek stared at the Battlemaster. How could he have been so stupid? The question echoed on several levels. Cyborgs usually showed about as much emotion as a land gator. What could have prompted Carcharoth to spout this ill-timed, melodramatic claptrap?

Whatever it was, it possessed him still. "Stop! Be silent!" he cried once more, but now the women would not heed him. Before he could launch another verse of his own maunderings, Titus the Breedmaster hurried up to him and whispered urgently in his ear. Carcharoth tried to shake him off, but Titus set an arm around his shoulders— as if in friendship—and steered him out of the refectory. Not just the women but also the few Soldiers in the hall stared after the two Cyborgs as they departed.

Carcharoth had succeeded in one thing: he'd stopped the keening chorus after all. But the hum of gossip that rose to replace it could have been no more reassuring to the powers of the Citadel.

"What's wrong with the Battlemaster, mamma?" Gimilzor asked, and then again when she did not answer. "What's wrong with the Battlemaster?"

"I don't know," Chichek said at last. The admission frightened her.

# • CHAPTER THREE

"Why me, Lord God, why *me*?" Hammer-of-God Jackson muttered into his new beard. Then: "All right, Lord, I'll take up this cross." Not that he had much choice. The Lord God of Hosts gave you a burden as heavy as you could bear, neither more nor less. You carried it to Heaven's gate, or let it crush you down into Hell.

His leg was hurting worse than usual today, and he had the beginnings of a headache.

*I've got the grandfather of* all *headaches*, he told himself, looking out over the plain. It was lower here, despite the mountains; they were still heading east, but the southwestern turn to the Shangri-La Valley and the passes was close. Lower, warmer, and wetter than the high steppe; the grass was nearly knee-high before the advancing horde, and it left no bare ground between tufts. Incredibly rich pasture, for the steppe. That was fortunate, because there must be—

*Two hundred thousand fighting men*, Hammer-of-God thought. Almost all of them mounted, although there were all kinds of men down to primitives dressed in land gator armor and swinging stone hammers. Plus the warriors' wagons, their yurts, their women and children, their remounts and muskylopes and yaks and sheep and the odd herd of longhorn cattle. The dust was like a stormcloud above them as far as he could see, right to the horizon. Dun-colored masses of them, straggling clots, or here and there the geometric regularity of a disciplined column. Reddish light winked back at him from helmets and odd bits of armor, from the steel of lances and the burnished brass ornaments of a clan chief, from a woman's dowry-

..... of silver coins. The sound of their hooves and feet
.... voices rumbled endlessly, like distant spring thunder
that never ended.

*Two hundred thousand fighting men at least.* Perhaps
one tenth of all the males on the steppes of Haven
between sixteen and sixty. Far and away the largest army
the planet had ever seen—and more pouring in every cycle. Thousands upon thousands more. There might be half
a *million* by the time they reached the Citadel. *And we'll
need every one.*

"Why *me?*" he asked again, a little more loudly. The
Seven were in charge, but he was their military advisor.

Barak bar Heber laughed at his back, grinning unre-
pentantly when Hammer-of-God wheeled toward him.

"You've been around us Bandari far too long," Judge
Chaya's son said, grinning at him. "Picking up bad habits.
We're the ones who argue with God—it's a tradition."

The Atlas reared at his back, baring white fangs at
heaven; it was Dimday, only the huge reddish globe of
Cat's Eye above and the sister-moons floating about it in
the dark blue sky. The Pupil was centered today. It seemed
to leer down at him, watching like the Lidless Eye of the
Dark Lord himself. Eager to see these fools break their
hearts and bones against the walls of the Citadel, die beneath the weapons of Its chosen people.

"You'll argue with *anybody,*" Hammer replied, clapping
him on the shoulder.

Kemal, heir to the tribe that had been Juchi's, leaned
both hands on the pommel of his saddle and looked down
at the horde. "Magnificent," he said. "Not since the time of
legends has such an army gathered."

Hammer-of-God looked at him out of the corner of his
eye. Juchi's tribe had been allies of the Pale for a long
time—tributaries now, since the Bandari rescued them
from chaos and hungry neighbors after Juchi died. Kemal's
father-in-law Tarik Shukkur *Khan* led them; but Kemal
had chafed under the velvet bonds of the protectorate.
And he was no fool . . .

"I am surprised," he said, confirming Hammer-of-God's estimate, "that the Sauron bases on the way have not given us more trouble. There is, what, a thousand of the enemy in each? Three thousand then, not counting Quilland which we passed early in the jihad."

Hammer-of-God smiled, and answered with a question: "How much stronger is an army of ten thousand than one of a single thousand?"

"Ten times?" Kemal said, surprised and suspicious. Most warfare on Haven was raiding parties of a few hundred, at that.

"No, over one *hundred* times more powerful. The strength of an army increases by the *square* of the numerical superiority, other things being equal. Archer Jones, a great warrior and scholar of Ancient Terra, writes thus in the books that Piet preserved; and I've found it to be true. So even if one Sauron equals ten or twenty or thirty ordinary men . . ."

Kemal nodded thoughtfully; he detested Hammer-of-God, but had never made the mistake of underestimating him. "Still, why haven't they done *something*?" he said. "We bear down on the Citadel, the heart of their people upon Haven."

Barak smiled unpleasantly. "Creeping feudalism," he said in Bandarit. Kemal's command of that language was good, but not complete. When the nomad prince raised his brows, the Bandari amplified:

"What happens when a *khan* sends a garrison and a relative to govern an outlying province?"

"Ah, so." Kemal snorted understanding. "In a generation, the outlying province becomes independent once more—under the son of the kinsman sent to command it."

Barak continued. "Back on Old Sauron, they had all the technology of the Ancients. Men could fly from one side of a world to another in hours, so a whole world could be commanded as a clan chief rules his yurts. Here even the closest of the northern Bases is months of travel across bad steppe country. The Bases on the Great Northern Steppe were founded back in Diettinger's time, during the Wasting. Their garrisons have been native-born for three hundred and fifty T-years. The Bases are their homes, the homes of their children, their wives, their fathers since the time of legends."

"And however fearless they are as single warriors, they won't risk the survival of their true homelands," Kemal said.

Hammer-of-God touched reins to his horse's neck, and the three leaders rode slowly down the hillside, their mounts picking their way carefully between stones. Iron and leather clattered on their weapons and harnesses. Both younger men listened carefully as Hammer spoke:

"Angband was the furthest base westward—they paid heed to the Citadel only in name. Quilland is a little more under the Citadel's thumb. Dyar more so, and so on as you move east. But none of the Bases on the High Steppe is under the Citadel's real command, the way the settlements down in the Valley are. You can't move armies across the steppe, not unless whole peoples move as we are doing now—and behind us we leave desert where a bird would have to carry its own rations. As long as the Bases know we're moving on, they won't strike at us with any force."

He looked up, met Kemal's narrow black eyes. "And you, Kemal bar Kaidan, are learning rapidly."

A complex of emotions ran through Kemal's eyes, although his face was expressionless. His father Kaidan had died at Hammer's hands; but, before his death, Kaidan had ruined the tribe after Juchi left, and Kemal himself had abandoned him; his uncle Tarik *Khan* had called in the Pale to save the remnant.

*Kemal* bar *Kaidan*. That was the Bandari patronymic; *bar* for a son, with the father's name, *bat* for a daughter, with the mother's. His tribe were subject-allies of the Pale now, but the Pale didn't like ruling foreigners. Many Bandari had married into his people, wedding the widows and orphaned daughters of men slain in the civil wars and invasions after Juchi's fall . . . and, not incidentally, securing their grazing and water rights. He himself had spent much time in the Pale, and his young sons attended school there. The *kapeteins* were famous for their patient planning. His descendants could be *aluf kumpanie*—chiefs of a Bandari clan, not *khans* of a subject tribe. Could be . . . and while he chafed at lost independence, to be a clan chieftain in the Pale, his people with an equal say in the election of the *kapetein* . . . that was wealth and power beyond most steppe chieftains' dreams.

He nodded acknowledgement of the point. It was something to consider.

"Well, the meeting won't wait," Hammer said, clapping him on the shoulder. "Let's go and look confident for the *hotnots*."

Kemal did not quite stiffen. That word would be an insult . . . if the two men considered him a *hotnot*. He knew enough of Hammer-of-God Jackson to know that no insult was meant.

"So? You *aren't* confident?" Barak said.

"Not every Christian's a bliddyful," Hammer replied dryly.

Castell City lay at the confluence of the Jordan and the Alf, where they came together to form the Xanadu. Because of its location, it had been an important trade center since CoDominium days. The *Dol Guldur* had struck it with fusion fire during the Wasting, but as soon as men could come there without dying of radiation sickness, they'd begun to rebuild. These days, they sold little lumps of greenish glass as amulets to give strength and courage. A few were even genuine souvenirs of the blast.

They *had* sold such amulets, Sharku thought. Now, though his two Regiments were still a good many kilometers outside Castell City, he saw the smoke of its burning rising high into the gray-blue sky of Haven. No nuclear blast had raised this smoke, but it was no small conflagration, either.

Sharku turned angrily to Mumak. "Fire. What has Lagduf

been playing at back here?" he demanded. "He's had enough time to pacify the city."

"It's a big place, Castell City," Mumak said placatingly, "and city fighting is hard work. Too bloody many places for rats to hide in and skulk through. Then they jump out and try and bite you in the ass."

"It's not sport any more," Sharku said. "We don't have time to play games with the barbarians."

"Who could have thought the cattle could fight like this?" Mumak said. "Using the rebellion in the west to pull us away from the real action—" Admiringly, he added, "You saw that coming, when nobody else did."

"I saw it. No one would listen."

"They listen now," Mumak said. "At least these do." He gestured to indicate their Regiments. "Even Ghâsh listened."

"Now we have to convince the Citadel—"

"If we're lucky. Maybe they already know. They'll listen, Sharku. They don't know how to deal with this. Ghâsh didn't know. I don't know. But you do."

*And if I don't?* No time for doubts. Any hesitation would lose everything.

There was gunfire ahead. From behind a stone fence a few hundred meters off to the north, somebody shot at a Soldier with a black-powder weapon: not one of the rifled breech-loaders the Bandari had introduced to the valley, but a local taking a potshot with his hunting musket. Sharku's head whipped in that direction. A couple of troopers leaped the fence and killed the man before he could reload and shoot again. Sharku couldn't tell whether they used knives or rifle butts or bare hands, but they didn't waste ammunition on him. One of them jumped up onto the fence and waved to show the job was done. "Any of ours hurt?" Sharku shouted to him.

"No, sir," the Soldier answered. "You couldn't hit your mother across the table with one of those lousy guns." He jumped down and loped east again.

"Not even a delay," Mumak said. "No problem."

"Not this time," Sharku said. "But put enough lead in the air and some of it lands where you don't want it to."

The pop-pop-pop of small arms sounded unduly cheerful as Sharku's men made their way into Castell City. Some of it was more black-powder fire, some short, purposeful bursts from the Soldiers' assault rifles. Mumak looked around in awe at the wreckage. "They've made a desert out of this place," he said. "Maybe old Lagduf hasn't been farting around after all."

"They may have made a desert, but they haven't turned it into peace," Sharku said. "That was the point of the exercise." The devastation was impressive. Dupar Street, down which the regiment cautiously advanced, boasted hardly one building that hadn't been damaged by fire. Bullets pocked surfaces that hadn't burned. The air stank of burnt wood and burnt meat—and dead meat that hadn't burned, now going high.

A couple of swarthy kids, almost man-high, in layer upon layer of rags came up out of the basement where they'd been sheltering. They kept their hands high and well away from their bodies—they'd learned that Soldiers shot first and didn't bother with questions afterwards. "Food, sirs?" one of them whined.

Mumak reached over his shoulder into his pack, pulled out a fat chunk of smoked muskylope haunch, and tossed it to the youngsters. They salaamed in abject gratitude, then snatched up the meat and disappeared before anyone else should spot their prize. "You're too soft," Sharku said, not for the first time.

"Can't be a herdsman without cattle," Mumak answered with a shrug. "I just hope they don't fight over it."

Weary, grimy Soldiers cheered the new arrivals. "We get some relief now?" one of them called hopefully. "I've had enough of grubbing through the ruins, I have."

"We'll all be out of the ruins soon," Sharku said, which made those who heard him cheer louder. To Mumak he added, more quietly, "That doesn't mean it's over, not by a long shot. It just means we have to do the fighting where it really counts, not waste ourselves here."

The one good-sized building in the town that seemed to have survived more or less intact was called, for no reason Sharku understood, the Club. Lagduf made his headquarters there; the place also served as infirmary, canteen, and as barracks for a good part of the regiment. Sharku thought that was putting too many eggs in one basket, but Lagduf had gotten away with it. To give him his due, he did keep sentries spread out well beyond the range of any weapons the barbarians were likely to be able to bring to bear on the Club. Any merely normal man who thought he could sneak through that ring would merely get his funeral in a place he didn't expect. Inside the building, Sharku greeted several men he'd trained with. A good-sized crowd gathered around him as he explained his mission to the local commander.

For a Soldier, Lagduf was on the stocky side, with shoulders that made Sharku glad he didn't have to wrestle against him. He greeted Sharku with a nod and a sharp question: "Have you come to help us put this miserable place in order? We could use three times the manpower we have, I tell you that for a fact. The last time I saw you, you were a Chief Assault Leader. Come up in the world?"

"Yes, sir," Sharku answered. No harm in recognizing Lagduf's seniority. "We're just here in transit—we've been ordered directly back to the Citadel. They're under attack there, too. The Bandari are behind it. They armed the farmers in the west end of the Valley, and they've set all the plains tribes in motion, too. It would be a wonderful piece of strategy, if it weren't aimed straight at our heads."

Lagduf let out a dismissive snort. "Cattle against the Citadel? Let them come. It saves us the trouble of going out onto the steppe to cull them."

"It's not like that." Sharku wanted to kick the Regiment Leader—or else pound his own head against the ferroconcrete wall. He'd run into the same blind spot, the same unwillingness to take the cattle seriously, when he'd argued against Carcharoth before the Council. "The Bandari are *dangerous*. It's not just that they have better technology than the rest of the folk out there beyond the Shangri-La Valley; they have an ideology, too, and a sense of history. They plan for the long term, and they've been setting this up for a long time. The regiment I'm taking back could use all the help it can get. I wouldn't mind having yours along, too."

"Not bloody likely," Lagduf said with another snort. "We have our hands full trying to hold this place down, I tell you. When we first got here, we couldn't go down the street without somebody taking a potshot at us. We've put a stop to most of that shit, but we've had to pull the town down around the cattle's ears before they'd start paying attention to us. If we pull out now, it'll all flare into rebellion again, soon as we're gone."

"That's not the point—sir," Sharku said. Lagduf was a good officer of the old variety, good at holding off the enemy, good at enduring the boredom of occupation duty. But no thinker, no strategist. Were there any strategists left among the Race? *Am I the only one?* "If Castell City rebels again, that's a nuisance, and we'll have to spend some time and some blood putting things to rights. But if the Citadel falls—if the Citadel falls, we might as well be cattle ourselves, because we can't possibly get back all the things it has in there: more toys than we've worried about in generations, unless I miss my guess. The way the Bandari have outmanipulated us so far, we'll need every one of them before the end, too, or I'm dead wrong—which is just what I'm liable to be."

Lagduf turned to his own men, who had drawn up behind him to listen. "Did you ever hear such an alarmist?" he said, pitching his remarks to them and not to Sharku. "When have cattle beaten the Soldiers?"

"Sir, if cattle hadn't beaten us, we wouldn't be in exile on Haven now—we'd be ruling the Sauron State out there beyond the stars," Sharku said. "Where we belong now!"

Lagduf's glare was venomous.

Sharku turned to address all the Soldiers. "The Citadel is in danger, I tell you. I can use every man possible at my back. What you're doing here is slapping a bandage on a scratch, nothing more. What you need to be doing is turning aside the stroke aimed for the heart. Are you with me, Soldiers of the Race?"

"You are insubordinate," Lagduf said in a voice like ice. "I realize you have been under stress, so I will give you a moment to recognize that fact."

Discipline and subordination ran deep in Soldierly training. Almost, Sharku apologized to his superior and let Lagduf retain control of the situation. But Sharku had seen too many shortsighted men put the Race into the predicament in which it had now found itself. He had protested; they had overruled him; he had obeyed. All at once, obedience snapped.

"I am going on to the Citadel with my Regiments," he declared. "I will gladly accept all volunteers from forces in Castell City to accompany me." He looked at the Soldiers crowding round. "Would you gamble the Citadel and everything in it? And for what do you risk everything we have left in this world? You can go on as you have, slaughter cattle until you're no better than cattle, but you doom the Race!" He raised his voice, as if he were a nomad chief haranguing his men, whipping them up into a frenzy before he took them out to fight. "Who's with me? Who will come to save the Race, now, when it must be done?"

Lagduf folded his arms across his broad chest and gazed scornfully at Sharku. He plainly expected only silence from the Soldiers of his regiment. "I'll report you for this, stress or no stress," he snarled. "If you live, you'll get the shit detail to end all shit det—"

"I'm with you!" An Assault Leader stepped forward. "I'm with you, sir. What we're doing here, it's just a waste of time."

"Muzgash, you'll pay for that!" Lagduf yelled.

Muzgash stood like a rock.

"Me too," Mumak said. "But you knew that."

Another Assault Leader came out, with a dozen behind him. "We're with you." Then Vizgor, Assault Leader of the scout detachments. "Count us in. If we don't take care of the Citadel, we can kiss our ass goodbye."

"That's right," another man said, saluting Sharku. "I'll come along." And more, voices blending together too fast to count. "To the Citadel!"

"You've got 'em," Mumak said cheerfully as Soldier after Soldier came over to Sharku's side and abandoned the commander under whom they'd served. "About time some people get to hear straight talk, don't you think?"

"Time and past time," Vizgor shouted. "We're all with you, Sharku."

Five of Lagduf's men ran outside to shout word of what was happening to the men on patrol. Soldiers of the First Regiment, Sharku's first command, ran into the building. They brandished the rifles they'd taken from the Sons of Liberty. "This is what we're fighting! And the only one who knew it was Sharku!" a Soldier shouted.

And more came in, carrying their own weapons. The word went through the Regiments. Sharku was in command. And death to anyone who didn't like it.

Lagduf wasn't finished, but he was careful not to draw a weapon. "This is my command!"

"No more," Mumak said.

"By what right?" Lagduf demanded. "By what authority?"

"It's in Mumak's magazine," Sharku said. "And if you're lucky I'll be able to keep it there."

Mumak grinned and stamped his assault rifle butt against the floor. Another Soldier took that up, and another, until a hundred rifles drummed a rhythm of war and death.

"I have orders," Lagduf said. "How can I carry them out if you steal my men?"

"Your orders are changed," Sharku said. "They were bad orders to begin with. You fight well, Regiment Leader, but what good is it to carry out the wrong orders? I bear you no bad will, Lagduf. This world is changing, and it's past time for it. We're the future of the Race. Join us."

The drumming rifles were louder now. "Who appointed *you* Threat Analysis Computer?" Lagduf demanded.

Sharku swept his hands in a wide gesture to indicate Mumak and the shouting Soldiers. "They did."

Mumak held up his rifle. The drumming ceased. "Lagduf, the TAC didn't see what was happening. No one in the Citadel understood what the Bandari were up to. The TAC, nor no one in the Citadel understood the connection between the rising in the west and the attack from the steppe on the Citadel. Sharku did! And no one listened, and we're paying the price for that. From now on we trust Sharku!"

"Sharku!" the Soldiers shouted.

"Join us," Sharku said. "Join us, Lagduf."

Lagduf stared at him. He'd clearly lost. It was almost unthinkable: Soldiers did not talk that way to their superiors. But Sharku just had, with the troops behind him.

"Where is Deathmaster Ghâsh?"

"Cleaning up in the lower Valley. I have his approval."

"As if you needed it," Mumak said. "Come on, Lagduf, flip that land gator, or spear it. But decide fast."

"We'll go to the Citadel," Lagduf said. "I agree. But I'm senior! It's my command." But his voice failed him, and he heard laughter.

"Gather your men," Sharku ordered. "You can pick a hundred to hold here. I'm taking the rest with me. If a hundred Soldiers can't do that, the Race is too far gone to be saved." He raised his voice. "Mumak, take charge. I want these Regiments ready to march in four hours."

"Sharku!" Mumak shouted.

The shout was echoed in the room, then outside.

"Sharku!"

# • CHAPTER FOUR

Like ripples from a stone cast into a pool, rumor spread outwards. What the refectory knew now washed up in Nûrnen a few hours later. Oftentimes rumor was garbled, that being the way of such things. This rumor, though, was too big for garbling to matter much. It raced through the city that had risen to serve the Citadel, came to rest in the taverns that lubricated Soldiers and Nûrnenites alike.

At one such, a dive called the Sozzled Stobor, Strong Sven held forth. Gesturing with a cup of tennis-fruit brandy, he declared, "We got nothin' to worry about. Those horsefuckers from the high plains'll never get past the Citadel. By Allah or Jesus or whoever you fancy, we'll scavenge from their carcasses for the next five T-years."

From behind the bar, one of the serving-maids, a wide-faced girl named Raisa, said, "Aye, you'd be the one to think so, wouldn't you?"

Several people chuckled, at the bar and at the tables close by the fire. Strong Sven had a large infusion of Soldier blood, which helped account for his nickname. Most folk had to be careful about alluding to it. But he was sweet on Raisa, and took from her what would have angered him in someone else's mouth.

He said, "How can we doubt it? We fleece the steppe-rats, too, after all, when they ride through here so their drabs can drop their pups. You think they're going to whip the Soldiers?" He chortled at the very idea.

From the safe anonymity of a crowded table, some-body—Strong Sven couldn't pick out who—said, "One of those steppe rats, and a blind one to boot, booted your ass, you son of a Sauron."

Strong Sven felt the tavern grow silent around him. Rage surged in him, and mortification, too. He'd mocked Juchi the Accursed when Juchi came through Nûrnen, mocked him and paid the price for it—old and blind though Juchi was, he had a lot more Soldier blood in him than Strong Sven did. Sven had needed more cycles than he cared to remember to rebuild his fearsome reputation.

He thought about taking on the whole table at once. Reluctantly, he decided against it: seven or eight men sat there, and several of them looked tough. Not even a semi-Sauron cared for odds like those. Besides, touches of Sauron blood were anything but unknown in Nûrnen; even the jokester might have his share.

So Strong Sven managed a halfhearted laugh and said, "Shit, if I'd had a Gatling like the ones out in front of the Citadel, it never would've happened."

"Yeah, but they say the Jewboys are ridin' with the steppe nomads," someone else from that full table observed. "Who knows what they've got?"

Another silence fell, this one thoughtful. The men of the Pale had earned solid respect in the Citadel, both for their strength and their cleverness. The Bandari Pale was halfway around the world and had never paid tribute to the Saurons, but everyone knew how they'd aided Juchi to take the Sauron Base of Angband on their borders.

"I don't care if the Bandari are with 'em," Strong Sven said. "They took a pissant little outpost ten thousand kilometers away, but they can't take the Citadel."

"Maybe not," Raisa said. The Russki flavor she gave her Americ deepened, as it did sometimes when she had things on her mind. "But what if they . . . get past it?"

Now the silence told of horror. If the steppe horde got past the Citadel, through the pass it warded, they'd come upon—Nûrnen. The city that served the Citadel had no wall to protect it. For one thing, nobody had imagined it would need one. For another, the Saurons would not have permitted it even had someone imagined the need: from behind a wall, the folk who served them might more readily have rebelled against them.

But without a wall, the Nûrnenites were as naked to the nomads as Raisa was when Strong Sven came to her little room over the bar. And the nomads had scores to settle. Ever since Nûrnen grew up after the Wasting the Saurons inflicted on Haven's older settlements, its inhabitants had profited by gouging the plainsfolk when they came into the Shangri-La Valley. Haven's steppes were thin of air, too thin for most women to bear their children to term. The tribes for a few thousand kilometers about must use the Citadel's pass—and pay heavily for anything they bought in Nûrnen. The warriors of the steppes were proud and violent men, but the Nûrnenites treated them as savages to be tricked and mocked, with the Saurons to prevent reprisal. Memories of that sort of treatment were long.

But there was more. Even Strong Sven felt a chill, as if from a cold wind off the Atlas Mountains. Nûrnen existed for the convenience of the Soldiers. If the plainsmen got past the Citadel, what sort of vengeance would they wreak on those who had helped the Soldiers hold down Haven?

The wind that blew up Strong Sven's back grew icier still. He wondered if his name had ever found its way up onto the steppe—and knew it probably had. The bards who wandered from encampment to encampment had been embroidering the tale of Juchi the Accursed for a generation now. His exposure on the culling field of Angband Base, his adoption by the nomad tribe of Dede Korkut, his unknowing slaughter of his Sauron father and marriage to his mother—how could any bard resist it? And what better detail of Juchi's heroic death than his victory over a half-Sauron bastard just before he and his sister-daughter Aisha met and slew the Cyborg Battlemaster Glorund? Juchi had died in that encounter, but Aisha lived—lived and raised the steppes to vengeance. She led the horde that bore down on the Citadel. She would not forget Strong Sven's mocking words or his attack on her blinded father.

What vengeance would the nomads wreak on him personally if they knew he was the one who'd reviled their accursed Juchi, the same Juchi whose desiccated fragments still stood impaled by the side of the road just outside of town?

As was his way, Strong Sven covered alarm with bluster. "Never happen," he said loudly. "Never fucking happen. The Soldiers, they'll chew those fur-hat bastards to rags. Like I said, we'll all get rich off the stobor pickings. Hey, sweet thing" —he reached out and stroked, almost fondled Raisa— "gimme another brandy."

He drank till his head buzzed and the tavern seemed to roll and sway whenever he moved his eyes, but the fear would not leave him.

"Well, *I* believe you, Shuli," Barak said soothingly. "But she's got a belly like she swallowed a pumpkin; she can't do much harm from behind that even if she *is* a Sauron. And a Cyborg."

Shulamit paced like a caged tamerlane, up and down in front of the three horses; they were all wearing nosebags, and munched stolidly as they ignored her. *Like the bliddyfuls running this joke of a* hotnot *army*, she thought savagely. Her hand caressed the pistol-grip of the Sauron assault rifle; she had not let it out of her reach since it had been awarded to her at the ceremony. The three of them had ridden off to these rocks for privacy, there was none back around the headquarters tents and the households of the Seven. Too many servants, guards, hangers-on, all creeping round and listening, waiting for a chance to serve or save—*may their dear loyal souls fry*.

"Well, whose fault is it she's about to pup—" She turned on her heel and jutted her chin at Karl. "—*daddy?*" she finished, voice dripping with sarcasm.

"She didn't tell me she was going to get pregnant," Karl said.

"Nu? Maybe you forgot what usually causes it? Your papa never tell you about that part?"

They were standing nose-to-nose now, windmilling their arms; it was hurtfully familiar, almost nostalgic. Karl had been her first lover; she'd always assumed they'd marry in a few years—until he went sniffing after the Sauron bitch like a long dog in rut. Sigrid had used and dumped him—the memory of what she'd seen, when she stumbled on the two of them at the hot-springs of Cliff Lion Oasis burned her yet—but she wasn't about to forgive him. Just yet.

"*Shut up!*"

Barak bar Heber grabbed them both by the back of the neck; the fingers jabbing into Shulamit's flesh above the collar of her jacket seemed like articulated metal rods. Normally that would have been a futile thing to attempt with Karl bar Yigal, who had far more than usual of the genes of the Founder's people, but Barak was three-quarters Sauron by blood himself. Years older and more experienced to boot. Karl gave a tentative heave and settled down as he realized it would mean a real fight to get away. Barak shook them both, then held them motionless until they relaxed.

"All right, you *nunikim*," he grated at last. "*Maybe* you're right, Shuli. She *smells* a bit like a Sauron, but there are a lot of mixed-bloods down in the Valley . . . maybe you're right, though. In which case, this little *wildichaver* here was hooked by a very big land gator himself. A Cyborg can play games with your mind, who knows what a Cyborg female can do. So have a little consideration, eh?"

Shulamit opened her mouth, considered for a moment, and shut it with a snap.

"Well, Ruth bless us with her *wisdom*, a *thought* has penetrated that thick little skull! Shall we be a little less righteous for a while? Hmmm?"

He shook Karl in his turn. "As for you: at your age, all boys think with their pricks—myself included, back when. It's no disgrace, but it's no great honor, either. You're not dipping it now, boy, so *think*. Develop your brain beyond the level of a land gator ganglion! You're the one who got close to the *shisk*. Really close. We've got evidence now, from the tame *hotnot* Shuli found. Now, talk."

Karl glanced down at the toes of his boots, face twisted in concentration. When he looked up, the heavy bones under his mahogany skin were somehow more prominent; for a moment both the others could see a shadow of the man he might be in another decade, if he lived.

"She was strong," he said, in a voice just a touch above a whisper. "She lifted me. . . . I didn't hold back at all, and I didn't hurt her. That's never happened." He stopped, hunting for words. When he spoke again it was less than a whisper. "She was strong, very strong."

"*So*." Barak's face was long and lean, usually open and friendly as well. Now the skin stretched tight over it, making it a thing of slabs and planes and angles. He knew exactly what Karl meant; his own heritage gave him a similar problem with normal women. "We'll ask that lady some questions, after this battle." The grin that followed was feral and precise. "But since she's swallowed an anchor, she won't be going anywhere, will she now?"

Gently, as if to a child, Breedmaster Titus said, "Battlemaster, we need to take additional steps to ensure the security not only of the Citadel but also of the breeding population it contains."

Carcharoth nodded. He kept his eyes fixed on the death's heads Titus wore on his collar tabs. The Cyborg emblems seemed to steady him. He knew he hadn't been thinking as clearly as he should lately. Too much had happened too fast. *Overload*, he thought. It was one of the risks of being a Cyborg.

With their breeding and biomechanical implants, Cyborgs thought faster, farther, and wider than ordinary men, just as their bodies outperformed even those of regular Soldiers. But their achievement had its price. When a Cyborg dismissed data, he dismissed them completely. That was how Glorund, Carcharoth's predecessor as Battlemaster, had died: he'd decided Aisha could not be of

Soldier stock, and proved vulnerable when she proved she was.

Carcharoth's problem was similar, but deeper. His mistake had been believing the Threat Analysis Computer and so assuming the rising in the west end of the Valley had nothing to do with the *Volkerwanderung* sweeping down from the steppes. Now he knew beyond doubt he'd been wrong. The conflict between what he was forced to view as truth and his previous lifelong confidence in the TAC, a confidence central to his whole belief structure, was shaking his connection to reality.

He knew that. Given enough time free from additional stress, he might be able to repair the damage. He wasn't being granted that time. As best he could, he fought the process. But the war went on at levels different from those he was used to consciously controlling. And every skirmish lost left him with fewer mental resources for the next one.

Titus said, "Given the limited forces at our disposal, Battlemaster, how do you recommend we safeguard women and children? Without them, the Race is doomed regardless of success in the field."

"Yes." Carcharoth studied Titus' death's heads again. At a purely tactical level, he still functioned well. The answer took but moments to compute: "Confining dependents to the Inner Keep for the duration of the emergency will allow maximum protection with minimum diversion of manpower resources from combat. I suggest the most genetically valuable—Soldier-born women, their children, and the most promising of the others."

There were tens of thousands of ordinary tribute maidens and their offspring in the Citadel, but the Soldier-born women were the core of the breeding program, rare and precious. Only one in three births was female, and only a minority of those were suitable for reproduction. Back on Old Sauron, the children had been conceived in laboratories, and many brought to term in artificial wombs. Such refinements were long vanished on Haven.

"Excellent," Titus said. "I trust you will draft the appropriate orders?"

"Yes." They formed themselves in Carcharoth's mind. Very likely they'd already formed themselves in Breedmaster Titus' mind, too; he must have been relieved to find his Cyborg counterpart capable of action after all.

Carcharoth wondered why Titus was not going through the same process of mental sorting out (coldbloodedly rational though he was, he didn't care to think of it as a progressive deterioration). When he turned the still-formidable force of his mind on the question, its answer came back quick and clear: *responsibility.* Titus hadn't given the commands that put the Citadel at risk; Carcharoth had. He was paying for it.

Oh, but the rebels, the nomads, and above all the Bandari, they would pay, too. The Battlemaster waited till Titus, having finally had enough of nagging him, gave up and went away. Then he drafted the orders the Breedmaster had requested of him. That didn't take long; when he put his mind to something—when he was able to put his mind to something—he still performed with Cyborg efficiency.

Even as he wrote, he knew the orders would create grumbling among the Citadel's women. They grumbled enough already; he'd heard that in the refectory. Had someone tossed him a piece of stainless-steel small change, he'd have broken the carpers' necks for them. Some of them, no doubt, hoped the Citadel would fall so they could resume the louse-plagued, hungry, fear-ridden existence they'd enjoyed up on the steppes.

"By the *Fomoria* that became *Dol Guldur,* I'll show them," he muttered. Had Titus or any other death's head heard him, he would not have stayed Battlemaster another heartbeat; a Cyborg far enough gone to start talking to himself was in no condition to retain his command. But Carcharoth was not yet far enough gone to slip where his peers would notice.

His thoughts slid back to the flame thrower. As he'd

explained to Dagor, it was a highly specialized weapon. Far more often than not, an assault rifle made a more useful tool. But the terror a man wrapped in flames engendered ... Carcharoth got an erection just contemplating it.

The long-dead man who'd shaped the mythos from which the Race, by coincidence of planetary name, had drawn so much, that man had known of the fear fire forced on foes. So many of the powers on Sauron's side in those battles had used weapons of flame: the Nazgul with their flaming swords, the Balrog with his lash of fire.

A slow smile spread across Carcharoth's features. Was not the flame thrower a lash of fire against the enemies of the Citadel? The smile got broader. He'd burn them all. The smoke from their pyre would mount high into the heavens, and the Race would rule supreme over all Haven forevermore.

When you got right down to it, Carcharoth thought, *Battlemaster* was an insipid title. *Balrog of the Citadel*— now there was something to inspire fear all the way to the Northern Ocean.

With the cunning he still retained, he reminded himself the time to propose the change in nomenclature was not yet ripe. Once the nomads had been incinerated, though, who could have the effrontery to speak against anything he proposed?

*No one*, he told himself. *No one.*

# • CHAPTER FIVE

"Ah, Shulamit?" Karl said.

"Yes?" she replied, reining in her horse.

Barak moved on ahead, his horse breaking into an easy trot as he pressed a leg to its side and shifted balance. The horde had halted, most of it—the rear was still breaking camp when the vanguard was pitching tents—and they were on the fringes, in open space between widely scattered yurts. A dozen warriors from a far-northern tribe were killing a land gator that had gotten too close; the beasts were very bold after months of following and eating everything from foundered horses to the stray child. This one was big, nearly ten meters long. It looked like a stout oblong oval on four columnar legs, the same sandy-reddish color as steppe of native grass, the front of the oval split back for a third of its length, edged with teeth like gems. The warty skin was studded with organic sapphire too, under the crusted, lumpy surface; when the Chukchi riders loosed the arrows from their heavy recurved bows the armor-piercing shafts sank only a few handspans deep with a sound like iron splitting rock. Thick red blood flowed in sluggish trickles down from the puncture points.

The land gator gave a hissing bellow of distress, something like a steam engine with a bellyache, but the arrows bristling from it like spines had not slowed it down much. Not by the speed of the sideways snap that almost caught one rider as his mount skittered aside, or the lashing strike of the tail. That was edged with knife-sharp scutes, and the horse it struck at jumped back with a squeal of fear. The other Chukchi swept around, firing again. The big animal

halted, swinging its notional head—there was no neck—
and the independently pivoting eyes, round and the size of
plums in their high sockets of bone. Land gators had virtually nothing in the way of brain; they were an evolutionary
relic, far more primitive than drillbits or muskylopes. They
were too stupid to be afraid. They did understand pain,
though. This one had had enough; it turned its head
toward the distant mountains and began to lumber
clumsily away.

The Chukchi closed in, firing again and again. One
arrow went *chunk* into the elbow joint of a foreleg. The
land gator bellowed again as it collapsed at one corner
and began walking in a circle around the pivot of its
ruined leg.

"Shulamit?" Karl said again.

She looked over at him, raising an eyebrow. They were
both in full kit; Hammer-of-God had insisted on War Zone
regulations, but he had his helmet off, and the dimday
light cast ruddy tones across his brass-colored hair. Shulamit felt a complex of emotions she could not name; they
seemed to be located just under her breastbone, and made
her armor too tight.

"Um, I want to apologize," he said, meeting her eyes
with a visible effort. "I did something stupid. I'm sorry."
He smiled, like Byers' Star coming up on truenight morning. "Will you forgive me?"

*For sniffing after the Sauron bitch because she was in
heat?* Shulamit thought. *For not believing me? For not believing me for* five months *while she swelled up with her
repulsive spawn, which will be the first Sauron named fan
Reenan, Piet forgive us?*

"Yes, I'll forgive you," she said.

He reached out a hand to her. The smile crumbled
when she slapped it aside.

"I didn't say I'd forgive you *yet*," she snapped.

"Yeweh give me strength—why *not*?" he shouted. "I
*said* I was sorry!"

"*Because you haven't suffered enough yet!*" Shulamit

screamed back, shaking a fist under his nose. Then she wheeled her horse around and spurred away.

Karl bar Yigal sat in the saddle watching her, the dust and grit of her departure stinging his eyes and making them water. He sat that way until her mount vanished behind a herd of muskylope, and until he heard a sound behind him. Laughter.

He turned. A couple of the Chukchi were laughing at him, resting their bows across their thighs and hooting with mirth, their broad flat faces creasing. Karl nudged a heel into the side of his horse and rode up to one of the warriors; the man's face had just enough time to change as the Bandari gripped him by the belt and hoisted him out of the saddle. The others shouted at him in their incomprehensible Siberiak dialect, going for their sabers or knocking arrows. He hoisted the man above his head one-handed, bringing a wheeze of protest from his horse, and then pitched him at two others ten feet away. All three went to the ground thrashing, and one of the horses staggered off a few paces and collapsed itself. Karl dismounted, ignoring the shouts of anger from the other Chukchi. Instead he unlimbered a weapon slung at his saddlebow, a forged-steel mace as long as his thigh with a serrated steel knob the size of a small child's head.

The warriors milled, hooting and yipping and calling to each other as he marched toward the land gator. When it paused in its obsessive circling to snap at him he jumped straight up over the lunge, landing with his legs braced on either side of its mouth and both hands gripping the warhammer. The mace came down and landed on the low-domed surface of its skull, rebounding with a ringing scream of protest. The metal could rebound, but flesh and bone could not; grayish tissue spurted out through cracks in the jewel-armored hide. Karl struck twice more; the last time he withdrew the macehead, it came out with a wet *shluk* sound.

"*Keep* the bloody thing," he snarled over his shoulder, as he marched back to his horse.

❖          ❖          ❖

The big tent's sides were pegged out; it was a calm trueday in late summer, a good ten degrees above freezing. There was still a dense crowd around the clay model on the five-meter by five-meter table; as each new *khan* or *noyon* and his aides got a good look there was more spitting and invocations of Allah, Buddha, and the spirits at the perfection of it. A scale model, of the Citadel and the mountains about it, of the Karakul Pass through the Atlas and the beginning of the lowlands beyond, with Nûrnen sitting right at the edge. More detailed maps were strung from stick frames around the tent, showing the approaches and every facet of the Sauron defenses in immense detail, all of it the fruit of centuries of painstaking espionage and record keeping. Caravans from the Pale had come this way; even more individuals of the People had, often in disguise, and every second or third one had secret training and instruments.

Hammer nodded *well done* at Sapper and his aides. More of them now, people and goods had been streaming in from the Pale. It wasn't particularly difficult to overtake the horde, not if you were moving fast without grazing herds and families to slow you down.

"Khans, *ghazis*, enemies of the Saurons and their Dark Lord," Hammer said.

Silence fell, a deep hush of respect. The commanders bowed with helmets under their arms, or saluted in the manner of their various tribes and nations. Even Chaya inclined her head. It was like the glow of a glass of good brandy by a warm fire; Hammer could feel the pain in his leg fade, and the gnawing anxiety. Even the weird not-quite-real feeling he'd had since Chaya spoke to the tribes last truenight faded a little. It had been eerie, the tall figure in white lifting her arms on a high rock above a sea of faces that stretched to infinity.

*First things first,* he thought. "Khan Oyuk Tepe of the Mongur Kipchaks, come forth," he snapped.

That *khan* did; there was another murmur at the bandaged wounds he bore, and more still at the two guards who held him by arm and shoulder. Another Kipchak prince of high rank walked beside him, weaponless as well and with a nervous sweat on his flat brown face.

"Some of you have heard, and the rest should: *Khan Oyuk*, to whom is assigned the vanguard, took his men forward without orders."

"I could not restrain their—" the prisoner began. His voice sank under Hammer-of-God's glare, until the loudest sound was the snapping of guy ropes against the canvas roof.

"Bullshit," Hammer snarled in the homely Americ of his youth. Then he shifted back to plains Turkic:

"*Silence, dog!* You couldn't restrain yourself at the thought of paddling your paws in the loot of Nûrnen! So much for your oaths to the Seven."

He turned to the other commanders. "What is the penalty for those who break ranks to plunder before the battle is done?"

The growl that followed might have come from a pack of stobor closing around a wounded camel. There was a rattle of expensive steel-splint armor as hard callused hands closed on saber hilts, and a collective half-step toward the luckless Kipchak noble. Any steppe warrior knew the answer to *that* question.

"And more than that, this fool had no better idea of *how* to get to Nûrnen than to ride past the outworks of the Citadel; he lost a thousand men. A thousand men!" Hammer half-turned on his heel and bent slightly to glare into the nomad's face. "How many Saurons did you kill, thief and son of a thief? How many?"

Oyuk was no coward. "None, as you know," he snapped back. "The Gatlings caught us in the open—the sons of Shaitan can see in the dark!" The guards forced the nomad down on his knees, and stepped back. Hammer kicked him with calculated viciousness; it hurt, but Oyuk collapsed, wheezing.

"Thus giving them their first victory of this war," Hammer snarled. "Giving heart to all their followers. Giving them a thousand heads—the heads of brave men who deserved to die better than at the orders of a greedy thief and fool."

"Could you do better?" Oyuk snarled.

"I *will* do better," Hammer replied; in the same instant, he drew the Citadel-made revolver from his belt and shot the smaller man through the chest. "I will not charge fifty-meter concrete walls and Gatling guns with sabers and bows. I will not tolerate disobedience."

The body dropped, kicked twice, voided its bowels, and went limp. The smell of blood and shit rose on the summer-warm air. The smoking muzzle of Hammer's weapon turned on the younger nomad.

"You are now *khan* of the Mongur Kipchaks, Suleiman Tepe," he said. "Can you do better than this dead dog?"

Suleiman was a man of thirty T-years or so, hard-faced even by nomad standards, and evidently quick on the uptake.

"Command me, lord!" he said, bowing low.

"Good," Hammer replied. "Take your place." Casually, he tucked the weapon back and rested one foot on the dead body.

"Now," he went on, "even this stobor food beneath my boot could get something half-right. We're not going to take the Citadel by storm, and if we sit down to make a siege on the steppe outside the Karakul Pass, we'll start starving to death in about three days." Haven days, almost two T-weeks. "While the enemy draws on the wealth of the Shangri-La. By the end of the sixth day, we'll be eating our horses."

Hammer drew his saber and used the point to trace a circle around the Citadel. It stood proudly in the mountains on the west side of the center of the Karakul Pass. To its east the narrow Pass wound over a high saddle between the Atlas Mountains and the Girdle of God Range. The Pass wound south from the Steppes down to the city of Nûrnen at the northeastern edge of the Shangri-La Valley.

"We need to *circumvallate*—" He stopped, groping for

a Turkic word. "—We need to establish a complete ring around the Citadel, and for ourselves, win access to Nûrnen. With Nûrnen in our hands, we can eat. And the enemy cannot."

"Much loot in Nûrnen," a Cossack leader said. "By Mary and the Saints, I passed through with our tribe's women, and the Sauron-loving arselickers charged us ten ounces of gold for four months *camping* in an open field. Merchants so fat that grease ran from their mouths when they looked up at Cat's Eye made us pay a dozen sheep for a man's-weight of flour—ten times what they paid the farmers for it."

There was a chorus of similar complaints. Nûrnen had a monopoly of half a dozen necessities for nomads taking flocks or pregnant women or trade-goods into the great lowlands, and its merchants and traders used that power ruthlessly. The Saurons approved; the more wealth that was concentrated in the Citadel's dependent city, the more resources they had quick access to.

"Gold, yes," Hammer nodded, stabbing the air above the tiny streets on the clay model. "And silver, jewels, spices, drugs, fine rugs, blooded horses." He could see eyes narrowing and hear lips smacking. Life on the steppes of Haven was very hard, and wholehearted greed was a survival characteristic. "More than that. The harvest" —his sword took in the area west of Nûrnen— "of the richest lands on Haven, and it's just past harvest-time. The tribute will be streaming into Nûrnen for sorting and forwarding to the Citadel. Steel and copper and brass, grain and cheese and meat, livestock and cloth. Herds of fat stock fed on planted grasses. Grazing for all our beasts . . ."

*And the souls of men*, he thought ironically. Some of the nomad *khans* were practically mooing with lust at the catalog of wealth. Hammer judged his moment, then nodded to one of the Bandari regimental commanders; there were nearly three thousand fighters of the People here by now.

"How do we get past the Citadel?" the man said, tugging absently at the long black braid of his hair. "Their

Gatlings command all the open ground in that pass."

Hammer grinned like a stobor and shifted his sword-point south on the relief map.

"There are trails passable on foot, a few on horseback, through the northern foothills of the Atlas range." He indicated an area at the northern approach to the Karakul Pass. "The Saurons control them by patrols—but thanks to our little diversion off in the western Shangri-La, they have not even enough men here to man all the gun-bunkers in the Citadel itself. We'll push through, making a road for wagons as we go. Then" —his saber cut through the hills, then southwest— "we bring up the siege weapons and hit the ruins of the old Gates with wave attacks from here and here." He pointed to northeast and northwest of the old Gates of Paradise, ruined generations before by earthquakes.

"We move past the Citadel—fast—to Nûrnen. With the materials in Nûrnen, we can throw a C-shaped ring of field fortifications around the Citadel; if the old men and boys there come out and fight us, we'll swamp them with sheer numbers."

The young Bandari raised his hand again. "*Aluf*, two points. First, what about Saurons in there, the blockhouses in the hills? We can't *count* on them all being gone. Second, what about those field Regiments? They're going to come back mighty damn fast, once we sit down around their homes and women."

Hammer nodded. Those were good points. Actually, the Saurons would have done well to spend more time on fieldworks in those hills, but that was *Soldati* strategy for you. Aggressive to a fault, move forward, strike fast, crush. With the Citadel as an invulnerable base of maneuver and its normal garrison to send out strong patrols, the hills would be a worse deathtrap than the open ground under the fortress walls. The Citadel didn't think in terms of being stripped of all its maneuver forces and thrown back on a static defense. "If we can take Nûrnen and establish our ring, the field brigades will break their teeth on it;

between the rebellion, and the way we'll strip the areas near the pass of supplies, it'll be a month or better before the field brigades can get back here. To make sure we get through the hills, I'm sending in our finest leaders," he said, with a slight smile.

The Pale commander reached back and gripped a shoulder in either hand. Barak bar Heber and Kemal of the clan that had been Juchi's came forward on either side. "With picked assault troops. And Sapper—"

"Djinni," a chief distant from the table muttered.

"—has something new from Clan Gimbutas. A *secret weapon*." That brought grins and more spitting and oaths. "Have no worries. Nûrnen shall fall before the next truenight!"

"*Woe.*"

Chaya's voice, the thin reedy whisper that was so unlike the matter-of-fact tones of the Judge he had known. Hammer felt the hairs try to stand erect along his spine, and he was sure that every other man in the tent besides the corpse beneath his foot felt the same sensation.

The Judge stood, her eyes focused on something beyond the tentpole.

"Woe unto Nûrnen, the bloody city; earth is full of her iniquities. Woe unto Nûrnen, the bloody city, for she shall fall—and who shall weep for her?"

The tall figure in the white robes swept out of the tent, and a vast rustling sigh went through those of the horde near enough to see. Her voice rose to an astonishing shout:

"*Woe unto Nûrnen! She is fallen, and her children shall be scattered like the dust!*"

Hammer shivered, turning back to the commanders. "Prepare your men for battle within thirty-six hours," he said quietly, as a long swelling roar of exultation rose from those who were listening to Chaya's impassioned speech. "This isn't going to be easy—but we're going to win."

Temujin was pacing in the little foothills' hollow. He looked much better now, with the bruises given a month to fade; you could believe he had been born a prince of his tribe, a slim narrow-waisted young man with the broad shoulders of an archer. Kinsmen with the horde had outfitted him, from curl-toed boots to embroidered chamois coat and astrakhan-wool cap, with a good plain saber at his side. His face was the color of old amber and handsome in a blunt-featured way, and he walked gracefully, without the bowlegged waddle many steppe-dwellers had on foot. There was wary respect in his glance when Shulamit reined in and swung down from the saddle in a jingle of iron.

*She-tamerlane*, he thought. Deadly and unpredictable, for all she was so young. All haBandari women would as soon hand you your testicles on a knifepoint as look at you, but this one was worse than most.

"What results?" he asked.

She spat something in a guttural, choppy language he could now recognize as Bandarit, if not understand. From the expression, it was something obscene.

"Barak believes us, but won't do anything until after this battle; doesn't want to bother the commanders, I suppose. He says the bitch isn't going anywhere, not with that belly. *Karl* believes it too, for what that's worth. Which is nothing. She'll get away, I *know* it! Yeweh and the spirits of the Founders curse her with boils and hemorrhoids."

Temujin sighed and nodded. He had complete faith that Sigrid would get away, pregnant or no. He was also uncertain whether that angered or reassured him. When he looked up again, Shulamit was staring at him thoughtfully; the back of his neck prickled a little as he saw she had the grip of the assault rifle in her hand. The muzzle was pointing straight at him, ready to tear him in half with a twitch of her finger.

"And it's a time for paying debts," she said grimly, baring her teeth.

*Oh, no, not again!* he wailed inwardly, as his hand made a minuscule movement toward his sword. He had killed three men in duels, who called him "Sauron's dog," including the one who struck him while he was bound. It had been very good to be a free man, not knocked about and threatened with torture—perhaps too good to be true. *All the* tngri—*I must have been a* monster *in my last life to deserve this!* The haBandari wildcat must hold him responsible for setting Sigrid out on the steppe to begin with. Unfair!

"Drop the swordbelt," Shulamit said flatly. "Not a word—just drop it. Throw it aside. The boot-knife too."

Temujin obeyed. The air felt cold on his sweating face, despite the late summer warmth of the trueday and the still air of the little hollow where they had arranged to meet. He was suddenly acutely conscious of the spicy smell of the bracken beneath his feet.

"Down. Down, I said!"

He went down on his belly, hands behind his neck. "If you're going to kill me, at least let me die standing, you mad bitch," he said.

"Shut up. Roll over; keep your eyes closed."

For a moment there was nothing but a muted clanking and rustling. With a sinking feeling he thought of someone preparing knotted cords and sharp little sticks. *What did I do to deserve this?*

"You can look now."

He opened his eyelids, blinked them shut again, and stared, bug-eyed. Shulamit was standing over him, entirely naked, a silhouette against Cat's Eye, tying back her hair with a thong. Then she sank to her knees, straddling him, and grinned.

"I figure what I owe you is about twenty minutes of extreme happiness," she said, unfastening his belt. "That's what I got when you came up with her name . . . you can move now."

# • CHAPTER SIX

The senior mare was close to foaling. Sigrid finished determining that the mare was well and the foal was as it should be, and went on to one of the younger, and less gravid, mares.

The yearling that she had taken from Katlinsvale, now a gangling two-T-year-old, came up behind and nibbled her hair.

Time to start training that one. She knew about the halter and the lead. She would need more if she was to be ridden. Sigrid had not decided yet. Her potential as a broodmare was priceless, but in between foals she should be of other use. Anything else was inefficient.

They were all in excellent condition, barely run down from their T-year on the march. And Sigrid was avoiding less pleasant considerations.

Soldier heads on spears. Soldiers killed by this army of mongrels and madmen. There were Bandari with assault rifles now. They talked of taking the Citadel as if they really could do it.

*Never,* said Soldier pride.

*Impossible,* said the Cyborg brain, shutting out data that made cattle a threat to Soldiers.

*All too possible,* said the gestalt that was Sigrid, assembling data with tireless efficiency. Hormone changes from pregnancy affected it; she had no illusions about that. But she could still put two binary units together and get binary ten.

She draped an arm over the filly's back and rubbed the horse's nape, frowning at the data running behind her eyes. The fetus rolled and kicked, demonstrating admirable technique. The Frystaat-Soldier combination was turning out even better than she had hoped. He was maturing early, physically. She could expect equally impressive neural development.

It was a pity that she had not had access to the laboratory in the Citadel in the early T-months, when she could have made the modifications that engineered a Cyborg from superior Soldier stock. What materials she had with her were enough to ascertain that he was healthy, carried no overtly lethal recessives, and was developing ahead of schedule, but still within acceptable norms.

She had noticed the habit pregnant women had of resting a hand on her belly as if to protect it. She was doing it now. She took her hand away and went back to rubbing the filly's nape.

Soon she was going to have to admit something.

She was uneasy.

The little bitch watched her constantly. Wherever she went, the bitch seemed to be, fondling her captured rifle and glaring in a manner that, no doubt, she reckoned formidable. She made no secret of what she thought. The word Sauron was usually a part of it.

So far no one seemed to believe her. Sigrid knew better than to think that that would last.

And then?

Fight her way out if she had to. Cattle had a kink about pregnant women. Soldiers did too, for that matter. It was hardwired into the system. It made them protective. And they persisted in thinking that pregnant meant delicate.

She was off balance, but she could compensate. She was ungainly, but she was a poor Soldier if an extra few kilos up front could cancel her fighting abilities. It was useful to let cattle think that it had, to stay among her horses when there was a skirmish, to wear an aspect that shouted noncombatant.

Her back informed her that it was tolerating its load for now, but by the time she came to term, it was going to be displeased. If it had been up to her to engineer the perfect Soldier, she would have rearranged the reproductive system and found a better way than this to carry a baby.

She said as much to the one who had been standing in what he probably fancied was deep shadow, breathing like a bellows and wrapped in a breathtaking combined stink of lye soap and land gator blood. He stopped breathing. He could hardly stop stinking.

"It was half dead when you killed it," she said. "Whose head were you bashing in? Or did you care?"

"She says you're a Sauron."

Sigrid almost smiled. "Does she? And who is that famous she? Your Judge with the senile dementia? Your bint with the planet-sized chip on the shoulder?"

Karl burst into the light, but stopped short, hands working, face shades darker than usual. "You are. Aren't you?"

"Will you club me to death if I say yes?"

His eyes dropped to her middle. She rested her hand on top of it. And smiled.

He howled like a tamerlane. "I should have cut my balls off!"

"You should not," said Sigrid. "Your genes are by far the best thing about you."

"You . . . ice . . . cold . . . bitch."

She studied him. "You could probably give me a fight. But I would win."

It would have been characteristic of him to spit something else equally uninspired, heave for breath a few more times, then bolt. He surprised her by staying put. "That's my child, too. Don't you forget that."

"Never for a moment," she said.

Karl stood glaring at her, but gradually going gray. Abruptly he turned and ran. Somewhat later, she heard the sound of retching.

Bandari, she had noticed, had a horror of Soldiers that amounted to phobia. Interesting, considering what led them on this march. This reaction was extreme, but preferable to the alternative, which was attempted murder.

She did not regret driving him to it. He should forget his Bandari delusions of fatherhood. This child was a Soldier. So he would be born, and so he would die.

And if the Citadel fell . . .

She would get it back. If that was Soldier arrogance, then so be it. Blind arrogance had set Soldier heads on spears. Open-eyed arrogance tempered with caution would serve her until she had something better to work with.

She had already considered and discarded assassinating the leaders, or at least the madwoman who led them. That would not dissipate the horde. She would only make a martyr. And martyrs above all were the wrong thing to make in this kind of war.

Karl, having gagged up his supper, was gone. She thought of calling after him to tell him where his little bitch was—rutting in the grass with a Mongol who appeared to have done her a favor. But that would have been petty. Pettiness was inefficient. Which was rather a pity, but she could not help her conditioning, any more than she could help the gnawing in her stomach. She signaled the she-dog to guard the horses, and, followed by the he-dog, went in search of her own supper.

Barak chopped his hand backward and the column behind him sank to the ground. To his ears, the rattle and clank of iron and stone was as loud as thunder; worse, he knew it would be just as loud to the Saurons ahead. If there were Saurons ahead. There were *probably* enemy soldiers ahead; they knew the horde was close, and this was one of the obvious ways through the hills to the south of the Citadel and the Karakul Pass. High enough to be chilly, even on a trueday noon in late summer . . . some of the chiefs had been surprised they didn't wait for darkness. Barak snorted silently; how long was it going to take them to realize that the Saurons could see in the dark?

He moved forward, harness muffled to prevent any clatter, Sauron assault rifle at the ready. Shulamit was beside him; she was almost as quiet, rag-wrapped saber across her back and the same alien deadliness in her hands. Other rifle-armed followed, with Sauron weapons or Pale breechloaders. A squad of Sapper's pets followed them, carrying boxed instruments. The hills narrowed in around them as they moved, turning from tumbled rock cut by gullies to a canyon, with sides that closed in and rose. Signalers dropped off as they progressed, keeping each other in line of sight; the rock turned from old granite to softer volcanic tufa and lava, cut into fantastic shapes by wind and water, red and yellow and iron-red and black. The level of the ground rose as they pressed westward, and a wind was coming up from the valley. It smelled of wet and greenery, and of the dry canyons of the pass as well, and of men. A fair number, quite close. Sweating. Human norms, and the slightly blander, less salty scent of Saurons. Tools on rock sounded, and metallic clanking he could not identify; that should cover their approach, if they were very careful.

Barak made a hand gesture. Everyone stopped, and the last in front dropped to their bellies. They crawled forward through dirt and soft pumice dust that scratched at the insides of their noses, until they could look out. Behind him, the riflemen moved softly to take up positions upslope and down, wherever there was good cover and a clear line of retreat.

The Saurons were setting up behind rock *sangars*—one-man breastworks—a couple of hundred meters beyond this narrow spot. The cliffs here would make it easy to outflank a blocking force and fire down from above; the broader spot the enemy had chosen had a dropoff on one side and an unscalable overhang on the other. *Good choice*, Barak thought. Picks and shovels were flashing. His eyes went into telescope mode, and the scene flashed out at him. A dozen Saurons, and twice that of human norms—they must be laborers from Nûrnen, helping with the entrenchments. Several of the Saurons looked preadolescent, and the one with Assault Group Leader's collarflashes had only a fringe of gray hair above his ears and neck. There was nothing substandard about their equipment, though; every man had an assault rifle—some of the outlying bases were making do with bolt-action models these days—and they were setting up a portable Gatling gun, with a huge sheet-steel tub of ammunition. Rifle pits were being dug, and a stone *sangar* for the Gatling. Boxes of grenades were being carried forward. In Sauron hands, grenades were about as bad as a mortar, and he wouldn't be surprised if the Saurons had one of *those* too.

Barak made another hand signal. The last engineer unpacked his box of tricks. Part of it was a shuttered lantern for signaling back down the line to the forward base. The rest was crystal lenses and brass wheels and turning screws, all on a tripod that itself could be carefully adjusted. Barak knew the cost of them: he had been an officer in the *h'gana*, the army of the Pale, after all. About the price of five hundred good horses or ten thousand sheep, endless skill by the finest artisans on Haven, shaping and filing. Well worth it, since the ability to judge distances with precision was half the secret of the Bandari military "magic" the tribes feared so much.

"Got it," the engineer whispered. He had the lanky build and ash-blond hair that sometimes cropped up in Clan Gimbutas; there was a Balt strain among them. "Got the *meshgah* pinned like a beetle on a card."

"Send it," Barak said.

He slid his assault rifle through the narrow slit between two rocks and focused his eyes again. Behind him, the lantern clattered as the engineer squeezed at the handle and so worked the slats over the flame and mirror. Sure enough, the gray-haired Sauron turned and looked, squinting. Then his eyes flared wide, and Barak's finger stroked the trigger. *Crack.* The rifle gave its love-tap to his shoulder, nothing compared to the black-powder models he was used to. Barak could generally hit a man at five hundred meters snapshooting; prone, with a steady rest and this fine piece of Sauron engineering, the thousand or so were nothing. The copper-jacketed bullet punched the Assault Group Leader back like a jointed doll, blowing out a fist-sized exit hole where the back of his neck had been.

The rest of the Bandari opened up. So did the Sauron Gatling, even though they had to spend a second or two to finish securing it to the mounting. The savage *rrrrrrrrt–rrrrrrrt* of the six-barreled weapon slammed echoes back from the jumbled hills around them. Fifteen-millimeter slugs savaged the volcanic rock in front of Barak's position, and he rolled backward spitting out pumice dust and blinking to clear his eyes before crawling to a new position. The engineer was lying on his back, tranquilly making notes on a pad.

"Hope Sapper gets that bloody thing into position pretty damned soon, or we'll be needing Piet's direct intervention," Barak snarled to him. As if in counterpoint, a scream came from the cliff to their right and a Bandari sniper fell from his firing post, pinwheeling through the air to land with a tooth-grating *clump*. Two more rounds hit him on the way down; the Sauron was taking no chances. "And the Founder helps those who help themselves."

"Sapper will come through," the man replied. "Hell, Hammer-of-God's watching him, isn't he?"

"Just pray they don't undershoot."

"Up here ought to do," Sapper called, pointing ahead and then wheeling his horse and riding westward to the platform he had selected.

"About bloody time," Hammer snarled.

"The men are working very hard," Aisha said. "They are not accustomed to it."

She nodded down at the trail, unconsciously laying a hand on her stomach. Karl Haller put an arm around her shoulders with something of the same protectiveness, and Hammer harumphed from the base of his throat.

They *were* working hard. The new-made road stretched back five kilometers, to where the main camp of the horde butted up against the hills, directly northeast of the Gates of Paradise. Almost hidden in the dust of the workings, and not much of a road, just the boulders rolled out of the way and the fist-sized rocks stamped down and covered in gravel, then watered and rolled. Not arrow-straight, either; Sapper's people had laid it out for minimum grade and maximum speed. Still more than good enough for wagons and heavy transport. Men swarmed ahead of it like ants across spilled beet sugar, slamming at rock with crowbars and sledges and improvised tools of a dozen sorts, digging with their hands if nothing else was available. Twenty thousand of them at a time in continuous relays, with tribeswomen carrying endless loads in baskets, on their heads or slung between two. It was amazing what that many pairs of hands could do, even when they were unused to any labor that involved getting off their horses.

Everyone wanted to get into the Valley, into Nûrnen.

Rations were short already, and little grass was left within a day's journey of the entrance to the Karakal Pass.

"I'm going down and seeing them get the *Ariksa* in place," he said.

The weapon was being hauled up by a twenty-pair hitch of muskylopes, and a hundred haBandari troopers besides, pulled off road duty for something that needed skill as well as raw muscle; that was besides the twenty or so who made up its crew. Six more of the weapons waited back in camp, but there was only room to deploy one here. They'd bring the others up once they were through the hills. Once they'd run past the Citadel they could sledgehammer their way in from both sides, with the horde to pin the Saurons down and the siege mortars to blast them out. The walls of the Citadel itself would be impregnable, but their field fortifications wouldn't.

Hammer ran a critical eye over the *Ariksa*; as a secret, it had never seen action before, but he had been involved in the planning and execution, of course. There was a special six-wheeled articulated wagon to carry it, man-tall wheels rimmed in steel and tired with woven drillbit gut. On that was a circular platform of welded steel plates and bars, none thinner than a man's palm. Endless trouble and expense. Above *that* was a complex arrangement of wheels and gearing, with a steel rod in the center the height of a man and the thickness of a strong man's arm.

The whole thing was heavy, and that was not counting the ammunition in the carts coming up behind. The smiths of Eisenstaadt, the Gimbutas Clan headquarters town back in the Eden Valley, had worked on it and its siblings for sixty years, experimenting and adjusting at a cost that set two successive *kapeteins* and their councilors wincing. All for an opportunity like this.

One of the Bandari officers heaving at a wheel left off and came over to meet him, flipping a casual gesture of salute. Except for a harness supporting breasts that scarcely needed it she was stripped to the waist, her thick arms and blocky torso glistening with sweat where it wasn't plastered with the dust that made a mask of her eyes; they were bright blue, glittering like the silver medallion bouncing between her breasts. A couple of the nomad roadworkers stopped to gape at her as she scratched under her halter, until someone shouted them back to their tasks. The wagon ground on, with a slamming rattle as one wheel rolled over a larger-than-average rock and crunched down an inch. The ground shook.

"Marija bat Yentle fan Gimbutas," she said. "Glad to be here; we could follow your track by the bones and scavengers all the way from Cliff Lion Springs."

Hammer nodded. That was a compliment, of sorts . . . and you had to live up to your reputation.

"Glad you're ready to go right into action," he said.

"This *mamzer*" —she jerked a thumb over her shoulder— "my grandfather, my father, and my mother all worked on it. I've been wanting to fire the bliddy thing in action all my life!"

He nodded silently, and the teams heaved again. Up ahead, Sapper's squads were working to level a place for it, and from further ahead still they could hear the crackle of

gunfire. Gunfire and something else, something that
sounded like a powered saw cutting stone. That would be
the Sauron Gatling that Barak had reported. Hammer
smiled thinly, and several of the nomads working nearest
made warding gestures behind his back. The road ended
here, more or less, with only the largest stones pushed out
of the way. The big wagon lurched and slowed, and more
haBandari swarmed forward to steady it and roll it the last
dozen meters.

Few of the nomads would be willing to associate with
such technology, reeking of djinni.

What followed was as smoothly choreographed as a
Piet's Day dance. Jacks went onto the corners, and the
coulter pins of the wheels were pulled out; pairs of workers hammered them off the axles and rolled them away;
and the gears ratcheted as the wagon-turned-platform was
lowered onto the prepared bed of rocks. They paused for
an instant to check the levelling as it touched down, then
pounded long iron stakes through slots in the frame to
secure it. Hands spun the wheels, and the long steel rod
dipped. Nearer to Hammer, tarpaulins were stripped off
the ammunition cart. Each shell within was two meters
long, a stubby cylinder with fins at one end and a blunt
rounded head at the other. Moans broke out from the
nomads, for on each iron casing was painted the symbol of
the atom. Panic sent them surging back.

Hammer grinned. Actually, there was nothing inside
the shells but good old-fashioned black powder, mill-
ground to a coarse peameal consistency as for blasting
work. There was, however, a *lot* of powder—and it never
hurt to use tribal superstition. *Hellmouth, they think*
accounting *is magic,* he mused. Marija bat Yentle came
back, wiping herself down with her shirt and then shrug-
ging into it.

"We're getting the portable crane up," she said. A shell
went into the cradle, swung over and up and turned; waiting
hands guided it, and it slid down with the pole travelling up
the central hollow until it disappeared altogether.

"Still seems odd for a projectile weapon not to have a barrel," Hammer mused aloud.

"Oh, it's got a barrel," Marija said. "The cylinder inside the shell is the barrel, the pole is the piston-head, and when you let off the propelling charge" —she brought her hands together and then swung them apart— "gas expands and pushes the piston out of the cylinder. It's called a 'spigot mortar,' and we spent years piecing it together from hints in bits and pieces of ancient works—had to reinvent it, really. Bloody *hell* getting the tolerances close enough to make, ah, sorry, sir."

Hammer waved indulgently. Sapper and his chief aides were consulting over pieces of paper; messages flashed up and down the line of signal-lanterns. Sapper himself turned the wheels, and the huge weight of the shell swivelled, light and precise. Then he clamped the end of a long blue cord that ran from its base into a small mechanism of wood and brass, and hopped down to walk over to Hammer-of-God.

"Marija." He nodded to the officer. "Hammer—you want to do the honors?"

Around them haBandari were scattering back, taking cover. The nomads dropped their tools and followed with considerably more speed, as soon as translated explanations told them why. Hammer took the igniter in his hands and held it aloft.

"One—"

"Two—"

"Three." His fingers clenched.

Nothing dramatic happened, just a fizzing as the friction-primer inside lit the slowmatch. He turned and walked away slowly, letting his limp show a little, and stopped to stretch before he stepped behind a rock some distance away. Aisha was there—he scowled at that—and Chaya, and Kemal watching with bright curiosity in his slanted eyes. No night-terrors with *him*; he was a downy one, and dangerous. They all craned their necks around the edges of the rock. Thirty seconds, Sapper had said. The

sound of the Gatling came clearly, now that everyone was
holding their breath and the work-parties had stopped in
their labors all the way back to the camp. Everyone was
watching . . . even the spies who were undoubtedly among
them, probably slipped in from Nûrnen last truenight;
nobody could keep an accurate headcount in this mass-
migration masquerading as a war.

Hammer-of-God Jackson felt a sudden deep happiness,
pleasure sweeter than he had felt since his wife died, as
deep as the pain had been when his son's wound went gan-
grenous. Whatever happened, he was *here.* He had led an
army to the gates of the Citadel; he had mustered a host
against Antichrist. Chaya was the prophet; Aisha the voice
that had lashed the plains people into rage and shame: old
Barak back in the Pale had seen which way the wind was
blowing with those shrewd little eyes of his and sent what
was necessary along. But *he* had organized it, he, plain
Hammer-of-God Jackson of no clan, Jackson the share-
cropper's son, the dumb Edenite, the peasant. His name
would be there in the histories and the songs. *Hammer-of-
God.* God's hammer to smite the wickedness of the
Saurons, to humble their pride and might.

*BWAAAMP.* The ground moved and hit at his feet; he
reached out a hand to steady himself against the rock.
Dust puffed up; a great pancake of it about the *Ariksa,*
mingled with the rotten-egg stink of burnt powder. An
arch blurred through the sky heading toward the north for
a few seconds, then another crash—louder, but muffled by
distance and the rocky earth between. The Bandari stood
and cheered at the cloud of black smoke and dust rising
from the unseen target. The crew rushed out and began
dancing around their weapon, leaping on it and kissing it
and yelling endearments. More slowly, the nomads joined
the celebration, until Hammer turned and roared; officers
passed it down the chain of command, and in ten minutes
the picks were sounding on rock once more.

"That," Hammer said, his hands on his hips as he stared
north, "ought to take care of that."

# • CHAPTER SEVEN

"Three. Four."

Shulamit tossed the grenade backward over her head, over the lip of rock to her rear. It went off with a sharp *crang* as she rolled three paces to the right and whipped around to point her rifle down the steep slope. The Sauron—he looked barely thirteen, but death if he got in here with her—was still plastered to the rock, but his right arm was missing to the elbow and blood ran in sheets down his face. She blinked with surprise at that. It would have been *impossible* to catch it and start a return throw in that time. Her finger moved of its own volition, pumping out three shots into the body only ten meters away. It jerked and peeled backward, slithering down the rock. Another bullet from across the open space cracked by close enough above her head to feel the passage, and a line of white fire creased one buttock.

"*Yeeeee!*" she shrieked, tumbling forward. The rocks smashed at her, although the armor took most of it; she came to rest behind a half-boulder, jammed tight halfway down the slope. It took a minute of wiggling before she could touch the injury. *Flesh wound*, she thought with relief, no worse that half a dozen scrapes and minor cuts she'd gotten today. *Bliddy arsecutter Saurons*, she added, as it began to sting. A hand's width over and it would have smashed her pelvis, or cut her spine. The second frightened her more than the first.

Then the world seemed to end. The rock came alive and pitched her back and forward, and there was a sound that drove needles of pain in her ears. Then near-silence, and a

cloud of dust that rasped at a throat and nose already raw.
She hugged at the rock for the count of thirty; there
seemed to be a rumbling to the north that increased as she
swallowed. *My ears are numb. Something was so loud it
numbed my ears.* Things started to patter down out of the
sky around her, fragments bouncing off her armor and
making her helmet ring. Shulamit blinked and coughed
and spat, pulling herself up on the rough surface of the lava
boulder until she could peer across at the Sauron position.

The ground looked wrong. Where there had been an
overhanging cliff and a dropoff was now a cone-shaped fan
of debris, with scree still bounding and hopping across the
surface as it shifted. The sight was so strange that it took a
moment to sink in, as did the towering column of black
smoke that was beginning to flatten out at its top. Then
voices came to her, faint and tinny: the other haBandari,
cheering. Barak was not just cheering; he was *capering*,
and whirling the engineer around in a helpless circle. She
realized what it meant and started cheering herself.

"It means we'll be through the hills by next truenight,"
Hammer said flatly. "We've smashed half a dozen of their
posts in the Atlas Foothills, and we're pushing through
against the rest. It's costing us—thousands of dead
already—but they can't stop us.

"They can't hold in the open because we'll swamp
them, and if they try to hold a squeeze-point we can blast
them out. We'll have to attack through the pass itself as
well, the ruins of the Wall. That will cost heavily, but we'll
be able to come at them from both ends. The Saurons are
no fools; once we've blasted out enough of their strong-
points they'll pull everything they've got back into the
Citadel itself. We'll push the road through, and then—"

The inner circle of the commanders was in his tent, sip-
ping at tea or something stronger and looking at the
beaming Sapper and his protégée Marija. Cat's Eye was
down, and Byers' Sun was near the western horizon. The
lantern hanging above them cast its yellow light, kindly on

faces worn with strain and worry. Across the steppe to the east the campfires sparkled like a galaxy in turmoil, farther than the eye could see even from this high place.

"And then?" Chaya said quietly. It was her normal voice; beside her, Aisha and old Karl relaxed visibly.

"Nûrnen falls," Hammer said flatly. "Then for a cycle or two, chaos. *Walpurgisnacht.*" He inclined his head toward the tentflap; outside, the horde was chanting, convinced that the spirits themselves had promised victory. The sound was like heavy surf beating on a cliff.

"Not the Lord God Jehovah himself come down from heaven with a thunderbolt in his hand could control that bunch, when they see a city with no wall spread out like a feast in front of their eyes," Hammer added. "There must be a third of a million of them, now—of fighting men alone."

The sweep east had emptied the Great Northern Steppe; now the tribes of the northeastern highland plains, nearer to the Citadel, were streaming in. Mad with greed and hate and memory of ancient wrongs. The Lidless Eye had rested heavily on those lands, since the very beginning when thousands had died building the fortress walls of the Citadel. They were numerous, too, being so close to the best birthing grounds on Haven.

"We can't lose the foodstuffs!" Kemal said sharply. The Pale commander made a mental note; this was one who had learned the lessons on logistics.

"I'm making plans," Hammer said. "We've got some good troops here, ones who'll obey orders, enough for that at least. Essential supplies will be secured at once. Besides, we won't have to feed all the nomads."

"Why not?" Aisha said hotly. She tended to defend the plainsmen; well, she came of their blood too.

"Because not all of them are going to stay to dig trenches and watch the Citadel," Hammer said patiently. He thrust his hands under his belt and walked to the entrance, standing with his legs braced and throwing his words over his shoulder. "Enough will, of course."

"But think. Half these *hotnots* come to the Shangri-La every year or two, with the tribute and with their birthing women. They've *seen* it. The towns in there, the villages—they don't have walls, they don't have weapons, they *don't know how to fight.* Not the lands the Citadel ruled directly. They've always had Sauron garrisons. The richest land on Haven, naked as a cootch-dancer at a caravan *serai.* What does every two-legged stobor on the steppe wet-dream of, while he's crouching in a freezing yurt in the middle of a ten-day blizzard in midwinter, eating grass soup and rotten horsemeat?"

They all nodded. Hammer went on. "The Kara Asva, the Chukchi, the Kulogulu Yaik—half of them will scatter out into the Valley lands. By hundreds or scores, Hell-mouth, every would-be bandit chief who can talk ten riders into following him; and a lot will take their families, too. They'll pass over that land like a plague out of the Bible—like a wind of fire, burning and killing, breaking down the dams and canals and the mills . . . They'll infest every patch of rough country or woods for years, even if we *lose.* Dam' little those lands are going to yield for *anyone.*"

Silence reigned; even Aisha's fierceness was daunted.

"What have we *done?*" Chaya whispered.

Sharku pulled up for a rest. Five minutes of heavy panting, a pause to let his blood and his tissues reoxygenate, and he'd be ready to go on eating up klicks. He'd picked a good spot for it: the middle of a broad field of growing barley, with no trees or rocks or fences for nasty locals to use for cover. There weren't a whole lot of such stretches hereabouts. The land was valleys and gullies and mean little hills—ambush country. He didn't like that, not even a little bit, but the maps said it ran on this way for a good stretch of distance north of the Jordan. Going around would have cost time, and he didn't think he had any time to spare.

Mumak paused for a blow beside him. "Where in the ass end of nowhere are we now?" he asked. "When we get back to the Citadel—if there *is* a Citadel when we get back—I swear I'm never gonna move again, except maybe to open my mouth so the tribute maidens can drop in slices of fruit every now and then."

"You mean you're going to make the girls get on top all the time, too?" Sharku said, and skipped back before Mumak could stick an elbow in his ribs. "As for where we are—we're within a few hundred klicks of Falkenberg. Three-fifty, maybe; that'd be my best guess."

"I know that much. Even I know that much." Mumak looked comically offended. He was extraordinarily good-natured for a Soldier, which led some people to mistake him for stupid. He played on that, though Sharku knew better. He went on, "What I meant is, which particular set of cattle infests this stretch of territory?"

"Damfino, not offhand. Whoever they are, they'll probably hate us."

"It's a good bet," Mumak said. "Everybody we've been through seems to; we've done a lot more fighting on the way back than we did coming out." He wiped a sleeve of his field-gray tunic across his forehead. "Maybe we ought to let the nomads down off the steppe and into this nice farm country, give the peasants a reality check. After a dose of Turks and Mongols, they'd worship the ground we walk on for the next thousand years."

"Well, they don't worship it now." Sharku pulled a map from the inside pocket of his tunic. "If I were a Cyborg, I'd have all this shit memorized."

"Yeah, but you wouldn't know what to do with it once you had it," Mumak said.

"Isn't that the sad and sorry truth?" Sharku sighed. "Well, let's have a look. If we are where I think we are, this is the country of the Klephti."

"Oh, I've heard of them," Mumak said. "Talk a funny language, use a funny alphabet—it's not Roman or Cyrillic, but it kind of looks like both of 'em. They have a name for being brigands, if I remember right."

"I think you do—not that it proves much," Sharku said. "There's not a tribe on Haven that ended up here because their umpty-great-grandparents were nice people." He looked around. It was quiet, very quiet. "Where are all of them? We should have seen some by now—farmers and such running for their lives, if nothing else. Where are they?"

"Don't know," Mumak admitted. "I was just counting my blessings. After all the time we've wasted fighting odds-and-sods, I figured empty country was just the break we needed."

"It is," Sharku agreed, "if it isn't empty because it's filling up ahead: filling up with trouble, that is." He called to a couple of troopers loping by: "Spread the word—let's pick up some locals and find out what's going on. When things get too easy, I stop trusting them."

"If we haven't learned that one by now, it's not because Haven hasn't tried teaching it to us," Mumak said. He glanced over at Sharku. "You ready?"

"Ready enough," Sharku answered, and swung into the ground-eating Soldiers' trot. He hadn't been moving more than a couple of minutes when gunfire rang out to the north and east. As if that had been a signal, more shots came, again from the east, but this time to the south as well. Automatic-rifle fire answered the single booms of the locals' flintlocks.

Scouts came dashing back toward the officers, who ran near the middle of the long, thick line the three Regiments of Soldiers had formed. "It's harassing fire, sir," one of them said, "nothing worse than that. Do you want us to make a real fight of it, or just go on?"

Before Sharku could answer, Lagduf said, "We'll just go around them, stay out of range, if it's only harassing fire. After all, we are short of time if we're to make it to the Citadel."

Every word he'd said was true. The tone in which he said them made Sharku want to bust him in the teeth. He might as well have said, *Well, you're the one with a land gator up your backside, so I suppose we may as well humor you.* Sharku decided not to make an issue of it, nodding to show the scouts that what Lagduf had said was what they should do. Keeping Lagduf functional as a subordinate when he was still formally a superior was enough of a pain in the fundament as things stood already.

No more than a few minutes later, Sharku regretted doing things the easy way. The Klephti delivering the harassing fire were on the high ground to north and south. By avoiding them, the regiments on the way back to the Citadel squeezed together and entered a wide, shallow valley that led to the east, the direction in which they wanted to go.

From the heights at either side of the valley, horns made flatulent noises. More horns from the eastern end answered. That end was blocked off with a barricade of turf and stone and timber. Behind it, a good many Klephti hunting muskets of one flavor and another whooped and shouted unintelligible defiance at the Soldiers. A couple of them started shooting, though even the scouts were far out of range of their weapons. Plumes of black-powder smoke rose into the sky.

Lagduf turned to Sharku. "Well, what do we do now, *sir*?" he asked. He'd made the suggestion that put the Soldiers in this pickle, but he was right: it remained Sharku's responsibility. The first thing Sharku wanted to do was add another item to the list he was compiling of what he owed the Bandari. The Klephti hadn't been troublesome when the Soldiers moved west. They still knew that, however tough they thought they were, the men from the Citadel were far, far tougher. But now, with rebellion flaring all through the Shangri-La Valley, and with the Soldiers bloodied and in apparent retreat, they wanted to get in on the action. *We'll give them all the action they want*, Sharku thought.

His answer to Lagduf came out cold and precise: "We are going to storm that position, Regiment Leader. We are going to go straight through it, slaughtering those barbarians until they stop resisting us. Then we are going to continue on our march to the Citadel, as fast as may be."

"It will be expensive, *sir*," Lagduf said. "They're just cattle, and they don't look to have any of these fancy weapons you've made so much of, but that is a strong defensive position. We'll take casualties we could avoid by swinging around them."

"Then we'll take casualties," Sharku said. Ever since the heliograph that led to the Soldiers' pullback had come in, he'd grudged every wasted second. He continued, "I would rather arrive with half my men in time for them to do something useful than come in with all of them too bloody late. And I don't think we have a lot of time to spare."

Lagduf shrugged. He was making his list, too: The Blunders of Sharku, chapter and verse. If the regiments got back in time to help save the Citadel, Lagduf's list wouldn't matter. If they got back too late, the list wouldn't matter, either, in a different sort of way—nothing would matter then, not if you were a Soldier. But if they came storming back eastward only to find that the Citadel hadn't needed their help, not even a little bit . . . then Lagduf's list would matter, quite a lot. About the best Sharku could hope for then would be to pull permanent steppe duty, with one cycle off at a grimy Firebase every seven T-years or so. At worst, they'd take a last couple of sperm samples for the freezer and then euthanize him. That sort of thought kept his mind occupied when things weren't going as well as they might, which seemed to be most of the time lately.

He didn't have time to worry about it now. Raising his voice, he said, "We are going to attack that position. Flankers, you'll try to get round it on the high ground to either side and deliver plunging fire. Main force, we'll advance in line to within our effective range, then a barrage to make them keep their heads down, then fire-and-move till we go over the barricade. After that, I do what you want, but do it in a hurry. I want to knock these buggers out of the way so we can get on with our important business. Questions?"

Nobody said anything. Sharku flipped off the safety to his assault rifle. That small click seemed signal enough for the advance. The Soldiers loped forward. Behind their barricade, the Klephti yowled and whooped to see them come. They were short, swarthy men, many with fierce mustachios waxed to stand out from their faces. Most of them wore red bonnets—Sharku couldn't find a better word for the headgear—with black pompoms hanging down from a string. He tried to guess their numbers: about as many men as he had, he thought. His lips skinned back from his teeth. Even with a barricade in front of them, even numbers was long odds.

Before long, their shouts became a one-word chorus: "*Malakas! Malakas!*"

Beside Sharku, Mumak said, "I've heard that in taverns now and again. Means something like 'jerkoff,' doesn't it?"

"You'd know better than I would," Sharku answered abstractedly. He was studying the officers or nobles—leaders, whatever the Klephti called them—riding back and forth behind the barricade. He could see more of them than of the men they headed. Instead of the footsoldiers' muskets, they carried lances, with a brace of pistols and a saber on their belts. Some of them wore wool leggings, others knee-length kilts or skirts. They had peculiar shoes: carved from wood, with pompoms like those of the local headgear on the toes. Some of them wore iron helmets; one or two had iron breastplates as well. Against other barbarians, they looked well able to take care of themselves. Against the Soldiers—everybody would find out about that pretty damn quick. The Klephti opened up when the Soldiers were within about half a kilometer of their field fortification. "Hold fire!" Sharku called. The locals would have to be lucky to hit anybody at that range with what they were using. A couple of men swore—as Mumak had said, put enough bullets in the air and some of them would be lucky.

Another hundred meters forward and Sharku fired the first burst himself. A Klepht reeled back from the barricade, clutching at his shoulder. An instant later, the rest of the Soldiers began shooting, too. One of the officers slid bonelessly off his horse and crumpled to the ground. All along the locals' line, cries of pain went up along with the smoke from their weapons that helped screen them and made good shots annoyingly hard to come by.

The Klephti had balls, no doubt about it. They fired their muzzle-loaders as fast as they could, hunkering down behind their wall to reload after they'd let each bullet fly. They weren't tactically blind, either; their nobles spotted the Soldiers' outflanking maneuver right away, and detached bands of men to go out beyond the ends of the barricade and try to bar their foe's passage.

Still, the flanking parties drew less fire than the main body of Soldiers. Before long, they were in among the Klephti who'd been sent out to stop them, and that was that. The Klephti had long bayonets on the ends of their long muskets, and a few Soldiers got stabbed, mostly men busy fighting already when a Klepht they hadn't spotted leaped out at them from behind a rock.

But however good the Klephti were, that just meant they died in place. They didn't run; they went down swinging. But before long, almost all of them *were* down, and the Soldiers were sweeping past the rest far faster than mere barbarians could hope to run. Brave to the point of madness, a group of mounted officers charged the Soldiers; lances and muzzle-loading horse pistols against assault rifles and enhanced genes that made the Soldiers as quick as horses and much more maneuverable was another unequal contest. They might as well have been charging tanks. Along with the groans of men, wounded animals' squeals made the battlefield hideous.

Sharku paid only peripheral attention to these fights. The frontal assault was proving as costly as he'd feared. The only good thing he could see about the injuries his troopers were taking was that the unrifled muskets of the Klephti fired round balls that did not mushroom or tumble in a wound and tear up the pierced tissue. But inexorably, the Soldiers drew closer to the logs and stones and earth set up to bar their way. As they approached their fire became withering. Brave as they were the barbs soon learned that they had barely time to pop up and find a target for their smoothbores before uncannily accurate answering fire found *them*. Even though they were willing to die if they could take a Soldier with them, mostly they just died. Individually, each Klepht was at least as good as the barbarians further west, but, thanks to the Bandari, the westerners had had much better gear. Gear counted, too—and the Soldiers had better gear and better men. But even ten to one or twenty to one meant too many Soldiers lost to the Race.

The first Soldier sprang up onto the barricade. The Klephti stabbed up at him with those long bayonets, then reeled away as he emptied a magazine into them on full automatic. They hadn't seen much of that before—the Soldiers had been firing on semiauto to conserve ammo and make each shot more accurate. But when you wanted to clear out the landscape right around you, spraying thirty rounds into your unfriendly neighbors all at once was the way to go about it. The Soldier jumped down onto the eastern side of the wall. Two other troopers leaped over it right after him. They fired long bursts, too. Klephti went down like ninepins. They had the genes of heroes in them . . . they didn't break until the Soldiers on the flanking parties started pouring in heavy enfilading fire. Then, at first a few at a time, then in mass exodus, they started running back toward the apple orchards and pine woods behind their position.

Suddenly, or so it seemed, no more Klephti were on their feet behind the barricade. A few stragglers were pelting off toward the woods, from which the occasional musket round still came. Sharku considered. Would the survivors give him any serious trouble as they continued their journey east? No bloody way, he decided: if they hadn't lost better than three quarters of their force, killed and wounded, then he was a Bandari. Which meant . . . "Let's gather up our hurt, rig litters for the ones who can't walk, and get moving again."

Lagduf scowled at him. "We ought to leave behind two or three companies, put the fear of the Citadel in these stinking cattle for good."

Sharku answered. "I've already taken casualties here. Trading men for time, for *nothing*. But I'm not going to trade men. Is that understood?"

"This is insubordination!" Lagduf blustered.

Sharku looked at him steadily. Mumak, on the other hand, spoke. "Don't *you* take that tone with the Death-master, Regiment Leader," he snapped.

In an instant, that title was in every Soldier's mouth: "Deathmaster! Deathmaster! Sharku Deathmaster!" The swelling roar, backed by Soldiers' lungs, was far louder than the war cries the Klephti had raised.

Sharku finished Lagduf's demoralization: "After what just happened here, Regiment Leader, I don't think the Klephti are going to give any Soldiers who pass through here after us a hard time. Do *you*?"

Lagduf surveyed the abattoir the battlefield had become. He shook his head.

Inside a quarter of an hour, the Soldiers were east-bound again. From then on, the Klephti left them severely alone. Every so often, a trooper would call out "Deathmaster!" as if he liked the sound of it. The cry would ripple up and down the line, then die away, only to start up again a few minutes later.

Sharku liked the sound of it too.

# • CHAPTER EIGHT

Regiment Leader Ufthak stood at the edge of the crag, and looked down at the mouth of the Karakul Pass. From this distance the cattle milling before the Gate looked like ants stripping the bones of some giant beast who had slumbered far too long and fallen to an ignominious fate. It wasn't hard to see that carcass as the Sauron Unified State, not with over a third of a million enemies swarming before the Karakul Pass.

The wind tugged at his feet and he shifted to gain a better purchase on the rocks. He was inside the third courtyard of the Inner Citadel on a claw of rock too tenacious for even the raw weather of Haven to have tamed. It had also become known as the meeting spot of conspirators and lovers not eager to have their conversations overhead by the ubiquitous Threat Analysis Computer.

Not that there might not be a hidden microphone sculpted somewhere in the natural rock formation; however, the screeching wind made it difficult most of the time even for Saurons with their enhanced hearing to hear words shouted only centimeters away. Now, with the corroboration from Sharku's heliographed message about the Pale's involvement in the Shangri-La Rebellion, it appeared that everyone had been granting the TAC more infallibility than it had ever deserved.

The approaching sounds of leather soled feet on rock warned him of approaching visitors. He turned to see Gimli the Archivist, one of the six members of the First Council, and a short squat man he couldn't remember ever having seen. Unusual for Ufthak, who prided himself on knowing more about the comings and going of the Citadel than the TAC.

"Welcome, Archivist. If anyone questions why we are here, say it is to witness the cattle who have come to view their graveyard."

"Were it only so," Gimli answered, the last words turned to a whisper by a passing gust. "If Carcharoth continues underestimating these Bandari cattle, it may well become our graveyard."

"Yes, and if he hadn't sent Sharku and the regiments to the ends of the world—but enough of this, it all has been said too many times before, by ourselves and others. The damage has been done and now we must keep the Bandari dogs out of the henyard."

"These rocket mortars they used on our fortifications have changed the equation," Gimli said. "Without these static defenses, even the Battlemaster admits there is little we can do, with only two garrison battalions, to stop so many warriors. I have asked for, and received, the Battlemaster's belated permission to open the Weapons Vaults for armaments that will keep the cattle from breaching the Pass."

"At long last, some sign of sanity from our esteemed Battlemaster. What about the First Council? Why have they not insisted upon this days ago?"

"They are a revered and august group, but, unfortunately, far past their prime. Also, they fear the Battlemaster and his arbitrary authority. And, like too many of our fellows, they look upon Cyborgs as infallible; a mistake the first Diettinger warned us of before and after the Cyborg Revolt. Most of the members of the First Council believe a Cyborg can do no wrong; for them, to think otherwise is to cast uncertainty upon the Sauron ideal. Only the sight of cattle entering the Inner Keep could make them reconsider their cherished beliefs."

"Should the cattle make their way successfully through the Karakul Pass, Nûrnen will fall like an overripe Finnegan's fig. Unless Sharku relieves us, it is possible the Citadel itself may be in peril."

"Nûrnen stands in their way."

"We cannot rely on Nûrnen. The Battlemaster has stationed half of the 16th Battalion to hold the pass, the other half to fortify the city, a thankless and hopeless job. Carcharoth is holding the 17th in reserve here in the Citadel. The wiser among our stalwart allies flee the city like rats from a burning hut. Two hundred and fifty Soldiers, bolstered by old men and youths, to hold a thousand times that many—another of Carcharoth's follies!"

"How have things become so bleak? I had not known."

Ufthak shrugged. "The Battlemaster relies on the TAC."

"It has not been wrong before."

"Are you certain?" Ufthak asked. "Sharku believes otherwise. We have lost no battles in the past because we have been stronger than the enemy. This does not mean we have fought efficiently, or even intelligently. Sharku has examined a dozen previous campaigns and shown how we might have won with fewer losses and less expense. Now it is late. Perhaps too late, even if Sharku arrives in time."

"I hadn't realized things had grown so bleak."

"Few know the true military situation." Ufthak shrugged. "Unless some miracle weapon resides in the Weapon Vaults, we may find ourselves in peril regardless of all Sharku can do."

"So you said before." Councilor Gimli nodded. "And so I have brought one who may be able to help. Techmaster Thorin is one of those who guards the vaults."

The short, stout man stepped forth. Few outsiders would have recognized him as a Sauron; Ufthak, however, noticed the carriage and certain other subtle cues that told him he was in the presence of another Sauron. Not a Soldier, but, nonetheless, a Sauron. A Citizen. One unchanged from the times before they came to this world.

"Greetings," Thorin said. "Word of your exploits and Regiment Leader Sharku's have reached even those of us who labor unseen and unheard to keep the Citadel well and functioning."

"Sometimes one forgets just how large the Citadel truly is, Techmaster, and how many labor in its behalf. Your people have declined both in numbers and status under this long period of Cyborg ascendance. There are those of us who look for a return to the Founder's ideals of a new Sauron homeworld, not a backwater run by Cyborg masters with little understanding of destiny and the machines that will enable us to rule the stars again."

The little man's eyes shined. "You echo the dreams of those who labor below."

"I say what my leader tells me," Ufthak said. "For me, I am content to follow Sharku."

"Regiment Leader Sharku," Gimli said.

"For now that is his title. We can hope for another. I speak from his works. His discourses."

"We have seen some of those works," Thorin said. "Now they are no longer available. The Battlemaster forbids them, and harries them from view."

"We have more," Ufthak said. "From those who work the heliographs. From his wife. His accounts of the campaigns in the Valley make interesting reading. Would you like to be included among those friends?"

"I would indeed. Certainly, I know many who could be counted as new friends of our young Regiment Leader. Most have already heard of the Ranker who predicted the conspiracy among the Bandari to split our forces and relieve the Citadel of its protection, even when the TAC said otherwise."

"This is good to know. There will be an accounting for these and other errors when Sharku returns. It is good to know now that he has allies throughout the Citadel. His friends will be remembered."

For the first time Techmaster Thorin showed real passion. "There are many of us who have believed for a long time that the leadership here has been asleep. If we are to truly turn this world into a new Homeworld, we must regain the power and knowledge of our ancestors."

"Maybe," Archivist Gimli added, "this cattle attack is the wakeup call we've needed."

"Indeed it is," Ufthak agreed. "And it will be up to us to prepare the way for the new order."

"Is there anything we can do?" Gimli asked.

"We? I know one who can." Ufthak smiled slyly. "It is my understanding, Archivist, that Regiment Leader Sharku is a direct descendent of Galen Diettinger. We shall need proof of this if we are to restore the Founder's principles to the Unified State."

Gimli looked thoughtful. "I had not heard this. It must be well hidden."

"Hidden or not, it must be found if—"

"I understand." Gimli looked out at the field of the dead. "I had not expected to see so many enemies this close to our gates."

"That is the first group. There are far more coming."

"I see. Indeed—Ufthak, the Citadel holds many records. We don't always see them all."

"Sir?"

"But one of my predecessors often said that there has been so much inbreeding in the Citadel that every Sauron alive is in some respect related to Galen Diettinger and the Lady Althene."

"Then you should have no difficulty in providing the proof we need. Meanwhile, I will inform our supporters of this new and important discovery."

The Archivist looked at Ufthak as though he were seeing him for the first time. "It is an abuse of my office if I manufacture false lineages."

"I would never ask you to do that, Archivist. Certainly it would be a disaster if anyone suspected it. Yet we need proof that Sharku numbers First Soldier Diettinger among his ancestors. I can't imagine that such a task would prove formidable to a man of your skills."

Gimli looked at the fields of death again. "And there are more coming?"

"Soon."

The Archivist sighed. "I shall comb the records most thoroughly, Regiment Leader. I'm sure I will be able to find all the proof we will ever need."

"Good," Ufthak said. "Now Techmaster. What do we have in the Weapons Vaults that can stop these barbarians?"

"Those vaults have been sealed for a long time, Regiment Leader. We don't know everything that we will find. Some of the—relics—we have tended for lifetimes, but they decay. But there are also the records and plans."

"So?"

"We have had no time for more than a cursory inspection, Regiment Leader. However, we have already found some items of interest. There are machine guns that fire bullets of greater caliber and with far more speed than our Gatlings. We have already begun to unpack them and make ammunition as described in the manuals. We have instructions on poison gases, one called 'nerve gas' that sounds as terrible as any weapon ever made. Unfortunately, it would take weeks to make up the stocks. Many of the chemicals and reagents are in short supply in the Citadel stockrooms."

"Anything else?"

"The Battlemaster has ordered—"

"I no longer care what the Battlemaster has ordered. I speak for Sharku." He looked both ways, and said, quietly but forcefully, "First Soldier Sharku."

"First—you're mad!"

"No. Battlemaster Carcharoth is mad. And his orders have nearly destroyed the Citadel."

"You plan—"

"You need not be concerned. I want to know what is in the vaults."

"I will tell you when we know more."

"Yeweh Shield of the *People*," Barak murmured in awe. Shulamit knew exactly what he meant. She had heard of the great Wall all her life—the story of its building and its fall were ancient legend, like Babylon and Egypt and Earth—but seeing it was something altogether different. For long minutes the eyes refused to believe that it was a construction at all; the scale was wrong, it was like *hills*.

Kilometer after kilometer, from the northern foothills of the Atlas right across the ragged gash of the Karakal Pass, anchored in high cliffs to the south. Once it had been a series of huge interlocking wedges; now it was more like a row of rotten teeth, like the jawbone of a fallen god. Even the *stumps* were dozens, maybe scores of meters high.

She and the others of the advance party were coming at it from the western side of the Steppes. Far ahead lay the stone-paved Sauron road that ran down from the Citadel to Nûrnen. It was still dimday, and she could see the dark flood of nomads fanning out before them through the Atlas Foothills.

*brrrrrt.*

Red fire stabbed out. The Bandari party was still outside the Gatling's range but flattened instinctively; screams and shouts of *Allahu Akbar* echoed back from the monumental ruins. The humans ahead seemed as tiny as ants, a scurrying mob of drillbits.

Barak swung down from the saddle. "Margulis," he snapped. "*Get* that thing moving. The rest of you—what are you waiting for, the Saurons to throw rocks so you can build a sheep pen? *Avrithai!* Follow me!"

The Bandari dismounted and fanned out; unlike nomads, they were trained for combat on foot as well as on horseback. They darted forward, working from rock to rock. Shulamit adjusted the sights of her Sauron rifle and flopped down behind a boulder; ahead of her was a tangle of felt-clad bodies. The heavy 15mm Gatling slugs had torn heads from bodies and limbs from torsos, sawing open rib cages and bellies until the raw stink of it was nearly enough to make her gag. *I should get used to this. This is war.* Stobor cried somewhere, the smell of food fighting against the fear of man and giving an edge like hysterical laughter to their pack-howl.

There had never been a war like this. The rocky slope ahead of her was *covered* in bodies, clumps and windrows and pieces slung headlong. Shulamit slid the muzzle of her assault rifle between two leaves of stone and sighted

carefully. Breathe in. Breathe out. *Squeeze* the trigger
when you breathed out. Squeeze. Squeeze. The rifle
tapped her shoulder and spat brass cartridge cases. She
could see the rounds flicking at the stone around the firing
slit of the Sauron bunker. Others of the People were
opening up all around her, with Sauron weapons or the
single-shot rifles of the Pale. She whipped the rifle back
and rolled aside; none too soon, as Gatling fire sawed at the
rock where she had lain. Heavy bullets went *crack* between
the leaves of rock.

Shulamit leopard-crawled to a new firing position.
More nomads were charging by; thousands of them, all
across the defile. She saw a green banner with the crescent
moon go down; another man snatched it up and carried it
forward a half-dozen paces before Sauron bullets hammered him to the earth. Another picked it up, and another.

"*Allahu Akbar! Gur! Gur!*"

The yelping warcries were louder than the snarl of
Gatlings and assault rifles. Shulamit bounced up and ran a
dozen paces upslope and forward, under cover of a tribal
warband; when she dove to earth and fired again, they
were gone. Only a few hundred meters to the first of the
Sauron pillboxes—

Something went by overhead. She buried her face in
her arms. *Whump.* The ground pounded at her breasts
and belly through her armor. Grit flicked between tight-
squeezed eyelids; she blinked them open and blinked
again to clear her vision. The beautifully balanced Sauron
weapon came up easily, but the bunker ahead was tumbled
stone.

"I wish Karl were here," she muttered.

The blocks of stone shifted, tumbling in dust that
puffed red-white beneath fading Cat's Eye. She fired again
and again as the Sauron fought to free himself; the half-
seen figure jerked and stumbled. Those might be her
bullets, but there were scores of Bandari firing at him—
and many more nomad bows and *jezails*. She dashed
forward again. Stocky fur-clad men with yataghans and

sabers swarmed over the ruined bunker. One flew backward, his face a red blur, and then the others were standing in a circle. Their blades rose over their heads as they lashed downward. A few seconds, and a blond head rose on the point of a spear.

Exultant shrieks echoed from the ruins of the Wall, from the scores and hundreds close enough to see. Shulamit dove into new cover just as another bunker further up opened on the victors and chewed them into rags of bone and flesh, some of them moaning and whimpering. The Bandari girl's eyes were open—round and wide—but she squeezed the eyes of her mind closed as she clicked the magazine free, slid it into a pouch and retrieved another. It was not until she'd pulled back the charging handle that she realized there was someone else in the depression.

Two someones. Barak and Sannie; he was tying off a bandage around her upper arm, fingers impossibly agile and neat in the darkness stinking with cordite and black powder and blood all around them.

Shulamit rolled on her back. *I really wish Karl were here,* she thought again. *Even if I had to be wounded.* The thought made no sense, but the yearning was real. From here she could see quite a ways down the paved road; the *Ariksa* was set up there, behind moveable bulwarks of thick timber and drillbit gut. As she watched one moved forward, scores of muskylopes and men heaving and pulling. Sauron bullets plowed the dirt around them, and some fell, but the range was long and the shielding tough.

She groped her canteen free and sipped. The water was shockingly cold on her raw throat.

"Why—" she said, and coughed. "Why don't the Saurons have something long range?" It was a bit better when she talked of impersonal things.

Barak looked up, his last touch gentle on Sannie's shoulder. "A Sauron with a sword or rifle is worth twenty, forty ordinary men," he said. "But all the reflexes in the world can't outrun an artillery shell. If the Saurons had built

cannon, others would have tried—us, certainly—and
when both sides had distance weapons, their advantage
would go down. They're probably regretting that line of
thought right now."

His strange eyes probed the fire-shot darkness ahead of
them. "Not long now. We're nearly to the crest, through
the old Wall."

*Karl*, Shulamit thought. *Don't get your bliddy arse
killed. I need you.*

The Sauron *caught* the head of Karl bar Yigal's warhammer. Karl was faster than most men, much faster—but the
Sauron's hand hadn't seemed to move at all.

He hadn't been expecting the force behind the blow,
though. Bone shattered in his hand, and the tall man
lurched. The backswing stroked the serrated head of
forged steel into his temple. Brains and blood spattered on
stone.

The sight didn't make Karl wince any more. He had
time to notice the others around him; nomad and Bandari
were both looking at him in awe, and nobody objected
when he stripped the Sauron of his weapons and slung the
assault rifle over his back.

"Come on, then," he said, pointing upslope.

They were on the western edge of the pass, climbing
over shattered volcanic rock and the frost-crumbled concrete of the Wall's foundations. The Citadel was visible to
the south: ascending circles of black stone wall and the
long spike of the Inner Keep rearing up against the rock
chimney that formed the base of the cliff extending to the
top of the Atlas range, the roof of the world, above them,
all lit by the dreadful unnatural light, blue-white and
actinic, like a model through the clear air on the slopes of
the Atlas to the west. Below them the pass was packed
with attacking hordes. It was like watching a wave breaking
on rock, as they washed against the interlocking fire of the
Sauron bunkers. But here it was the wave that advanced,
crying out and killing as it died. Behind them the Bandari

mortars crunched forward, setting up for another bombardment.

"We're above them," Karl went on—the original officer was dead. "Nobody but single scouts up here. We can finish them off and take some of the flanking bunkers from above." He drew a deep breath. "Follow me."

"I've never seen anything like it," Hammer-of-God said in awe. "The hand of the Lord is on them."

A Sauron pillbox blew up on the slope above, a huge globe of orange fire against the night; for a second men and parts of men were silhouetted against the stars. Probably suicide. The bunkers were cunningly placed, dug into the ruins of the Wall, mutually supporting. They could do little against a *sea* of men indifferent to death. The bunker beyond fired until the lapping curve of bodies choked the gunslits. Bandari staggered up the rocky slope with something slung between them; they dropped it on the bunker's roof, bent over it for a moment, then dove away. A red-shot pillar of black erupted; when it cleared, the steel hatches had vanished in a writhing tangle of reinforcing rod shocked clear of shattered concrete. Another wave of nomads broke over the pillbox, this time leaping down into the hole the satchel charge had made.

A Sauron emerged. He was fighting, too strong for any number of men to hold when the space for hands on his limbs and body was limited. Each blow with fist and knee and foot and butting head killed, yet more climbed over the bodies to reach him. Some of them had steel in their hands. More *plucked* at him, and in a few seconds the Sauron warrior's body was nude, pale beneath the stars— then streaked with blood. He disappeared beneath the scrimmage, and then showed again . . . or pieces of him did, held aloft in triumph over screaming bearded faces.

"Hand of God?" Chaya asked, beside him on the hillock. "I've never doubted God, but this makes me a believer." He looked at her. "In Hell, General Jackson."

"Men run to Hellmouth as to a bride's embrace,"

Hammer-of-God said with simple faith, and a lifetime's experience of war. "It's Adam's sin, turning us from grace."

From here they could see across kilometers: the whole U-shape of the Karakal Pass, up to the fortress itself perched on the mountain's slope, and west to the saddle where the ground fell away to Nûrnen. And the ground *moved*, moved in a dark carpet that shone with starlight on a hundred thousand swords. The Bandari siege-mortars were islands of order in that swarm, turning northward to duel the Citadel's outerworks into silence as the horde went by in a torrent. A torrent that screamed in exultation as it passed the Seven and their standards, echoes booming back and forth between the mountain walls, falling in dimuendo from the giant fragments of the Wall. The sound was like nothing human, a white-noise roar that shivered in bones and guts.

A tongue of flame shot out from a bunker outside the Citadel's Wall: a flame thrower, one big enough to drop an arc of fire spilling across a hundred meters. There was a sharp smell, like—tar. Flame spouted again.

# • CHAPTER NINE

In the distance, Senior Assault Leader Bogdar's ears were filled with a roar that reminded him of an avalanche he'd once heard while on duty in the Devil's Heater. Individual crashes and bangs hurtled out of the ear-splitting roar much as boulders had bounced around the edge of the avalanche. Only this was no tumbling wall of stone and rock; this was a wave of living, dying human and animal flesh. With only one thought: to kill every Sauron it could find, including himself. More dangerous by far than any river of mere rock.

If the cattle rumors were to be believed, this horde was a divine wall of steel and flesh sent to scour the Saurons from this world. Now that he heard its scream it was hard to remain as aloof as he had been two days ago in the barracks room when he'd been given his new assignment.

The Karakul Pass twisted its way through the Atlas Mountains, like a giant seam. It was the result of an ancient earthquake that made even this disaster seem infinitesimal. The Pass itself twisted its way through the Atlas Mountains for over twenty kilometers, in some places as wide as half a kilometer, in others only eighty to a hundred meters wide.

Scratch's Elbow, as this kink in the Pass was called, was a giant overhang that almost crossed the entire width of the divide. Bogdar's orders were to stop the nomad army dead in its tracks. Their bunker straddled the trail between the Elbow and a sheer granite cliff that stretched farther to the sky than even magnified Sauron eyes could see.

The bunker was a ferro-concrete box with firing slits for

four Gatlings and dozens of assault rifles. This morning two of the Gatlings had been replaced by what Cyborg Rank Bonn had called machine guns, ancient weapons from the stars that had arrived with the *Dol Guldur,* and still smelled of the muskylope lard they'd been preserved in. A third had been emplaced behind a hastily erected wall on top of the bunker. According to Cyborg Bonn, the range of the 30mm machine guns was on the order of two kilometers, almost two thirds of the way to the next turn in the Pass.

Using the high-powered optical telescope left for him by Cyborg Bonn, Bogdar was able to see ahead to the next bend, where the pass was almost a quarter of a kilometer wide, and where a hundred-man Sauron company made a thin gray line.

A line that had better hold; otherwise, Bogdar's bunker was the last defense of the Pass between the nomad horde and the city of Nûrnen. A peaceful trading city with no fortifications, other than some hastily dug earthworks that were still in the early stages of construction. Most of those working on the Nûrnen defense were cadets or retired veterans.

Not that Bogdar's platoon didn't have support, four Soldiers crouched in emplacements carved out of living stone along the eastern slope about 15 meters above the Pass. These man-sized notches had been there since CoDominium times, so legends said, built by the Valley Lords to keep the nomads out of the Shangri-La, Haven's one and only treasure.

Each of the four Soldiers were armed with flame throwers, another of the weapons brought out of the ancient vaults. They'd been held in reserve for the return of the Empire or a major uprising. Bogdar laughed, remembering Battlemaster Carcharoth's predictions. This was major enough . . .

If the First Council and the Battlemaster had listened to Assault Group Leader Sharku, the blood of the cattle horde would be flooding the steppes in a river of red, while the Soldiers pleasured themselves their women.

Instead, all five of the Citadels' regiments were down in the southern Valley, thousands of kilometers from where they were needed. Only two half strength battalions had been left behind to face the greatest threat to Sauron hegemony since the Succession Wars. And in command of the Citadel was the very Battlemaster who sent the strength of the Race far to the south.

Most of the junior officers Bogdar knew agreed that it was time the full Council did something, even if they had to restrict Carcharoth to permanent breeding duty and put the old geldings on the First Council out to pasture.

Still, it would not have been such a disaster had the Battlemaster not ignored the field reports and gone to the ancient vaults earlier. No, his pride and blind faith in the Threat Analysis Computer had led him to ignore all contrary evidence, send away the only Soldier who did see the big picture, and any other commander that threatened his command. It was only when the dreaded Bandari mortars destroyed half the pill boxes guarding the Citadel's flanks that Carcharoth began to treat this invasion as a serious threat to the Sauron Unified State.

Only then had the Battlemaster sent the guardians into the Vaults where indeed they had found some marvelous weapons, but also found too little time and too few techs to do more than assemble a few of them. Nor had there been time to establish more than a patchwork defense for the Pass. Nor enough *petroleum*, as it was called, to fuel more than a dozen of the flame throwers. Four of them guarding the passage to his bunker.

Suddenly the burp of a hundred assault rifles and a dozen Gatlings resounded through the stone walls of the pass, for a moment stilling the roar of the horde.

He could smell the sweat of his squad in the dusty air and now a new odor, the coppery tang of freshly spilled blood. The bend in front kept the horde out of sight, but he could hear the roar of the horde grow, now drowning out even the burping Gatlings.

"Check your loads," Bogdar needlessly reminded his

snipers. They were armed with scoped, single-shot rifles accurate up to three and a half kilometers, far more accurate than were needed here. "Remember, shoot *khans* and Bandari warriors only. Leave the grass eaters for the machine guns. Once they realize our position they will bring up the mortars; I want you to kill as many of their techs as possible."

"Yes, sir," an elderly Assault Leader replied dryly. This was Soldier work, work they'd been bred for and trained for a lifetime. Let the dung burners come and learn why the Saurons had held this pass for over three hundred and fifty years.

Then the wall of living, multicolored flesh came into sight. At three kilometers it appeared as though it were spraying a red froth. Estimates this morning had put the number of nomad effective at 320,000, not counting camp followers. Using his enhanced telescope, Bogdar could see that the froth was a spray of blood and tissue that was coloring both sides of the pass. It was hard to discern one warrior from another in that press of bodies; it appeared that most of the bullets were ripping a half dead mass of tangled bodies.

When the wall reached the barricade, it appeared to halt, and, for a few moments, to turn in on itself; then, suddenly, the barricade and one hundred Soldiers were gone.

Part of the wall itself.

For the first time Bogdar felt anxious; sweat beaded on his forehead, his stomach knotted, his knees began to tremble. *Is this fear?* How strange to feel a new emotion. *Is this what cattle felt when they saw death before them?* Surely his command would die, like the company ahead, unless the machine guns could tip the balance. The magic of Old Sauron against the nomads' gods.

"Fire Gatlings," Bogdar ordered. In this alley of death, the Gatling effective range was far greater than in the field, since many of the shells would bounce off the sides of the Pass and find the enemy in such a target-rich environment. The machine guns, with their far greater range, were to be held in reserve.

Now he could make out individual horde members, a Cossack in shiny mail and a Bandari in articulated boiled-leather armor. He heard a loud report and the Bandari catapulted off his horse and against the stone cliff. The two Gatlings tore red ribbons through the front of the horde but didn't appear to slow it at all. Horses and men ran down or over the fallen like natural obstacles.

The death cries, screams, yells, gunshots, had all blended themselves into a single noise and Bogdar wondered if he would ever hear individual sounds again.

At the one-kilometer mark painted on the wall, a single black line painted on the side of the cliff, he ordered the assault rifles to fire. The additional twenty guns stitched a line of red across the front of the wall but didn't slow its momentum for a second. He had planned to wait until the horde reached the half kilometer mark before ordering the machine guns to fire, but decided by then it might be too late and gave the order now.

The machine guns with their heavier bullets ripped into the front of the horde, chewing it up into fist-sized hunks of flesh and leather. Then the flame throwers sent out huge tongues of fire. For a time, the wall appeared to come to a complete halt. The odor of burnt flesh was now added to the almost overwhelming smell of cordite inside the bunker, and black powder coming from the horde.

But the nomads with their Bandari weapons were taking a toll on his command, too. The trooper next to him spun backwards, with the back half of his skull removed. He used the respite to count casualties, three dead, one with a sucking chest wound, and four more with injuries that might put a human norm out of commission but not a Soldier.

The wall appeared to writhe again, and he put down his assault rifle and picked up the telescope. By Diettinger, the cattle were building a wall of boulders and dead horses and men to hide from the rain of 30mm shells. They had stopped the horde!

Bogdar ordered the machine guns to stop firing; there

hadn't been time to produce more than fifty thousand rounds per gun, almost half of which they'd already fired. The Gatlings kept up their rain of fire, as the impromptu barricade grew, shooting rounds off the cliff side to ricochet into the cattle farther down the Pass. The writhing of the cattle as they died showed it was having an effect. *Maybe they could stop the horde right in its tracks?*

The snipers were still firing at will and Bogdar directed their fire to a group drawing a giant six-wheeled wagon through the Pass. *Maybe he wouldn't need to use their surprise after all?*

The Bandari wagon came to a halt, about two kilometers away; just out of effective Gatling range. Now they were assembling one of their deadly—what had Cyborg Bonn called it—*spigot mortars*, yes, that was it. Now it was time to show them what the machine guns could really do!

"Machine gunners, target the Bandari mortar. Destroy it and its crew." The guns began to chatter, cutting a swathe through the barricade and the living wall of flesh.

The nomads at the barricade actually tried to turn and run, but there was nowhere to go. The Pass turned into a killing floor. The bullets tore into the log abatis the Bandari had placed before the wagon, sending the Bandari engineers scattering, only to fall from sniper fire. The strange, bullet-shaped device they'd been raising suddenly toppled and exploded, and at least a thousand nomads died in the explosion. More would have died, but for the wall of once living human and horse flesh that absorbed most of the blast.

Bogdar had never seen such killing, and doubted this world had since the landing of the *Dol Guldur.*

For the first time, the horde actually pulled back, drawing past the barricade where a hundred Soldiers had given their lives. "Cease fire."

"We've broken them!" a Soldier shouted.

The dead were heaped across the Pass in piles as high as the bunker itself. Bogdar estimated the casualties at well over twenty thousand men with easily as many horses and muskylopes. If they could stop this horde, their names would live on as heroes as long as the last Sauron heart beat.

The sudden silence was almost as oppressive as the noise had been. The Senior Assault Leader would have liked to believe they were retreating, but the wall had only pulled back, not broken. *What are they doing behind that curve of rock?*

The machine guns were both down to less than fifteen thousand rounds each. They'd have to conserve their firepower. The Gatlings and assault rifles had all the ammunition they would ever need. Looking at his watch, Bogdar was surprised to learn that over a half hour had passed since the horde had first overrun the barricade.

He shifted uneasily in his seat, trying not to think about the dead-man switch he had now activated. This next attack would see either victory, or a blazing death. Either way, Bogdar promised to send many thousands of nomads to the Wind.

There was a sudden spume of dust from around the curve, and then an explosion that almost threw him off his seat as the eastern half of the bunker collapsed. Smoke and debris filled the room; his ears were ringing and he touched them only to find his fingers dripping blood. A quick survey revealed that the mortar round had taken out one of the machine guns, probably the one on top of the bunker as well, a Gatling gun, and half his platoon. He wasn't surprised when he looked through the aperture to see the nomad horde less than half a klick away.

His dazed Soldiers began to pick up their weapons and resume firing. The rate of fire was sporadic and not at all effective until the remaining machine gun splattered its rain of death. The single gun was not enough to do more than slow the horde down. The nomads were now in range and slugs and arrows were beginning to pierce the firing slits, taking casualties. One of the flame throwers sent out a roaring finger of flame until a sharpshooter took him out with a well-aimed shot, sending the still burning flame thrower tumbling into the horde.

Then the machine gun, its ammunition expended, stopped firing. The remaining Gatling continued until the horde was upon the bunker, lances and spears thrusting through the firing slits. Two more Soldiers went down, and suddenly the horde was over, around, and coming into the bunker.

Bogdar felt something slam into his chest like a hammer, and looked down to see an arrow buried half-way into his chest. He willed his capillaries to staunch the flow of blood that threatened to fill his right lung. A slug tore through his shoulder like a red-hot poker, as three Bandari emerged from the rubble of the eastern bunker. He took two out with his assault rifle and another with his bare hands, pulling the Bandari like a child into a fatal embrace with the arrow half-buried in his chest. Bogdar's head was beginning to grow light.

*It's time,* he thought, as two more Bandari emerged with half a dozen nomads. The horde was over him, by him and now with him. He fell off the dead-man's switch and waited for the explosion that would send the entire Elbow tumbling down on the vanguard of the nomad horde.

His last thought was that no Soldier had taken so many enemies with him into the darkness since the Final War. Maybe they would remember him after—

"Wha's that?" Strong Sven said, letting go of Raisa's waist. He had felt the room rock and heard a bone-rattling crash. The Sozzled Stobor was warm and close tonight; a quarter of mutton sizzled over the fire, and smoky lanterns threw more warm yellow glow over the taproom. Sven felt a little dizzy as he got up. He had been spending every evening here for the last couple of days, two T-weeks, drinking as much as he could afford and cursing the Soldier blood that made it so expensive to get drunk. A Soldier could guzzle popskull 'till it came out of his ears and not take enough to forget. Strong Sven was not quite so resistant, but it was close. His work sweated it out of him—he was a stonecutter and miner, like his father and grandfather before him—but for the first time in his life Sven welcomed the work. You could drown fear in sweat, almost as easily as in vodka or clownfruit brandy, and much more cheaply.

The low roar of conversation died, fading away under the smoky rafters. Sven walked carefully to the door, and threw it open. Despite the truenight chill and the spatter of late-summer rain falling on Nûrnen, the street was crowded, a circling mass lit ruddy by the torches some carried. They seemed to be mobbing around a man who shouted incoherently, babbling something about Jews and doom and Soldiers. Strong Sven peered closer; his nightsight was good. *Mischa Jenkins*, he thought. A laborer, one of the ones the Soldiers had taken to build fieldworks. The conscripts had gone willingly enough, since they were helping to defend Nûrnen as much as the Citadel.

Sven felt something grasp under his breastbone and squeeze. Recklessly he jumped down into the crowd, barely conscious that some of his tavern cronies had followed. Men scattered back from his shoulders, or his fists if that did not suffice; he grabbed Mischa by the scruff of his jacket and half-dragged, half-carried him back toward the tavern. At the top of the steps he paused, since the doors had been flung open and a bright puddle of yellow light spilled out, across the veranda and the upraised faces and the cobbled street beyond. Mischa was dead-pale and sweating heavily, eyes darting in his whiskery face. Sven snatched the bottle off the tray Raisa still carried and handed it to the other man. He jammed it into his mouth with shaking hands and drank convulsively, Adam's apple bobbing.

"*Shut up!*" Sven bellowed at the crowd. "*Let him speak!*"

Then he snatched the brandy away from Mischa. Roughly, he shook the smaller man and asked, "Where are the Soldiers? Did they let you go?"

"Dead. All dead," Mischa said hoarsely.

"Talk sense and stop babbling, man," Sven barked.

Mischa seemed to pause, took a deep breath and licked his lips. "Give me the bottle," he said. After another swallow he spoke loudly, half-turning to the crowd.

"They took us into the hills. We dug, built pits, hauled rock. Then the enemy came."

"The horde?"

Mischa shook his head. "They were behind. We could hear them—kilometers away, we could hear them. One of the Soldier scouts came back and said they were so many, he could not count them—they covered the plain beyond *his* sight. They built a road through the foothills as they came."

A sigh went through the crowd, like wind through trees. Their eyeballs shone in the lamplight, and the sound of their breathing was heavy. Doors and windows had opened, all up and down the street.

"Then the fight started. The Jews, it was the Jews—the Soldier in command, the Senior Assault Group Leader, he said haBandari. They had rifles that struck as far as the Soldiers—and captured Soldier rifles, I could tell by the sound. They killed the Leader. Then—then—" He stopped for a moment and stuttered. "Then *the mountain fell. The mountain fell.* The blast threw us to the ground, we were half a kilometer away—the cloud rose up, the mushroom cloud—the Jews have the Hellfire bombs, Star bombs like the old ones told us when were children, they're real, and the Jews have them, the Jews have Hellfire!"

Mischa was shrieking, clawing at his own face, the blood mingling with tears. "The Saurons ran away, back to the Citadel, all that were left alive. I ran—I hid among the rocks from their scouts—I ran here—the Jews have Hellfire bombs, and the horde is coming. Right on my heels. The horde is coming. They are coming *now!* They are coming *now!*"

Thunder banged and rattled from the south, as Mischa tore out of Sven's grip and ran down the street, howling like a stobor. The crowd dissolved in a rush, running—running anywhere and nowhere, and their shouts carried the news across the sleeping city. Screams broke around Strong Sven, as he stood motionless. Some were in his ear, Raisa's voice:

"Sven, Sven—what shall we do, what shall we do?"

He put his hand across her face and pushed, turning away. *I must hide*, he thought numbly. His mind was becoming clear, very clear. Where could Strong Sven hide, he who persecuted Juchi? *The horde is coming.* They would turn him over to the nomad women; he would be T-months dying. Wait. Wait. The Jews were with them; he could bargain with the Jews, everyone knew the Jews would bargain. What his father had told him, the old workings—from his grandfather's father, in the old days. It had never seemed anything valuable, just an old family legend. Dangerous, even, if the Soldiers found out, so he'd never spoken of it to anyone. Yes. If he could hide long enough to find the Jews—

Strong Sven began to run.

*Nûrnen screamed.*

That was always how Shulamit would remember the Sack: people screaming. In rage, or fear, or pain; people screaming, darkness shot with flame, smells of blood and roasting meat and the nasty stinks of things that should not burn. The main streets were packed with the first spray of nomads, only the forerunners, but already thousands of them rioting through on foot or horseback. Smashing glass for the sheer luxury of it, dragging out armfuls of plunder and then throwing it in the dirt to dart away for more, dragging out women, too. Riding down fleeing Nûrnenites, hooting with laughter as they shot or stabbed with their lances or swung shamsirs at the townsfolk who ran, or cowered, or tried to fight with household tools or sticks. The solid wedge of haBandari cleaved through the shaggy steppe-people like the prow of a ship through water, shouting for way or lashing out with riding-whips and bowstaves and the iron-shod hooves of their horses.

She stood in the stirrups and looked back. The way up

to the pass was lit with fire; from burning bunkers, from
burning flesh and clothing, with the muzzle-flashes of
thousands of firearms. That was beginning in Saurontown,
in the high part of Nûrnen nearest to the Citadel, as well.
*I'm glad we're not up there,* she thought. That was mainly
retired Saurons, but . . .

"*Istrafugallah!*" A nomad chief on foot limped up to
Tameetha bat Irene and grabbed at her bridle. "Brother,
your help; these other pigs have no order and think only of
plunder. The sons of Eblis hold the street down from here;
in the name of the Beneficent, the Lovingkind, aid us."

"Saurons?" she said sharply.

The man looked up at the sound of her voice and hesitated. Tameetha bat Irene fan Tellerman was in her late
thirties, with a dark, weathered face and no curves that
showed through her armor—an old associate of Hammer-
of-God's in the *Sayerets,* the Scouts, and an officer of
caravan guards by trade when she wasn't working officially
with the army of the Pale. But her voice was a woman's.
The nomad went on:

"No, ah, *khatun.* Nûrnenites, but a Sauron leads them.
There."

He pointed as they came around a corner. It was dark—
any city was, in truenight—but there was enough firelight
to see a rude barricade across the avenue. Farm carts,
piled cobblestones, the gaudy travelling coach of some
merchant, its yellow-painted wheels spinning as it lay on its
side. Bodies lay in the street before it, and more mounted
nomads milled around just out of arrow range. As they
watched, a rifle spat from behind the wagons, the distinc-
tive sharp *crack* of an assault rifle on semiauto. The
nomads broke backward in a medley of curses and neighs,
leaving more men and beasts kicking on the slimed cob-
bles.

Tameetha nodded as they edged their horses backwards. She looked up at the house to their right; it was big
and fronted on both streets. Her hand indicated the second story, moved in precise signs every Bandari child

learned. *Windows. Shoot on command. Simultaneous.*

"Shulamit, Kostas, Schalk, Jakoba, Coenraad. You—"

"Barachuk *Khan*."

"Barachuk, get your people ready."

Shulamit swung down and dashed up onto the porch. Then she hesitated for a second. There were panels of *glass* in the door of the house at the corner—colored glass in the shape of flowers and beasts. It was beautiful work, as good as anything in the Pale, but strange. Beside her Coenraad bar Johannes snarled impatience and raised his boot. Before he could kick, Shulamit reached out and clicked the latch. The door swung open, and she felt an irrational lightening of the spirit as they crowded in and went up the stairs. Everything was quietly rich and disturbingly alien, ceilings too high, far too much woodwork, the adobe brick of the walls covered in smooth plaster and printed wallpaper.

Silent hand-signals sent them to windows overlooking the barricade. Nobody raised their head, not yet, not with a Yeweh-damned Sauron down there. Coenraad raised one finger. Two. *Three.*

She bobbed up and braced the forestock of her rifle against the windowsill. Full automatic; she hosed the entire magazine down into the crowd behind the tumbled vehicles and furniture. Beside her, the Pale rifles spoke their deeper boom, and the smell of burnt sulphur drifted on the cold draft from the street.

"*Yip-yip-yip-yip*—" Barachuk *Khan*'s Uighurs poured down the street, setting their horses at the barricade in a flourish of curved swords and stabbing lanceheads. For a moment there was a boil of motion around it, then all was still.

Shulamit swallowed, reloading her weapon and slinging it.

"Here." Jakoba bat Katarina called to her. "Look at *this.*"

A box of scarves spilled across the bed; for the first time, Shulamit realized this must be a bedroom. It was a bit odd to think of Nûrnenites with bedrooms . . . which was silly when you thought about it, but she'd always pictured them flogging slaves, or bowing and scraping before the Saurons, or whatever. The scarves were beautiful work, fine linen embroidered with a flamebird, picked out with gold and silver thread. *This must be a woman's room,* Shulamit thought. There was a crucifix on one wall, and an opened closet with dresses; it looked as if they'd left in a hurry.

Tameetha's voice called from below. Jakoba tossed half a dozen of the scarves toward her; feeling a little guilty, she stuffed them into her pockets and up under the edge of her cuirass and knotted one around her neck. *Actual plunder*, she thought. *I am growing up.*

Nobody was left alive behind the barricade. The tumbled dead didn't look like soldiers, just dead people—all ages, though, thank Yeweh, no children. A few were women, in clumsy-looking dresses, a little like what Edenite women wore back in the Pale. Tameetha gestured them back and drew a double-barreled flintlock pistol from her saddlebow, aimed carefully and fired at one figure—the one in Soldier gray, although he was already covered in swordcuts and had half a dozen bullet wounds to boot. His head was bald and fringed with a few white hairs; it burst like a dropped melon when the heavy lead balls struck it. Shulamit looked away, concentrating on getting her boot into the stirrup as she remounted. Behind them were yelps and smashing sounds as a spray of nomads found the house she'd fought from. Her horse snorted and sidled, and she ran a hand down its neck.

"*Hotnots* got his rifle, Yewehdammit," the Bandari commander said, looking down at the dead Sauron. He must have organized this defense himself. The Uighurs had vanished into the crowd; the street was filling rapidly.

She bit open cartridges, rammed them home, primed the pans of the massive pistol with a flask from her waist and reholstered it.

"Now—" She took out a map. "Should be—"

They turned into a side street for a moment, quieter than the main avenue—the looters hadn't had time to spread out much, yet—but darker than Gehenna. It was truenight, not even a sister moon up, and smoke-palls hid what stars there were; they came out into a larger avenue, then back into the shadows and narrow ways. The leader kicked her horse closer to one building that had faint light coming from its windows.

"*Aluf*," Schalk bar Yoachim complained. He was a young man, with a gingery beard. "What is this place we're looking for?"

"Machine shop, the *Ras Aluf* said," she replied absently, pushing back her helmet a little to peer at the tilted paper. "Bliddy big, this Nûrnen."

Shulamit felt herself nodding, peering around at the buildings—most of them three or even five stories tall, though this neighborhood was shoddy. All that she had seen of Nûrnen was dirty and unplanned by the standards of the Eden Valley, but it was *huge*. There must be a hundred thousand people living here. *Were living here*, she reminded herself, swallowing. That was as much as the capital, Strang, and the other big Pale towns put together several times over.

A fat man in an apron was sprawled in the street with blood and gray matter still leaking from a split skull.

The young Bandari trooper shifted reins and rifle. "Ah, *aluf*—the *hotnots* will get all the good stuff and the fun!" he complained, his voice jagged with excitement.

Tameetha folded the paper away. "Got it," she muttered, then grinned and cuffed the trooper across the ear; his helmet rang.

"'Good stuff'?" she said, chuckling.

It was an unpleasant sound, and her teeth shone wet under the brim of her helm; Shulamit felt an urge to look away. Tameetha was a fine commander, cared well for her squadron, had experience and all that . . . but there were times when she strongly suspected that Tameetha bat Irene fan Tellerman was *not* really a very nice person by her parents' standards. Besides being, she was pretty sure, bent.

The officer held out a clenched fist with the pinkie extended, tapping Coenraad on the nose. "Boy, when your mother's milk is dry on your lips, you can tell Tameetha how to loot—or tell Hammer-of-God Jackson." Her arm chopped out toward the roar from the nearby streets.

"Let the *hotnots* do the dying; not all the Saurons or Sauron lovers in this town are dead yet. And then—these *gayam*—what are they stealing? Gauds and trash, sequined underwear from whores. All they're going to get, *boy*, is junk—and sore stomachs and aching heads, hangovers and the galloping clap. What do you think *Kumpanie Gimbutas* will pay for Sauron metalworking lathes, even fourth-hand ones the Citadel sold to Nûrnen? The Hammer is sending us out for the *real* loot—only The People and their friends are going to do well out of this. That's why all our regiments are out posting guard while the *gayam* riot."

Her grin grew wider and she chucked him under the chin. "You stay with Tameetha and obey orders, boy, and she'll make you *rich*. Then you can buy all the fun you want."

Another scream, this one from above their heads. Shulamit's head whipped up, looking up past the sign that showed a stobor lying on its back with a stein in one fist. A woman had climbed out the short ledge by the second-story window. Her long flaxen hair streamed in the hot wind from the fires, and her dress had been ripped down the front to her waist. She screamed again as a figure appeared in the window, a troll-blocky man in felt and furs, his face a mass of tribal scars beneath a peaked sheepskin cap. He shouted at the woman in a Turkic dialect Shulamit could barely follow, shouting again in wordless rage as she edged further away and cowered with her eyes screwed shut. When his hand came out of the window his shamsir was in it, and he leaned far out for a cut that would slice her in half at the waist.

Shulamit's rifle was slung; no reason to waste precious ammunition outside serious combat. Her bow was ready.

She drew and loosed in a single fluid movement; the meaty impact of the broadhead was clearly audible, pounding home over the leaning man's collarbone and sinking to the feathers as the point sliced through lungs, heart, and liver. He dropped out the window and slid down the slanted shingle roof over the veranda to drop across the horse trough outside the inn. Shulamit sat with her bow still up, not quite believing she had just killed a man—an ally—so quickly. *I didn't even decide to do it*, she thought.

"Oh, *shaysse*," Tameetha swore, drawing the pistol again. She cocked it by bracing the hammers on her thigh and pushing down, then shot both barrels into the window as other figures appeared there. Arrows followed the buckshot as the rest of the squad reacted, and another Turk flopped out to lie bent across the windowsill. A third came bursting out of the ground-floor doors with saber in hand, and stopped dead as an arrow cracked into the boiled leather of his breastplate, angling down through the lower gut. He was close enough for Shulamit to see his face clearly, much younger than the first and with fewer of the ritual scars. Slowly he slid down the doorpost and sat, touching the fletching. Behind him the four blades of the arrowhead sparkled, wiped clean of blood by their passage through padding and armor on the way out.

The woman on the ledge had her eyes open again, darting from the Turks to the shadowed figures whose horses stamped below.

"*Pajalsta!*" she called, her voice quavering. *Mercy*, in Russki. "*Pajalsta!*"

Tameetha swore again in the same mild tone and hung her helmet from the saddlebow, transferring her pistol to her left hand along with the reins. Shulamit saw her blink at the girl, purse her lips and nod, then nudge her horse into a walk until it halted underneath the fugitive. She called up in the same language:

"You want to come along, *shisk*, or take your chances there? Look lively, I haven't got all truenight." Her gauntleted hand reached up.

The woman—girl, Shulamit saw, a little older than her-self—seemed to pause for a moment, met Tameetha's eyes, then nodded in her turn. She gathered her skirt in one hand and groped cautiously down the shingles, sat on their edge and reached out to grip the offered glove and swing down to ride pillion behind the commander.

"It's an ill wind blows nobody good," Tameetha remarked to Shulamit in a conversational tone, shifting the Nûrnenite girl's hands to a more comfortable grip around her waist. "You might think before you get me into a fire-fight, next time, though. Now, we've got a job of work to do before we rest."

The rescued girl turned enormous haunted eyes on Shulamit for a moment, before she buried her face against the armored shoulders in front of her and clung as if to squeeze out what she had seen.

"Right, you stainless heroes," the commander shouted. "Down there, two lefts and a right—follow me!"

Behind them the young Turk wept slowly into his lap, the arrow jerking with each sob.

## • CHAPTER TEN

Carcharoth prowled the outer reaches of the Citadel like a cliff lion ranging its territory in search of prey. The heavy flame thrower pack on his back, the dangling nozzle and trigger mechanism protruding forward over his shoulder, should have impeded his grace, reduced his walk to something heavy and lumpish. But no. He wore the clumsy weapon as if it were as much a part of him as a cliff lion's paws, a land gator's jaws.

Dagor had trouble keeping up with the Battlemaster. Unless he spoke to Carcharoth, the Cyborg paid no attention to him. Carcharoth's eyes didn't simply see—they scanned. If a sentry on the outer walls stood so much as a centimeter out of place, if a watcher's gaze wavered even a degree or two from its appointed direction, the Battlemaster gave him the rough edge of his tongue. Ever since the day when the Bandari began hammering the Citadel's outposts with their spigot mortars, Carcharoth had become as dangerous to be around as mercury fulminate. Pillars of flame-lit smoke on the southern horizon where Nûrnen lay did nothing to improve his temper.

Even Dagor hesitated now to address him. At length, though, he asked, "The jihad can't really harm us in here, can it?"

The outer walls of the fortress were thirty meters high, and the thickness was immeasurable—the Citadel was really one gigantic building, granite blocks, mass concrete and sections chiseled from the living rock of the Atlas.

Juchi's son looked down at the steep rocky slopes below and shuddered. He'd seen battle and death—who did not, on Haven? But there were wagon cartloads of bodies being dragged away from where the horde labored to throw protective ramparts around the Citadel, and more tumbled across the steep rising ground toward the fortress proper. Faint with distance even to his enhanced ears, he could hear the screams as more were driven forward to the work—Nûrnenites, from their dress, with guns to their rear and ahead as well. The line of earthworks was more than just a wall; trenches zigzagged out from it, and minor redoubts for the giant . . . *spigot mortars*, was the phrase Carcharoth had used . . . which hammered back at the outworks gun-bunkers.

As he watched, a huge mortar-bomb landed just short of a Gatling position among the outworks. When the smoke and dust cleared, the Gatlings opened up again; the heavy concrete and fieldstone fortifications were proof against anything but a direct hit. The protective bulwarks around the mortar jerked and stirred as hundreds of men grasped them from the inside and levered them forward; some fell as the 15mm bullets chewed at the surfaces, or ricocheted beneath. More herded forward through the trenches to take their place, and still more levered at the base of the heavy weapon. It was a battle of ants against tamerlanes, and there were more ants than the tamerlanes had paws to swat.

*The plainsfolk never had a single will to drive them,* he thought. *And never the skill to direct their hands. But they pay a heavy price already, and the Citadel itself is not touched.*

"And the best of the folk are in the Inner Keep," he went on aloud. That towered up behind him, at the center of the semicircular Citadel. It was a spike hundreds of meters high, dwarfed only by the sheer vertical cliff it rested on.

The Battlemaster's eyes fixed on him for a moment— and when they fixed, they held *still*. Dagor felt impaled by the force behind them. "Aye, we should be proof against mortar bombs here. The physical concerns me less than

other things. There's treachery in the wind, lad, treachery."
His nostrils flared, as if to scent it.

Dagor stared at him. Carcharoth had always been of
remorselessly literal mind. To hear him speak in metaphor
was as uncharacteristic, and therefore frightening, as
Hammer-of-God Jackson losing his religion might have
been. Dagor asked, "Has the Threat Analysis Computer
warned you of the risk?"

Like any plainsman, he thought of the TAC as an oracle:
Chaya, say, in electronic disguise.

"The Threat Analysis Computer?" Carcharoth threw
back his head. The laughter that ripped from his throat
reminded Dagor of the cry of a stobor scenting prey. "Titus
sits at the TAC these days, not I; were it but a little less
machine and he a little more, the two of them might be
wed. He seeks to learn from it what I already know: a great
burning is on the way." He stroked the nozzle of the flame
thrower as if it were the tender flesh between a woman's
thighs.

"A burning? Here?" Dagor looked at stone and concrete and metal all around. Of the whole of Haven,
nowhere seemed less flammable.

But Carcharoth nodded. "Aye, a great burning. The cattle of the steppes shall pass through the fire and all will be
burnt—*holocaust*, in the ancient tongue. I shall see to it
myself. Aye, they build their worthless fortified circles out
there, but I, Carcharoth, I shall show myself the lord of
their rings."

Because he'd been brought up away from people of his
blood, Dagor lacked the skills drilled into them from their
infancy: he still started in surprise, for instance, and his
face gave away far more than a proper Soldier's would
have. Till the crisis hit the Citadel, he'd been training with
boys a third his age, learning to master the abilities printed
on his genes. Most of the boys were better than he. He was
done resenting that, and had buckled down to learn as
much as he could. Before he came here, few had thought
him worth training in anything.

Now the discipline he'd acquired paid for itself. Before he started learning how to put his body under conscious control, he surely would have drawn back a step from Carcharoth. The Battlemaster didn't sound like any other Soldier he had known. He seemed more like a shaman who'd gone out into the steppe alone, eaten a double handful of mind-blinder mushrooms, and then come back to his clan with his head fuller of visions than sense.

*Not the TAC*, Dagor realized. *It's Carcharoth who reminds me of Chaya.* Like his sister/aunt, Carcharoth had come to the place where he was seeing more with his mind's eye than with the two that looked out on the real world. Such folk had been touched by the finger of Allah; they saw visions, and sometimes the vision became truth. Exposing fear before that fiery, searching gaze would have been fatal.

And yet, merely by accepting Dagor for who he was rather than the cursed result of a sin-filled union, Carcharoth had done more to make him feel at peace with himself than anyone since the day his mother Badri slew herself and Juchi plunged the brooches again and again into his own eyes. How much did he owe the Battlemaster for that gift?

Enough to make him say, as gently as he could, "Should you not carry on the war as one fought with everything here within these walls against the armies from the steppe? Surely not even you, sir, could hope to defeat them by yourself?"

"I do. I shall." Carcharoth sounded eerily sure of himself. "I am the instrument of the Race, the goad to subdue the cattle of this freezing, stinking world. Your will is free, lad—you may aid me if you wish. Stand against me and you too shall be consumed." He stroked the nozzle of the flame thrower again.

Under the veneer of impassivity he'd labored to acquire, Dagor knew cold terror. Carcharoth seemed more like a father to him than any man he'd known since Juchi, blind and moaning, stumbled out of Tallinn Valley.

No more denying it, though: the Battlemaster was not just behaving erratically any more. He had, without question, gone mad.

The impossible had begun to happen.

Nûrnen had fallen.

If Sigrid had been any other Cyborg, she would have gone catatonic or run rogue. Cyborgs did not calculate the impossible. Irrelevant data, data that did not connect with anything useful, were discarded, erased, forgotten. And Nûrnen overrun by hordes of howling cattle, the Citadel manned by women and children, the strength of the Soldiery lured half around the world on a wild-drillbit chase, was so profoundly unlikely that it counted as fiction.

So was her position. She was not bound—that would have taken stronger ropes than anything the cattle had— and she was under no restraint, but there was an assault rifle trained on her and a pair of cold Bandari eyes behind it, and a grin that flickered whenever Sigrid happened to glance that way.

Sigrid had brought it on herself. She had called it biding her time. The truth of it was, she had been vegetating. She had shut down her logical faculties when they persisted in running scenarios of Nûrnen taken and the Citadel besieged. Or worse—the Citadel taken from behind, by certain ways that she knew. She did what she used to scorn in males of her breed: she excluded data that did not suit her comfort.

Some things were important, some were not. The week before had been important. Two days outside of Nûrnen, when the army camped to rest, before the assault on the Gate, her eldest mare had shown herself ready to foal. Sigrid scouted a place that would do, a slight rise and a cairn of stones uninhabited by inimical wildlife. It was defensible, just, from the army of predators and scavengers that followed the human horde. The army was breaking camp as she separated her little herd from it. She did not worry about being seen. She was known as a horsetrader, not a fighter, and she was rather publicly pregnant. No one would care that she had finally decided to go her own way before things got too interesting to get out of.

The mare knew her business. Sigrid had to do little but keep an eye out for prowling predators.

The foal was born quickly, as if it were eager to have a look at its cold new world. It was wrapped in a silvery caul and followed immediately by the mass of the afterbirth; before Sigrid could move to help, it had kicked its way free and wobbled to its feet, diving blindly for its mother's teat.

Young horses were quick to find their feet, but Sigrid had never seen one as quick as this. It attacked the teat like a hungry tamerlane. Its mother investigated it calmly and began to lick it dry. It was a bay like its sisters, with a thin blaze and a white forefoot.

Sigrid moved in carefully. The mare's ears went back, but she offered no further threat. Sigrid ran hands over the foal's forequarters, taking care not to touch the rump and trigger the kick reflex. It was a colt, well made, no perceptible defects. In a day or two, she would be able to judge more conclusively, but she thought that it would be taller than its sisters, and more finely built.

The thin air of the steppe gave it no trouble, nor did its mother begin at once to hemorrhage. Again, time would tell. But Sigrid was nine parts certain that the mutation had bred true. If the colt could pass it to his get, then she had a priceless resource: a herd of horses that could breed on the open steppe.

This was joy, this thing that made her heart beat so uncommonly hard. She was grinning like a Bandari. She suppressed a completely preposterous urge to whoop.

"So that's your secret," said a deceptively quiet voice. She looked up from the colt into the face of Barak bar Heber. There were other faces behind him, including one that struck her as inevitable. More to the point, there were rifles, trained on her. Joy congealed into cold stillness.

"They can all foal on the steppe?" Barak asked. His rifle

was slung behind him. Sigrid's was in Bandari hands. She had laid it with her pack when the mare began to foal—stupidity beyond belief, and worth every moment of misery she suffered for it.

She could still fight her way out. It would not be easy. She would almost certainly take a bullet, probably more than one.

That danger would have been negligible.

Except.

She straightened slowly. Her hands were on her belly.

Advertising it. Protecting it.

Barak's brows quirked. He understood. She shifted her feet infinitesimally, drew an unobtrusive breath.

A rifle-barrel jabbed her in the gut. "Go ahead, Sauron," said Shulamit. The rifle was aimed, by design or by accident, at the baby's head. Her finger twitched on the trigger.

Sigrid calculated options at panic speed.

"Put that thing down," said Barak. He was smiling his easy Bandari smile, but his voice had the crack of command. Shulamit snarled and obeyed.

Sigrid stood still. If she moved, she would rip Shulamit's head off. And that would get her killed, and the baby with her.

"Yes," she answered Barak's question of a minute or an age ago. "My mares can foal outside of valleys."

"And you," he said. "Can you . . . ?"

"My system prefers a higher air pressure than can be found here," said Sigrid.

He noticed what she was not saying. "Such as that in certain sealed rooms of the Citadel?" he asked.

"You know of such?" she inquired.

Shulamit spat. "Stop your lollygagging and spill it. You're a Sauron. I know a man who names you Cyborg Sigrid of the Citadel and calls you the Breedmaster's daughter. What's a nice girl like you doing in a place like this?"

"Is she incapable of speaking in anything but ancient cliches?" Sigrid asked Barak.

Barak aimed a look at Shulamit. It did not cow her, but

it shut her up. "I hadn't heard that there were Cyborg women. Even Sauron women are reckoned by some to be a myth."

"Or a legend," said Sigrid. "Like your mother."

He stiffened. The smile wiped itself from his face. He looked every inch the Soldier for a moment, before he remembered again to be Bandari. "How do you know—" He stopped himself before Sigrid could. "Of course. You'd know the bloodlines, wouldn't you, if you were the Breed-master's daughter."

"I know yours," she said. She lowered her voice almost to subvocal. Maybe to protect his secret until a better moment presented itself. Maybe simply to thwart the Ban-dari bitch. "I can tell you your father's name."

"My father's name was Heber," said Barak, but in the same register—below the range of human hearing.

"I postulate that he was a Soldier named Gorbag. He disappeared at the proper time, and you carry certain of his gene-markers. His was a good bloodline. Not a great one, not command quality. But better than some."

For a moment she knew, hoped, that he would lunge. But he had better control than that. His eyes were flat. He had learned to hate her, then.

She shook her head with sadness only part feigned. Aloud, so that the cattle could hear, she said, "You have me, I grant you that. Do you plan to assign a platoon to guard me? Can you spare that many?"

"I could put you in chains," he said.

She shrugged. "It would take me a while, but I would get out of them."

"Even if those chains are forged of honor and not of steel?" She looked at him. He did not seem to have gone mad. "Give me your word," he said, "that you will do nothing to hinder our assault on the Citadel."

"I may be the Breedmaster's Cyborg daughter," said Sigrid, "but I can hardly prevent three hundred thousand fighters from doing whatever they have a mind to do."

"Three hundred and fifty, actually," Barak said. "With

the pass open we've almost made up the nomad losses. But I had in mind something a little more subtle. Such as sneaking into the Citadel and alerting your kin."

So had she. She should have expected him to know it. "Did you? And I thought you might be plotting something even more subtle—such as using me to open the gate."

"So I had," he said affably. "I don't suppose you're that easily corruptible?"

She was silent.

He smiled wryly. "And if that isn't acceptable, would you consider giving us a fighting chance? Such as putting us onto a back way?"

Still, silence.

He seemed not to have expected anything else. "Of course not," he answered for her. "I could threaten your baby, I suppose, but believe it or not, we Bandari stop short of open atrocity. We'll do it the hard way. Unless . . . ?"

"No," said Sigrid.

"Give me your word, then. No treachery for one T-month."

By then they'll have the Citadel or starve. And what is a promise to cattle? But he didn't think of himself that way. She smiled, remembering words once written by the Lady Althene, who would no more have kept a dangerous promise to cattle than she would explain her actions to the family cat. He blinked, dazzled, which made her smile the wider. "And no chains?"

"No chains," said Barak. "But you'll be watched. You'll pardon the insult, but . . . necessity . . ."

"Necessity," she said without irony. "Yes. One T-month."

"We'll have to take your weapons, I'm afraid. And your horses. We'll take good care of them."

"What do I keep?" she asked.

"Your life, Sauron," said Shulamit.

Barak shot her another look. "Your life, yes, and your belongings that are not weapons. Your dog, too. I don't think he'd let us separate you."

"You ask a great deal," said Sigrid, "and leave me very little."

He shrugged and spread his hands in an eloquent Bandari gesture. "Can you blame us? If you're a spy, you've seen enough to condemn you a hundred times over. If you're not, it's no more than common sense to keep you out of it while we win our war."

"If you win it," said Sigrid.

"We will," he said, then paused. "Well?"

She did not need to take as much time as she did. She had processed all the data. Some of it was actively painful. But even if the worst scenario played itself out, she would be alive. She had full knowledge of this army, its leaders and its strategies, thanks to her perambulations through every camp and along the march. She was of little value to the Citadel now. Later . . .

"I give you my word," she said.

"A Sauron's word," sneered Shulamit.

"A Soldier's word," said Sigrid. "Take it or leave it."

"I take it," said Barak. They clasped hands on it: the clasp that tests strength. His eyes widened. Her own smiled. He looked a little less cocksure when she let go, but he still had the upper hand, and he knew it. She granted him that. For the moment, she accepted it.

And Nûrnen fell. Sigrid was kept out of the battle, but no one tried to stop her once the city was taken; not even the countless women who keened along the way, beside the tumbled nomad dead.

*They have lost more in one cycle than we have killed in ten lifetimes,* she estimated clinically as she walked down the road through the pass. From the sounds to her right, they were losing more still—but the earthworks were already over man-height, good enough protection from the battered outerworks. In Nûrnen, the initial enthusiasm of the sack had faded under the combined influence of exhaustion, satiation, and hard Bandari discipline. There were still too many revelers to deal with all at once. They had set fire to the Soldiers' Quarter—no wonder they were bitter, judging from the degree of damage. It looked as if heavy weapons, doubtless another Bandari surprise, had been brought up to shatter the buildings when each became a fortress. Now citizens who looked too much like Soldiers were as likely to be raped and killed as to be rounded up and questioned.

The Bandari were busy; she saw wagon after wagon packed tight and leaving on the long trail back to the Pale. They were generous to their barbarian allies with coined silver and other goods. The wagons were full of things much more valuable than money—machine parts, alloys, books. What they could not steal, they destroyed with methodical efficiency, unless it was likely to be immediately useful. What was useful, they *prepared* for destruction.

Shulamit was watching Sigrid. She had not drawn that duty as often as no doubt she wanted, having had plenty to do in the battle and the aftermath, but she had managed an hour here and there, spelling the rota of guard dogs whom Barak had set on watch.

Her rifle's safety was off. Sigrid could have taken her a dozen times over; cattle concentration was weak compared to a Cyborg's, and the little bitch was starting to show the effects of too many hours without sleep. But Sigrid had given her word. Oaths sworn to cattle were worthless.

The city, as a city, meant little to Sigrid. As the chief tribute center of Sauron domination on Haven, it meant much, and its sack twisted her stomach into a cold knot of rage.

The savages were raping it. Orders were out that there was to be no wanton vandalism, but drunken Mongols cared nothing for orders. She saw one draped in a lace shawl with a copper cookpot on his head, swilling something out of a jug and bawling a Turkic love lament. His brother, or one like enough to him to be his close kin, was raping a girl to the beat of the song. Shulamit looked as if she would have loved to bash his head in; but if she did, she would lose sight of Sigrid.

Sigrid did the honors for her with a single swift kick. The man's head burst like a melon. His brother stopped singing to gape down at him. Sigrid drove his nose into his skull.

It was small, that pleasure, but it sufficed. Sigrid stepped over the body of the would-be singer and went on. Although it was truenight, the sky was afire. Manmade fire. Sigrid's eyes suffered almost as much from it as from the full light of day. Still, she could not keep from looking at it. Her feet and her enhanced senses negotiated the maze of streets, choosing a path that avoided the worst of the sack and the scattered fires. The best loot was taken long since. The men who wandered in and out of broken doors brandished lesser treasures: a woman's gown, a hat with a ridiculous length of plume, a child's hobbyhorse. One villainous-looking Turk, wearing enough beads and gauds and bones of his own to mark him a chieftain, ran along a rooftree balancing an enormous, still ticking clock. "Is this honorable?" he howled to the street, the roof, the blazing sky. "What honor is there in this? I will have honorable loot!"

He fell from the roof still howling, landed on his feet like a cat, and ran off without abatement of his litany. And also, Sigrid noticed, without losing his grip on the clock.

She paused where he had landed. The few looters in the street had gone off after their chieftain. There were people barricaded in the houses, but they were not about to investigate the sudden quiet. The air stank of smoke, sweat, gunpowder, blood.

This street ran almost straight for a distance. Beyond it, beyond roofs and walls and several klicks of no-man's-land, loomed the black rock that was the Citadel. No lights shone there. There would be guards on the walls—old men or boys, or women. Sigrid would have been there if she had not defied the Breedmaster's orders and gone questing like a man, searching for something honorable to mark her passage into adulthood.

Her lip curled. Honorable loot, honorable accomplishment. Was there any difference between them?

The treasure that she had found was taken, held in Bandari custody. The treasure that she carried in her body was bound with her to this captivity.

She glanced at her watchbitch. Shulamit stared back, near blind in that light, but not near enough.

The baby drummed a tattoo on the dome of her belly. She quieted him with a hand. Soon, she promised him. Soon.

"Got a *gayam* who claims to have something valuable for you, Hammer old *chaver*," Tameetha said.

It was still dark, the beginning of dimday. Hammer-of-God blinked eyes that felt as if they were lubricated with ground glass and glared at the Bandari woman.

*She* looked as if she had found a chance to rest, and like the tamerlane who swallowed the prize sheep besides. He had known and worked with her for years, without any liking—Tameetha had her reasons for spending most of her time outside the Pale—but with a good deal of respect. He decided that she was unlikely to interrupt this nightmare without serious reason, and she *had* secured the target he assigned her. He wished all the others had; there were only so many Bandari troops to hand, and few others who could be trusted to guard a grain storehouse or a waterworks while the nomads made merchants dance on coals until they told where the gold was buried. In Nûrnen, there was likely to be a good deal of gold. . . .

"Who is it?" he growled, pouring himself another tea. Jehovah and His Son and the Spirit of Harmony, but he could use a drink. Impossible; he'd been up too long. The last thing he needed was to relax, if he did they wouldn't wake him the next cycle even if they used one of Sapper's *Ariksas*. Most of Saurontown was still holding out, and the outworks of the Citadel were being a bloody—in every sense of the word—impediment to the huge labor teams working on the circumvallation. *It'll keep our logistical problems down*, he thought bluntly. "And it had better be important."

They were talking in the meeting room of what had been Nûrnen's mayoral palace, quite tasty, even by the high standards of the Pale. Lots of carved wood—always a luxury on this dry planet—a marble fireplace, paneled walls with paintings, good rugs—and all intact. Hammer had come straight here to establish his headquarters, and the mayor had been quite cooperative to protect his family from the savages rampaging outside. Quite cooperative, it hadn't been necessary to make *him* dance on coals to produce spectacular results. *Bind not the mouths of the oxen who tread out the grain*, Hammer quoted to himself, then forced his aching mind back to business.

"Name of Strong Sven," she said, and laughed at his start.

"Yes, you'd better keep Aisha from hearing the name— the one who tried to slap Juchi around and got a broken arm for his pains. Found him hiding in a cellar at the machine shop, of all places, after I woke up. Had, hmm, a witness to confirm some of his story. He claims to know something but won't tell anyone but a high-up."

Hammer nodded; it was his only hope for a reward, or for pardon or whatever he wanted to ask for. It would have to be spectacular information to save Strong Sven's life, in *this* army.

"Bring him in," he said, levering himself erect with both hands on the table. Sitting was almost as bad as walking, on his leg, and it let him know with a blaze of pain that made him grind his teeth.

Strong Sven was a big man, as tall as the commander and much thicker through the shoulders, with only the faint beginnings of a beer gut. There was no arrogance in him now as he bowed low between two of Tameetha's troopers, Shulamit and that *sklem* Karl; a local girl of some sort was hovering in the background, wrapped in a Pale-made military cloak. She stepped quickly over to Tameetha's side, staring at Sven with what Hammer judged to be a mixture of fear and spite.

*People are complicated*, he sighed. "Talk, Sauron's arselicker," he said ominously. "Every man should confess his sins before he dies."

He had judged correctly; this was a man fear would

always rule. "Lord—please, lord, I can tell you what you need to know. I've always hated the Soldi—the Saurons, they've oppressed us without mercy, please, let me tell you what I know!"

Hammer nodded, rubbing his jaw to hide a grimace of distaste.

The whistling, nasal dialect of Americ the Nûmenites spoke was unpleasantly reminiscent of the Sauron accent, but that was not the reason for his displeasure. *Got to use a pitchfork to shovel cowshit,* he thought.

"Everyone knows the Jews are God's Chosen People, I know you'll give me justice—" Sven babbled on, bowing toward the banner of the Pale that stood against the wall: six-pointed star over the leaping springbok, flanked by burning swords.

"Then it's a pity you're talking to a Christian, isn't it?" the commander replied, kicking the man as much to shut off the sound as to inflict pain. Strong Sven whimpered and closed up around his bruised stomach.

"Judge Chaya bat Dvora leads us, and Aisha bat Badri, and the rest of the Seven—but I'm not going to break their sleep for some Sauron bumboy's prattle. I'm General Jackson, and they call me the Hammer-of-God, dog. Now speak!"

Sven straightened up. "For your ear only, General." Unwillingly, Hammer stooped. Then his face went rigid at the hurried whisper, and he rose, wheeling.

"Put this man under close arrest. *Nobody* is to talk to him until I return. You—summon the Judge and the Seven. *Now,* man, *now!*"

# • CHAPTER ELEVEN

Carcharoth held to his temper with all the remaining strength of his mind . . . which was still considerable, in a familiar situation.

Facing down the Council which nominally oversaw the operations of Sauron-on-Haven was familiar enough. Galen Diettinger had not been a Cyborg; in fact, he'd put down an uprising of Cyborgs not long after the *Dol Guldur* had landed. It was the First Citizen who was supposed to rule, with the Council to advise him.

No strong heir from the Founder's direct line had emerged for generations. Over the years, the Battlemaster had usurped most of the First Citizen's power and the Council's as well. It happened bit by bit, but the change was steady over the centuries. Cyborgs were a myth of terror to the cattle of Haven, but they had mythic resonance among the Soldiers as well. A Cyborg was the logical culmination of the genetic creed of Sauron. The Battlemaster's was a competitive position, and ordinary Soldiers seldom bothered to compete with Cyborgs, believing it a waste of time and effort. Cyborgs made no effort to correct that impression.

But Diettinger hadn't been a Cyborg . . .

Carcharoth looked around the circle of aged, worried faces and concealed his contempt. "We have suffered setbacks," he said.

Gimli the Archivist snorted. "This Council agreed," he said, looking up at the holo of Galen Diettinger on one wall, below the great banner of the Lidless Eye, "that the uprising in the western Shangri-La was the first priority. It seems that the minority was correct, and it was a diversion."

"No. The judgment was logical given the facts available at the time," Carcharoth said smoothly. Like all his kind, his voice was full and rich and carried overtones of sincerity, command and conviction—it was engineered for just those purposes.

"Perhaps it was logical, then," Councillor Haggard said. "But now we know differently. We will gain no tribute from Nûrnen in this generation. Or the next."

Carcharoth made a gesture of dismissal. "Regrettable but not fatal. We are recalling Deathmaster Ghâsh and his expeditionary forces. These are temporary reverses."

First Citizen Ansel Diettinger could not hide the contempt in his voice. "Loss of Nûrnen is scarcely a *reverse*, Battlemaster. It is more in the nature of a *catastrophe.*"

"This setback will be remedied when the new forces arrive. The TAC estimates not more than three hundred thousand cattle troops before our walls. We have killed more than ninety thousand and they have not tested our strength. The Citadel holds, and Deathmaster Ghâsh comes with his forces. There is no reason for concern, First Citizen." He made the title an insult. "Our only problems will be sanitation when we seek to dispose of the dead."

*They will burn,* Carcharoth thought. He knew that thought showed in his eyes; he could smell the faint chemical traces of anxiety in the sweat of the Council members, hear the slight acceleration of their heartbeats, see pupils dilate. They had been trained for generations to defer to Cyborgs. This would be no exception. *When the cattle are destroyed, I will sweep this antiquated farce out of existence.* One of the Sauron Role Models, the Ancient Napoleon, had done something very similar with . . . what was the name? Carcharoth's data-retrieval system was still functioning: the Holy Roman Empire. "Unless this Council wishes to remove me from my post as Battlemaster?" he asked flatly.

He eyed Gimli and his group. Any opposition would come from them. There was none. They still feared him. As they should.

◇ ◇ ◇

The Chairman of the New Soviet Men and the President-pro-tem of the Sons of Liberty withdrew to the next room, shutting the thick door tightly behind them. Even Soldier hearing couldn't hear what they whispered to each other.

The Soldiers were here under flag of truce, but their regiments weren't far away. There was fear in the smell of the rebels around the walls, the nobles of the *politburo* and the Ranchers who ruled the Sons of Liberty—as much as anyone ruled that group. The room itself had been the garrison commandant's residence. It still stank of cordite and black powder and old blood, and one corner showed sky where *something* had blasted the thick stone and morticed beams apart. The Soldier force here hadn't been large, but it had died hard.

The two cattle rulers returned; the Chairman's face was impassive for an unaugmented man's, his little blue eyes flat above the grizzled gray brush of beard that swept down over the shimmering silk of his high-collared shirt. The President didn't try to hide his hatred, a beak-nosed weathered man slung about with weapons, one of them a captured Citadel-made revolver.

"Nyet," the New Soviet rulers said.

"No." The President's voice was equally flat in his harsh twanging dialect of Americ.

Another Sauron might have seen that Ghâsh was startled, but to an ordinary human he was motionless.

"You are facing total defeat," Ghâsh said. "It is unreasonable to continue your resistance."

The President smiled. "If we was reasonable, we wouldn't have rebelled in the first place."

The Chairman stroked his beard and nodded. "Your demands grew beyond all bearing. If you have troubles elsewhere, good."

Ghâsh tapped the dispatches. "The Bandari have been using you as pawns," he said. "Do you not realize the nomad horde is *past* the Citadel? They are coming down through Karakul pass, spreading out into the Shangri-La. It is what they have sought for generations. Do you want *those* as your neighbors? Compared to them, our yoke is light."

Some of the other cattle in the room stirred and murmured.

"Nyet," the Chairman repeated, and the President nodded.

"We know what it's like fer farmers to have the fur-hats on their borders," the President said. "Like havin' giant rats fer neighbors . . . mean ones."

"Then why will you not end this foolish rebellion?"

"We figgure," the Americ-speaking leader said, "that you'll beat the fur-hats anyhow. Only it'll cost you more and weaken you more if you have to worry 'bout us too. Or if you *lose*, you'll kill enough of them to weaken 'em so we can handle them. It's a long way from here to the Citadel, anyhow. The nomads are there *now*. But you're *here* now. If you want peace, get out, we won't stop you."

"*Da*, the Zhid dogs have lied to us," the Chairman rumbled. "But we expected that; this is political struggle, no? You cannot expect us to surrender just because it would be convenient for you."

"Your losses have been heavy," Ghâsh said.

"We expected that."

The President nodded. "So've yours been. Hundreds to you is worse than thousand and tens of thousands to us. Especially when you need the troops elsewhere."

Ghâsh gave no sign of his feelings that unaugmented men could hear. Every minute was critical . . . for the Soldiers. The cattle could afford to wait, and they intended to take full advantage of the fact.

"As you say. We depart. But you will do more than not oppose us. You will assist us on the way. Transportation and supplies. Otherwise we will burn both your capitals to the ground."

Ghâsh could hear the faint sound of teeth grinding together.

❖         ❖         ❖

Deferential but insistent hands had waked her, draped furs over her shoulders. *Save them for the children*, Chaya started to say. But she, even she, shivered. And there were no children in this house.

At least, not yet. She shivered again. Her mother Dvora had had these odd flashes of knowledge, and her mother before her. It was her mother's blood in her. . . . *Her mother was Badri*. She was Sauron.

What happened to Saurons who didn't die fighting? She had had stray reports, had promised herself that one day for her son's sake she would find out . . . no time now. Was she almost out of time? Since Nûrnen fell, she had drifted in and out of waking dreams, punctuated with lights and her own voice and eyes, concerned or awed, watching her.

Lights flickered about her, automatic courtesy in the night as Hammer-of-God had her conducted to the mayor's study. She didn't need the lights. Yet. And they reminded her of Nûrnen, burning down. *Woe unto the city* . . . no, not now.

She heard other voices, sleepy, apprehensive, and didn't need the keen hearing she still had to put names to them.

*What have we done? What have I done?* Each hour, she knew more until the waking dreams drew her as strongly as a drug—and drugs did not work that strongly on those of her blood.

She paused on the threshold of what had been the mayor's study. Light the color of oil glinted off the wood, off the model that Sapper and his officers had lugged into the room. Karl and Aisha stared down at the model, and near them, young Kemal, determined to grow himself from *khan* into General. His friend and vassal Ihsan stood behind him as if on guard.

Barak rushed in . . . and Sannie, from a different direction.

Trouble there? Not for her only son, borne with such pain. And even Sannie, one of the Seven, was dear to her now.

Around her, voices rose and ebbed. "Tameetha brought this one in . . ."

"Him! He spat on my father's name in Nûrnen. I should . . ."

"Aisha, dearheart . . ."

"He claims he hates Saurons? He lies. He made a boast of sharing their blood, but my father . . ."

"Lady, by my mother's grave I didn't know . . ."

"My father lies unburied!"

"Shut *up*, traitor!" Tameetha interrupted. "You saw the girl outside—her name's Raisa—confirms the story, and she'd like to scratch this one's eyes out. I'd say that's more than a lover's quarrel. Lovers—feh! Man like him would make you want to be a virgin again and stay one."

"*Yongk*, shut his face for him . . . no, we're not going to kill you yet, animal, not as long as General Jackson here says. You want to live? When he says talk, you talk."

"Judge Chaya?" Hammer's voice.

And Barak's. "*Amah?*"

"What have we done?" Chaya whispered aloud.

Aisha turned to her like a child seeking her mother's voice. Poor child, she had had all too little of that. Like all of them, she was going on too little sleep, especially now; but still, she glowed, not just from torchlight, but from the presence of the man at her side and the life that swelled out the Turkic garments she had thrown on, a splendor of scarlet and gold that bespoke lavish tastes in the mayor's wife.

The dreams hung temptingly in Chaya's consciousness—Heber as a young man, spring in the Pale, Barak as a baby. She pushed them away.

Hammer-of-God lurched over to the model of Nûrnen. Chaya winced in sympathy for the General. He was younger than she but lacked her pain overrides. He made do on willpower.

"When this is over," Aisha hissed, "Strong Sven is *mine*. He dishonored my father." She pressed forward and spat accurately on the man as he knelt, hunched over his belly. The stink of urine rose about him.

"There's worse dishonor than that. You will avenge it

all," her husband told her. "But first, love, listen." Hand on her arm, he led her back to a chair. She could have broken free; she could have broken his arm as easily as her father Juchi had broken this coward of a Strong Sven's arm, but she let him seat her as if she were an invalid or a princess, and she even smiled.

"You wouldn't have waked us for nothing," Chaya said to Hammer-of-God. "What does this . . . creature have to say that's worth keeping him alive for, let alone waking me up?"

Hammer's stobor grin stripped exhaustion from his face. Strong Sven cringed further, and Chaya almost laughed. *A Jew and a judge and a Sauron all in one, and I won't deal, is that it?* "Karl," he beckoned to young Karl, "you and Shuli take him out and dump water on this dog. He's not housebroken. Then get us some food and go away."

They dragged him out, shutting the door on the babble of his curses and pleas. Moments later, they returned, dumping a wetter, cleaner, and—hard as it was to believe it—more frightened man on a bare spot on the floor.

Pale-faced servants followed them, setting steaming bowls and pitchers and cups anywhere documents could be shifted from the huge table.

"Take something with you," Tameetha bat Irene told Karl and Shulamit. They loaded hands and a pocket or two with food and herded the servants out.

Karl Haller beckoned to Chaya. *Eat something.* Typical *mediko* who'd been too long among Bandari, who always wanted people to eat something. Barak and Aisha joined her, and then they were all dipping with a kind of ghoulish coziness into the common bowls while Strong Sven watched, breathing through his mouth.

Aisha raised an eyebrow. She picked up a bowl from the table—it had been clean a day or so ago—dashed its contents into the fire, and filled it. Then she set it before Strong Sven.

"Let's see you feed, dog," she hissed. "With your left hand."

Kemal and Ihsan looked faintly revolted. A petty revenge, Chaya thought, but they didn't want the traitor passing out on them.

Using his left hand, Strong Sven shoveled in the grains and meat. Aisha watched every mouthful until he finished. She did not offer him a second bowl.

"Now, dog," said Hammer-of-God, "*howl for us.*"

"I am a miner, lord, like my father and grandfathers before me. Up in the mountains, where the air is thin and the shafts are narrow . . ."

"Who've we got there?" Hammer-of-God snapped.

"Nazrullah *Khan*," Kemal had the name a second before Barak. One of the *mujahedin*, Chaya identified him. Her memory lapsed back into the waking dream of time and place that so pleased her and surfaced with a Terran name: *Afghan.* "Kin, feuds?"

"This lot keeps itself to itself," Barak cut in. "Some rumors that centuries ago, they were hand in glove with the Saurons. Any man who says that aloud doesn't get to say anything else. I wouldn't team them with the Russkis. . . ."

"What about Shamyl?"

"They are of the faithful," Ihsan shrugged. "It is no matter."

"Someone get them. Also Gasim, Ilderim *Khan*, Suleiman Tepe—let him *earn* his title—the other leading *khans*. See if you can find anyone of the men of Bod we can talk to. Doesn't have to speak Americ, but *good* Turkic . . . his life could depend on it."

"I'll go," Sannie volunteered.

"You'll go nowhere," Hammer-of-God snapped at her. "You are by-God one of the Seven and you don't run errands. Besides, didn't I hear somewhere you've a head for heights?"

"Grew up in the hills, sir."

"She's good," Barak put in. "Doesn't pass out as fast as . . ."

*One not of our blood.* Chaya gazed at the model of

Nûrnen, the Citadel, and the rocks. Moses was supposed to speak to the rock, but he struck it, and his death poured out with the water. *Open*, she commanded silently, but the stone kept its own secrets . . . mottled stone, easily worked until touched with fire. Laced with small, rich deposits of copper, platinum, iron, gold. By now, the miners of Nûrnen and the *mujahedin* had probably honeycombed those hills.

Chaya felt her lips stretch in a grin worthy of a death's head. "There is a way, isn't there? A secret way into the Citadel."

Hearing the secret with which he had hoped to buy his life tossed out like that, Strong Sven almost pissed himself the second time that night. Kemal's and Barak's grins made them almost look, God forbid, like brothers. And after a moment, Aisha began to laugh.

# • CHAPTER TWELVE

"Not long now," Mumak said. "Three hundred kilometers. If the bridges are still up we'll have the Citadel in sight by tomorrow night, Deathmaster."

*Deathmaster.* Sharku nodded agreement. Not a rank given by the Council, or anyone else in the Citadel, but by his own Soldiers. His original two, Regiment Leader Laduf's command from Castell City, another force from Firebase Three, and every man Firebase Two could spare from the defense of Falkenberg. It would leave little enough in the Valley, but that hardly mattered with the Citadel in danger—and now that the New Soviet Men understood what the Bandari were up to, there would be new alliances there.

Effectively four Regiments. Easily a Deathmaster's command . . .

"Signals stopped days ago," Mumak said thoughtfully. "Last message said there was an attack on Nûrnen and recalled Deathmaster Ghâsh. Lady Althene! Nomads at the gates of Nûrnen!'

Sharku nodded again. It was unthinkable enough that the heliograph had been interrupted. That could mean anything. A relay station taken with its crew besieged inside. Or—or the Citadel, with all its strength down here in the Valley might already have fallen, the armory sacked, women and children dead, Chichek and Gimilzor dead in their blood with a hundred enemies dead around them. At least that many—

Or the nomads could have broken against Nûrnen, with no danger to the Citadel at all. The TAC might have been right, and Carcharoth had cut off the signals himself, luring him on—in which case he'd have a cold welcome.

Odd. His future depended on disaster to his home and all he loved.

It hadn't been an easy passage. The journey back through the Valley had been even more hard fought than the drive down to Firebase Six.

Hard fought, but not as costly. On the way down, Ghâsh had allowed the officers to lead from the front, and far too many were killed because they hadn't realized how good the barbarian rifles were. Not just rifles. Discipline. Tactics. They'd taught a costly lesson.

Mumak held up a hand. "Gunfire, Deathmaster. Heavy guns, not all ours."

Soldiers in the forward ranks slowed to a walk and displayed the clenched-fist signal for their comrades to do likewise. A messenger ran up to them. "Nomads, Deathmaster. Assault Leader Vizgor estimates at least a thousand."

"Which nomads?"

"Not known to us, Deathmaster. Their banners show horsetails with yellow streamers."

"Yellow Chin," Sharku said. "From the far northern steppes. Their domain ends a thousand kilometers north of the Citadel."

Mumak looked puzzled, then nodded in comprehension. "The TAC never hinted of an alliance that large."

"No. Messenger, tell Assault Leader Vizgor to take command of the advanced party and sweep them out of our way. The rest of the force will continue the march."

"Sir." The messenger ran back to the front.

"Nomads west of the Citadel," Mumak said. "You've been right all along. This is a lot more than the usual migrations. Sure you don't want me to deal with this?"

"No. Let Vizgor show what he's learned of the new tactics."

"*Your* new tactics, Deathmaster."

"My new tactics, then. Another change long due. We've

lost too many officers looking for glory, Mumak. Glory! As if there were glory in risking Sauron lives to barbarians!"

"The Race needs glory, Deathmaster."

"Not against barbarians." He looked up at the baleful glare of the Cat's Eye. "Out there is glory. Not here on this stinking prison world!"

Vizgor's messenger trotted up to Sharku. "All is ready, Deathmaster. Final orders?"

"One. We want none to escape to take word back. Assault Leader Vizgor may take increased risks to accomplish this."

"As you say, Deathmaster." The messenger ran back, his easy lope carrying him faster than a trotting horse.

Up ahead the lead battalions had separated, while the first group of the main party had dug in to form an anvil. The nomads had seen no more than a hundred Soldiers, and couldn't know what they faced.

Vizgor listened to orders, then waved two groups of Soldiers to envelop the barbarians. In the valley below the nomad leaders had seen the unmounted Saurons on the hill above, but there was no panic.

"They have horses," Mumak snorted. "They think to outrun us. Deathmaster, these are clearly from very far away indeed."

"They'll learn," Sharku said.

Vizgor looked back to the commander, got no word, and turned to his junior leaders. "No burning. No fires," he said. "No warning to any ahead of us." It was clear that the nomads still didn't know what they faced. Herds of lowing cows, baahing sheep and insatiable goats grazed delightedly on what would have been somebody's next crop of rye. Men in fur hats on horses and muskylopes kept the herds heading roughly northwest. Behind the animals came the clan's yurts, with children playing on the wooden platforms that supported the domes of felt and with bored-looking old men or women driving teams of draught-muskies down the path of devastation the herds had created.

Between and behind the yurts shambled Caucasoid-looking people on rawhide leashes: farmer-folk the plainsmen had already scooped up in their rampage through the Valley. They'd end up slaves or concubines or tortured to death for the hell of it.

All eyes swung toward Vizgor. He raised his arm, then dropped it. The lead elements swept forward, as the encircling forces took positions on either side of the enemy.

It was not a battle. It was not even a massacre. It was an extermination. The outriders went down at once, most of them without ever knowing how they'd died. The rattle of gunfire hardly even disturbed the plainsmen's herds; the animals must have heard enough shooting lately to grow used to it.

Vizgor briefly examined the accouterments of a nomad who'd fallen off his muskylope after taking a three-shot burst across the chest. His longarm was a muzzle-loading flintlock, a smoothbore that fired round balls. He couldn't have hit a house at a hundred meters with it, or hurt the house if he did. He had a pistol in his belt and one more in each boot. They were similarly ineffectual.

*Gatling fodder*, Vizgor thought. The Pale must have used up these savages by the thousands in forcing their way past the Citadel. But when they had tens of thousands to spend, who cared?

Then he was running again, toward the cluster of yurts. He was inside assault-rifle range when the nomads got the idea that something was wrong. That was much too late. A few shots went off; he heard the dull bangs, saw the clouds of black-powder smoke rise. After the serious fight the western rebels had put up, it wasn't even a skirmish.

The only survivors of the raid were those of the nomads' captives who hadn't accidentally stopped a bullet. They greeted the Soldiers like heroes, shouting "Rescuers!" in Americ and Russki and three or four other languages. A very pretty blonde spread herself on the ground in front of Mumak, offering the only thanks she could give.

Mumak turned aside. "Isn't that the way it goes?" he said to Sharku. "They loathed us till they found out what we were holding back. All of a sudden, we don't look so bad any more."

"What else is new?" Sharku answered, the same bitterness in his voice, his mind too glossing over the fact that it had been Saurons long ago who had smashed Haven and its people into this low-tech hell—and *kept* it there for their own inscrutable purposes.

Along with the plainsmen, their herds went down in great numbers. The Soldiers gorged on raw meat, and cut off more slabs to carry with them. It was a welcome relief from the pemmican that fueled their hard-burning metabolisms on most long journeys.

Less than two hours after the attack on the nomads began, the last Soldiers were loping toward the Citadel again. Sharku wondered what would happen to the cattle and sheep they'd left behind. He supposed the local farmers would keep some, slaughter the rest—keeping meat was rarely a problem on Haven, you just dug down a few feet and it got cold. The farmers would live fat for a while—unless more bands from the steppe rolled over them. He could see pillars of smoke to north and south, clans lucky enough to be out of the way of the returning Soldiers. There were more and bigger fires to the east.

Twenty klicks closer to the Citadel, the Regiments encountered another nomad clan eager to seize part of this rich land for its own. This time, the Deathmaster barely bothered with spoken orders. The outflanking parties moved as if directed by thought alone. The slaughter that followed was just as complete as the first one.

Here, though, the Soldiers took a casualty: a trooper got a smoothbore ball through the muscle of his upper arm. He seemed more embarrassed than pained; his sectionmates ribbed him unmercifully.

Here, too, one of the plainsmen on a fast horse tried to escape the maelstrom and bring warning to his fellow nomads. Laughing, a Soldier ran after him. He paced the rider for a few hundred meters, taunting him for not going faster. His jeers made the plainsman knock an arrow and shoot from sheer frustration; he might have hit, too, had the Soldier not dodged aside and caught the arrow out of the air with a boyish whoop. The nomad managed to fire a pistol while the Soldier closed with him. He missed, of course, and the Soldier dragged him off his horse and killed him.

"Come on, Snaga," Sharku said, pulling the Chief Assault Leader off a writhing plainswoman. "We have serious work ahead of us."

"Oh, very well," Snaga said testily. He broke her neck with a quick twist, yanked up his trousers and buttoned his fly, going from rapist to soldier in the space of about fifteen seconds.

Sharku wanted to say something sharp to him, but all that came out was, "Just make sure you don't do that with any women from the Valley. Having our own cattle on our side may give us an edge."

Again, the nomads' captives had rapturously welcomed the Soldiers as liberators. Even if it was just a case of the devils they knew versus the ones they didn't, Sharku wanted to wring every gram of use he could from it—and it was logical, too. The Soldiers wanted to keep their cattle fat and healthy; the nomads regarded them as so much wild game to slaughter.

The steppe barbarians, no matter how numerous, could be handled. They had no capacity for forethought, planning, coordination. The Bandari puppet-masters behind them . . .

Truenight continued long past the time when dawn would have woken any Terrans who had survived their own world's wasting. Warriors stood, squatted, or sat where they could in the mayor's study, which would probably never be the same, even if they could get the stinks of sweat out of the rugs or oil the scratched paneling smooth once more. No servants were admitted: the youngest of the warriors were proud to fetch food or light or other men, whom they regarded jealously as if their mere presence might snatch honor from their grasp.

Nazrullah, *khan* of the men who still called themselves *mujahedin* as well as *Pathan*, stood with his back to Strong Sven. No one wanted to look at him. "Yurek," he mused. "Son of Abdullah. Back . . ." His eyes closed and his lips moved. "Our *qadi*, our judge, could reckon the years better, but it is said that Yurek learned many secrets when he sat at the feet of Dihtahn Shah."

Hammer's bleared gaze locked on Chaya's, compelling her attention. *Is it true?* He knew the tribes' speech as well as she. It was confirmation he wanted of her.

She gave it in a word. "Diettinger." Commander of the *Dol Guldur*, founder of Sauron-on-Haven.

"Sweet Jesus," the General said. "The little bastard isn't lying. I shall find a way. Or make one." His eyes kindled. "We shall smite them hip and thigh, as David smote the Philistines."

*Jesus never said that.*

There was a way. A way through the mountains and into the beating heart of the Citadel, to cut into it and still it, please God, forever.

And if they struck fast enough, not even Cyborgs could withstand them.

"Question, sir!" Barak almost snapped into a brace that would have done his blood kin in the Citadel credit.

"You've got Nazrullah's word . . . no, *khan*, I'm not tired of living and I'm not a fool. I believe you. But you're not talking foothills here. You're talking the Atlas range, the very Wall of Allah. There's no air up there, or not much. How do you know he's not telling us about a way that'll get us all killed?"

"It hasn't killed the *mujahedin*," Kemal interrupted. "They're used to it," Barak replied. "That's why we've brought the Tibetans in. Now I can probably breathe it, too. Sannie, too. No, don't give me that, Kemal. I've seen Sannie climb where strong men would black out. But that doesn't leave very many of us for heavy climbing or fighting . . ."

"Well, dog?" Kemal snapped at Strong Sven. "A man is talking to you. Look up when a *man* speaks!"

He obeyed, glowering. *Better watch that one.*

"Have you been there?"

"Not I, great lord, but my grandpa . . ."

Kemal spat on the floor.

"Brother." Nazrullah spoke up. "Have you ever heard of a thing called 'overpressure'? Our *mullahs* tell us that the warm air rising from the floor of the Shangri-La Valley meets the cold air moving down the mountains and in from the seas, breeding fast winds. Our village lies on a plateau where these winds are trapped. . . ." He was barrel-chested, vigorous, despite the exposure to nearly lethal altitudes. His eyes squinted from exposure to the light, but he had none of the skin cancers that constant life in thin air could create. What he said could be true.

"Now and only now you tell us what you have known for hundreds of years. The air is only slightly thinner than in the Valley?" Chaya spoke up. "You do not need the Valley if your women are to bear live sons? And yet, you served the Citadel. Why?"

Her eyes met Nazrullah's. They kindled into rage at the slur, then cooled. *A crafty one. Good that the others know this.* "Were you not Judge and *ghazi* and were we not all oath-kin, it would be death to say that. It is true that years ago, we served the Saurons. *Khan* Yurek guested there and was treated with honor. But it was an honor tainted with blood and fear. The accursed Saurons . . ." he spat " . . . threatened us with their weapons. But you Bandari have those weapons too."

He cast an awed glance at Sapper, who appeared to be asleep.

*So our only traitor is the one who ran from Nûrnen?* Not so, Chaya thought. There was this Temujin, whom Shulamit had in charge and who had fled the Citadel—or, more likely, been allowed to leave. He had brought word

that the blonde horsetrader with her face like a blade and
her arrogance, akin to Chaya's own, at the oath-taking was
not only from the Citadel, but a Cyborg, pregnant, God
help them all, with a child likely to be of Piet fan Reenan's
blood. And then there was the man of her own blood,
Dagor, her brother and nephew, wherever he was.

"Long ago," Nazrullah went on, "we decided that less
closeness to the Saurons meant more honor—even if they
killed us for it. So we walled up the old ways, and they did
not pursue us."

The Bandari General nodded. "I see. But you remember them, too? Thought so. Sapper?"

The engineer snapped to full awareness, shown, in this
case, by opening both eyes. He was like her, Chaya
thought. He only seemed to be sleeping. "Pick me out
three of your toughest who have done any climbing.

"Then I want all of you to meet with Nazrullah. Take
this" —Hammer-of-God gestured at Strong Sven— "prize
pup of ours with you. Better collar him, I'd say, so he
doesn't run or squeal. If I find he's been talking to anyone
not in this room, so help me. . . . Right. Find out everything you can about the rock and what the Saurons might
have used to seal it."

"Ferrocrete and . . . they might have had supplies left
from the Wasting . . ."

Hammer-of-God shuddered. He had heard the old
tales of the Holocaust. A fire brighter than a thousand
suns. . . . "What else may they have?" Hammer-of-God
asked. "Hellfire?"

"Whatever they have, they didn't use it to save Nûrnen,"
Sapper said.

Hammer grunted, slightly relieved. Indeed, if the
Saurons had ancient weapons, they would have used them
on the quarter-million enemies camped around Nûrnen.
"You'll need to build some charges. And your boys will only
have the one chance. . . ."

Nazrullah bowed to the General and the Seven.

"C'mon, Marija, boys," Sapper said. They followed

him—Ladslas, Algirdas, Kosti—as children would follow a conjuror. Ladslas and Algirdas grabbed Sven and ushered him roughly out with them.

Then, as Chaya had known it must, bloody hell erupted in the filthy study.

"You send *boys* and a woman on a mission like this?" Gasim of the Golden Tamerlanes said.

"I shall send" —Hammer-of-God leaned fists on the table— "those men and women judged best suited for the job. I shall send those whom I see fit."

Kemal opened his mouth to protest. *Quiet, fool*, Chaya breathed at him.

Shouts of how dangerous, and therefore how honorable this trip up the mountains was, boasts of personal prowess, and offers to take on the Citadel singlehandedly—Chaya wished she could shut her ears.

"And I shall refuse those whom I judge more valuable elsewhere. The Judge . . ." He shook his head. "She is our head and our heart. Aisha and Karl of the Seven shall not go; she bears a child, and we need them here."

"I would like to go." Aisha's eyes flashed.

On anyone else, Hammer-of-God's glance at Karl would have looked like a plea.

"I want you here," Karl said.

*Not good enough.*

"We need you here." Valiantly, he tried again. "Only you can reclaim your father's bones. And his honor."

*Oh, well done!*

Aisha bowed her head. "As you wish," she said.

The General went on hastily. "Kemal and Ihsan will remain. Tameetha bat Irene will remain. Marija will remain. I will not sacrifice all my best commanders."

So Barak and Sannie went. Chaya saw them join hands, their eyes glowing.

"And," the big Edenite went on, "I shall lead. Barak will be my second in command. Nazrullah will come . . . if he wishes."

Another eruption of shouts. The Afghan *khan's* eyes

glowed. "Command me, Aga Shah." Hands flicked in tribal diplomacy, which the General returned.

"Let Barak lead," Karl Haller said flatly. He gestured at Hammer-of-God's leg. "You're as drunk on glory as the *hashishayun* get on smoke. You've soldiered your whole life. . . . This is a job for young men."

"I tell you, I'll make it. And if my body doesn't, my spirit will. I *will* be there to see the Citadel fall, by the strength of God and the spirits of Ruth and Piet and all the *prkn'az.*"

"We have all taken that oath!" Gasim shouted.

"This will be a new oath," the big General said. "A special one. Who swears this oath? Any fighter who can. *This* oath, though; only the bravest, the strongest, the craftiest, and the luckiest will be privileged to swear it. It will be secret for now, but I swear by Judge Chaya's honor that the names of all who take it will last until the Cat's Eye shuts for the last time!"

Weary, Chaya shut her eyes. A lifetime ago, she had thrived on such conferences, reveled in her ability to plan and to master and manipulate the people she ruled. Now, though, Hammer seemed as fey as Piet himself, when he sought not death but undying glory by fighting a Cyborg.

He was old for a soldier. And tired. She could sense his exhaustion, twin to her own, despite her Sauron blood. Karl Haller was right; he should no more make that climb than she herself. He'd sprung this on them without letting them have a chance to shout him down, damn the man.

But she knew what he would say. She could almost hear him say that it was rotten doctrine to send a commanding officer off on a raid. But who else could goad the tribes, yet keep them from killing each other? Only the man they hated, feared, and respected above all others. He'd argue that he *wasn't* the commander of the horde, that the Seven commanded. "*I am a hammer in your hand,*" he had said once. He'd scare hell out of the Seven and his own staff by saying that, sooner or later, they'd have to learn to do without him. And he'd point out that he, of all people, would

be able to know what in the Citadel could be used and
what must be destroyed.

He'd have a host of reasons about as large as the army
that shouted his name as often as it did the names of the
Seven, and they'd all back him in his stubbornness. His
*bliddyful* stubbornness that, dammitall, made a kind of
sense.

And too, what a chance for Barak to learn his skills!

She shuddered at that thought. Then words and memories thrust the truth beyond those pretexts into her
thoughts. She tried to brush them away, but they stormed
her consciousness. She resisted. Then others, known lifelong and much loved, sought utterance and she yielded.

*"Piet fan Reenan"* —she began the traditional words,
recited at the Spring Festival— *"was the wisest man I ever
knew, and the saddest. In his last illness, he told me that the
final irony of his life was that he, a historian—for that was
how he thought of himself, not as a soldier or ruler—had
outlived history. I asked him if our story would not be preserved for the generations yet to come: surely our wars and
our wanderings, griefs and loves, the peace we made and
the people we brought to being, all this would live? Yes, he
said; but not as history, because history was the product of
civilization. When the Saurons came, Haven stepped out of
history, into the time of legends. It was as myths, archetypes, legends that we would be remembered, not as
human beings. Our children and children's children would
live once more through the endless turnings of the great
cycle of myths."*

Once again, it would have been tempting to drift. Chaya
almost thought she could see Piet's *anima* wavering before
her. It took on more substance as she looked. The eyes lit,
and behind her she could see others. Ruth, before she
aged so rapidly and died. Ilona, with that scar on her face.
They were smiling at her. *Not unworthy then?* she asked
them. *Even with my Sauron blood?*

*You are my true daughter*, Ruth's *anima* told her. *I am
proud of you.*

*Advise me*, Chaya pleaded. *I am old and sick, and they think I am mad. I wander in the dark. Tell me what to do.*

She heard Piet's laugh in the no-time in which her consciousness floated, felt his lips on her forehead.

*Think of a myth, Chaya.*

The shadowy figured disappeared. She let her head loll forward.

"*Amah?* Drink this." The rim of a cup pressed against her lips. "Quiet, all of you!" (Never mind that Karl Haller shouted for quiet right by her ear.)

She lapped at the liquid in the cup. Pure water. Abruptly, she began to laugh then, just as quickly, ceased as she saw the near-panic in the *mediko's* eyes.

"She has thought of something, haven't you, Chaya?" Aisha knelt beside her and took her into her arms. Bless the girl, how warm she was.

"That I have," Chaya looked down into Aisha's face. God was merciful to fulfill her wishes here at . . . *think of a myth, Chaya*, Piet's voice interrupted her.

"Gideon," she whispered. "Gideon and the three hundred." Some of Aisha's brightness faded. Did the girl really think Chaya had wondered so far that she wouldn't recognize the people around her? Fear flicked Chaya briefly, and a memory of the horsetrainer Sigrid's pale face. *A Sauron of the Citadel, are you, girl? I'd like to know what's in that brain of yours. And what I face.*

"Gideon, *amah?* It's . . ."

Chaya chuckled. "An old story from our Books, Aisha." *Tell us a story?* Would that comfort them? She wondered. *Go to the rock for comfort; there is none in me.* Still, if it would serve . . .

"Uh, Judge? General Jackson?" Tameetha bat Irene stuck her head into the study. "Begging your pardon, I'm sure, but we've got something."

When no one snapped her head off, she entered the room. Odd, Chaya thought, after the looting of Nûrnen to see her so . . . uncomfortable. Obviously, this goes beyond the war, or she'd be turning to her officer.

"What is it, Tameetha?" Chaya asked.

"It's like this, Your Honor. We've found the body. Juchi's. Along with a sign saying that the peasant Yegor and a failed Battlemaster are up there with him. They're all in pieces."

Aisha lunged to her feet. "My father . . . did you touch him?"

"Steady there, Aisha." Karl Haller had her shoulders in his hands.

Tameetha met Aisha's eyes without flinching. "We took the sign down. It didn't seem right, keeping it up. I've got a couple troops standing guard there right now. But I thought I'd come to you first."

Aisha whirled toward her husband, who raised a hand to touch her forehead as if testing for fever. "We promised you, didn't we, Aisha?"

"I have to take him down," she said. Her breathing was fast for a human, let alone a Sauron. "I have to. I swore to give him back his honor."

She raised her hand, on which the ruby ring with which she had been married blazed. All the light in the room seemed to center on her.

Chaya saw Karl Haller grimace. Aisha was pregnant—a late pregnancy, much of it under harsh conditions. He'd have had hard things to say about any woman's exposing herself to whatever contagion there might be in those corpses—let alone his wife. *What about a battlefield?* Chaya thought. He'd already lost this one.

"Let me go, husband," Aisha pleaded. "For the sake of my honor, which is now yours. And the honor of our son."

"If it *is* a son," Karl said, and grinned at the way Aisha and the *khans* stared, shocked that he might not automatically prefer one.

"You shall go, Aisha," he told her. "Your father shall have his honor redeemed, and you yours. But you will be guided by what I say."

Aisha stood before the stakes holding the pieces of her father's body, flanked by the Battlemaster she had killed and the peasant who died because he had encountered her thereafter. She remembered how her father had screamed when Glorund broke his arm, then his neck. She remembered how her broken ribs had felt like coals, searing against her lungs and the furious irritation she'd felt at the peasant—Yegor, his name was—for all his crisscrossing.

Just look what it had gotten him.

Just look what it had gotten her.

Her hands went to her belly.

"Father?" she murmured. "Do you see? Do you? Your son . . . he lives. . . ." though Allah only knew where Dagor wandered when he had spurned the prosperous, peaceful life that Judge Chaya had implored him to take up. "And soon . . ." Her voice faltered like that of a very young, bewildered girl. " . . . do you see? This is my husband, a wise man. A good man. Your son consented. And soon, you will have a grandson."

Tears ran down her cheeks. She should have been shrieking. Any woman in the tribe would have, she knew.

*Badri would not.* There were some griefs that went beyond the proper wails of mourning.

She knew, too, that onlookers would expect her to speak, to say something to inflame their spirits. For, of the Seven, she was the Voice that had stirred the tribes to war.

There was an emptiness in her that had nothing to do with her belly or the fulfillment of her vow. Against all hope, she had accomplished what she had set out to do.

*Now what?*

"Aisha?" Karl's voice in her ear, calling her back to the life she had made since her father's death—and to the future she had won.

"I was thinking," she said. "Even a blind grandfather might have adjusted a grandson's hand upon his first sword. I have so much now. And he? Nothing at all. Not even a grave."

"He'll have that now. And the honor he lost . . ."

" . . . That was taken from him."

She started forward to remove the dismembered body from the stakes that held it.

"Aisha," her husband said, "you gave me your word. I owe Juchi a son's duty. Let me honor him in this."

She started to glare at him. He had tricked her, somehow, tricked her into yielding what she had sworn she would never yield, her right to bury her father with her own hands. *You raised an army that took this city. Is that not enough for you that you must risk your health and that of our child?*

A wife was supposed to obey her husband in all things. He had asked her compliance in very little. Here, before the soldiers and the *khans*, he reminded her of her word. He tricked her into consent. She had a mind . . .

And then, he smiled at her. "I'm your *mediko*, too, Aisha. Your father would want you to look to the health of your child."

"His grandson!"

"Whatever you say—so long as you will listen to me in this."

She glanced over at Chaya, sister and aunt. "I will help him take my brother's body down," the Judge promised. "The tie of blood shall be kept. And I tell you, as Judge, that you have done all you vowed, and more. Such a deed that your name and his will always be remembered."

Chaya's voice went strange again. She'd done that too often lately.

Aisha felt the baby stir in her womb. "As you wish," she said. *Not much longer, little warrior.* She knelt and spread out a carpet, intricately knotted of faded silk, on which to deposit Juchi's body before it was buried.

"What about the other two?" Tameetha asked. She sniffed, oddly fastidious for a woman whose trade was arms. "We'll bury this poor sod of a farmer. But you want that Cyborg taken down too?"

*Let him go on rotting,* Aisha started to say. Then she paused. Even before the blood that had run from Juchi's mouth had dried, she'd known her duty. *Bury him.* And, though it had galled her, she and the peasant Yegor had buried him and the Battlemaster in one grave. Ill and half-mad as she was, she had known what was right.

She still did.

"Bury the farmer," she said. "It were a kindness to give him more respect than he had in life. But the Sauron? Do we even know how they treat their dead? If I may, sister?"

"Go ahead," Chaya said.

"If this were a matter of a feud between tribes, we might return the body. . . ."

Tameetha snorted.

"But with Saurons . . . put him in a coffin and bury him at my father's feet. Like his dog. Then mark the place. The time may come when the Saurons wish to know. And if not, it's good for the army to know what I learned here. Even Cyborgs can die. I have killed one. . . ."

The acrid tang of some alcohol with herbs in it masked the charnel stink of the bodies. They were swiftly removed and hidden from sight. And smell. Battlemaster and peasant were hustled off to their graves.

And Aisha followed her father's corpse to the funeral she had stirred all Haven to win for him.

• **CHAPTER THIRTEEN**

*Think of a myth, Chaya.*

*I have,* she told the voice in her head. *Juchi, for one, and how Aisha fought to have him buried, for another.*

Now it was time to return to Gideon.

Gideon, Chaya thought several meetings later, would have recognized the situation. Must have been quite a fight when you announced you needed fighters—but only three hundred? And how did you pick them when you had a Citadel to attack, a town to sack, and a half million tribesmen to keep from killing themselves while they killed Saurons?

*Which was worst, Piet old boy? The planning, the battle, or the aftermath?*

She didn't quite dare to cast her mind free again, for fear that the old, old warleader might answer her.

"What is your Book to us?" shouted Suleiman Tepe. He had more balls than brains, that was for sure, seeing that not long ago, Hammer-of-God had executed his *khan* and held a pistol to his own head.

"It is not just the Book of the Ivrit or of the men of Eden," Nazrullah cut in. *Smart man, that. Literate.* "The hills are full of such stories, chief among them the tale of Iskendar *Khan.* Long ago, bandits told him that to take their fortress, he must grow wings. So he chose out three hundred men, bound them with the oath of death commandos, and sent them up the cliffs to victory and undying fame."

*An invitation to high-altitude suicide,* Chaya thought. Irresistible. How did you select three hundred out of the tens of thousands of honor-mad lunatics who would clamor to be allowed to swear away their lives? *Must be getting old to be this cynical*, she told herself. *What have I done what have I done what have I done* keened in her consciousness like a widow of the tribes, veil pulled over her eyes.

*What I must*, she snapped, setting the phantoms adrift. She had a problem to solve—selecting death commandos. And, as each *khan* or clan leader shouted out his claims, she paid them the tribute of her full attention.

"One at a time!" Hammer was roaring, pounding on the table for quiet in which separate claims could be heard.

*How did you choose?* Even if the camp didn't teem with spies, if you announced a mission of great peril, chances were you'd have not three hundred but thirty *thousand* honor-mad tribesmen clamoring to volunteer. With their guns and their knives and, Yeweh help us, all their noise. And Gideon's option of selecting only the men who drank a certain way—there wasn't a body of water near Nûrnen that was big enough or clean enough to allow that many warriors to drink from at once.

"It is not only honor," Hammer was saying in Turkic as fine as Chaya had ever heard, "but undying glory. For those of us who scale the Wall of Allah to drop upon the Godless Saurons as they sleep shall be not as *hashishayun*, for they are mortal. I have slain them. We shall be *fedaykin*, death commandos."

The shout that went up was one of pure excitement. *Want to run for office, General? You have a great future ahead of you, Piet help you, as a politician.* The Edenite's voice turned reassuring, the way he might encourage a recruit before his first battle.

"We swore as brothers, and well I know my brothers have the hearts of cliff lions to drop upon the Godless and harry them. You will all find peril enough, honor enough, reward enough. But as you would not use an axe to carve bone, I must choose those of you best suited for *this* fight."

They would learn, yes. Those whose hearts did not

burst with effort, or whose bodies did not freeze or limbs blacken, or who did not reel and fall from high peaks. There was no time to learn. They needed mountaineers or those familiar with the hills. Nazrullah's people. The few Tibetans who had ventured from their peaks and were willing to risk allying not just one life but all their lives with the horde. Those tribes and clans—Gasim's and Shamyl's and Suleiman Tepe's among them—who ventured into the hills at need. A few of the Bandari shepherds who had chased flocks up past Haven's wretched excuse for a treeline.

Still, too many. And too little time. From time to time, messengers called Hammer-of-God or Karl or even Aisha away to other tasks. At such times, Barak took over, as if Hammer groomed him as a replacement. *What does he know that I don't?* Chaya thought. *Perhaps he really means not to come back.* They could not afford to lose him. They could not afford to lose *any* of the leaders. And she dared not allow fear, for it was fear she felt, to interfere with her judgment.

If she were a Cyborg, she could put it out of mind. She was not. She tried.

Cut the group further. Age, health, wounds . . . how far could you go? There were always special claims; every *khan* had a special claim.

"I am not too old to go," Gasim declared, breaking into an explanation of mountain sickness. "And I tell you, go I shall!"

"It is said," Nazrullah said, "that you have need to go. That so your tribe might live—and I honor you for the sacrifice—your own daughter went with the tribute maidens to the Citadel."

Gasim's face went white, then flushed with the sort of anger that washes away pain. *That will teach you to interrupt,* Chaya thought. Let them rant. She would watch. The Seven would handle it.

"I have no daughter!" Gasim spat.

"No?" Nazrullah raised an eyebrow. "There is still, there

is always the tie of blood. Your daughter is your daughter, even if you must kill her for unchastity."

"And what do you know of it, you who *bought* your women's freedom from . . ."

"Were it my child in the Citadel, I would seek to reclaim her from what she was sent into, as—so it is written—the lady Bortei was regained by Temujin from his enemies— him they called Chingiz *Khan*, Emperor of All Men. And I should bring her sons to my hearth and welcome them. For they would be blood of my blood."

"They would be *Saurons!*"

"Mingling the blood is not always bad," Karl Haller put in. "I beg the *khans* not to quarrel. As the General says, there is honor enough for all—and I speak as a man who is not to go."

Another wrangle for the next day's meeting, *after* the palisades were inspected outside and a myriad of other tasks: why were some women allowed to be considered when so many warriors vied for the post? Chaya sighed. Sannie, secure of her place as a member of the Seven, kept silent. The shouts and the boasts went on. Far too long.

Time was not their friend, Chaya told herself for what she vowed was for the last time. To her mind, too many people knew now of the meetings that had nothing to do with camp or horde or fortifications. And others, who knew less, were skilled at drawing conclusions—like that Sigrid. She raised her head.

"Draw lots," she said. "Let Yeweh—or Allah—decide." That was far too close to *kill 'em all and let God sort it out*, but it would do. With as much dispatch as there had been shouting before, smooth stones were gathered. Some were marked— less than three hundred, if the truth be known, since some places were already filled. Hammer-of-God as leader. Barak as aide and, God Yeweh forbid, second in command. Sannie. Lobsang and his people. Nazrullah and a son of his. Shamyl's eldest son. Gasim. Suleiman Tepe. Ladislas and Algirdas. Sapper. Be-Courteous and Smite-Sin Jackson, cousins of Hammer and even more dour, if that was possible.

And then, told only that their leaders required it, the fighters considered most fit to storm the Citadel's unguarded back each drew from the box in Chaya's keeping.

And they had their list. It was not the band that any one of them might have chosen, Chaya thought, scanning the blotched and crossed-out scroll. The lots had turned up some damned strange candidates. *Even among our own.* A couple merchants turned fighter. A *mediko* or two—along more for their climbing and weapons skills than for any chance they'd have to save life.

The further Sharku ran, the closer to the Citadel he got, the more nomads he and his comrades eliminated, the more he worried about the future of the Race on Haven. The Bandari had put everything they had into this assault on the Citadel. If it fell . . . if by some dreadful mischance it fell, how would his people be able to rebuild their lives? All the technical knowledge on Haven was concentrated there. If it were destroyed, no one knew enough to reconstruct it.

They would never go back to the stars. This world would be prison and grave to the Race forever.

The realization chilled Sharku. *How could so much go so wrong so fast?*

"Not so far, now, Deathmaster." Mumak's voice held little of the concern that he must have felt.

"Not far at all," Vizgor echoed. "Then we'll show them, Regiment Leader."

"I think we will," Mumak answered. He looked significantly at Sharku. "He will, anyway."

"Nice to know you've got confidence in me," Sharku said.

"Oh, we have that," Mumak said. He raised his voice. "Don't we, lads? Let's hear a cheer."

"Sharku!" Vizgor shouted.

"Sharku!" the staff ranks answered. "Deathmaster!"

The road stretched out ahead. "Increase the pace,"

Sharku said. "If you've got the breath to shout, we're not marching fast enough."

They were still cheering as they broke into a loping trot.

Another day to pack, to gather the charges, to assemble the food, the ropes, and the sturdy hooks and spikes for hands and feet that Nazrullah scorned as luxury, but that they might need; and the three hundred assembled before those of the Seven who remained behind.

They gathered in the largest room of the mayor's house, which happened to be a basement. A fire and the press of bodies took the chill off. Closely guarded and wearing a heavy collar, Strong Sven was held nearby until needed: until then, it was thought, his presence would only pollute the assembled *fedaykin.*

"Brothers." Hammer-of-God's voice all but purred in the silence. "And sisters, in no less honor. When we swore to the jihad, we made oath in word and blood before the Judge and the entire host. Today, we swear the oath of *fedaykin* in secret, known only to the God of Battles and to those who rule us. I would ask each of you to swear today, in the silence of your own hearts and souls, not to flinch, not to falter or to betray your brothers by action or inaction, but to go forward until you take the Citadel or death takes you. I further swear that *none* of us shall return until the Citadel falls.

"Do you so swear?"

There was a murmur of assent. Then, the General walked over to Chaya. Trying not to favor his weak leg, he knelt and looked up at her. *The irony had gone from his face,* she realized. As much as the men he had spent a lifetime fighting, he believed in this. *For what you believe it may do,* she thought, laid hands on his head, and seemed to bless him.

He rose and looked at his *fedaykin*, his face oddly happy. "*Khans* and princes and simple warriors you have all been. Today, you claim a title more rare and more glorious. And I tell you, I could not ask for a finer group to live and die among."

He drew his sword and the firelight shone on the blade.
"God with us!"

Then, detaching the scabbard from his belt, he snapped
it and threw it into the fire. The others followed suit. And
the flames, fed by some trick of the engineers, blazed up to
consume them.

"Let's go," he said simply. They broke ranks, to disperse
and meet at the appointed place among the tumbled rocks
of the foothills near a disused entrance to the mines. Barak
strode from the room without a backward glance. Someone handed him Strong Sven's leash.

And then they were gone.

# • CHAPTER FOURTEEN

In small groups, the *fedaykin* were passed by the block-aders in each tower. Watched by armed guards, they crossed the ditches that circled Nûrnen, then approached the old mine entrance to the northwest, where the Atlas Mountains reared up to defend the Citadel. Engineers had pried away the boulders; with any supports that remained from the long-ago days of the entrance's use carried away, it looked no different from any other cave.

Hammer-of-God stood at the entrance, Barak with him, counting and checking names and faces against their lists and memories. "One traitor in our midst is more than enough," the General remarked.

"That's it, sir. All present. Ready when you say."

The Edenite looked out over the Valley. The wind cooled eyes tired by too many nights without sleep. Tainted by smoke and dung and blood it might be; as he prepared to enter the mine, it seemed better than brandy.

By the light of Nûrnen aflame and the twinkling of thousands of campfires, he could see the defenses he had caused to be built. A good plan. Circumvallate. Attack from secure positions. Send the tribes into the Shangri-La Valley, and isolate the Citadel. It might even have worked, given time. But time was every bit as much their enemy as their friend. If they could strike directly at the Citadel . . . he grinned mirthlessly and wondered if he would ever see the stars again, or the sky.

"It is not all darkness," the *khan* Nazrullah said.

Something Hammer-of-God had read during the godawful six months he had spent on his back recovering from the *last* time slipped into his thoughts. *Above all shadows rides the Sun, and Stars for ever dwell. I will not say the day is done nor bid the Stars farewell.*

He shrugged and entered the mine. "Move, dog," someone hissed. There was the sound of a kick, then Barak's voice.

"What if you break his ribs? We need him fit to climb for now."

They took the first leg of the climb in darkness, Nazrullah herding Strong Sven forward, Barak at their side, the strongest climbers spaced out along the line of march.

When they had gone so far into the side of the mountain that not even the hindmost could see the sky, they found shielded lanterns cached. They cast as much shadow as light over smoke-streaked stone tunnels, hacked out of the rock, then hardened by exposure to fire; but they were better than stumbling in the darkness, doubled over in some of the passageways, but always heading upward. Toward the mountains, the secret ways, and the Citadel.

From time to time, the rock shuddered slightly. At one point, they had to wait as four men cleared rocks from their path.

"Water somewhere," Barak whispered. The shaft caught his words and amplified them.

"Watch for ice, then," Nazrullah said. "Is there ice, dog?" Strong Sven gabbled assent. They proceeded more slowly. After awhile, the rock changed from the friable, variegated tufa of the foothills into a tougher stone. Now they had entered the Wall of Allah. Despite their exertions, they were cold. The unevenly cut tunnel pressed in upon them. Breathing grew more difficult as the path rose upward more and more steeply.

"Not long." Nazrullah barely sounded out of breath. Some of the others were panting audibly.

They must make what time they could now, Hammer-of-God knew. When they reached the uppermost stages of the climb, they would have to rest about a quarter of the time, assuming that they could. And they would have to assume that, any instant, they could be attacked by men stronger, faster, and better able to see, hear, and even breathe here in the heights.

Damn. If he were shorter, his leg wouldn't hurt as much. He bared his teeth at the pain and realized that, once again, he was grinning.

The men nearest him pressed against the wall and let him pass. His leg didn't hurt as much.

He edged up to the head of the line and signaled for a halt. Taking out his knife, he showed it to Strong Sven. "Don't think to lose us in these mines," he warned. "You have no food, no light, no blankets. You would wander in the dark and cold until you died. When do we reach your secret way?"

Where . . . where . . . Strong Sven sounded willing, if sullen. There was a cache, a corridor intersected by several others. Some of it may have fallen away by now. From there, if you had the right guide, it was possible to reach. . . . But it was far away, very high. . . .

"We'll see," Hammer muttered. He had no stomach for torture, but he'd let not-so-strong Sven think he did.

And they climbed. They had a very bad moment when someone gasped for breath and sank to his knees. But it was panic and breathlessness, not gas buildup in the tunnel. Briefly, they stopped to eat, to rest, then kept on, always upward.

Finally, air blew in upon them from above. Cold air. Night air. Air from outside.

"Kill the lights!" came a hiss, and the lanterns were shuttered.

After awhile, the tunnel widened. Part of the rock wall had fallen open to reveal the sky. They saw starlight up ahead. *Above all shadows rides the Sun and Stars for ever dwell.* . . . Sweet suffering God, the light was beautiful. The cache—empty, more's the shame—of which Strong Sven had spoken lay open, but the passageways stretched out before them.

The traitor pointed. "That one."

Having no choice, they followed him. When they could no longer see the sky or smell night air, they dropped.

"Good rock, good walls. We built this part of the tunnel," one of the *mujahedin* told the man next to him. He didn't know that Hammer-of-God was nearby, so he was probably telling the truth. Thank God for small mercies.

Watchers, chosen in advance, rubbed their hands together as noiselessly as possible while the others wrapped up and slept. Or tried to. It was very cold. The thin air brought them strange dreams.

"Too good to last," Sharku said to Mumak after the Soldiers' regiments wrecked yet another clan group of nomads.

They paused; this was as good a spot to consolidate the spread-out travel formation as any, if they were to make maximum speed from here to the Citadel. There was a good road now, and engagements with the nomads were getting frequent enough to slow the separate columns down.

"Ah, well, what isn't, Deathmaster?" Mumak answered philosophically. "Sooner or later, the news of our coming had to get ahead of us. Even though we travel faster, this close to the Citadel, the plainsmen are jammed so tight, one clan against the next, that we bloody well can't smash one set of 'em without the nearest other bunch gawping while we do it."

"Now all of the bastards know we're here. Nothing's going to be easy any more."

"Nothing's going to be *as* easy," Mumak corrected. "We haven't had much in the way of trouble yet, and I don't expect we will, not until we get back to whatever lines the Bandari whoresons have thrown up around the Citadel. You'll deal with those, too, once we get there."

*They all think that. Well, it's what I wanted.* They came up to a river, one of the many that flowed into the Jordan, the big stream that drained most of eastern Shangri-La

Valley. The stone-paved Citadel-built road ended in the concrete stumps of a bridge. Most of the timber structure lay in the stream, with white water foaming around it.

"Nomads didn't do that," he said grimly. The piers had been cut through neatly by explosive charges shrewdly laid—and then the wreckage blown up again, to destroy any surviving long timbers. Good building timber was rare this close to the Citadel.

"No, they didn't," the scout who directed them upstream to the ford said. "Shod horses—haBandari. In, blew it, got out again, two cycles ago."

Sharku and Mumak nodded. *They're building up an account*, Sharku thought. Aloud, he asked: "What's this one, the Rapidan?"

"No, the Rappahannock," the Soldier answered. "The Rapidan is next, then the Trebia, then the Scamander, and after that—"

"—the Marne," Sharku finished for him. "I remember." He'd spent a lot less of his career in the long-pacified Valley than most Soldiers. He was an Intelligence officer by training, specializing in the plains nomads. "Once we cross the Marne, we ought to be in sight of Nûrnen."

More herds—lowing cattle, sheep that cropped the grass down to the ground, broad-backed muskylopes longer on horns than brains, furry stinking two-humped camels—chewed their way through the farmland between the Rappahannock and the Rapidan. Seeing that country stripped raw made Sharku want to slaughter every plainsman he could find, but no time now. Push through, kill whoever got in the way, bail out the Citadel . . . everything else faded to insignificance.

Past the Rapidan, the going got easier. Suspecting a Bandari trap, Sharku was suspicious of anything easier than it should have been. He soon satisfied himself, though, that his suspicions were groundless this time. The going was easier because the nomads, once warned that the Soldiers were coming, fled as if before the wrath of Allah. They'd swarmed into the Shangri-La Valley for pasturelands and loot, not to stand up against a Deathmaster and the largest single force the Citadel had mustered in several lifetimes. The ones who wanted to fight were back in Nûrnen and the siege-works around the Citadel.

The land between the Trebia and the Scamanader proved even more empty than that between the Rapidan and the Trebia. Burned-out farm buildings and ravaged fields showed the nomads had been through, but there was worse damage. Once they had to detour around a huge mudslide that had taken out the road when a major dam burst open. Towns smoldered, wrecked to the foundations, and the local populations were gone—pyramids of heads or corpses charred in their homes, or marched back toward Nûrnen.

A belt of forest—Terran firs, mostly, their short, flat needles so dark a green as almost to be black—stretched east of the Scamander. Sharku ordered a halt for rest and reconnaissance; anything might have lurked in that gloomy, forbidding wood.

"See?" Sharku said. "This is what we buy for clearing out that rats' nest of New Soviet Men in the trees at the other end of the Valley."

"You're right," Mumak said seriously. "If they'd killed us outright instead, we definitely wouldn't have to be doing this now."

"An odd view. Kerak. Pick some escorts," Sharku said. "And let's see what's out there."

"Let me go, Deathmaster. You stay here," Mumak said.

"Another time." Soldier rank was functional—if you weren't needed to oversee, and had a skill, the skill got used. Besides, as the Sauron Role Model named Rommel had pointed out, a commander had to *see* the situation to give accurate orders. Particularly now that electronic gear was so scarce. *And it won't hurt to have the men see I'm still one of them.* "I need to look over the route. You're in command. Assault Leader Kerak, lead off."

The recon patrol swam the Scamander naked but for camouflage body paint and belts with knives, in the chill darkness of truenight. They were there to scout out safe routes through the forest, not to advertise their presence with gunfire. And besides, what deadlier weapon was there for close-in fighting than a Soldier's body?

The patrol split up into two-man teams once on the eastern bank of the river. "Open country again about five klicks east," Sharku reminded Kerak. "We shouldn't have a lot of trouble finding our routes. Nomads aren't likely to go poking their noses into a forest."

"No, but the Bandari might." Kerak's hand dropped toward the hilt of his fighting knife. "Deathmaster, I hope they have. Your new tactics save lives, but I owe these a debt I want to pay in person, not just at rifle range."

"A good way to get killed."

Two kilometers into the woods, they came up to the edge of a good-sized clearing. Till then, everything had been quiet. Sharku said, "We can be more thorough if we split up. You go right and I'll slide around to the left. We'll meet on the far side, fifty meters behind that stump there."

"Right you are." Kerak's green-brown-painted body vanished among the mossy tree trunks. Because he could see farther into the infrared, Sharku's eyes followed him further than an ordinary man's would have, but soon he disappeared even from the Regiment Leader's view.

Sharku semicircled the clearing, found the stump on the far side. He was a little surprised Kerak wasn't waiting for him fifty meters in; he'd given his scout leader a good start. When Kerak didn't show up after five more minutes, Sharku was more than surprised. The prickle at the back of his neck whispered something was wrong.

He started back around the clearing in the direction Kerak would have taken. He'd been relaxed before, not expecting anything but trees and woods creatures. Now he moved with every bit of woodcraft and combat caution he could muster. If something had happened to Kerak, it could happen to him, too.

He drifted forward again, one slow, cautious step at a

time. His eyes found—nothing. His eyes . . . there, amid some ferns, lay a body. Had he not been able to use infrared, he might not have noticed it, for it was daubed and streaked in green and brown like his own.

"Kerak." Again his lips moved silently. His scout leader's head lay twisted at an unnatural angle. Whoever had ambushed him had broken his neck, as Snaga had broken the neck of the girl he was raping when it was time to move on.

But who—or what—could treat a Soldier so?

Something stirred in Sharku, something so old and strange he needed several heartbeats to find a name for it: fear. It wasn't the fear of death or mutilation on the battlefield; he'd met that demon many times, and had its measure. This fear bubbled up from a place deeper than genetic engineering could touch.

So, a man, then. In spite of his alarm, Sharku kept enough Soldier arrogance to be confident he could beat any man of the cattle who didn't have a gun. He stood up, took two steps into the clearing. "One of us is going to kill the other," he said, first in Americ, then in Turkic. "Shall we make a proper duel of it? I am Sharku, Deathmaster of the Citadel. Whom do I face?"

Silence on the far side for a long moment. Then the bushes over there stirred. Out came a warrior in dull brown tunic and trousers, with a cuirass of overlapping leather plates. Sharku needed a couple of seconds to notice the shape of breasts and the wide hips under the clothing. The woman bowed to him. "Tameetha bat Irene fan Tellerman, *aluf* of the Bandari," she answered, in a guttural dialect of Americ. "I'll nail you too, *mamzer*, if I can."

He knew he was staring. Some surprises, like some fears, ran too deep for the control genetic engineering brought. "*You* killed Kerak?" he blurted.

Her hawk face split in a mocking grin. "Bet your ass I did, *soldat*. Found myself a tree trunk to hide behind, waited till he came by—fool was humming to himself, told me right where he was at—broke his fucking neck. He never knew what hit him. With a little bit o' luck, I'd've scragged you too." Her features clouded. "Even Piet only got the first one, though."

To most Soldiers, the remark would have meant nothing. But Sharku's specialty was Intelligence. He'd become familiar with the Bandari legends. Their folk hero, Piet van Reenan, was supposed to have slain a Soldier (some version he'd heard said a Soldier *and* a Cyborg) in single combat before he died himself of some massive bodily overload.

It was, Sharku admitted to himself, just possible. Van Reenan had been of the Frystaat blood that kept cropping up among the Bandari to this day. The Soldier took another look at Tameetha. Wide shoulders, especially for a woman, scanty subcutaneous fat that left the muscles he could see defined like a man's—she carried a goodly number of those genes herself. She might have broken Kerak's neck. She might break his, too.

"By your Three Faiths, Bandari," he began, and saw her eyes widen ever so slightly at his knowing and using that oath, "you've really gone and buggered this whole stinking world, do you know that?"

"Fuck you and your muskylope turd of a mother, Sauron," she said. "You've no bliddy business talking about buggering Haven, not after what your kind did to it when they got here."

"It was here for the taking. We took it," he said. It was strange, talking to a cattle female—no, a female barbarian warrior—but he might learn what else they faced before they reached the Citadel. And Bandari liked to talk. And talk. . . . "The only difference between what we did to Haven and what you Bandari did to carve out your stinking Pale is one of scale. We were stronger, so we took more. Methods? After what you've done here, you'd better think twice before you squeal about the moral advantage."

She glared. He'd hit a nerve. "We didn't use Hellfire."

"But we did. And how many of your friends died on the way here? None of your own, but how many plainsfolk?"

"*Hotnots*," the Bandari woman said dismissively. The

word and the way she said it raised echoes in Sharku's mind: he would have said *cattle* in that exact tone.

"Besides, when has a Sauron ever given a flying fuck about what happens to the nomads? They—"

In the middle of the sentence, without change of expression or voice, she plucked a knife from her belt and threw it at him. She launched herself behind it, another blade in hand.

Sharku was fast enough to knock aside the thrown knife, but he couldn't do that and pull out his own before Tameetha was on him. She struck upward, to rip his belly and seek his heart. He grabbed her wrist, arrested the point bare centimeters from his skin. She was, he realized with something approaching horror, almost as strong as he. Her left hand grabbed for the knife he hadn't been able to draw.

He chopped her hand aside. Real hand-to-hand combat, as he'd discovered before, was a much less orderly, much less precise business than the practices on neat padded mats back at the Citadel. Close-quarter fighting between Soldiers and cattle rarely lasted long enough to give much of a corrective. *Have to do something about that*, whispered the one percent of his mind not actively engaged in fighting.

Tameetha butted, trying to break his nose with her forehead. He ducked; the blow landed on his own frontal bone, and shook them both about equally. His thumb found the nerve plexus inside her knife wrist. He squeezed with everything he had. That should have crushed a bone, but Frystaat genes built bones to stronger patterns than was usual on Haven.

Even if it didn't do just what he wanted, he got enough from that squeeze: it forced the tendons of her hand to open so the knife fell out. *One less variable*, he thought. He was beginning to have her measure. She was well trained and—yes!—far stronger than he'd ever imagined a woman of the cattle could be, but she wasn't very fast, at least not by his standards. And she was not used to fighting anyone near her own strength, which he was.

The fight didn't last long after he realized that. He won a groan from her when he wrenched her arm back at an impossible angle. Then he landed a solid kick in the pit of her stomach, the tough lames of her armor buckling under the force. She folded up and crashed heavily to the grass. Without wind, with internal injuries that must be bleeding, she still tried to rise. He kicked her in the neck. She went down again, strangling with a crushed larynx.

He stared, aghast; he'd intended to break her neck like a stick, give her what she'd given Kerak. *Maybe this is better*, he thought, *she'll suffer more.*

He shook his head. He wasn't Snaga: he killed because he had to, not for the sport of it. Warily, lest she hurt him even as she died, he approached with drawn dagger.

The wariness saved his life. The rutch of a bowstring and the *hunnn* of exhaled breath as the archer loosed had him crouching and diving backwards, rolling away as the arrow went *thock* into a tree. Another followed before the sound had died.

Sharku cursed as he flitted noiselessly around the clearing. The Bandari were probably doing the same thing he and Kerak were—scouting ahead of a larger force. They hadn't brought firearms for the same reason his assault rifle was back in camp, to avoid noise at all costs. Bows did not make much noise, however.

Two more figures in mottled leathers darted across the clearing to where Tameetha lay; they held bows in their hands with knocked arrows. The bows had pulley-wheels at the tips. Sharku's reports estimated their range at up to three hundred meters. One Bandari knelt beside Tameetha's thrashing form as the other stood guard.

"Vanished Homeworld," Sharku muttered. No wonder the Bandari ranked next in might on Haven to the Soldiers if they made even women into warriors like that one. And, of course, they had the enormous advantage of being able to point to the Soldiers as the greater danger, so their own machinations and crimes went unnoticed till too late.

Physically, Sharku wasn't damaged past scrapes and bruises that would quickly heal. He moved slowly, taking his time to go east through the woods again, past the spot where lingering IR warmth and scent indicated the archers had waited.

Keeping at maximum alert as adrenaline drained away took all the control he had over glands and nerves. It paid off, though: not far from the edge of the woods he scented horses, then heard a quiet stamp as one shifted weight. Four of them; and a man, in dark leathers like the ones Tameetha and the bowmen had worn. This fellow was less wary than she had been.

The Bandari was still trying to soothe his horses when Sharku hit him in the side of the head with what was just short of a killing stroke. He sighed and crumpled, and the horses broke free and galloped away into the open field to the east. Sharku slung him over his shoulder like a sack of barley and started back to the Scamander on a wide arc around the clearing where he and Tameetha had fought. If fate was kind, having a Bandari prisoner might begin to make up for losing Kerak. Even with field techniques, the Soldiers could tear what they needed to know from his carcass.

By the time Sharku reached the river, the prisoner was starting to squirm. Swimming with an uncooperative captive would be more trouble than it was worth. Sharku hit him again, not quite so hard this time.

The trip back across the Scamander showed how worn he was. He wondered if the river was trying to rise up and drown him, but the real foe was his own exhaustion. That made him wonder, too, how many of the Soldiers were close to their breaking points.

*We can't break,* he thought as he wearily splashed up onto the western bank of the Scamander. *We still have too much work ahead of us.*

Everything had gone wrong—the Citadel bypassed, the Gatling nests that should have warded the pass blasted by the cursed mortar the Bandari had fetched, Nûrnen burning, works going up to keep the Regiments now in the west end of the Valley from rescuing the town or the Citadel . . . all in all, it was enough to drive a man mad, especially when that man was the one who had ordered the Regiments away from the Citadel in the first place.

Carcharoth's smile stretched slowly across his face. Nothing could drive him mad, not now. He was mad already.

Part of his mind knew it and still struggled against it. The rest, though, the rest had tipped onto that slippery slope the moment he realized the TAC, in which he'd placed his trust, proved fallible after all. Let a Cyborg's most basic assumptions be overthrown and everything they supported would eventually crash down with them.

The outer shell of the Battlemaster's persona still held, though even it had cracks—he'd seen white all around the edges of Dagor's eyes, as if they were those of a spooked horse. Still, the wild Soldier clung close to him; he'd done a good job of establishing a master/disciple relationship before his own degeneration had made further advance along that front difficult. Now, even while Carcharoth paced the battlements of the Citadel's outer walls, in his own mind he moved more through the misty world of legend than the mundanity of the siege. As reality faded within him, the archetypes of the mythos the Soldiers— the Saurons—had fostered reached upwards into his consciousness. The flame thrower he often carried seemed more and more a part of him. It was right that he should have the power to enforce his will with a whip of fire.

His eyes went to the mountains on whose skirts the Citadel sat. He laughed. A sentry—a youth who might make a Soldier if he lived—gaped at the spectacle of a Cyborg snickering. Carcharoth turned on him. "What would you have me do, boy? Bury myself with vain labor at the Threat Analysis Computer like that fool of a Breedmaster?"

"N-no, sir," the boy stuttered.

Carcharoth laughed again. You'd have to be a madman to think anyone would climb those peaks and take the Citadel from behind. Who would bother even to scan them, when the air ran out before the mountains did?

And yet, high on the slopes of the Atlas Mountains, where only a madman would think to find enemies, he spied motion. Even he doubted it. But where common sense had run out of him like beer from a cracked cup, his senses still functioned on a level of animal perfection. He saw what he saw: men, attenuated by distance even to his Cyborg's sight, toiling upwards.

*What are they after? So small a force could scarcely endanger or even distract the Citadel in direct assault—and there were five thousand meters of sheer cliff between their position and the Inner Keep. Too many were up there to make a reconnaissance party; a handful would have sufficed for that.*

Carcharoth's mentation implants still worked, after a fashion. Methodically, he searched through everything he'd ever learned for connections between the mountains and the Citadel. In microseconds he found one, in the most literal sense of the word: some time not long after the Citadel was built, a tunnel had been dug from the fortress up to . . . a point not far above where the climbers labored. Records showed the workers had been quietly killed after the work was accomplished, and then three generations later the tunnel had been sealed with a ferroconcrete plug.

The cattle had a purpose, then, and not mere reconnaissance. They wanted to sneak down a long dark tube and give the Soldiers a surprise, did they? He turned to the TAC and sent a message to the Duty Officer: THREAT TO INNER KEEP THROUGH CLOACA TUNNELS. PREPARE AND DEFEND.

EXECUTE.

The Battlemaster's smile was enough to make one of the young sentries recoil in horror. Carcharoth made a mental note of that, to settle accounts later. Now, he was busy.

He all but flew down from the wall, then trotted across the parade ground at what was close to full sprint for a non-Cyborg. He didn't have the flame thrower on now; he'd left it in a little chamber a couple of doors away from Interrogation. But it was, for where he was bound, the perfect weapon.

With the vivid projection lent him by his Cyborg enhancements, he saw the bandits crisping in flames like moths diving at a candle, heard their—brief—screams, smelled flesh cook and char. The imagined odor made his mouth water.

He pushed past Soldiers and tribute maidens and their brats as if they did not exist; for him, they might as well not have been there. Then a man called after him in accented Americ: "Where away so fast, Battlemaster?"

As few would have, that voice pierced his fantasies, brought him back a moment to the here and now. He said, "Come with me if you care to see, Dagor." Then he pressed on again. By the footfalls behind him, Dagor followed.

A procession of two, they hurried past the corridor which held the armored room wherein dwelt the TAC— and, these days, Titus as well. Carcharoth's lips drew back from his teeth in a snarl of contempt. Let the Breedmaster manipulate useless symbols if he would. Carcharoth had no need for symbols. He'd come across what was real.

Deeper into the heart of the Citadel he pushed, following the map in his mind as if it had been projected in the air in front of him. When at last he pulled open a door, its hinges squealed in rusty protest but could not withstand his strength. Dust lay thick inside; no one had come here in many years.

"Where are we, Battlemaster?" Dagor asked in a low voice that fit the gloom of the surroundings.

Carcharoth did not answer, not with words. He undogged a door that stood against the far walls. That was thick metal, salvaged from the hull of the *Dol Guldur* itself, still spotless after the centuries. When it came open, it revealed a tunnel cut into the living rock. Cold, musty air flowed out of the tunnel and engulfed him. Without hesitation, he plunged into the opening.

No light had shown there since the cattle cut it not long after the *Dol Guldur* came to Haven and the Citadel was raised. Nor did Carcharoth carry torch or candle. Nevertheless, he could see. His own body radiated enough infrared to give his enhanced and cybernetically augmented eyes a source of illumination.

He advanced slowly even so. The footing was treacherous; cracks and crevasses had opened in the floor. Dagor stayed on his heels. The wild Soldier was no Cyborg, but he had the glowing infrared image of Carcharoth to follow.

After curving down for a time, the tunnel began to climb.

Here parts of the way were rough, natural bubbles in the volcanic basalt. The Battlemaster nodded in grim satisfaction. This was the way he'd thought it to be.

"Where are we?" Dagor repeated.

Carcharoth pondered. Having someone fully appreciate his brilliance might be pleasant. He deigned to explain. "Long ago, we opened this secret way up into the mountains. The secret was kept too well among us; I doubt anyone but I knows of it now. But the Bandari, curse them, have somehow found it from the other end. The records say the tunnel was blocked, but I doubt that will hold them. Thus I shall meet their would-be raiders here deep underground, where the advantages will be all mine."

"But, Battlemaster—" Dagor had nerve, if he dared protest to a Cyborg. Stammering a little, he went on, "Shouldn't you have told someone before you set out on this course? What if you fail?"

"The Balrog stands forever alone. So it is written, so shall it be."

"I don't understand," Dagor said, and then, after a moment, "Do you—do we—Sau, uh, Soldiers then have legends too, like the tribes of the plains? I hadn't thought so until just now."

"Not a legend. Say rather deeper truth."

Dagor said, "Battlemaster, shall I go back and fetch aid for you?"

Carcharoth considered. Part of him wanted to fry Dagor for his presumption. Watching a gout of liquid flame crisp a man would be . . . pleasant. But no. Though the madness in him grew with every heartbeat, it had not yet consumed him. Not quite.

And he knew the error he had made, and the price a Cyborg who made such an error must pay—alone. Regretfully—he would have liked someone to see what was all too likely to prove his last stand, to weave it in among the legends of the Race—he said, "Aye, tell them if you feel you must. And Dagor—"

"Battlemaster?" the young wild Sauron said. But, though his voice doubted, Carcharoth saw that some deeper part of him understood.

He finished, "If any man save I should come alive from this tunnel . . . avenge me."

"It shall be as you say, Battlemaster." Dagor looked away. Trying not to reveal his emotions, Carcharoth judged. The genetic material might have been promising, but the training—just for a moment, the Battlemaster functioned very much like his old self. The youngling's training, he thought, should have been much better and would require improvement if he ever expected to make anything of himself.

Dagor fled down the tunnel, toward the men—and the women, and the children—sheltering in the heart of the Citadel. When he presented his back to Carcharoth, the Battlemaster again all but flamed him down—the impulse to exterminate a fleeing foe was strong, strong. A last time, he mastered himself. Dagor was not the foe. The foe lay ahead. Carcharoth resumed his advance, looking for the perfect place in which to lie in wait for the enemy.

Three T-days into the climb, the first man died. The

guard whose watch he failed to relieve went to check on him and found him cold. They wrapped him in his blanket and laid him out with care along the side of the tunnel. Someone grumbled that one of the other commandos might welcome the extra warmth.

"We don't get that cold," Sannie hissed. "Sir, what do you think?"

"Leave it. God knows, I'd like to come back and retrieve his body, give it decent burial," Hammer-of-God muttered.

"He lies in the finest tomb on Haven," Nazrullah said. Sannie nodded, saving her breath for the climb. She smoothed the coarse wool over the dead man's face. Her own fingers had not swollen as much as those of the other *fedaykin*. It made them clumsy. In his nightly meditations on "what could go wrong," that reminded Hammer-of-God to check on the engineers' gloves. If *they* lost fingers in this climb . . .

Vertigo took out another man; a rockfall caught one Tibetan woman and the three men of different tribes who tried to dig her out and were caught in a second shower of jagged rocks.

No one fell behind. Shamyl son of Shamyl began vomiting and complained of agony in his right side. The *medikos* among the death commandos whispered together about attempting surgery, but the young mountain man disappeared one rest period when the lanterns were out.

Iskendar of the Silver Hand—Alexander the Great— had lost more of his three hundred. But he had won his battle. Now the air stabbed in their lungs. Hammer-of-God's leg ached, then numbed with the cold. It took as much courage as anything he had ever done to examine it for signs of blackening. He would not allow himself to die, he vowed, as slowly as his son had when his wound rotted. He would make it look like an accident. And still they climbed, up past the roughest of the walls into a passage where the walls were smoothed out, symmetrical. Sauron work, no doubt. Barak leaned up against the side of the tunnel, listening. "Damned water," he grumbled.

"Don't complain," Sannie told him. "We may run short."

"The sound masks anything else that might be there," he complained. "I can't *hear*."

And it wouldn't have mattered much if he could. They were all jumpy, all imagining noises and voices and lights that weren't there. It was the thin air.

They passed out of that tunnel under open sky and wind so cold that it practically froze their eyelids shut. Already they were higher than you'd have imagined anyone could climb and live. This, Nazrullah said, was the level of his village.

Gasim muttered something about coupling with *afritahs*, rather than women, to which the Afghan replied with an obscenity about yaks and plainsmen. Barak swiftly distracted them.

Not long now, Strong Sven reported, wheezing. He began to go more and more slowly, muttering to himself, weeping on occasion as he sought to remember. "Do you regret your bargain?" Hammer-of-God wanted to ask one of any number of times. Easy enough to release the traitor from it. He had not been pleasant company.

He became speedily less pleasant when Barak, Gasim, and Nazrullah began to question him. "I *told* you," he wept. "Up ahead. There's a rockfall. You have to move it. . . ."

"You expect us to listen to that, get ourselves killed in an avalanche?"

"Behind it is the seal. Move it—if you can." His voice was thin with malice as well as exhaustion.

The engineers spent what seemed like a frozen eternity poking and prodding at the rockfall when they found it. Any one of those stones might be the keystone to a collapse. Ultimately, the engineers couldn't be risked. Volunteers pulled the rocks aside. "That patch is artificial," Hammer's cousin Smite-Sin Jackson said. He scraped away at it with a knife blade. "Ferroconcrete, just as we thought." He tapped the rock wall with a hammer, then started to scrape.

"What's that?" someone asked. "Who scraped against something?"

Barak pressed against the rock. "Nothing there," he said. "Just the damned water."

They spent the rest of that waking period working in shifts—very short shifts. Removing rock. Digging into the living rock, planting their charges, then pressing back huddled together, as much as possible, as the fuses were laid. They held themselves immobile.

Hammer-of-God flexed his leg, not wanting it to collapse if he had to move fast. "Be ready," he whispered. Certainly, the explosion might be heard and the concussion felt through the rocks. The time it took to draw and shoot might be more time than the Saurons would let them have.

"Now!"

Smite-Sin touched fire to the fuses, then flung himself, gasping, to safety in the bend of the passage. Prayers and imprecations that the Saurons consider this another quake or rockfall hissed upward in the silence as thin tracks of flame raced toward the charges.

There was that heart-stopping moment that kills engineers wondering if their explosives were going to work this time. And then, fire and explosions tossed them about like beans in a jar. Coughing, gagging, and tossing aside broken rocks occupied them for what felt like an eternity. The engineers edged out, poking at the rock face.

"Is it going to hold?" Barak asked.

"Can't know till we try it." For once, Be-Courteous didn't have a whole speech prepared. They were all shivering a little from reaction.

"Let me go first," said someone. Hard to tell who it was in the dark, when your ears were still ringing and everyone had a blackened face.

*I lead.* The words were on the tip of Hammer-of-God's tongue. *Son, there are two kinds of leaders. Those who lead from behind, if you can call "leading" what they do, and those who lead from up front.* But he wasn't the man for this job, he knew. He was the only one who knew that, sometimes, you had to order other people into danger it would be easier to face yourself.

He growled something that the man could take for assent or approval. Then he added "Take *him!*" The wall breached, their traitor suddenly became a whole lot less valuable, except maybe as protection for a brave man. Strong Sven's leash was passed to the new leader.

The passageway ran on—level now, thank God, given the way they were all coughing from the powder and the rock dust. You could tell the difference in the way the Saurons built for themselves . . . steeper gradients, fewer handholds or stopping places. They didn't need such things themselves and clearly saw no reason why they should build them—or order them built—for anyone else.

Barak stopped so suddenly that Sannie bumped into him.

"I hear . . . something," he rasped. "We're not alone in the tunnel."

# • CHAPTER FIFTEEN

Carcharoth flexed his shoulders, as if under the weight of the flame thrower. In fact, though, he half expected to spread vast black capelike wings. He could not feel them. That did not mean they were not there. "Carcharoth is the Balrog, and the Balrog is Carcharoth," he whispered. "The cattle of the steppe shall learn this to their sorrow. Oh, they shall."

He didn't know how far up the tunnel he'd come. He was beyond caring about things like that. All he knew was that he had yet to reach the perfect ambush point or to encounter the cattle—no, they sounded like muskylopes drunk on fermented tennis fruit—coming his way. A single red imperative ruled him now: to slaughter as many of those who sought to come up the Citadel's back passage as he could. In some small way, he might yet redeem himself for the blunders he had committed.

Awareness of those blunders still ate at him poisonously. Increasingly, as he strode through what would have been darkness illimitable for any ordinary man, himself as Battlemaster faded and himself as Balrog, creature of fire and smoke and dread, grew. The Balrog too had been the last of its kind, fighting against those who disturbed it in its ancient home and refuge from overpowering foes.

He skipped lightly over a two-meter crevasse, landing on the balls of his feet, flexing his knees to take the shock of coming down with the heavy flame thrower strapped onto him. The metal tank rattled against a buckle as he came down. He scowled. Some of the cattle ahead were not quite cattle, were men with Soldiers' senses . . . like

Dagor. Some of them, if myth were indeed fact, were Dagor's closest kin. He frowned. It would have been a telling show of weakness in the Battlemaster, but who could say whether Balrogs showed what they felt?

He should have flamed Dagor after all. He was sure of it now: either flamed him or forced him to come along. Too late, too late. The wild Sauron would betray him, as he'd already betrayed his own kin. He was sure of it. But what was his certainty worth these days? He'd made mistakes on large matters, so why not on small as well?

Then all such worries left him. Some earthquake, not so long ago, had torn a great rift in the heart of the mountain—twenty meters across, easily, and deep beyond any reckoning. The Soldiers had bridged it with an arch of stone no more than half a meter wide—plenty for those of their blood to walk on surefootedly, but little enough, over that chasm, to take the heart out of most cattlefolk. His mental image of the tunnel showed no such bridge, which meant only that it had been made after record-keeping began to look unimportant when set against the day-to-day struggle for survival. The Race had grown sloppy since the days when it came to Haven.

"A redeemer, I shall be," Carcharoth murmured.

In their quest for day-to-day survival, though, the Soldiers had been thorough. By the bridge, on the side nearer the heart of the Citadel, they'd built a breast-high bulwark of fitted stones, to give defenders a perfect firing point against their foes.

"A firing point indeed," Carcharoth said. He smiled. That wide grin was a more telling sign of his decay than the earlier frown had been—a madman's smile, pure and simple.

Dagor almost sobbed with relief as he came up to inhabited levels once more. Had he been out on the steppe, he would have screamed his news to everyone he saw. Since he had been in the Citadel, he'd learned Soldiers went about things differently. He looked this way and that for a person in authority. *If I don't find one soon, I'll start screaming anyway*, he thought. *Let them make of it, and of me, what they will.*

Luck, for once, was with him. Here came Titus, escaping for a moment his closeting with the TAC to fuel his body. "Great lord!" Dagor said, and then, again remembering where he was, "Breedmaster, sir!"

Titus looked at him, looked through him. As always with the Cyborgs, he had the sense of being weighed and found wanting. Here it was doubled, for he was Carcharoth's pet, and he had seen Breedmaster and Battlemaster were uncertain allies and certain rivals. But Titus seemed as perfectly controlled as ever as he said, "What is it you wish of me?"

Now Dagor spoke urgently, his words tumbling over one another as he gasped out the Battlemaster's discovery. "Not cattle. Bandari warriors, coming through the tunnel. We need to send a force into the tunnel right away, come to Carcharoth's aid," he gasped.

"No," Titus answered, and Dagor gaped at him. For a moment, behind those cold, gray-blue eyes, he saw the wheels and gears spinning. They spun very fast. After what could have been only a heartbeat, the Breedmaster went on, "The Battlemaster commands until dismissed. It is entirely possible that the Battlemaster will be able to dispose of this entire raiding party single-handed. And if he does not—" If Carcharoth couldn't handle the raiders by himself, Titus would be rid of his rival.

Titus resumed: "If he does not, then it is to our advantage to have the raiders come out of the tunnel and into less restrictive quarters. The more open the field, the more the Soldiers enjoy the advantages of speed and maneuverability. In the tunnel, the raiders would inevitably fire straight ahead, and would as inevitably inflict casualties. We are better adapted to a game with more options."

"Soldiers?" Dagor said. "You have—we have—no Soldiers here, only women and children."

"They are of the Blood. They shall suffice," Titus said. The upward curl to his lips was entirely artificial.

Dagor knew as much. Somehow that made it only the more frightening.

"You've been hearing water as long as we've been climbing," Sannie said to Barak.

"Quiet! I tell you, there's something out there. . . . You saw the map—pull the plug, proceed along this corridor, tunnel, whatever, and then there's the chute down into the innermost Citadel. Yewehdammit, quiet! Something's coming up!"

He drew his sidearm—Sauron issue, awarded after the first battle—and edged forward in the line, moving as fast as he could.

Hammer-of-God signaled people into readiness. This is what he had helped train the boy for, independent command. His stomach clenched as it always did before a fight. He usually relaxed into a sense of freedom where mind and body meshed more smoothly than at any other time. Not this time, though. Not with old enemies as allies, not with Saurons to be fought.

"Hold up! Hold up!" The urgent call came from ahead.

"Bring more torches. Yeweh, there's a cursed chasm here, looks to go down all the way to Eblis."

"Ropes? Grappling hooks?" The question came in Turkic. Hammer-of-God blinked. A bliddy *hotnot*, starting to think like an engineer? If that sort of thing happened more often, it might end up being more dangerous to the Pale than the stinking Saurons were.

The first voice spoke again: "No. There's a bridge here, though one fit to make your stones crawl up into your belly. One step wrong and you find out how deep the pit is."

"What's that on the far side? Fetch up another torch, somebody." A pause. "Looks like a cairn, maybe. Can't really see, not in this stinking light."

Barak spoke: "I know whom to send to find out. Let

Strong Sven lead." He spoke with grim satisfaction. Hammer-of-God nodded. The wretch had outlived any need for him, but if anything across there was dangerous—and in Sauron country, the bet to make was that *everything* was dangerous—he could still be useful one last time.

Strong Sven might have been part Sauron in blood, but not in spirit. He began to blubber: "No, great lord, not me!"

"Pass him up to the front."

"No!" Strong Sven cried.

"Shut up," Hammer-of-God said implacably.

Up Strong Sven went, passed from one hand to another like a sheep to the knacking house, bleating at every step. "I've got it!" a voice said at the very edge of the chasm. The accent was Edenite: Be-Courteous. Hammer-of-God's lip curled scornfully. If Strong Sven had a gram of whey in him, he'd fight for his life, but no—

But yes. Strong Sven grabbed at the leash and tugged. It snapped, and he lashed Be-Courteous across the face with it once, then again. Be-Courteous tried to dodge, overbalanced, and then, with a scream, he plummeted. . . . *Bliddyful heart*, Hammer-of-God thought. Dear God, anyone but him. Maybe there'd be a miracle. No chance. They found out one thing about the chasm: it was too deep to hear the thud of a body when it hit bottom.

Beside Hammer-of-God, Barak was cursing, practically weeping. "You couldn't have stopped him," Jackson snapped. "Now get back down!"

The younger man stretched out close at his shoulder. He wasn't breathing fast, and his heartbeat didn't pick up, not even when they looked out.

Dear God, they'd come out into a Godrotted cavern. The path they must take—couldn't be more than fifty centimeters wide, if that much, and they'd have to cross it single file. Miss their step, overbalance, duck, Hell, do anything but go forward, and there was only a sheer drop into endless blackness. His eyes watered, and he blinked furiously.

Strong Sven dashed across the bridge toward the cairn, babbling, pleading, begging. . . . He was part Sauron, too; maybe his ears spoke to him of what Barak's had also sensed: that they were not alone in the tunnel. "I brought them to you, Great Lord, noble Soldier, the Jews, the tribes, the cursed wild men . . ."

A tongue of flame lashed out and enfolded Strong Sven. Screaming, burning, he fell into the abyss. You couldn't hear his body hit, either.

From behind the cairn, a voice spoke in the Sauron dialect of Americ. "Is that the latest story? Not good enough. I heard them. So confident Titus was that the Citadel was safe. I gave the orders to satisfy him, but I knew that only I could check on its safety. . . . I . . . Carcharoth, the Balrog, the Redeemer of the Race."

*Jesus wept.* Carcharoth. Not just a Sauron, but a Cyborg Battlemaster. He sounded old. He sounded, when you thought about it, more than a little *meshuggeh.* An aging Sauron whose mind was going, Hammer-of-God thought, matching his voice with that of . . . *I'm going to fry, and I left my army to . . . Oh God. God!*

However old the Sauron was, though, and however crazy, he had all the cover in the world and a weapon Satan would have been proud to use. How were they going to winkle him out?

"It throws *flame,*" whispered Smite-Sin, stating the obvious, the horrific.

"Little man, it burns disobedient cattle. It will burn you. I will burn you, I, Carcharoth, Balrog of the Citadel." Age had not blunted the creature's supernal hearing.

"It throws flame," Smite-Sin repeated. His voice had stopped shaking as he applied his skills to the problem at hand—staying alive against a Cyborg. "But it's got a limited supply of whatever fuels it."

"There is no end to my power!" Carcharoth shouted. "Come to me! Come one, come all! You shall learn the truth."

The trouble was, they had to do it. If they were going to

enter the Citadel, they had to pass the Battlemaster. "Here's what we do," Barak said, his voice eerily, inhumanly calm. And why not? Jackson's mind gibbered. Barak was Sauron, too. He went on, "The ones with automatic rifles open up, make the Cyborg keep his head down. While they're doing that, we rush a part across. Yeweh willing, some of them will make it, force him out of his hole there—"

"It's the best chance," Hammer-of-God agreed. "But it's not what you'd call a good one. And you're a shooter, not a charger, you hear me?" He put his arm over the younger man's shoulders. Time had been when his voice alone would have restrained Barak.

"*Ja*, Oom Hammer," Barak said. "We'll do it your way— for a while." A pause. Then Barak shouted, "Who here is brave?" It nearly started a riot but he shortly had his death chargers. It took only a few minutes to complete his rudimentary dispositions.

"Come on!" Hammer screamed. "Riflemen—fire! *Fedaykin*, forward! For vengeance! *Am Bandari Hai!*" There was no point in silence now and the hope, at least, that a howling mad charge might get at least a few of them across the bridge.

War cries shrieked up—"*Allahu Akbar!*" and "*Am Bandari Hai!*" and God knew what all else. The commandos sprinted single file out onto the narrow strip of stone. Behind them, assault rifles snapped viciously. When the first to charge was nearly across, Carcharoth rose, just a little, just for an instant. A hissing roar like a land gator's, but magnified a thousandfold, sounded even through the gunfire. A great shaft of fire engulfed the men. They were burning, up and down the length of the bridge, leathers and furs and hair, oh God, their very skin was crisping. Well back in the tunnel, the heat beat against Hammer-of-God's face.

The mouth-watering, appalling smell of roasting meat filled the air as, in their writhing agony, the living torches tumbled from the bridge, one by one. Bare seconds after they had begun the charge, it stood empty, inviting.

"Come to me," Carcharoth crooned.

They hadn't gotten him. And how many swept away? Twenty-five had charged. And for nothing.

*No, not quite,* Hammer-of-God thought. As Smite-Sin had said, the flame thrower could carry only so much fuel. But how much was so much? The only way to find out was to keep throwing bodies at it—literally, putting out a fire by leaping into it.

"Will they go forward again?" Barak whispered.

Beside him, Jackson shrugged. The flame thrower tested his courage, too, which angered him. But he knew the difference between dying for a purpose and throwing his life away. He tightened his grip on Barak's shoulder, not sure the younger man had learned that lesson.

They took more time readying the next assault, forming the attackers well behind the tunnel, positioning the riflemen to better advantage. Again the assault rifles crackled forth, again the attackers made the best speed they could across the bridge, this time well spaced, forcing the Cyborg to spend a burst of flame for each victim. Their war cries ringing, some sure of Paradise and *houris*, some of seeing Yeweh face to face, some of a happy rebirth, they charged madly.

Carcharoth incinerated them, one and all. "I am the Balrog, flame of Udûn!"

Hammer-of-God wouldn't have bet more than a jug of piss that the Sauron wasn't the demon he thought he was. Bullets didn't seem to want to bite on him, that was certain.

The third group formed. "If this one fails, I will be with the next," Barak said. He shrugged away from Hammer-of-God with effortless strength to show the old war leader he meant what he said and could not be stopped.

*God, are You listening to me?* Jackson asked silently. He'd spent a lot of time talking to God, and a lot of time listening to Him, too. Now, for the first time, he wondered if his deity was listening. Did God and His angels sleep?

What did it take to go forward, knowing you were going into sure and hideous death? Whatever it was, the *fedaykin* had it. The third group, spaced a little more tightly as they learned through bitter experience the limits of the Balrog's flame, advanced over the bridge. As before, Carcharoth let the leader get nearly across, then crisped with individual bursts. How many gone? Near a hundred now. "I am the Redeemer!" Carcharoth shouted. "Through me, the Citadel lives!"

He was crazy, but that didn't make him wrong.

# • CHAPTER SIXTEEN

They were brave, braver than Carcharoth had imagined their kind could be. He admired that courage—it made them enemies worthy of his fire. He only wished he had more fire to give them. The tank on his back was lighter than it had been, lighter than it should be. Even so, he'd sent scores screaming into the abyss. And Dagor had gone back to warn Titus. Even if he finally fell here, the Citadel would not be surprised by this devious thrust from behind, from within. He had accomplished his mission. For a Soldier, there was no higher satisfaction.

But why should he fall here? True, the cattle had wounded him with their weapons, but the wounds did not kill him, and any wound that did not kill, he could ignore for as long as need be.

And how could any wound be mortal? He was not merely Carcharoth Battlemaster, he was Carcharoth Balrog. When the flame thrower he carried on his back ran out of fuel, would he not strike fire from thin air with his fingers? Was he not as near immortal as made no difference?

"Come to the oven," he cried. "Come and be burned! Come to me!"

"My turn," Barak said quietly, and slid toward the next group of silently forming men. Hammer-of-God tried to hold him back, tried with all his strength. Barak broke his grip as easily as if he'd been a clingy toddler. He took his place somewhere near the back of the line. Jackson consoled himself, just a little: had he not grabbed Barak,

Chaya's son might have been at the fore.

The men lined up for the fourth assault on the bridge, and solemnly clasped hands, one with another. They had seen what had happened to their friends, to their brothers. That they were ready to go on together, death-sworn though they were, spoke of men's—what? Courage? Idiocy? Hammer-of-God Jackson, for once, had no sure answer ready to hand.

The covering fire picked up again. Hammer-of-God prayed for a lucky bullet, a killing bullet, to find the Cyborg at last.

Heads bowed, leaning forward as if against a wind with snow in it instead of fire, one by one the commandos advanced across the bridge. Hammer-of-God noticed he was not breathing. The lead man was almost to the far side, almost, almost . . .

Again flame wrapped warriors in incendiary embrace. But this time things were different. Each tongue of flame, though fatal to its target, fell short of the last. Carcharoth's curses were music to Hammer-of-God. The Battlemaster had wasted fuel toasting Strong Sven, who really did want to betray the raiders to him, and now had none to spare.

Men fell spinning, screaming, into the crevasse. But one, the last, to whom the flame gave only a partial molten kiss, stayed on his feet, hideously burned though he was.

"Barak," Hammer-of-God whispered. This was worse than he'd imagined, worse even than falling to your doom after the fire got you. To stay alive, to keep trying to fight— Not for the first time, he saw what Sauron blood could do.

A scream of anguish went off by his ear. He reached up, snagged Sannie as she started after Barak far too late, and tripped her up so she fell heavily against him. "Don't cry, *myn mooie meisie*," he muttered. It was his eyes that were wet, though. "Go, Barak," he heard himself praying. "Go on."

Flame thrower empty at last, Carcharoth committed a last act of insanity: he leaped out onto the bridge, defying the enemies of the Citadel alone and weaponless, save for himself. Torchlight showed blood from three or four wounds on him, but only a heart shot or a head shot would kill a Cyborg dead, and even then you couldn't be sure.

And Barak still moved, as he fought for a few seconds more life . . . three, no, two steps more, to close with the Cyborg. . . . My turn next, Hammer-of-God thought, and scrambled to his feet. Going forward now was a relief; dying in battle held no terror for him.

Barak and Carcharoth grappled. In his madness the Cyborg had forgotten that Sauron genes were not confined to the Citadel. Barak seized him in a way that left him open to any of a dozen killing counters the Battlemaster cared to make and—jumped, still grasping his prize, into the Abyss.

*"BAARAAAAK! Am Bandari Hai!"* Hammer-of-God's voice rose to a deep-throated roar.

The commandos roared with him. One by one, they ran across that perilous, blackened bridge toward the Citadel. The thin air slashed their lungs like surgical steel, and they shouted all the louder to try to drown out memories of screams of burning men.

No more flame lashed out. No other defenders waited for them on the other side of the bridge. And after a time, the thin air and exhaustion muted the *fedaykin's* first blind rush of grief and rage.

So, when Sannie collapsed to her knees, retching dryly, Hammer-of-God signaled a halt. His hand was shaking.

The *fedaykin* flung themselves down. Some shook. One or two curled up, temporarily—he hoped—rejecting the unbearable. He heard the whirr of a prayer wheel and a low-voiced chant. Only the Tibetans would have that much breath left.

Pain stitched itself across his chest. *Not now, God. I've got an appointment with some Saurons. You'll have to make do with the leftovers.*

Barak would have laughed at that. Oh God, Barak. It was his son dying all over again. He'd put his whole life into those boys, into every soldier he'd ever trained.

*If Barak were here to laugh, maybe he could simply give*

*in, lie down, let it go . . . what am I even thinking?*

Sannie sank down nearby. He felt bodies at his back as others of the death commandos pressed in. *They are my brothers and my sisters*, he thought. *My kin, more than those in Strang. We are bound with blood and worse than blood. With fire.*

Hammer-of-God saw Sannie gather herself to speak and braced himself.

"General, when we enter the Citadel, I remember that the plans—if Sven wasn't lying—said there's a very narrow door. Just as with the fire bridge, we'll have to go to through one at a time." Another deep breath. "Barak is dead. I wish to follow him. I'm going first. As one of the Seven, I claim the right."

The argument that erupted was waged in whispers, not shouts, but it was nonetheless heartfelt and vicious. "A woman leading the way?" The glory-drunk fur-hats were squabbling over the right to plunge into a second furnace.

Their post of greatest honor a post likely to be held very briefly—albeit for the rest of someone's life. She claimed it; it was therefore hers, and they could say what they wished.

She was of the Seven; she did not have to request where she could command.

Who would have thought it, that the lanky girl from the farm down the road, the girl who loved a Bandari and left her home to soldier with him would turn into a woman who could meet the eyes of so many angry men and simply repeat: "It is my right."

He was proud of her, and that made it even worse.

He gestured the *fedaykin* abruptly to silence.

Say what you must, her eyes commanded him.

"We'll see," he told her. "First we scout. Then we'll see. I just worry about whether anybody in there knows we're coming." Their lives depended on the answer. Carcharoth back there had been crazy as a bedbug—crazy as Chaya, his mind whispered. If he were as out of it as he seemed, he might have gone in thinking he could take out three hundred of the best of Haven all by his lonesome. Battlemasters didn't have to answer to anybody. With a little luck—suffering Jesus, just a little . . . But how could the Cyborg know and no one else? How indeed. Still, his solitary appearance argued for it.

A tunnel, angling downward, almost a chute into the innermost heart of the Saurons' strongest keep. They'd have to hit it fast and ready to fight. Sure, there were mostly women and children in the innermost keep, but some of the women were Sauron and all of the children. Furthermore, some women of the tribes had gone over in mind as well as in body. They would be armed. They would fight, Jackson thought. How well would they fight? He didn't have any way to guess. No matter what nonsense Shulamit babbled about Sigrid, you didn't see Sauron women out on the steppes. If they fought as well as Shulamit, that would be bad enough.

*Don't think about it*, Hammer-of-God warned himself. They are enemies, not women like Chaya or Aisha or Sannie here . . . faces rose up before him. There would be Soldiers, too. It would be good to kill Soldiers, if he could. He must. Because beyond the innermost fastness stretched the rest of the Citadel. With the TAC, the machine that foretold the future like a prophet or a skilled gambler. He had seen the rusting hulk of the one at ruined Angband. Badri had used it to help bring down those walls. What Badri had used, he could use—or destroy.

And if he couldn't, Sapper's men could.

They padded through the tunnel. It narrowed until they were practically bent double—no problem for the others, but Hammer-of-God's back was on fire and his leg threatened to give out. He ignored the pain. All Haven vanished as he focused on the tasks before him, the space right in front of his eyes.

And finally, the way was blocked. By the dust that lay thickly everywhere, it had been blocked a long time. Carcharoth must have found another way in.

"Blow it," Hammer-of-God ordered the engineers.

With one arm, he gestured *everyone back up* as best he could in the passageway. It was deliberately cramped so that fighters would have to approach one by one. The engineers could widen that entrance, but there was no denying it. Someone—one or two someones—had to go through it first and face whatever was going to be shooting from the other side. And their chances?

He'd lived through a couple such squeezes himself and called himself a lucky man. Maybe not, though. Because this time, with Barak gone, he knew he couldn't be the first to go through. "Maybe, General, if they saw a woman, they'd be surprised, and I could get the jump . . ."

*Don't count on it, Sannie-girl.*

". . . just long enough for some more people . . ." Scuffling behind her, a profane objection from Smite-Sin, predictably enough, and hisses of "down!" from the engineers, who wanted to light the fuses.

In the flickering light, Hammer-of-God caught a glimpse of her eyes. Barak was dead. She had turned her back on her home. Where could she go?

Nowhere but forward.

"Take the lead, Sannie," he ordered. *And God bless.*

The door blew. Even before the rocks had stopped falling and the dust cleared, Sannie was through, screaming. . . .

God damn! Determined not to follow a woman into battle, Smite-Sin tried to push past her.

"Get back, Smite-Sin, you bliddyful!" Hammer-of-God shouted. Gasim and Nazrullah followed them out. He hurled himself after the pair of them, desperate woman and jealous man, but he was caught up in the rush, too old, too slow, too sore to get anywhere near the front. A pack of suicidal maniacs, he thought. At last he plunged after them, feet first through the gaping hole in the wall. Women's and children's mouths opened in what he knew were screams. His ears still rang from the blast. He couldn't hear them.

And not everyone was screaming. Intently they had

co-ordinated a defense, women and children as well as the few men. Sannie hit the ground. She would have come up shooting, but Smite-Sin fell heavily, fouling her legs, tripping her.

And a small woman with a round face that would have been flower-pretty if it hadn't been twisted in rage opened fire and cut them both down.

"Good shot!" The voice was high and shrill, piercing the deafness brought on by the explosion. Incredibly, a tiny child ran forward to snatch up Sannie's weapon.

"Gimilzor, get back!" the woman cried. Her voice bore an accent Hammer-of-God knew. The Golden Tamerlanes spoke that way, and every one of the *fedaykin* knew it.

One or two of them held their fire. Fools! It was the last thing they ever did. A tall, blond woman picked off Suleiman Tepe. She adjusted her aim minutely. At him, wouldn't you just know it. Time slowed, as it always did when his life went on the line, and he dropped and rolled. His leg shrieked pain. A bullet whined by his ear. Damn, she was fast. She too looked familiar. Ice walked through him. Maybe Shulamit hadn't been babbling after all.

Damn, were those *children* rushing him?

He lashed out with the barrel of his weapon and drew his saber to beat them away with the flat. If he weren't good enough to drive off a Sauron child . . .

The ringing in his ears had stopped. Behind him, he heard shouts. The calm part of his mind that let him plan even while he was fighting ticked off voices . . . Nazrullah, Gasim, Abdul, Rahman, Leshi, Lopsang . . . present, accounted for, and fighting like Hell, which was how this inner Citadel looked. Blood splashed the walls. Sauron blood was the same color as anyone else's: he saw plenty of both.

Then that damned woman with the pretty face and the bloody mind rose from a barricade she'd built of chairs.

She had a clear shot—or series of shots—at the entrance the *fedaykin* had blasted. In a second or two, she'd open fire. A few good shots and she might even stem the flood of men and women down into the Citadel. Blood already stained the floor from the speed of their attack. They still had a better-than-even chance of carrying this off.

But not if she blocked their rush.

One good shot, though, and she wouldn't be a problem.

*You're really going to shoot her?* he asked himself.

*Damn right.*

He raised his weapon. It would be close.

Gasim ran up beside him. *"Allahu Akbar!"* he screamed, which was predictable. Then *"Allah!"* in a voice of pure shock—which was not. And then, strangest of all, the *khan* of the Golden Tamerlanes cried out, "Chichek! Daughter!" Maybe he was going to ask Hammer-of-God to hold his fire. Jackson never got the chance to find out. Something slammed him in the side of the head, like all the muskylope kicks in the world boiled down to half a liter. Blood spraying from the wound, he crashed to the floor, the rifle clattering beside him.

It was a rare opportunity, Deathmaster Sharku thought with irony that was becoming characteristic these days. His Regiments had to build and fortify a camp on the old Roman legionary model, ditch, earthwork, and all. Necessity dictated it, of course, with this area of the Shangri-La Valley overrun with screaming nomads. The Northeast Valley hadn't seen war in centuries. Now most of it lay in ruins. Worse, the nomads had built enormous earthworks, fortifications to seal the Valley away from the ruins of Nûrnen and the road to the Citadel.

"Those bastards are all around us," Mumak said. He pointed south into the Valley. "Enough of them down there to keep Ghâsh busy a while."

"Or us, if we let them." Sharku examined the earthworks ahead of him. "Amazing. The Bandari have got those cattle doing real work."

Mumak grinned. "Glad to see you think that way. All this talk of enemy warriors, I was afraid you'd stopped thinking like us."

"I don't know why I let you talk to me like that."

Mumak grinned again, then turned serious. "Double walls. We're investing Nûrnen, and the rest of them have us surrounded. Reminds me of something I read—"

"Alesia," Sharku said.

"Right. Julius Caesar at Alesia. Ended right, though. Caesar cut off ten thousand right hands, as I recall." He pointed out to the plains. "There's more than that out there."

Hard fighting and sheer grim determination combined with nomad inability to carry out a real strategic plan even when the Bandari gave them one had brought Sharku's Regiments to the hills south of Nûrnen. Now his Soldiers were building double walls from mountain to mountain, sealing off the roads north into the Karakul Pass.

His troops, working with Soldier efficiency even on the edge of exhaustion, had the earthwork almost completed. The road to Nûrnen—the ruins of Nûrnen now—and the Pass was blocked. The hills to the south were rough and tangled, passable only to small parties. Small parties of nomads *were* infiltrating through there all the time, but they were so many less for the horde to use. They'd be a menace in the Valley too, but priorities were priorities.

His body was trying to tell him that he could relax a fraction, eat, sleep. His mind was still in combat mode, revving like a drillbit that has eaten its way clean through a mountain and hasn't figured out yet that it's gnawing on air.

Mumak pointed toward the Citadel. It was far into the pass, almost invisible beyond the earthworks surrounding Nûrnen. "Looks like a sally," he said. "Odd. I'd think Carcharoth would stay inside the walls. What's he doing out there?"

"What the TAC tells him to do, I suppose. Mumak, someone's got to study that thing. We can't trust it any more."

Mumak shook his head. "That's a Hell of a thing for us to admit."

True enough, Sharku thought. One of their advantages,

not just that the TAC gave good advice, but everyone, Sauron and cattle alike, knew it, knew in their very bones that the Race would never make an important mistake.

Except we did. This time, and the last three hundred years, ever since Diettinger died, we told the damn computer to show us how to hide, and it did, and what has that done for us?

"Hard fighting up there," Mumak said. "Maybe we ought to go help?"

"What for? The Walls are holding. There's half a million of those nomads crammed into this part of the Valley. Give them a week and they'll eat everything in it. Then they eat their horses, and each other, and they're all dead. All we have to do is keep them bottled up, don't let them get down where there are still crops to raid. Let the bastards starve."

"Goes hard, letting cattle run around in our city." He pointed to the ruins of Nûrnen. "Goes hard."

"It will go harder storming those earthworks. Mumak, it's time we learned strategy again, stop throwing lives away fighting cattle. Any Soldier wants to die for glory, can do it against the Empire, not cattle. This is our world! And we'll need every one of the Race to take it." He turned toward his headquarters tent. "Get some sleep. Truenight in an hour. We won't be able to do anything until it's light anyway."

He rubbed his eyes. They felt as if he'd washed them in sand and dried them with red-hot metal. His tent was pitched and waiting. The last meter of earthwork was packed into place. As he stood near the middle of the camp, still as a tentpole and about as central to the structure of the whole, he heard a raw voice bellow, "All right, maggots! Knock off!"

Sharku ducked into his tent. He wanted to sleep with a desire that was almost sexual in its intensity, but habit and Soldier discipline kept him awake, even after he'd choked down a ration packet and a cup of water and lain on his cot.

His ears tracked the movements of the camp: the posting of sentries, the dispensing of rations to men so tired they ate in slow motion, the rasp of snores as man after man succumbed to sleep. "Orderly."

"Sir."

"Bring in a night lamp after I'm asleep. Then get some sleep yourself. We've work to do, but for now, we can all use some rest." The last glow of Cat's Eye faded into truenight as he lay down on the bed.

# • CHAPTER SEVENTEEN

*Don't let them give you to the women.* It had been a maxim on the steppe for as long as Haven had been settled. It had probably been a maxim back on Terra of legend. Dagor had never imagined, though, that it might be a maxim in the Citadel, too.

His notions of what war meant still came from the steppe: you gathered and you ranted and you rode and you hoped your enemy hadn't found out about you—which he probably had, because of all the ranting you'd been doing—and then, eventually, you fought. Things didn't work like that here. Titus led him to a room with—what did the Saurons call it?—a microphone in it. When he spoke, his words were heard in every corner of the Keep, reverberating from the ceiling speakers the Saurons used to summon one another: "We have an emergency. All personnel, draw weapons and ammunition from the storage lockers at the end of each hallway. Personnel at levels H and below, approach the doorway in subbasement C. Approach with caution and be alert for possible raiders emerging through the door. Personnel above level H, hold yourselves in readiness for orders, and stand ready to respond to possible unauthorized entrance into the Citadel through other egresses. Execute."

"Are there other ways into the tunnel than the one Carcharoth took?" Dagor asked.

"Certainly," Titus answered, "but none they are likely to find. Still, if we concentrate all our resources at any particular place, that is a virtual guarantee the Bandari will come at us from a different direction. Thus I shall wait, and let them commit themselves."

Calm, methodical, careful: 'inhuman' was the word that sprang to Dagor's mind. Dagor shivered. He felt sure in his belly he had chosen the winning side, and hated himself all the more for it.

"I shall draw a weapon," Titus said. "Will you also take one, aid in defending the Race of which you are a part?"

"I—will," Dagor said thickly. His father/brother had died at the hands of a Cyborg, and here he was going into battle beside one. But the merely human side of his ancestry had abandoned him, with curses.

He saw Titus eying him and had the eerie feeling the Breedmaster was looking inside his head, feeling his doubts, the twists of his thought, even before he was aware of them himself. But then Titus spoke: "This is an annoyance. It diverts me from my examination of the Threat Analysis Computer. Learning how and why it came to be in error will save the Race many difficulties in future."

Dagor thought the difficulties the Race was facing at present sufficient unto the day, but held his tongue. The less he did to draw the Cyborg's notice to him, the happier he was.

Down at the end of the hallway, metal doors had been flung open. He and Titus got into the queue of old men, women, even children.

A tall blond woman with the help of a blade-thin boy was passing out assault rifles and thirty-round clips of ammunition. She smiled at Titus. "Here, Father," she said.

"Thank you, Sieglinde," he answered. "I am glad we have weapons left for me and for Dagor here as well. New to the Citadel though he is, he has done the Race a service."

"Good." Sieglinde smiled again, serene, happy. Dagor got the idea doing the Race a service was something she embraced at a level deeper than thought.

Breedmaster Titus leaned down and spoke in battle-tongue to the young Sauron. The boy nodded twice, then left at a quick trot without a backward glance.

He clicked the clip into his weapon, flicked the charge lever off "safe," and chambered the first round manually, as he had to. Everyone on the steppe knew the theory of using an assault rifle; few ever got the chance to put theory into practice.

Boom! The Citadel was made of concrete and steel. Nonetheless, it shivered, as if from an earthquake. "That was from above," Sieglinde said. Her smile broadened as an elderly Soldier, one-eyed, and with a hook at the end of his right arm, silently presented himself. Wordlessly they agreed that *he* should distribute arms, while she, freed of that undemanding task, should find someone to fight.

Titus dashed down the hall. The ceiling speakers came to life again: "Personnel above Level H, move to the sound of fighting. Below Level H, hold your ground for the present." Sieglinde ran for a stairwell and bounded upward. Dagor followed her. He did not think even the swiftest man with no Sauron blood in his veins could have matched her speed; he had trouble himself. But a lot of the women and even the boys and girls paced her.

Gunfire rattled ahead and above—mostly assault rifles, but a few black-powder weapons, too. Carcharoth might have been crazy, but he hadn't been wrong. The Bandari and their nomad allies were trying to bugger the Citadel from behind. Carcharoth hadn't lived, either. Dagor knew he'd have to wait till later to sort out how he felt about that. Another older man whom he had tried to take as mentor (as father, part of him whispered), had died.

In the stairway, Titus' voice spoke: "The invaders are at Level L and moving down. Estimate fewer than three hundred. Contain by sealing entrances to Level K and Level N, then exterminate. Execute." He sounded ever so faintly annoyed, perhaps still regretting that he couldn't get back to fiddling with the computer now, as he'd planned.

Instead of halting at each turn in the corridor and firing a burst around the corner, Sieglinde leaped through horizontal to the floor, her body aimed the new direction. Had there been an enemy in sight she would have fired a burst as she approached the top of her arc. As she gathered herself with tiger swiftness from the floor another Soldier was repeating her maneuver at the next turn. It was as if they had practiced this all their lives—as indeed they had, in squads and in platoons. The net result was that the main mass could pelt down the corridor as fast as their legs could carry them—until they actually met opposition. Small price that one Sauron might die in the process of that discovery; they were, after all, in a hurry. All at once, Dagor understood why there weren't any long straightaways in the halls of the Citadel: the fields of fire they gave would be too good. In the event nobody had to make that blind leap into live fire; they came to a wall whose opening onto the perpendicular was already bullet-scarred.

"Here is our perimeter," Sieglinde said, as if she'd found a tunic she was looking for. Not bothering to see if anyone carried a periscope, or even a mirror, she peered round the corner, quick as a blink. Her instructors would *not* have been pleased with this exhibit of youthful impetuosity. "Good. The first arrivals already have barricades in place." Hunching low, she ran for whatever shelter she'd seen. Dagor gulped and followed.

Bullets whined. Behind him, he heard the wet smack of one striking flesh. He dove behind an overturned metal desk, ever so cautiously looked out. Near the far end of the hall was another barricade. From behind it came cries of "*Allahu Akbar!*" and "Barak!" Barak his cousin/nephew . . . Would they have shouted his name were he not already dead, dead at the hands—at the flame thrower—of Carcharoth? Dagor bit his lip. But with bullets flying all around, with those men trying their best to kill him, what could he do but shoot back, if he wanted to live himself? Tears streamed down his face. "Allah preserve me," he whispered, knowing that Allah would not, and squeezed off a burst.

"Hold!" The word rang in Chichek's ears.

She stared at the plainsfolk and Bandari boiling out of the passageway like bread dough with too much yeast.

Hundreds of them, as Titus had warned. But there were hundreds with her, too, and more hundreds on the way. She did not know how many assault rifles and other weapons the Inner Keep held in reserve. Not everyone rushing to the fight was armed—but a Sauron woman without a rifle, could she but get close, was deadly to a man of the cattle, and would soon bear his weapon.

Was that her father? Allah and the spirits, it was, grayer and older than when he'd sent her off to the Citadel, but unmistakably Gasim.

Her finger shook on the trigger of her assault rifle. She had a bead on him. If she fired, she would surely slay him. How could she live with herself afterwards? But if she did not fire, how to live at all? She didn't think the invaders would stop shooting just because she did. And there was Gimilzor in the middle of the mad crush, fighting like the Soldier he would become—if the Citadel lived. And what was she to say to Sharku if she failed to defend their home, and her son, and herself?

Time seemed to stretch very slow and fine, as if she were a Cyborg. How she wished Sharku were here! He'd set things right. Then, all at once, time collapsed back in on her. After what had to be less than half a heartbeat, she screamed and fired.

If she'd done what she intended, a neat, short burst would have stitched its way across Gasim's chest. But the barrel of the assault rifle wavered, too—and after the first round, the magazine went empty. All the same, her father reeled backward, clutching his shoulder.

Tears blinded her as she fumbled for another banana clip. By the time she managed to stuff it into the assault rifle, it was too late. The enemy was upon her and her comrades.

She pulled the trigger anyhow. But she was new to war with automatic weapons, and had forgotten to yank back on the charging handle to chamber the first round in the magazine. She didn't know what was wrong; all she knew was that the rifle didn't work. It had a bayonet on the end of it. She tried to stab the nearest invader she saw, a tall, rawboned Caucasoid fellow with a face as stern as a *mullah's*.

He was fast and strong—not like a Soldier, but fast and strong enough, and also agile enough to dodge her thrust. Then he grabbed the rifle by the barrel. His face twisted. The barrel had cooled, but was still hot enough to burn. It didn't keep him from wrestling the rifle out of her hands.

She threw herself at him, not to get the rifle back, but because, just past him, Gimilzor was fighting with—and beating—a man three times his size.

The invader grabbed her, held her back at arm's length while she tried to kick him in the crotch. Somebody screamed *"Afrit!"* and pointed at Gimilzor. Somebody else gave her son a sharp stroke to the side of the head with a rifle butt. He sagged and went limp.

Chichek screamed then. "Hush, there," the man holding her said. "If you're Gasim's daughter, you ought to be able to figure out you're on the wrong side."

She tried to kick him again, with no more luck than before. "Liar!" she shrieked. "Should I love you bandits? You've just destroyed my life!" As he stupidly looked in the direction of her gaze, she stamped on his foot. He half-stumbled; his breath hissed out in pain. She broke free, tried to rush to her fallen son.

Gasim got to Gimilzor first. He clutched his grandson to him as if the boy were a bandage to stanch the bleeding from the wound his daughter had given him. Using Gimilzor as a shield, he broke away and staggered toward one of the chambers that gave off the passage. Light streamed into the hall from the room and others along the corridor, making up for some of that which was lost when fluorescent tubes were shot to fragments: those rooms looked out on the rest of the Citadel. Chichek went into them only at urgent need. Looking down from such a height made her giddy.

Now she did not hesitate, or rather would not have. But the invader who had seized her was made of stern stuff.

Instead of losing himself in his hurt, he snaked out a long arm and hauled her back. "War is not a game," he told her. "I am called Smite-Sin, and in you, woman and Saurons' whore as you be, I smite sin and sinner both." He spun her around and hit her on the side of the jaw.

The world grayed. Chichek staggered back, the iron taste of blood filling her mouth. More by reflex than by any conscious will, she lurched toward the hard-faced man, her hands clawing into fists.

"God has granted you the sovereign virtue of a hard head," he said; she heard him as if from very far away. He went on, "but I smite sin wherever I find it, again and again until it is gone. Also, I have not the time to linger over you. So—rest." Blurrily, Chichek watched the door behind which her father had taken her son slam shut after him. Like all doors in the Citadel, it was steel, or something stronger than steel. Getting Gasim out of there would not be easy. And her son, her son . . . Just then, the man who called himself Smite-Sin hit her once more. Gray flared into white, then drowned in darkness.

The night lamp cast pale shadows. Deathmaster Sharku came awake silently, barely opening his eyes, not moving, not changing his breathing. Someone was in the room.

"Sir."

He came fully awake. He worked to keep any expression from his face as he examined the figure sitting on its heels beside his cot, hands resting on thighs, pale gray eyes fixed on his face. It was an apparition out of Old Sauron, ash-fair and blade-faced even as young as it was—it could hardly have been more than seven T-years old, if that. A ghost? A Hero returned?

Superstition died, however, in the face of the apparition's scent. Stench, rather. There was an effluvium of lye soap and iron-hard water, and under it a ripe reek of sewers.

"The cloaca's still open, then?" Sharku inquired.

The child betrayed no hint of surprise. Sharku had a name for him somewhere in the files. He was pure Soldier blood, or close, with the true Nordic coloring, pale as ice—remarkable in a gene pool that had been tending heavily toward olive skin, dark hair, and epicanthic folds. "Yes, sir," he said. "Mostly, sir. I had to come out for a while where there was a blockage, and there were cattle raiding everywhere. That's why I'm so late, sir."

That much respect would have indicated parody in most children, but if this was who Sharku thought he was, he probably thought he was being casual. "I'll excuse you when I've received all your data," Sharku said. And after a pause, "Cadet."

"Cadet Harad of the inner barracks," the boy said, managing to sound both brisk and embarrassed by his failure to name himself properly when first reporting. Then, with a touch of pride, "Beast barracks, sir. The Nazgul."

Of course, Sharku thought. This child would be assigned to the best of them all, the one reserved for Cyborgs and for officer material. He had been hoping to see Gimilzor assigned there in a T-year or two, when he was ready.

Thought of Gimilzor made his gut hurt with longing to be back there, with the war relegated to nonexistence and life returned to its old round of extracting tribute, breeding Soldiers, and ruling Haven according to the tenets of Old Sauron.

He made himself focus on this boy who looked so little like Gimilzor, but sat and spoke and moved so much like him—so much as all the best of Soldier blood did. "You come from the Citadel," he said.

Harad nodded. "You've got a very nice camp here, sir. But one of your sentries is asleep. I would have cut his throat, sir, but I thought that might be exceeding my authority. I did tie his bootlaces together for him."

Sharku eyed the boy warily. The boy was deservedly proud behind a carefully cultivated, emotionless mask. Sharku thought that he might be grinning, in back there. Cocky little bastard. Good, too, at sneaking and scouting, if he'd made it this far, through the barbarians, through

Nûrnen, and then past Soldier sentries. Sharku nodded solemnly. "Well done, Cadet. Your report?"

"Sir," said Harad promptly, snapping to attention without losing the knowing look. Cocky, Sharku thought. Yes indeed. And why not? He was the Breedmaster's grandson.

"There's an attack on the Inner Citadel, sir."

*Great shattered Homeworld.* "In what strength?"

"Unknown, sir. Battlemaster Carcharoth detected an attempt to enter the Inner Keep through the old postern tunnel. He went alone to intercept it, and left instructions for defense in case he failed. When he learned this, Breedmaster Titus sent me to find you and report. I left immediately." The boy stood at attention, waiting for questions or orders.

"Orderly," Sharku called.

"Sir," a sleepy voice answered.

"Send for tea. A lot of it. And send for Deputy Leader Mumak."

Mumak eyed the young Soldier sitting at attention on Sharku's bed, and frowned a question.

"Harad. Breedmaster Titus's grandson. He's just come from the Citadel."

"I think there are some sentries who'll need to explain themselves," Mumak said.

"Let it be till after. He has a message from the Breedmaster. The Inner Keep is under attack."

Mumak froze in the middle of whatever he'd been about to say. "What do we know?"

Sharku shook his head. "Damned little. Titus sent the boy to find us the instant he heard there was danger."

"What should we do?"

For once, right action was not immediately evident to Sharku. "Let's think about what we know. Carcharoth is crazy, but he's still a Soldier. If he thought there was a real danger to the Inner Keep he'd do something about it."

"Maybe," Mumak said. He was visibly trying to stay as

calm as Sharku seemed, but worry flickered across his face and in and out of his voice. "But he sent us off to the south end of the Valley after you warned him. Sharku, he's *really* crazy. You can't count on anything else."

"If we give up this position, the war will go on a lot longer. And we'll lose a thousand Soldiers bashing past those earthworks. Maybe more."

"And if the Inner Keep falls?"

"Then there is nothing left worth fighting for," Sharku said heavily.

Mumak would hear no more; he held up his hand. "Deathmaster, command me.

"Four hours," Sharku said. "Wait that long to see if word comes in from Carcharoth or Titus. The men need rest anyway. Let them sleep four hours. Then we march on the Citadel."

"Who stays behind?" Mumak asked.

"None. We cannot leave enough to hold, and when we assault those earthworks the more we have with us, the fewer casualties we'll take. We go with everything we have."

"Down!" Sieglinde shouted. In the middle of insane combat, anyone else would have screamed. A grenade, gray smoke trailing from its fuse, flew down the corridor and exploded with a deafening crash a few meters behind her position.

Dagor had already flattened himself out on the battered floor. He hadn't been far from flat, anyhow. If you showed any part of your body, you'd end up with a bullet through it. The commandos who'd found their way into the Citadel were the best the Seven could send against it. The amount of slaughter they'd worked was astonishing. Most of the casualties were unarmed women, of course, but even so, the invaders were not your typical cattle by a long shot.

A shard of pottery from the grenade dug into Dagor's leg. He swore and looked back at himself. Blood flowed, oozed . . . stopped. Sauron genes again. If something didn't kill him outright, he'd just keep going.

Two women fired from a doorway. Another woman, and a boy who couldn't have had more than eight T-years, emerged from another doorway, dashed down the hall, and into the next chamber further up. Gunfire greeted them there. The woman reeled back; a burst had stitched her across the chest. But, a moment later, the boy waved: another room cleared. Containment was over. Counterattack had begun.

Bending double against rifle fire, Dagor sprinted up to join the lad. He glanced into the room, just for a second. Three commandos there, all shot. One of them still moved a little. The boy saw that, too, and put a round through his head. "Sorry, sir," he said to Dagor, no doubt thinking he was a proper Soldier. "It's the recoil on this piece." He brandished an assault rifle that seemed almost as tall as he was. "I'm just too damned light to control it properly."

"You did fine," Dagor said. He could get that much Sauron-flavored Americ out without giving away his accent, which might have made the boy shoot him for a commando. Gaping like a fool wouldn't help, either, though the boy (maybe with some help from the woman) had just taken out three of the best warriors the cattle could produce, and seemed chagrined that he hadn't made three perfectly clean kills.

"This is ugly fighting," the boy said. "Corridor by corridor, room by room." He shook his head; he hadn't been drilled out of all his emotions yet. Then he smiled, showing a gap where he'd lost a baby tooth. "But we're getting the hang of it, I think."

"Good," Dagor answered faintly.

If he'd been in a mood for what the Bandari called *pilpul*, he would have reckoned the fight one of nature versus nurture. The commandos had been trained for war since they could crawl, and they'd been fighting since they weren't any older than the freckle-faced killer beside him. They were tough and hard and deadly. Their foes in the Citadel, aside from the few actual Soldiers, had far sketchier training—but they had their genetic heritage.

Little by little, nature was coming out on top.

"Fire and move," the boy said, perhaps to remind himself, perhaps to get Dagor off what the Saurons, for some reason, called the dime. He and, a moment later, Dagor, stuck their rifles out the doorway and fired down the corridor, making the commandos keep their heads down and giving more Sauron women and children a chance to move forward against the foe.

The tactic saved casualties. It didn't save all of them.

One of the women moving up took what had to be two or three rounds in the belly. She folded up, but then straightened and vaulted over the furniture the commandos had piled up as a barricade. More rifles snarled at her. Even so, she smashed one bearded fighter against the wall and broke another's neck with a kick before she went down.

"Come on!" the boy yelled, and ran out into the corridor looking for nomads to kill. The children were the worst, Dagor thought dazedly as he followed. They made small targets, they played at war as if it were a game, perhaps not understanding that when you died, you really died dead, and they were as strong as ordinary men and a lot quicker.

Dagor fired through the barricade. He must have hit something, for a man's head appeared over the top, face twisted with pain. The boy in front of him blew out the raider's brains, then leaped over the desks and sprayed bullets all around. Dagor leaped, too, fearing to let the child get the better of him and also fearing that, once he reached the commandos, he'd find some of them were men he knew. Oh, but betrayal was rotten meat. There on the floor lay Nazrullah, blood pooled all around him, the back of his head blown away. Dagor dashed for more cover; the commandos were still shooting from the next barricade further back toward the place where they'd made their entrance—the corridor stank of powder and the iron tang of spilled blood and the death-smell, like an overfull latrine. But even as he ran, he thought about the proud Afghan lord, gunned down by a lad half his size with a freckled face and a missing tooth. Who would have thought the forces of the Seven needed to be warned against children?

# ● CHAPTER EIGHTEEN

When Hammer-of-God Jackson woke, he expected to be face to face with his God.

Instead he gazed on slaughter through a pinkish haze. Vastly disappointed and in great pain he brought a hand up to rub at his eyes. He felt damp stickiness, and held his hand in front of his face. It was smeared with half-dry blood, beginning to go black.

"Wounded again." How many times was this? He couldn't recall.

His hand went to the side of his head. Cautiously, it traced the furrow that plowed a valley through his scalp just above his left ear. A couple of centimeters to the right and he would have been explaining to God exactly what needed doing, and why, and how.

He sat up. Concussion: just moving left him sick and weak. But he was used to making his body do what he wanted rather than what it wanted. He spat on his fingers and rubbed at his eyes, getting the blood out.

Vision cleared, at least somewhat, he looked down at himself. His tunic was soaked with blood, and so, certainly, was his face, though he couldn't see that. He had pulled away from a large puddle of gore that lay all around him. Some must have flowed from him, but by no means all. He sat up amidst a welter of dead men—Bandari, Turks, Mongols, Afghan *fedaykin*. They had joined together against the Citadel; now they were joined together in death.

Gunshots echoed from down a corridor: a short burst, a few single scattered rounds, another burst. It was not the sort of firing that betokened fierce combat—it sounded more like . . . hunting.

Yet another burst of rifle fire, and then, after it, a shout of triumph. It was a woman's voice, or possibly a child's. Sannie might have cried out like that, but Sannie was dead. Nearly all of the defenders had been women and children. They'd been hideously ready when the raiding party burst out; the attack had failed, had to have failed. The triumphant voice was that of an enemy.

After the wordless shout came words, in unmistakable Sauron-accented Americ: "Is that the last of them?"

"Not quite, but damn near," another woman answered. "A few of them are still holed up behind the armor doors. We don't know which ones have hostages and which ones don't, so we'll take those slow and easy. Aside from the hostages, they can't do us any harm, not where they are." Cold-blooded practicality: if she wasn't a veteran officer, she could have been.

"They've done enough to us, the bad-genes swine," the first woman answered. "These whole two top floors trashed to Hell and gone, fires down lower—I wouldn't have thought the cattle were capable of mischief on this scale."

"None of us would," the second woman, the underofficer type, said. "They've done us a favor, you know? We've gotten lazy these past years, just letting things drift along, being content as long as nothing went too bad. That needs setting to rights, you know, or how is the Race better than cattle, anyhow? Blasted worlds, this might be just the wake-up call we need."

Hammer-of-God wanted to pound his head against the floor. The jihad had failed. The Seven had intended this raid to take the queen—well, the queens—out of a nest of stingers. If this woman's sentiment was widely shared, all they'd managed to do was rile the stingers up. Christ suffering on the cross, bored, drifting Saurons were more than Haven could handle. *What would come from aroused, wrathful Saurons?*

He didn't want to think about that. Sleep tempted him, but he knew that if he slept he'd never get up again. If the Saurons had been through here once finishing off dead commandos, his head wound had fooled them into thinking he was already done for. But he couldn't count on that now that those around him had cooled. Those bastards could see heat—and if they saw he wasn't cold enough, they'd make sure he got that way.

The first woman said, "This is a black eye for the Council, that's certain."

"Bugger the Council," her companion answered. "That's just what these stinking cattle have done to us, too. We need somebody who knows how to do things, not just sit around and wait until things get done to us. I just hope there's somebody like that left to the Race who's a plausible candidate for high command. If there isn't—" She didn't go on, but the first woman could fill in the blank without trouble. So could Hammer-of-God.

He got to his feet. There lay his assault rifle, where he'd dropped it when he was hit. He picked it up. His blood painted the magazine and the barrel. What to do next? He wished his wits weren't so cloudy. He couldn't play dead. He might hole up here, pot a couple of Soldiers if they came through that passageway out there all unwary, take some of those cold blooded monsters with him. That was tempting. He didn't mind dying as a martyr, but it struck him as militarily wasteful. He couldn't assume any of the commandos had survived, which meant Chaya and Karl and the rest couldn't know what had happened here . . . until too late. Not unless someone told them.

Given the choice between dying here and going back to admit failure, dying looked pretty good. He shook his head, and regretted that, but the pain helped blow away illusions. Failures of intelligence killed campaigns, killed them deader than anything he could think of. This failure was his.

*My failure. And my obligation to make it right.*

More guilt, but that was a comfort too, because it told

him what he had to do. Painfully he sat again and pulled off his boots. The effort made his head spin again. He knotted their laces together and hung them round his neck, then painfully stood and slung the assault rifle over his shoulder. A trail of bloody footprints leading back into the tunnel would be as good a way to sign his own death sentence as any. Later, well inside, he'd put the boots back on. With the rough stone there and the climb down, he'd need them.

The thought of the trek back to the Pass terrified him more than facing the Sauron women and children. It would be so easy to turn and fire a burst, go out fighting—

*My failure. And my obligation to make it right.*

It was all that kept him going. And before the high country there would be the stone bridge. If he couldn't cross that—All at once, he was monstrously sleepy. He picked his way into the tunnel. Five times he heard voices, but he was lucky enough not to be found. *Luck, but good or bad luck?* Finally he was among the rocks. He found a niche and lay down, curled up with the assault rifle for a pillow, and fell asleep at once.

When he awoke, he felt better. No, actually he felt worse. All the pain the concussion had blurred was now there in full force. But he was used to making his body do what it had to, and his wits were clearer.

No way to gauge how long he'd slept, not in the unending darkness of the tunnel. He took little shuffling steps now, his right hand on the stone wall. Carcharoth's mound of stones had been on the right side of the tunnel. When he fetched up against that, he'd know he'd reached the bridge.

He kicked something in the dark. It wasn't the stones, not yet. Slowly, painfully, he bent and groped after what he'd stumbled upon. At last he found it: a torch, discarded by the commandos as they advanced toward what they thought would be victory. He still had a lighter. Could he get the torch going? He did, and almost wished he hadn't. Light drove nails of pain into his head, but now he could see well enough to move faster.

He found another torch before the first one went out,

and then another, and then another. One man didn't need nearly so many as three hundred had—no, two hundred or so, for only those who survived the encounter with Carcharoth had come this far. That should have been a warning. They just hadn't realized how good the Saurons were once roused—and now they'd gone and roused them all.

When he came to the bridge, he looked up through the rock toward the heavens. "Into Your hands I commend myself, Lord, as always," he said, and strode across. He reached the other side safe, and took that as a sign.

Walking was pain. As he trudged on, he distracted himself by thinking of what he should say. The leaders—those of them not consumed in fire and blood in the tunnel or in the Citadel—had to know the truth. But if he told that truth to the nomads—what then? He went round that question a dozen times in his battered mind, and always reached the same conclusion: the campaign against the Citadel would collapse. The fight through the pass toward the Sauron fortress had decimated them as it was, and they had been afraid of the Soldiers before that. One more bit of bad news and they would turn on those who had led them into this disaster.

"And we would deserve as much, too," he said, where there was no one to hear the admission. But some things, once started, could not be stopped, not without worse consequences. And so he would have to lie.

Another man might have reached that conclusion far sooner.

But Hammer-of-God, whatever else he was, had always been a truthtelling man. In a crazy way, that was an advantage now: when he lied, the plainsmen would believe him. Whether he would be able to live with himself afterwards was another question. "Military necessity," he muttered, there in the torchlit darkness. No doubt the Saurons had used the same comforting excuse to help themselves go to bed at night after they bombed Haven back most of the way to the Bronze Age. Maybe it had worked for them. He didn't think it would work for him.

It was easier going now, downhill, and he could go faster because he no longer cared what happened to him. He'd taken rations and a canteen from one of the dead commandos, and he couldn't even remember the man's name, an afghan warrior who'd come with him across the steppes and stood with him to the last, and now—

The canteen had been empty for hours, when, at last, hardly believing it, he saw light ahead, light that didn't come from the torch. He could hardly believe he'd dragged his battered body this far. If he could just make the descent, he could . . . tell his lies and damn himself to all eternity. Letting go and falling would be easier, but he had never believed in the easy way.

Down below, men saw him coming. They gathered at the base of the mountain. He could hear them calling up to him, though he was not such a fool as to look down. He was operating on the very dregs of his strength now, and knew it.

Then, at last, strong hands grabbed him, steadied him, helped him the last couple of meters to flat ground. "What news?" men cried in half a dozen languages. "What news?"

"Rejoice," he said. "We conquer." Then he collapsed.

Sieglinde led her troop of women and children and one half-educated wild Soldier against the latest of several barricades. The ones behind them were spattered with blood and brains, littered with the bodies of invaders and, here and there, a defender or two.

*Here,* she thought. *Right here. In the Citadel.* It was hideous. If she had been a Cyborg she would have erased it clean out of her database. But she was a Soldier woman, a mother of Soldiers. Her elder son was somewhere, sent away by the Breedmaster. *To safety? Or somewhere worse than this?* Her younger sons, one still nursing, one not quite old enough to begin training, were under guard and please-Diettinger-and-Althene safe in the room some of them called the Core, deep in the heart of the Keep.

This barricade was even more fiercely defended than the ones before it. It was a dead end, and the cattle apparently knew it. They'd boxed themselves in, with a door behind them, leading to a room with no other exit. It was mated Soldiers' quarters, empty since its male occupant marched to deal with rebellion in the Valley. The woman who had been assigned to him had elected to go back to the unassigned women's quarters. She was somewhere among the defenders, Sieglinde recalled—keeping the newer or more recalcitrant tribute women from breaking out and joining the attackers.

All this flashed through her mind as she zigzagged, ducked, and fired, zigzagged, ducked, and fired. The wild Soldier, whatever his name was, Damon, Iago, Dagor, ran at her back, clumsy but reasonably effective considering. When she hit the barricade, he was half a step behind her, yelling something in Turki. Silly. Yelling was inefficient.

It got him up and over the piled-up bedsteads, chairs, and table. He put a bullet in the eye of the last defender, just before Sieglinde blew the man's head off.

His death had been of some use, in the short run at least. The door at the end of the corridor was fast shut. Sieglinde was reasonably sure that it was bolted.

She halted so abruptly that Dagor nearly fell trying not to crash into her. The others—just a handful now, what with all the fighting they'd had to do to get this far—came up more neatly, forming a kind of rank in the passageway. Soltar, son of Sofia and Regiment Leader Lagduf had a white, wild look around the eyes, though he kept a Soldier's stern expression. He was too young for this, really. His friend, the one with the freckles, was limping but still grinning as he leaned on Soltar's shoulder.

"Cover me," she said abruptly. She did not waste time in looking to see if any of them obeyed, but sprang toward the locked and bolted door.

Doors in the Citadel were built to last, but even they were hardly proof against a Soldier woman who really, honestly needed to get this nonsense over with before

Rhun woke from his nap and started screaming for his supper. Her breasts were aching already.

She slung her assault rifle and walked briskly up to the door, and slid the panel beside it. The keypad was intact. She shook her head. Cattle. No sense at all, and no more technological couth than a pack of stobor. She punched the code that Breedmaster Titus had assigned for this cycle.

The door hesitated, clicked, sighed, and slid open. Her rifle was in her hands again, clip loaded. She sprang into the room.

And stopped cold.

There were still a few cattle left alive and standing. They'd used up all the furniture in building the barrier outside; the room was empty of anything that might have provided a shield.

Except for one thing. One person. A graying Mongol poised on the broad sill of a window that looked on the Citadel below, clasping him to his chest. His head lolled, but he was breathing.

Sieglinde did not need to search her mind for his name. "Gimilzor!" That was Soltar, coming up behind her, and stopping himself before he said anything more.

"Yes," said the Mongol in heavily accented Americ. "This Gim'zor. I Gasim, *khan* of Golden Tamerlane. Daughter, mine. Son, hers. Grandson, not mine." He spat past the child's head. "*Not* mine! *Not!*"

"Technically," said Sieglinde in fluent Turki—she had had to learn it, the Breedmaster insisted, and it did make matters easier with the cattle women—"and genetically, he is your grandson. You're being very silly. You're also being very reckless. It's quite a bit more than a hundred meters down."

The Mongol *khan* gaped at her. She had taken him aback. But not enough. He stooped suddenly and heaved. Gimilzor was solid Soldier stock on his father's side, stocky Mongol on his mother's, but he was only a child, and Gasim was as blockily strong as a muskylope bull. Gimilzor hung limply by the ankles from his grasp. Between his fragile skull and the rock of the lower Citadel was only air.

Even the invaders stood frozen. Sieglinde thought she saw horror in the faces of one or two—but fierce glee in too many, and avid anticipation. "Yes," said one of the raw-boned palehaired ones who looked a bit like Soldiers. "Yes, drop the spawn of Satan. Drop him now!"

The Mongol ignored him, ignored everything but the weight suspended from his stiffened arms, and the words he spoke. "The rest of these *fedaykin* will go free, or the child dies."

"You won't kill your own blood," said Sieglinde, not believing it.

Gimilzor was beginning to come to a little. His face was still waxy, his eyes sunk as if in bruises. He struggled weakly. His grandfather shook him, nearly sending them both toppling over into space. He stilled. Was it deeper unconsciousness? Or dawning awareness?

Gasim's lips drew back from his teeth. "This is no blood of mine. This is the spawn of Eblis. Let my people go, or he falls."

Sieglinde's eyes darted toward Gimilzor's face. Blood had rushed to it, purpling it. His eyes were open, but they were blank. His mouth was shut. His hands hung down, slack, seeming relaxed. She would have thought him dead, but she saw his chest heave. "He's hurt," she said. "You're making him worse. Put him down."

"Only if you let us go," Gasim said.

The decision was not as difficult as the Mongol might think. She had been counting invaders and reckoning that this must be the last of them—no more than a dozen all told. If they went out and told their tale of defeat, and let the horde of cattle know how strong even children of the Soldiers were, it would serve the Citadel well.

What slowed her down was fear that Gimilzor was so still, and his grandfather might think him already dead, and drop him simply to be rid of his weight.

He was stirring again, gasping for breath. Sieglinde

spoke quickly. "Yes, go. Go tell what happens to cattle when they come to us. Only give us the child. He's none of yours, you say. Let us have him."

Gasim's arms had begun to tremble. His strength had limits, it seemed, and he was finally forced to admit it. "I stay up here till I see my people go out the gate. That's how far I trust you, Sauron. That's how long you'll have to wait before this demon's spawn is safe."

"Very well," said Sieglinde. Her voice, she was pleased to note, was as serene as ever. "Soltar, escort these . . . people out. Make sure they don't try anything. Dagor, stay with me."

That command hadn't been needed. Dagor stood rooted in horror as he watched the drama unfolding. An outcast himself, now watching the ultimate, a *khan* casting out his own grandchild. "Accursed," Dagor muttered.

Soltar indicated the door. "This way," he said, full Soldierly contempt for these cattle evident in his voice and his posture. "Come."

All of them came, all but the *khan* standing in the tall window, dangling his grandson over empty space. People had gathered below—women, children, noncombatants of the outer Citadel.

"Who's there?" someone shouted from below.

Gasim shouted down at them, a great bull's roar. "Lay a hand on my people and he falls!"

A voice rang up from below. It was deep, and cold as only a Cyborg's voice could be. "We understand."

And very probably he did. Gasim had not been talking quietly, and Cyborg ears were keen. Very, very keen. "You have the word of the Cyborg Rank Bonn that your companions will be let out unharmed."

Sieglinde wondered if the Mongol noticed what the Cyborg had not said. Probably not. If he thought that far, which was not at all a sure thing, he would be figuring to see his people out, then use the child as a shield again, and let him go only after they had both passed the gate.

Then, of course, rifles on the walls would dispose of

him. Killing in combat was a right and proper thing. If Gimilzor had died in that fashion, it would have been unfortunate, but he was a Soldier. But there was no honor in dying as the cattle did.

Gasim stood unmoving in the window. The trembling in his arms had increased perceptibly. Sweat ran down his face. When Gasim looked out the window, Dagor moved closer.

Sieglinde moved carefully, gliding toward the room's second window. Gasim's narrow eyes slid toward her, but he said nothing. She looked down. The people below looked up, a massing of faces, some dark, some pale, but all washed with the same gray horror. Some of the women were weeping. Silly things. What good did tears ever do? *And Dagor has moved closer still. Whose side will that pathetic turncoat take? A pet, preserved by a Battlemaster gone mad. Whose side will he be on?*

She saw the little knot of invaders come out from the lower gate of the Keep and cross the courtyard, then disappear into the second ringwall of the fortress. After an endless, breathless time they reappeared in the outer courtyard, still safe, still intact, still shepherded by the tall figure and the small one.

They zagged from level to level and from gate to gate. They kept better order than most cattle would, though it was feeble enough by Soldier standards. Probably they thought themselves proud in their retreat, walking with heads as high as they could manage, shoulders back, the wounded limping as little as they might.

They were nearly to the outer battlements above the final gate. It was still shut, the sentries standing above, rifles trained on the invaders as they advanced.

Down in the Citadel as in the room high above it, tension ebbed. One of Sieglinde's Soldiers ventured to draw a breath.

But Sieglinde kept her eyes on Gasim. He had not moved. He still held Gimilzor over the edge, still glared at Soldiers round about him and Soldiers below, fierce with the consciousness of his shame. Defeat. Defeat and a Sauron grandson, and his daughter gone over to the enemy.

Sieglinde had heard the footsteps coming, stumbling, staggering, but grimly persistent. So: one of the bodies in the corridor had been alive after all.

Chichek's voice rang behind her, shrill with fury. "Father! Let him go! *He is your grandson!*"

"He is not," Gasim said.

"Father!"

And Dagor sprang. They had forgotten him, the pathetic wild Sauron, but Sauron he still was. His right hand took Gasim by the throat, and for a moment he held the weight of both the old man and the boy. Then his left hand darted through the window to seize Gimilzor's ankle.

"No!" Chichek shouted.

Dagor drew Gimilzor into the room with his left hand. With his right he hurled Gasim out, down to the stones below. Then, with exaggerated care, he knelt before Chichek and laid the injured boy in his mother's arms.

He looked up at Sieglinde. "At your command, my lady."

Sieglinde acknowledged him with a salute, as to a Soldier. Then she turned to the window. "Bonn. You may see to your duty. Sharku's heir is safe."

There was a moment's silence from below, then shouted orders. In the distance rifles cracked at Bonn's command. No commandos would escape now to tell the tale of Soldier wrath, and Soldier vengeance.

Sieglinde turned to the still kneeling Dagor. "Get up," she said. "Soldiers don't kneel to anyone."

The commandos were gone up the Citadel's cloaca. The army settled to wait. Rags and tatters had torn loose to raid in the Valley, but the bulk of it sat at Nûrnen. And waited.

Sigrid waited with them. This, for her, was a different kind of waiting than before, a state of constant, almost subliminal alertness. The moment, the very moment, she found an avenue of escape, she would take it. Even if it meant fighting her way through the rota of guards that had been doubled and trebled around her since the commandos left—subtly, they might think, hanging around, keeping weapons just within view, never letting her out of sight.

The Seven made no great secret of their strategy. That their Edenite General and their Judge's son were gone, no one tried to deny. Easy enough to surmise where, and why. Either they were too arrogant to care about spies, or they did not think that it mattered if the Citadel, or the Soldiers storming back up the Valley, knew what they planned: goose the Citadel from behind, storm it from the front.

And then what?

No one was talking about that. The nomads figured to loot, grab, and get out. The Bandari wanted their revenge. They did not particularly care what they had to do to get it.

There was a remote possibility that they would try to kill Sigrid before she could make a break for it. She doubted that anyone but Shulamit seriously entertained the notion. She was pregnant with a fan Reenan, bastard or not—and Bandari were fully as obsessed with good genes as Soldiers were, however much they might profess the opposite. They would keep her until she gave birth, if the war lasted that long. Then—who knew?

She was free to walk in Nûrnen, if she wished—always with plenty of company, but it never got in her way. She was not to attempt to signal the Citadel—she had been told that by every new guard who came on duty, till she could recite the lines with the actors—but she was allowed to look at the frown of the walls, and to note the continued quiet there. The place might have been deserted, for all the notice the inhabitants seemed to be taking of the army that had overrun Nûrnen.

Sigrid had a room in the house appropriated by her Bandari guardswomen, with a lock on the door that was strictly for appearance's sake, and everyone knew it. She was even allowed to see that her horses were looked after, though not to go near enough to touch. The she-dog was still with them, she noticed.

The he-dog was never farther from Sigrid than the length of a nomad's spear. He was an effective early-warning system, even without her enhanced senses.

Four T-days after the commandos went out, Sigrid was lying on her bed, which she had stripped of its too-soft mattress and replaced with a soldier's pallet. She was neither asleep nor pretending to be, although her guards were free to think either or both. The baby, having danced a hora on her spine, as the Bandari would say, had stopped to rest.

They were dancing in the streets, too, singing and shouting. The intensity of the uproar had increased in the past hour or two. Sigrid had deliberately not gone out to investigate. Her guards were distracted—when she looked out, the phalanx was visibly thinner. A little longer and there might be few enough of them left to be worth breaking through.

The dog barked once, sharply. Sigrid had already heard the footsteps. She did not trouble to rise or to greet Shulamit. The Bandari had her rifle in hand, but something—maybe the dog's low growl—kept her from jabbing Sigrid with it. She was grinning from ear to ear, doing a little joy-dance made neither more nor less graceful by the rifle she kept trained on her prisoner. "We've taken your bloody Citadel. We've thrown mud right in the Saurons' eyes—and it stuck."

Sigrid kept her mouth shut, her face calm. Cyborg training was worth that much. So was Soldier pride.

The Bandari bitch was not going to spare her a moment of it. "Hammer-of-God came back," she said, "and he said, 'Rejoice. We are victorious.' Our death commandos, the holy warriors of Yahweh have done the impossible. The Citadel is ours."

"And what condition," asked Sigrid coolly, "was Hammer-of-God in, that he should have been quoting *that* line at your people?"

Shulamit's eyes flickered. She kept her bold face, but her voice was a fraction softer. Just a fraction—but enough. "He's got a wound or two. Scratches."

"Scratches? How many others survived?"

"Don't know. Hammer's still out. But he'll be all right. His head is hard—Saurons put up a good fight." That was grudging, but it was honest respect. "We'll be watching you now, Sauron. You can't even take a piss without one of us there to count every drop."

"Oh?" asked Sigrid. "Is there something you don't want me to know?"

"There's something we don't want you to do—like get loose and ride to anybody's rescue."

"Which means," said Sigrid, "that there are still Soldiers left to be rescued. I thank you for that information."

Shulamit jerked as if she had been struck. Her face went crimson. She spat—missing Sigrid, whether deliberately or not—and got out.

# • CHAPTER NINETEEN

Sharku's enhanced night vision leapt from one line of bonfire-lit fortifications to the next, and to the one after that. There were ten thousand campfires blazing in the dark of truenight, and Sharku did not like what he saw. "Those works will be brutally expensive to assault," he said.

Most of the command group remained silent; the truth of the Deathmaster's remark was obvious.

"They hold us from the Citadel, therefore they must be overwhelmed," Regiment Leader Lagduf replied sententiously. "Besides, there are only cattle in them. How can they hope to stand against us?"

Lagduf had never quite accepted Sharku as his commander. He obeyed, and was even gaining respect for the new Deathmaster, but he never neglected an opportunity to show that he considered himself Sharku's equal.

And yet Sharku could make use of Lagduf, who could lead when told where to go. It always surprised Mumak how Sharku could make use of everyone's abilities, not only friends, but those who hated him. Lagduf, for instance, who really did believe the Soldiers were invincible, and who would not hesitate to lead his Regiment blindly into battle—but who could get the Soldiers to follow him there, too.

"They can't stand against us," Sharku said evenly. "But these barbarian warriors—even men of the cattle—in good defensive positions can hurt us, if we are foolish enough to let them. The Race needs all of us, Regiment Leader." He stared moodily at the fortifications. "Those are good positions, and we do have to come to them. They will hurt us."

A quadruple ring of earthworks lay around the Citadel and Nûrnen, one facing in, the other three outward. Each ring included a ditch too wide even for Soldiers to leap across, with pointed sticks and other unpleasantly sharp objects sticking up from the bottom. The dirt from the ditches had been piled into earth walls, topped with palisades similarly made from sharp and jagged things. The palisades were tall enough and thick enough to let men maneuver behind them without much danger of getting shot. Moving around in front of them was going to be something else again.

The Bandari had made their nomad pawns—and probably the survivors of Nûrnen—churn up incredible amounts of earth, even for a third of a million pairs of hands. Sharku felt irony again. Had the Soldiers forced such a project on their subjects, all Haven would have heard the tales of cruelty inside a cycle and a half.

"Very well, let's consider it as a tactical problem," Lagduf said.

Mumak ignored the irony in Lagduf's voice. "What shall we do, Deathmaster?"

Sharku came down from the camp wall and gathered the command group around a map laid out on a field desk. "We have no further word from the Citadel."

"And they cheer," Lagduf said. "Bonfires. Shouting." The bantering tone was gone now. "Deathmaster, our families—"

Sharku put his hand on Lagduf's shoulder. "We'll see to them. If there were really anything to fear, old Titus would have sent a dozen messengers, enough to be sure one got through. He didn't."

"But we don't know," Lagduf said.

"We don't know," Sharku agreed. "So we'll have to go find out." He looked down at the map. "We had at least nine thousand effectives as of nightfall, with more due to arrive before dawn. By then we should be on the move. Senior Battalion Leader Guthril, you will take your battalion and the Second Battalion of the Third Regiment to create a diversion. You will attack on a broad front and break through anywhere you find them weak to penetrate to the second ring. Get in there and dig in. We'll give the barbarians time to digest that, and while they're sending everything they've got to throw you back, I'll take First Regiment through their left flank toward what's left of Firebase One. Then we'll take the tunnel into the Citadel."

"What makes you think the tunnel is safe?" Lagduf demanded.

"Cadet Harad used it," Sharku said. "He closed every one of the barriers behind him on the way through."

"So how will you get through?"

"We'll send up rockets from Firebase One," Mumak said. "They'll see it's us, and come get us. Nothing to it."

"And my orders, Deathmaster?" Lagduf said.

"You hold here, and be ready to assist Guthril. Junior Regiment Leader Guthril, if you get out of this alive."

"Sir." Guthril grinned. "Nothing to it. Lagduf'll come get me. Won't you, Regiment Leader?"

"Senior Regiment Leader Lagduf," Sharku said absently.

Lagduf grunted. It was clear he wasn't happy with the plan, but he didn't have a better one. It was also clear that if he accepted promotion from Sharku, he could hardly question the Deathmaster's orders.

"The important thing is to stay alive," Sharku said. "Lagduf will open the route to bring you out, and when he does, you will come out. Instantly. This isn't a fight for glory, and it's not to kill cattle. We'll kill enough of them later. Right now, we've work to do at the Citadel. Any questions?"

There were none. Marln, the Senior Battalion Leader who was, now that Mumak was First Deputy, the nominal leader of First Regiment beamed, as did Guthril. Senior Assault Leader Snaga radiated silent disapproval. So did a few of the other commanders; but they would obey nonetheless. That sort of discipline had always been among the Soldiers' greatest advantages—the problem was, the cattle seemed to be picking it up as well.

"Fifty minutes," Mumak said. Except for the bonfires ahead the darkness was complete, but they could hear the sounds of battle far to their right, as Guthril's force penetrated the earthworks, and Lagduf laid down furious covering fire. If the cattle didn't think this was Sharku's entire force, it wasn't from lack of enthusiasm by the other three Regiments.

Sharku knew a strange sense of fatalism as he waited his turn to action. Three T-months before he'd have been cleaning his assault rifle and making sure he had extra magazines where he could get at them in a hurry. Now he was in command—

But he'd have to lead. He could send men to battle, but if he went with them, he'd have to lead, because he had to be the first into the Citadel. With the First, the loyalists who'd follow him anywhere—and against any enemy.

Enough. Soon he would be *doing*, too busy to think. Thinking led only to complication and confusion. The results of action, one way or another, would be clear.

The battle noises from the southeast grew louder. Guthril was attacking in the sector directly south of Nûrnen. The barbarians saw the threat to the city, and were sweeping down toward it to protect their loot. Sharku waited in silence. The longer he waited, the fewer enemies he'd have to fight through.

And that would still be too many.

The land ahead was not so well defended as was the direct route to Nûrnen, but even so there were three rings of earthworks between him and the place the cattle called Sauron Town: Firebase One from the first days the Race had come to Haven. Now they moved along the periphery of those earthworks, moving westward into the hills, the Soldiers loping in their ground-devouring trot. Scouts out ahead of the main body made sure no men of the cattle survived to get word back to the warriors within the fortifications.

They reached the point Sharku had chosen for the attack. The enemy lay just ahead.

Officers of the Race did not lead through fancy speeches, nor did the Soldiers require them. Everyone knew what was at stake. Deathmaster Sharku waved his hand. First Deputy Mumak said one quiet word—"Forward!"—and the assault parties loped into the firelight and leapt down into the trench in front of the first palisade.

"Listen to 'em scream," Mumak said. "We surprised 'em all right. Heh, like they think we're sendin' 'em all to that Hell they're so worried about."

"Maybe we are." Sharku waved the Soldiers on.

Nomads popped up onto the fire steps behind the parapet to blaze away at the Soldiers swarming toward them. Clouds of black-powder smoke swirled like hellish fog in the lurid orange light of the fires.

Out in the darkness, beyond the firelight, Soldiers fired at the men behind the earthwork, trying to sweep it clean so their fellows could advance. Plainsmen screamed and toppled, but every time one fell to the ground two seemed to take his place.

"Amazing," Mumak said. "Never knew there were this many on the whole planet. How'd they feed them all?"

"They're eating our crops now," Sharku said. "And they can't have left much behind them. If we drive them away from here they'll all starve."

"Serve 'em right. Except Breedmaster Titus will want some of 'em for stock."

"I think there are enough to go around," Sharku shouted as another band of nomads came over the ridge. Grimly they shot them down.

"Keep them moving, Mumak," Sharku ordered. "I expect most of them will keep on to Nûrnen when they hear the fighting here, but we can't count on all of them doing that."

"No, and the ones that do come here are going to be the

smart ones," Mumak said.

"Good thinking. Look at all this stuff. Nomads wouldn't build breastworks. That's the Bandari's doing—and that's who'll come to see what we're up to over here, you can be sure of that." He stopped to point. "Who's that chasing nomads? Mumak, get those Soldiers off that. Keep them moving but when the fur-hats break, let 'em run." He raised his voice. "Plenty of chances for slaughter later. On to the Citadel. Home!"

"Sharku!" someone shouted. There were more cheers.

The first wave of Soldiers had torn down sections of the wall and knocked down many of the spikes. Sharku sent them ahead and waited for the second group, setting them to smashing a wider breach in the palisades, then moved forward again.

More Soldiers were down already than he'd ever seen in one narrow place. Bullets chewed the dirt around his feet and hummed by nastily; the nomads were stuffing their muzzle-loaders with heavy buckshot, lethal at close range. And along with the lead came a whispering danger no less deadly for being all but silent: arrows lofted by archers from the second ring of works. The range was long even for the nomad's composite bows and the barrage had to be random, but when enough shafts fell, some struck home.

Soldiers clawed their way up the dirt of the wall to close with the defenders. Some were hit and fell back, some were hit and kept on, some gained the crest. Most of the nomads had muzzle-loaders; once they'd fired, they couldn't reload fast enough to shoot again with the enemy clambering up at them. Some reversed their muskets and swung them club-fashion. Others tried cold steel, and some tried to run. Generally, any of the three options netted the same result.

A flintlock went off almost in Sharku's face as he grabbed one of the sharpened stakes at the top of the palisade. The report nearly deafened him; the muzzle flash played havoc with his augmented vision—the world seemed to go up in hot yellow flame. The bullet *craaack*ed past his head, so close he felt the wind of its passage.

But it missed, and the stake meant to keep him at bay gave him a handhold with which to pull himself up to the top of the earthwork. He stuck his assault rifle over the edge, squeezed off a long unaimed burst. By the screams, by the stink of blood and shit and fear from the other side, the enemy had been packed tight enough for many of his bullets to find marks.

He tore aside the stake he'd been holding and the one next to it, flung himself down on the inner side of the palisade. Soldiers in camouflage uniforms were already dashing toward the second ring of fortification, trampling the felt-clad bodies—many still writhing—of the nomads who'd tried to hold them back.

The Soldiers had worked a fearful slaughter. Off to the right and south, the sounds of hard fighting were still intense. "Wonder how many Guthril's facing? Sure don't make much difference here!" Mumak shouted from behind him.

From right and left and from behind the second palisade, more gunfire raked them. And, as they crossed the open space between the two rings, lofted arrows dropped down on them once more. Sharku realized that the enemy had sited his lines so archers from the second could bear on the first, and those from the third on the second. *The Bandari again*, he thought: the nomads weren't sophisticated enough to create killing grounds like that.

"What do we do now, sir?" Assault Leader Vizgor shouted in battletongue.

"On to the Citadel. Home!"

More messengers found him. "Guthril's at the second ring. Pinned down there."

"As expected," Mumak said. "Deathmaster, do you get the feeling they expected us here?"

"It was the obvious route," Sharku said. "Forward."

"Not that we have any flipping choice. All right, you

heard the Deathmaster. Forward. Go home, Soldiers."

Sharku wondered if anyone heard his orders. Or cared. It wouldn't matter; the Soldiers knew the Citadel had been attacked. It had taken iron discipline to keep them from going off on their own. They wouldn't need any more orders, because there weren't any clever orders to give. This wasn't a battle that would be won by tactics, it was going to be sheer hard fighting.

"We're losing a lot," Mumak said.

"Estimate?"

"Ten percent already out of action."

"Forward."

"Aye, Deathmaster."

They were approaching the second ring when an arrow pierced Sharku between the index and middle fingers of his left hand. He growled something under his breath as he willed away the pain. He snapped off the point, yanked out the shaft, *willed* the bleeding to stop, then moved his fingers. They worked—no tendons cut, then. He could forget that wound.

The second's pause gave him time to examine the arrow. It was not the usual handmade nomad product; the shaft was lathe-turned, the head stamped out of some thin sheet metal, the fletching crude.

*The Bandari again.* They'd used the manufacturing facilities in Nûrnen to turn out hundreds of thousands of shafts, cheap and simple but good enough for this massed blind shooting.

*I'm getting sick of that thought,* he decided.

He ran toward the second ditch, firing as he went. Harad stayed close behind him, as he had throughout the battle. Soldiers were already making their way through it toward the next palisade. One fell as he watched, shot through the head. No enhancements could do anything for that.

The nomads were still delivering enfilading fire from either flank. There was nothing to be done about that but get through as fast as they could.

They were at the second ring. As they had at the outer ring, the Soldiers who made their way through the spiked obstacle course clawed up the earthwork behind it, many of them tumbling backward with wounds before they could gain the crest. Here and there, though, and then in growing numbers, they used their superior firepower to drive the howling warriors back. One by one, Sharku among them, they dropped down onto the far side.

In the cold and dark of truenight, lit only by lurid watchfires and the stroboscopic glare of muzzle flashes, the fighting had a hellish quality Sharku had never known before. Like all Soldiers, he scorned religion as fit but for women and cattle, but now he had a referent for a place where lost souls might end up: somewhere like this, with noise and terror and anguish and—again—arrows falling like snowflakes to pierce fighters who never knew they were there until too late.

"Not the education I wanted," he said as he advanced. "Harad."

"Deathmaster." The boy was just behind.

*Three paces right flank rear. Good lad.* "We learn from mistakes. You learn from mine."

"Sir."

"Report," Sharku shouted.

"Thirty percent casualties," Mumak said from behind him.

*Seventy percent left. Enough?* The answer appeared in front of his eyes like a prediction from the Threat Analysis Computer: *Enough. Just.* Guthril's force had drawn enough of them, and now Lagduf would be renewing the attack. Not even the Bandari would be able to keep the nomads disciplined if they thought they were losing all their loot.

The enemy could not be strong enough everywhere along their perimeter, despite the massive fortifications. Augmentation and superior weapons gave the Soldiers tremendous fire superiority at the point of contact; the enemy's response was huge, but diffuse. And now they were at the third ring.

Nomads were up on the fire steps behind the barricade, blasting away for all they were worth. He heard the excited keening of women from behind it, which puzzled him for a moment—then he realized that they must be loading for their men. With a chain of four or five behind him passing forward new muskets, each warrior could keep up an almost continuous fire. Some of them had Bandari rifles, too; the muzzle-loading abortions that had defended the first two rings would never have put so much lead in the air, even in relays.

"More than ever," Mumak shouted. "Bastards are sharp, I'll give 'em that!"

Sharku nodded. In the time that the Soldiers had taken to get this far, the enemy had brought in more of their best troops.

"Still more facing Guthril and Lagduf," Mumak said. "Last messenger said they were dug in good, though."

And at some point the Bandari would realize that Guthril wasn't moving on Nûrnen, and Lagduf was only going to aid Guthril—but by then it would be too late. They'd be through. One more ring . . .

The sound of a bullet hitting frontal bone and then drilling through and making brain into blood pudding is strange, hard and wet at the same time. A couple of meters to Sharku's left, a Section Leader dropped his assault rifle and tumbled bonelessly to the ground.

*Time to show them that the accursed Bandari aren't the only ones who can come up with surprises,* Sharku decided. A shame they had so few.

"Grenadiers to the front!" he called. Officers took up the call and relayed it.

All along the axis of the Soldiers' attack, troopers reached into cloth bandoliers.

"Forward. Make ready. Prepare to throw."

"Throw!"

Soldiers' arms could duplicate a spring-driven catapult. Two-pound bombs arched out with mechanical precision.

They burst over the inner lip of the enemy palisade with sullen *crack* sounds and a malignant whine of shrapnel; nails, stones, bits of broken ceramic. The volume of enemy fire fell off abruptly, amid a chorus of shrieks. Many of them were those of women, the loaders who'd been handing up muskets, or children scurrying about with bundles of arrows.

Sharku paused at the edge of the ditch to spray the earthwork with fire. He had only a couple of magazines left. Somehow that ammunition had to last until he'd fought through this ring and on to Firebase One. His lips skinned back from his teeth in a cliff lion's combat grin. *It will have to do.*

A handful of Soldiers, one by one, made their way to the top of the third barricade, dropped over. Battle-cries from the other side turned to screams of fear. A Soldier at close range was a cattle warrior's worst nightmare.

*Bring all the reserves from the base forward now?* he wondered. But if they failed, the Race failed with them, forever. And he had to act *now*. Hoarse shouts arose: "*Allahu Akbar!*" and another one, "*haBandaaaar!*" The enemy commanders wouldn't be deceived by the diversion forever. They would channel more and more of their reserves into this sector and turn it into a killing zone.

"Prepare to throw! Throw!"

Another volley of grenades, and another, arched out from the Sauron front line.

He wanted to kill them all, slowly. He wanted to kill Carcharoth, even more slowly. And none of that mattered, only cold calculation: Could the Soldiers take this position?

*We must.* "Forward. Runner."

"There's only me, sir," Harad shouted.

"Take the word to the reserves. All units, forward. Execute."

"Sir," Harad said. He darted away.

Another volley of grenades, then axes against the palisade stakes, through—

A ghastly sight met him beyond the third palisade. The enemy had packed in their men—and the women who loaded for them—shoulder to shoulder, trying to match the density of the attacker's firepower. Five thousand grenades had wreaked a slaughter beyond comprehension; the darkened surface of the ground was heaving with screaming, moaning wounded for a thousand-meter stretch of wall. The reddish light of the bonfires made the blood seem black; there was enough of it, and enough ripped bowel, to stun his Soldier's sense of smell. The light volcanic soil beneath his feet was turned to mud.

*This will be the most fertile ground on Haven for a generation,* he thought.

"Form column of companies. Forward!"

And on, past the dead and dying. A few Soldiers couldn't resist shooting the wounded. Sharku wondered if they were acting in spite or mercy. Some of both, probably. "Move!" he shouted, and behind him Mumak waved the rankers forward. "Go. Go. Go. Go!"

"Deathmaster."

It still seemed odd to be addressed by that title—the first Soldier ever promoted to it by his own Soldiers. He could worry about the Cyborgs' reaction when he got to the Citadel. He faced the messenger. "Report."

"From Battalion Leader Guthril; diversionary force requests permission to withdraw. Senior Regiment Leader Lagduf is in position to support."

"Permission granted. Mumak, fire the signal rockets."

"Right, Sharku."

"Battalion Leader Guthril reports thirty percent casualties," the messenger continued.

*A high price. Now to make it worth paying.* "Tell Regiment Leader Guthril the word is 'well done.'"

And then more noises, this time from ahead.

"What?"

Mumak pointed. A Scout Leader was running to them from the dark ahead. "The Citadel has seen us, Deathmaster. They're firing in support. The enemy is scattering."

Sharku took a deep breath. "Let's go home."

# • CHAPTER TWENTY

Chaya looked at the ineffectual fireplace. Her Soldier blood should have kept her warm even in the bitterly cold room, but she was old, her blood had thinned—and that was scarcely the worst symptom of her decline. She saw, every time she looked in Sigrid's eyes, a fellow Sauron's empathetic awareness of the onrushing systemic collapse that was the Sauron version of dying of old age. A far better version, except while you were in the midst of it, Chaya thought grayly.

Karl Haller rose from his place by Aisha and piled fuel onto the fire: furniture too badly broken in the wrack of Nûrnen to be worth carrying off. Aisha, vastly pregnant, had cold feet. An irony, that: Aisha's courage had never flagged, not even during the long hours of waiting.

*Damn you, Hammer*, Chaya thought. *Report*. The building she had made her command post was thick-walled. It drowned out the shooting, looting, stabbing, rape—enough to turn her blood cold if she let herself think about it. Instead, inside that deteriorating thing she still called her mind, she created a vault and crammed all the bloody deeds that stained her children's hands, and then she locked it with all her strength.

The deeds cried out to heaven. She could hear them.

She rose and walked to the nearest slit of window. From it she could see the great sullen bulk of the Atlas range. She was not weak-witted enough to believe she could follow the progress of the three hundred *fedaykin* through the bowels of the mountain, following a traitor and a track as old as Saurondom on Haven toward their goal: the Citadel itself.

It had worked for Iskandar. Yewehdammit, she had heard Ihsan and Kemal declare that over and over until she was glad to send Ihsan away and stop that superstitious babble of omens and kismet, mixed in with garbled history: their resolute optimism was driving her even madder. It had worked for Iskandar, yes. But it had also worked in the stories that were at the very heart of the legend that the Saurons had created about themselves. *Third time pays for all*. That was in those stories, too. The trick was bound to fail one of these days soon—please Yeweh, not this one. It was irrational to assume that the Sauron defenses would not be at their strongest this close to their heart. But this entire war was mad, and she the maddest thing in it. When Hammer-of-God Jackson, who was far from sane himself, had demanded to lead, what could she do but assent?

Throw her best general onto the table as a forfeit, and hope that the price of the game would not be more than not she, but the Bandari themselves, could bear.

What was frightening was that she was sure, in bone and blood, that the Sauron leaders were thinking in precisely the same way about the Soldiers they expended.

She nodded her head across the cold air between herself and the Atlas Mountains. The sky was at its reddest before truenight, the Cat's Eye's glare more baleful than ever. *Honor to you, my enemy*. Abruptly, the room wasn't just hot but unbearable. She was burning up, and sweat was running off her brow and down her sides in a way women spoke of but that she was at least a generation too old to suffer.

"Barak . . ."

"Chaya . . ."

"*Ama* . . ." Aisha was on her feet faster than any woman with a stomach that big had a right to be, Karl following her, not knowing which one of them he should play sheepdog to first.

She brought her hand up to wipe her face. Long, thin, hard fingers; a palm with the lifeline deeply etched—she had expected, for an instant to see skin peel away, leaving charred sinews and blackened bones. She would have cried out, deep in her throat, but she could not breathe, her lungs were burning up, and she reeled . . . she was falling, falling like a shooting star, half-dark, half-red, and wholly dying . . . *burning, burning, burning.*

Karl's hands raised, grabbing her upper arms, steering her toward the couch he had ordered dragged in here in case, heaven help us, his Aisha's back hurt. A brave man, Karl, if turning rash. Must come from sleeping with a Sauron: he thought he could manhandle them.

To show him what was what, she pulled away and let herself topple into the nearest chair. The impact hurt her hips: no flesh on those bones now.

Karl was at her again, this time with water. She sipped, ran the water about in her mouth, and just in time, did not spit. Odd, she thought to find actual ashes in her mouth, not just the taste.

"I'm not dead yet," she croaked. *No? And why not? What have you to live for now that Barak is dead?* "Barak is dead," she murmured. And heard gasps all around.

*"Baraka."*

Wouldn't you just know that Kemal would see this as divinely inspired prophecy? Yeweh or Allah had nothing to do with it. And the word he chose sounded unbearably like the name of her son. Lightning, who had been struck, and who had fallen, and who was now dead.

Some time during that agony of waiting, Chaya knew she had eaten and drunk. Her ears hurt from Karl's nagging. At one point, stung by anger that threatened to blow the locks off that vault in her mind, she had whirled round and glared at him, raising her hand to swat the little man aside.

He had held his ground, and she had seen herself reflected in his steady eyes: straggling, graying ropes of hair, skin adhering to the blades of cheekbones and shoulders, growing thinner by the hour under her grimy white leather robes. All she needed was feathers and a rattle. She had submitted to his rule. She had even dozed a little, as voices rose and fell at the great doors that Kemal shut firmly after each knock.

A great roar sounded from outside them, bringing her fully conscious from the half-sleep, half-wakefulness in which the vision of Barak, blackened yet burning, dropping down into a great gulf, bearing his enemy with him, was never far from her awareness.

Kemal opened the door a sliver. The shouting increased, a joyous, insensate screaming that finally resolved itself. "Praise him with great praise!"

"It's Hammer-of-God," Kemal raced toward Chaya. Incredulous joy glowed on his face, almost erasing the deep-etched lines of anxiety and grief. "They got through. Allah be praised, *we've taken the Citadel!*"

The doors burst open, and the room erupted with dancing, shouting, crying people. Here, a woman of the Tibetans and a man of the Golden Tamerlanes slapped each other on the back; there, one of *kumpanie Alon*, a devout lot, bound black straps on arms and brow and muttered aloud; and in the very center of the howling mob, was Ihsan, Kemal's *anda*, with one of Hammer-of-God Jackson's arms draped over his shoulders.

The Edenite did not so much limp as control his staggers. His eyes did not track, and his lank straw and gray hair—there was a gray blight in that straw these days, and it was getting worse—was matted with blood. "Concussion," Karl muttered as Chaya came to the same conclusion.

He pushed through the crowd with the stubbornness of a much younger man and the sheer arrogance of a *mediko*. "Do you idiots want to damn-well kill him? Stand back. Let the man breathe!" he was shouting as he extricated Hammer-of-God from their midst. "Get them the Hell out of here!" he ordered.

Ihsan and Kemal, shoulder to shoulder and obviously relieved to see each other again, began to harangue the crowd. Karl grabbed Hammer-of-God's arm and slung it about his own neck. The general slumped down about a foot, almost oversetting the much shorter *mediko*. Aisha thrust herself into the crowd just as Chaya stood.

*Ghazi*, women murmured; *khatun*, said their men; and they bowed their heads and withdrew, drawing the doors shut behind them.

Wobbling a little, *oom* Karl dragged Hammer-of-God over to the couch and let him drop. He knelt and started to hoist the man's legs onto it, too, but the Edenite fought against him, against the rest, the care that Karl urged upon him.

Wiser than he, for once, Aisha brought Hammer-of-God water. Ignoring the cup, he drank from the pitcher until water poured down over his blood-stiff tunic.

"Not too much," Aisha cautioned, and took the pitcher away when she decided he might hurt himself. That is, hurt himself worse. He dashed his hand across his mouth and matted mustache, then covered his eyes.

"The light hurts his eyes," explained Karl, even though they had not lit the torches yet and truenight drew on fast.

"That isn't it," said Chaya. She walked over to stand before her chief general. "So, *nu*, Hammer-of-God?"

The Edenite pushed himself away from the sparse comfort of the couch. He wavered, but forced himself as close to attention as he could. Slowly, he drew his sidearm with the other hand, and laid it gently on the nearest table, muzzle facing him.

"Barak is dead," said Chaya.

Hammer-of-God nodded, then ground his teeth, regretting any abrupt movement of his battered, blood-caked head. Before he could say anything, though, the tumultuous celebration outside was suddenly quenched, as if a bucket of ice water had been poured over a fire.

The door flew open. A scout came rushing in, a raw-boned Edenite named Go-Forward Haller, his long, lean face touched with the same righteous certainty that informed Hammer-of-God's features. "*Aluf!*" he cried to Jackson. "The bliddy Saurons outside the works—they're hitting back at us, and hitting hard, trying to force their way through."

"*You* can't go." Several people spoke the same words to Hammer-of-God.

"God of Battles," he groaned. "Too much all at once." He started to shake his head again, but checked himself. Then, from some inner reserve of strength left long after strength should have been gone, he forced yet one more rally. Chaya watched with mixed alarm and admiration the way he drew himself straight, forced his wits to work once more. "You're right, curse it—I can't go. I'm crack-brained; if I tried to give orders, I'd just get my men killed. Kemal, Ihsan, take command. Go-Forward, lead them to the assault."

Go-Forward Haller's eyes were eloquently dubious. If he'd shouted, "They're *hotnots,*" he couldn't have made his meaning plainer.

"They're of the Seven," Hammer-of-God said heavily. "Everyone will obey them. Anyone who doesn't—any-one—will answer to me. Now go!"

"Go we shall, from victory to victory," Ihsan declared, the light of battle gleaming in his eyes.

Kemal drew his sword. Firelight flashed red from the curved steel blade. "Lead us to the fighting!" he cried to Go-Forward. The Edenite, caught up in the excitement of the moment, and also conscious of the wrath of Jackson, saluted him as if he were of Bandari blood. The three men rushed out of the room.

Hammer-of-God limped to the door, closed it, and came slowly, slowly back. "Just as well they're gone," he muttered, swaying again on his feet. "Now I can tell you the truth. The truth—"

"Barak is dead," Chaya said again. Her vision had shown her that much. What more had passed, there in the heart of the Saurons' Citadel, that she had not seen?

"And I alone escaped to tell you," Hammer-of-God whispered. He shut his eyes. His face twisted.

"You *alone?*" Chaya cried. She heard the shriek of the

ice eagle in her voice as it stoops to strike down on its prey.
"You alone escaped, and you come here in triumph to tell
me—to tell the Seven—that you've *conquered?*"

A new thumping on the great doors. Chaya flashed a
forbidding glance at them, but Karl fan Haller had already
opened them, was allowing two officers, one an Edenite,
the other a plainsman, into the room.

"Cousin—"

"Great lord, victor of the Citadel . . ." Both voices
assailed Hammer-of-God. He flinched, then controlled
himself.

"Go ahead," he said.

"*Khan*, we've seen Saurons up by the ringwall. What do
we . . ."

"You kill them, man," Hammer-of-God snapped. "What
do you think you do with them? Take five times their
numbers and kill them. They're trying to watch the fight
out on our lines, and we need to deny them the
intelligence. I want to see their heads on pikes before I turn
in, and believe me, I could use a night's sleep about now.
Strong-Arm, you go with these wo . . . worthy men."

"Cousin, the Elder says . . ."

Hammer-of-God glared. "Tell the old . . . tell the
revered Elder to get his prayerbook out. I'll be there for
the memorial service. Now, will you hear the whole story
before our leaders do? Get out!"

His cousin saluted and turned smartly. The tribesman
showed some signs of wanting to linger, but the Edenite
grabbed him by the arm—fortunately with his right
hand—and propelled him from the room.

"My own kin," muttered Hammer-of-God. "God help
me, I pour out their blood like oil upon the waters, and
there is no peace . . ."

"Hammer," Chaya turned to put herself into his line of
sight, "*what happened?*"

He winced again and opened his blood-shot eyes.
Chaya had seen that look on horses that had escaped burning stables—or the wrack of Nûrnen town.

"The children," Hammer mumbled. "The young ones, the bright ones. They come to me, and I throw their lives onto the pyre. Sannie led the charge, said it was her right after Barak fell."

Aisha's hand flashed to her mouth to stifle a whimper.

"He . . . fell?" Chaya asked.

"I should have burned too!" Hammer cried out. "I kill them, I kill children, but they sent them out after us, their women and their children alone, after the burning stopped . . .

"It's all fire, I tell you," he leaned forward, eyes level with Chaya's and boring into them as if trying to convey what still danced before his eyes. "They lined up. My legs gave, and I couldn't march with them. Lined up and advanced over the bridge, and he shot fire at them. And they fell like moths into a torch, down into the pit of Hell. . . ."

Chaya brought up her hand and backhanded her general across the face. He staggered back, but the couch caught him at knee height, and he sat abruptly. He was back on his feet again in an instant, swaying.

"You turning the other cheek, Jackson?" she demanded. "*Who* shot fire at them?"

"Another cursed Cyborg," he muttered. "Called himself Carcharoth and Balrog, some hellish names like that. Barak . . . he's like you, Judge. Too strong for me. I tried to hold him back, hold him for you, but he pulled free. He took a direct hit, but he got hold of the Cyborg and dragged him down."

A fist seemed to squeeze Chaya's heart dry of all blood. In an instant, the pain would start again, she knew.

"Hellfire, I tell you," Hammer said. "Who knows what other sorts of fire they've saved till now to use against us? Nazrullah's *mujahedin* told those stories . . . oh Christ, he's gone, with his guts shot out. . . ."

"General, *report!*" ordered Chaya, an impatient snarl in her command voice, as if she had humored him long enough.

"We have to get them out. Get out as many as we can while not letting them know . . ."

Chaya looked Jackson up and down as if she had never seen him before.

"So you lied, did you? The man of faith, the incorruptible soldier—a lifetime of truth and you make up for it at the end with a lie. A Judas-sized lie."

"I send my own kin into the fire. They'll trust them, trust my kin."

"They'll trust *you*," said Aisha. "Because they, even those of the tribes, know that you kill, but you never, never lie." Abruptly, she launched herself at the Edenite. "Liar!"

"Aisha, Aisha," Karl tried to restrain her. "Remember our baby. You've been through so much already, put our child through so much. . . ."

She had Hammer-of-God's pistol in her hand, cocked. He drew himself up.

"Too easy by half, niece," Chaya said. "Don't you see? The lying bastard's *hoping* we'll kill him."

She turned to Hammer-of-God. "I've never seen you when you weren't trying to die in some damnfool way or another. And *kapetein* Mordekai stopped you every time. Yeweh, I'm glad the old man's dead, but I'll bet his soul is weeping tears of blood."

The general threw up a hand.

"That got to you, did it? Then you're really going to like what I'm going to say next. *Put down that gun, niece.*"

Karl whispered to Aisha.

"I'm telling you, Aisha, put it down. Hammer, you're the one who loaded this damn 'your honor' title onto me when I wanted to give it up. So you can bliddywell take the sentence I mete out: Hear your judgment. Hammer-of-God Jackson, you are goddamnedwell going to *live*. I sentence you to live and to keep your mouth shut about this until we can't hide it any longer because someone by Yeweh is going to have to get my children home!"

Aisha laid the gun down. She put her hand on her belly, and her eyes got the inward expression that meant that the child within was moving once again. A fine, strong baby. Yeweh—or Allah—grant that it lived.

"It's worse," the Edenite said. "What the Elders said when I was a boy . . . I called them old farts and laughed, but I'd have done better to plough my fields and go to church. Allow one lie, one sin—and you beget a host of them. A host . . ."

He looked up. "We're not going to be able to get all of our people out, you know. What's the safest way to get them out?"

"Safe?" Chaya shrugged an aching shoulder. "You wanted safe, you should have arranged to be born some-place beside Haven."

"Jokes," complained Hammer. "All these years. Didn't you learn any more strategy than that? God of battles. *Civilians.* God forgive us. We're not going to be able to get all of them out."

"Gives you a problem, doesn't it?" said Chaya. "Gives you a problem right now. Right now, you're the one the king delights to honor, or would be if we had a king. But when they hear you told a Citadel-sized lie, they'll hang you higher than Haman—if they let you die that fast. So you'll need another lie to save your miserable life, as I've ordered you to so you can get our people home. So the same answer does for both problems: we've got all those inconvenient tribes with a passion for violence."

"God," said Karl. "When the lie gets out, what's to stop them turning on Hammer-of-God? Hell, they'll turn on all the Bandari!"

Chaya shut her eyes on a vision straight from the Hell of Old Earth: an anthill, roiling in civil war, its creatures sav-aging each other until a jackboot stomped them into the dust.

"No, they won't . . ."

"I won't let them . . ."

She and Hammer-of-God spoke simultaneously. Their eyes met. The first time he'd seen her, after Heber's death and the downfall of Tallinn, she had brought Gorbag's head into The Pale. She remembered pale, inspired eyes, somewhat mad even then, fixed upon her as if she were some chooser of the slain. And his disappointment when, in the years after, she worshiped law, not violence. *I'm sorry, old man. I've made a sad mull of things. But I'm not as sorry as you are.* But after all these years, the wheel had come full circle.

"The tribes aren't going to turn on the Bandari," she said flatly. "They *need* us to get *any* of them out."

"Besides," said Hammer-of-God, "I have a plan. Sort of a plan. It came to me, praise to the God of Battles, on the way out of the Citadel. We can take a good many of our forces, Bandari forces, down into the maze of tunnels under the Citadel. If anybody asks us what we're up to, why, we're sending reinforcements to the lads in the Inner Keep. No way for the plainsmen to know the difference till . . . too late."

He was gaining strength again. God help us, he was wrapping himself in the myth, once more, of the invincible, ruthless General Hammer. Ruthless indeed: for him, Ruth's Day had always been a matter of accounting, of settling scores, rather than true forgiveness. And with the strength he gained, he turned again toward blood and darkness.

"You should have had the Sauron blood, my lad. Not me."

He grinned the tamerlane's grin that no one could watch for long. "And we're going to give the tribes a big present. Something they've wanted. All the glory they can chew, and a huge fight."

Chaya held up her hands as if fending off his words. One of her hands caught the leather of her tunic, and she tugged, tearing it. *Mourning again, old hag?*

"We'll send them against the Citadel," said The Hammer. "Give them the jihad they've prayed for. The forces of light arrayed against the forces of darkness. The last battle."

"You can't be serious, man," said Karl. "There's two

hundred thousand tribesmen out there, plus their flocks and families. You can't throw them all into the meatgrinder...."

"Can't I?" asked Hammer. "Won't be me who throws them. They'll charge at it, blessing our names." His mouth twisted. So did Chaya's, with the beginning of terrible knowledge. Inexorably, he went on. "And you know it. And however many of their people are killed there'll be that many fewer to turn on the Pale. And that many fewer mouths to feed on the trail home."

Hammer's eyes slid to met Chaya's, a terrible, silent complicity. "I think," she said, "that Hammer-of-God wants to start moving . . ." her throat closed and she wanted to retch on the term that had just come to her ". . . designated survivors out as soon as he can."

The Edenite general nodded. He was up and limping back and forth, the excitement of impending action keeping him from stillness no matter how he needed it.

"And what if the Saurons have another devil's weapon?" asked Aisha. "Worse than the one they used to kill Barak? Allah have mercy, you'll throw people against them anyhow?" Faster than Jackson could stop her, she snatched the pistol from his holster and aimed it at his head again.

"Go right ahead," said Hammer-of-God. "You'll be doing me a favor."

"Both of you put a sock in it!" Chaya snarled. "We must get the People out. Yes, and the tribes, too, as many as we can. I want your opinion on whom we can trust, and how much we can trust each of your choices with."

"My namesake Karl . . . young Karl, that is," mused Karl Haller. "But warn him not to tell Shuli. She talks too much, and she spends too much time around Sigrid. Let a word slip, and that one . . ."

"We have her word . . ." Chaya broke off. *Barak* had held her oath. Sigrid was quite likely to be a mistress of casuistry, as well as, temporarily, of young Karl, and to decide that with the man who held her oath dead, the oath was dissolved.

"I want Aisha out of here," said Karl. "Aisha and our child—yes, darling, I am telling you as your husband: *you will go*. If God is with us, I will ride beside you."

"Karl fan Reenan would be useful in a general charge," Hammer said. "He's young enough to see the glory of it, and strong enough that he might even survive. But I'd like to get him out. He's in direct line, and I was sent out here to protect him, remember . . ."

"I remember a whole lot, Jackson," said the Judge. "Including that I have sentenced you to live. I have every intention of getting Karl out alive. And getting you out alive too."

*I should lead myself,* Chaya thought. *I've killed Saurons before.* She remembered Gorbag's hateful weight on her, remembered the feel of the spike as it pierced his skull, remembered the beginning, the begetting, of Barak her beloved who now was dead, dead and burned, burned with the Sauron who called himself Balrog. The memories were mixed in a hellbrew of emotion that threatened to tear her head apart.

Another prophet, not her own but strong, strong, flashed through her head: *Muhammad led his own jihad.* And she remembered, she almost heard, Piet fan Reenan's dying cry—*We are the kings who die for the people!*

"Yewehdammit, *why?*" the big Edenite erupted. "My life's no good to me, I've dragged my honor through shit, and I've betrayed every single person who ever trusted me!"

Chaya grabbed him by the shoulders and stared into his face. He staggered, then caught himself, submitting to that raking gaze. Chaya could see the madwoman reflected in the eyes of a man driven nearly mad—or perhaps beyond the line once again—and she forced herself to breathe deeply. She might not get a chance to say what she must again, and she meant to be believed and to have her words remembered.

"Hammer-of-God Jackson, take my children home."

The old man shuddered, then nodded.

"So that The People live. We . . . you . . . will face death on the road home. You will face blood feuds that make any we have seen look like Ruth's Day by comparison. And Yeweh only knows what may wait for you at home: a *kapetein*, please God, and troops dug in in case the Saurons or the tribes get there before you do. There may be no end to your road, no Pale, but a *fourth* Diaspora. But you will lead, and you will obey. Me, for now. The *kapetein*, when you return with my people. You will tell him what you have told me, and you will do what he says. So that The People live. Is that understood?"

Hammer-of-God nodded.

"Can't hear you!" she snapped like a good drill officer.

"Yes, *aluf!*" Hammer-of-God cried.

"So tell me again, why are you doing this?"

"So that The People live," he replied. "Ma'am."

"Let me hear it from you, Hammer!" Chaya ordered. "Say it loud. Say it so those bastards in the Citadel can hear it."

Hammer-of-God snapped to attention. The grooves about his mouth looked as deep as the furrow across his scalp that had saved his life when the Saurons, the Sauron women and children, charged. Tears poured down them, and the deep bark of his voice broke into a sob, then was rigidly controlled. "Am Bandari Hai!" he shouted. "*Am Bandari Hai!*"

Hesitantly, Aisha asked, "If Hammer-of-God takes home those we can salvage, who leads the charge against the Citadel?"

Chaya's eyes blazed.

# • CHAPTER TWENTY-ONE

The Bandari bitch was gone. Sigrid lay exactly as she had lain throughout, although the baby was kicking again with increasing insistence.

She told herself she was perfectly calm. She knew that Cyborgs did not deal well with the impossible. It wasn't in their programming, and they had to rely on the human elements, which their training taught them to suppress, for strategies to handle the completely unexpected.

The Bandari believed the Inner Keep had fallen, and that they were about to take the Citadel. Was this possible? It was far more likely that the Bandari were deceived, but that was itself an unlikely event. Who would do that, and why? Certainly neither Battlemaster Carcharoth nor Breedmaster Titus had any reason to deceive them. Therefore it was either true, or Hammer-of-God was the deceiver. That didn't make sense either, but it was still more probable than the other alternatives.

Suppose they had the Inner Keep? Only three hundred had gone, and it was beyond reason that more than half survived. One hundred and fifty to dominate thousands of Soldier women and children? That too was impossible, madness for them to believe they could accomplish it at all, and as to bargaining with Carcharoth, or, presuming him dead, Bonn, or her father Titus, the most they could hope for would be safe passage out in exchange for doing no damage. Certainly the Citadel would never surrender to threats of damage from a hundred and fifty indifferently armed Bandari. Whatever the Bandari and their allied cattle thought, the Inner Keep was not the entire Citadel; the heart, true, but the Citadel was not an empty shell for the cattle to root and trample in.

It took only a few seconds to make this analysis. Now what were her choices?

And what would the First Rank of the Citadel—whoever that would be, and whoever spoke for him now—do in response to this insult to the pride of the Race? Cattle in the Inner Keep? Even close to the Inner Keep? That news would shake the Council to its roots. Council and every Soldier, and more to the point, the women. If the Soldiers couldn't protect the Inner Keep, then by Althene it was time something changed. . . .

The Citadel was full of Soldiers. Very well: not full troopers, but with veterans and their families from Firebase One there were still tens of thousands of Cadets, children, retired veterans, tribute maidens, and thousands of Breedmates of pure or nearly pure blood. Sauron women. Not as many as the Soldiers, but not helpless, not fully trained but what training was needed for Sauron women to defend their homes and their children? The haBandari death commandos would be lucky if they died early.

Not even with aid from the tribute maidens inside—an improbable assumption, since many like Chichek would stand by their men and their children—could the Keep have fallen easily. There was no Bandari in this Citadel to bring it down from within by her treachery. A mere three hundred cattle could not have done what Shulamit was claiming for them—and Shulamit had admitted that Barak was dead. Who else had fallen?

What if Hammer-of-God Jackson had lied? What if— she realized was thinking in circles. That could lead to overload, and she ruthlessly stopped the chain of thought. *Insufficient data.*

And what was so improbable that an enemy soldier would lie. Disinformation was an honorable tradition in warfare. Haven—and the Soldiers—knew it well. *Dol Guldur* itself had been born of a massive, strategic lie,

concealing the true face of Old Sauron and its last ship,
*Fomoria*, behind a popular fiction and an illusion of piracy.

Even so, the concept of false data had never sat easily in
a Cyborg brain—even a brain as anomalous as Sigrid's.
Logically she comprehended its use, saw its advantages,
and availed herself of it when she could, as in her failure to
reveal her true origins to the Seven and their horde. But
she had not lied outright, simply let assumptions take their
logical course.

What she looked at now had all the flavor and texture of
a tremendous lie. The circular thought patterns began
again, unbidden.

*What do I want to be true? That it's all lies, the Keep has
not fallen, Hammer-of-God, who never lies, is lying. Probabilities? Insufficient data.*

Voices. The guards. Each day a different group, so that
she could not bribe or persuade them. Today's lot were
Ironmen from the Vale of Charlemagne. Obviously they
thought she was asleep.

"Praise him with great praise." The voice was tinged
with irony. "The Bandari and their General once again take
all the credit for this great victory. One of the serving
wenches at Chaya's palace told me that Hammer-of-God is
gathering a host of the Bandari to reinforce their commandos. Only Bandari."

"Why were the Princes and *khans* not told of this?"
asked the second guard. "Did they not choose mostly
among their own ranks for the first attack?"

"Yes, yes," the other guards muttered.

"Konrad, you know Frederick of the Prince's House
Carls. Has he heard of this new attack?"

"Frederick the Braggart has said nary a word. If a sigh
passes through Konrad's lips, it must then pass as
Frederick's wind."

"The Bandari act falsely. They want the glory and loot of
the Satan's spawn for themselves. Look who they have left
to guard the Daemon Cyborg, who calls herself Sigrid.
Even the young Jewess, who looks like a man," he paused

to cross himself, "and blasphemes in all her talk and actions, has left."

"That one I would like to kill myself," said the third guard, pointing an ancient blunderbuss at Sigrid's prone torso.

Another guard asked, "Is your firestick filled with silver pebbles?"

"No, Konrad. What do you mean?"

"According to Patriarch Mikhael, only blessed weapons edged with silver can slay the Cyborgs. All others resist the flesh of the Unholy."

"Superstition, Konrad," the first guard said. "Our Bishop Otto tells us that the Unholy die like other men. Have you not seen enough of their dead on the journey through the Pass?"

"Yes, but those were not *Cyborgs.*" Konrad finished.

"True," the other guards muttered, some pausing to cross themselves, others taking firm hold of the pommels of their greatswords.

"Cyborgs of the Lidless Eye," one muttered.

"Have any of you seen with your own eye unliving Daemons?" Konrad asked.

"No," said the first guard. The rest shook their head in agreement. Sigrid, feigning sleep, could smell waves of fear in the air.

*There could be only one reason why the Bandari took only their own into the tunnels while sending their allies against the walls. The Keep was not taken, and the Bandari were preparing for something else. What? It seemed too much to hope they prepared for retreat, but what else could they be planning? And what will they do with prisoners if they flee in disgrace?*

At that moment, pregnant or not, she knew she could have leapt off her cot and subdued all six guards without a scratch, but it was clear that the Citadel was no longer in danger. *I am, but that's a different matter.* For the moment she had time. The mare and her foal would be worth some risk—to herself. Nothing would be worth a risk to the Citadel. She listened again.

"Prince Viktor of the White Host will not be pleased. Why do the Jew dogs get the best spoils? Who lost fifty lances of Ironmen in the courtyard of Sauron Town? Where were the Bandari and their accursed weapons then?"

"Nowhere. There is word that they consort with Satan's Tools at the outskirts of Nûrnen."

"By Christ's Blood, not *Machines?*"

"Yes, the very Tools that brought the Unholy to our world after the Star Empire left. They have used them! They make weapons with them."

"Weapons made with the tools of the devils will betray any of the Righteous who use them," one officer said flatly.

"My bishop says that the Star Lords fled because of Blasphemy in the Machine Shops of Castell City."

"May God protect us from infidels!"

The baby kicked, hard enough to let the guards see movement. One of them drew his sword.

Not time to act, then. Sigrid held herself still. There would come a time. Until then, she had enough of the cattle's blathering, as the conversation veered away then to the breeding habits of various Havenite fauna, each more exotic than the last. *They were almost as bad as Bandari.*

Nûrnen, having fallen to fire and sword, had fallen a second time—into chaos. And Chaya was falling with it. She stared into the fire in the old council room of the Nûrnen Mayor's Palace.

*A black rain was falling . . . a rain mixed with ash and cinders. Poison, her medikos said, glaring at her out of reddened eyes as they bandaged the melted eyes of tribesmen and Bandari with a terrible tenderness and supplies that were running low.*

"Chaya! Chaya . . . where are you?" asked old Karl, his voice fearful. He had always looked years younger than his age, but the final stages of Aisha's pregnancy were putting them back again.

She waved him back. Chaya was tired. It would be good

to sleep now, but she had to wait for word on the Sauron offensive against the ringwalls. The Soldiers had started a mighty attack near Nûrnen; they had expected that. But not so many. *More mother's sons lost to this futile jihad.* Her name would be cursed as long as there was human life on the Steppes. The Judge who lied. Well, she would face her Judgment. Let Yeweh take his measure.

She drew a shuddering breath that only the rags of her old control prevented from becoming a sob. Karl perched like a stobor over a rabbit hole. She had a job to do for now. She would do it.

The door slammed open. Go-Forward Haller, with a red slash running from his right eye to his jawbone, stumbled into the room. "The Saurons have broken through to Sauron Town!"

"I thought they attacked Nûrnen," Karl said.

"This was another force. To the West. Where is Hammer, where is my General?"

"He is taking reinforcements to the commandos in the Keep," answered Karl. One more lie that Chaya did not have to mouth.

"We need him. They're through the third earthworks. Those were meant to keep the bliddy bastards in, not out. I need more troops."

"If they are already through, why do you need more troops?" Karl demanded.

"Who knows when they will return? They didn't just break through, they destroyed the forces there! Terrible losses. Grenades, thousands of them. Warriors, women, children . . . dead, all dead. Rivers of blood."

Chaya could see the piles of dead bodies clogging the third earthworks. She started to rise, but her legs gave way. *Undo it, Chaya.* With what? Her Barak was dead. Hammer gone underground. All her best generals dead or gone. But she must try. Here and now at Nûrnen, with the final jihad yet to come.

"Gather the reserve, Go-Forward. Rally the nomads, but don't engage the Saurons again. If they want into the

Citadel, let them go there, but protect the people. What of the attack on Nûrnen?"

"They're already withdrawing back to their earthworks. I am following them closely, lest they strike at our weakness there, but if they strike from Sauron Town we are doomed! I am no general. Where is my general?"

"As of now. Go-Forward, you are General," Chaya said. "Go. Go and do what must be done to keep our children safe."

Go-Forward bowed. "Aye! *Am Bandar Hai!*" Then stumbled back out the door with his aides.

Chaya turned to Shulamit. "Go, girl. Bring Sigrid to me."

Shulamit for once did not argue. Her face was lined with worry. Worry for the Bandari or worry for Chaya, Chaya did not know. She was only glad the girl did as she bid. There were things that needed to be said. And who better to say them to than one of her own.

Sigrid had seen Chaya's workroom before—had sat in it more than once as observer and exhibition: the captive Sauron with her enormous pregnant belly. Guards were thick around it, but the one who sat at the table inside, huddled in blankets, might have been alone for all the notice she took of them.

The curtains of this room were tattered, the wood paneling scarred and soiled now. Many of the tribes had brought in their standards and banners. Smoke-and-bloodstained, the tattered greens and crimsons and golds added a kind of unfamiliar grandeur to the room

The Saurons had denied their subjects any such symbol that might serve as a rallying point. They were short on symbols themselves—the Lidless Eye, perhaps.

Chaya did not look up when Sigrid halted in front of her, with Shulamit's rifle trained on her and the guards in a ring, weapons cocked and trained on Sigrid. When the old woman spoke, it seemed to be to the air.

"He is dead," she said.

Grief too deep for tears. Anger too potent for outcry. Words as stark as the face she lifted, as bleak as the eyes that fixed on Sigrid.

"My son is dead," Chaya said.

There were whispers, mutters, a choked sob. Sigrid ignored them. She set herself at parade rest, which happened to be almost comfortable for a woman in the late stages of pregnancy. "You know this for a certainty?"

"I see it. You killed him, Sauron. You in your madness."

"You too are Sauron," Sigrid said.

The guards lurched inward. Chaya sprang to her feet, blanket flapping, and howled at them. "Away from us! *Away!*"

"But—" one of the guards began.

Chaya's arm swept out. The Bandari woman barely ducked in time. "Leave us alone! Go!"

"But she's a *Sauron!*" Shulamit yowled.

Chaya stopped cold. "So," she said, "am I."

That got rid of them. They hovered still, and they left the door open, keeping Sigrid in their gunsights, but unless one of them had hearing to match a Soldier's, they were in privacy, she and this woman who was almost a Soldier.

Sigrid said nothing. Nor, for a long while, did Chaya. She seemed to have lapsed again into apathy, swaying a little on her feet, staring at nothing.

Then she said, "I saw him die. He did battle over the abyss. The fire took him, and he fell. Fell long, fell burning. Fell dead."

Her voice fell into a chant with the last of it, and she rocked, but her face wore no expression at all. Nor did Sigrid's, now that there was no need to pretend lack of control. "Extrapolation," said Sigrid, "may appear to be truth, if the mind is sufficiently disordered."

Chaya's rocking stilled. "Oh, you are a cold one," she said.

"I am what you were bred to be."

Chaya laughed like the hunting call of a stobor. "No. I was never bred to *that* level."

"I too am a Breedmaster's mistake."

Sigrid was not bitter, not after so long, but Chaya caught the edge of it. How not? "Does he regret you? I never regretted my son. Even for the pain he cost me."

"You are fortunate," Sigrid said.

"If I were fortunate, my son would be alive. I sent him into the mountain's jaws. I knew what they would do to him. In a way, maybe, I bred him for it. We make our myths however we can."

"Maybe he'll come back alive," Sigrid said. Not to comfort her. No, not for that.

"Only in myths do the dead rise."

Her hand flashed out. Sigrid let it seize her, pull her down. Its strength was terrible, even knowing that her own was greater.

"Stay with me," the madwoman said. "Stay, until the towers fall."

That wouldn't happen, but Sigrid waited, because it was preferable to wait here, where she could see and hear and process data firsthand, than in her cramped cell. A guard brought a stool for her to sit on, with a look that made clear that he did it for the fan Reenan in her womb and not for the Sauron that she was.

Chaya returned to her chair and sat as if she had forgotten Sigrid. She rummaged in the papers in the basket beside her. Sometimes she rocked. Occasionally she muttered to herself, disjointed fragments, half lucid, half nonsense.

Tribesmen came and went. They chattered of victory in the Citadel, and each time they did Chaya winced.

Others came for orders, and Chaya sent them to positions along the perimeter. Cavalry here. Troops with ladders at another wall. A great battering ram they had assembled in Nûrnen, and was now brought forward in the truenight until it was less than a kilometer from Firebase Gate at the southeast corner of the Outer Citadel.

It became clear what Chaya planned. She was setting

them for an attack on the Citadel, a mad rush against the walls.

*Insane.* But the nomads believed that they would be aided by Bandari from within the Inner Keep. When they touched the walls the Bandari would attack.

*Could it be true?* Doubts assaulted her again. What if the Bandari were somehow in the Inner Keep without anyone knowing? Could there be enough of them to cause trouble at a critical moment?

And Chaya spoke with certainty, with a perception that might have seemed uncanny to one who did not understand the thought processes of a Soldier. "We will conquer," said the Judge. "It is written."

Yes, Sigrid thought, it was written: in the convolutions of a senile brain. Her own calculations yielded other results.

Karl Haller had been in and out of the room a dozen times. This time he came in hurriedly and bent over to speak to Chaya.

"Go with Karl Haller," Chaya said. "Faithful-in-the-Lord, accompany them. Watch closely."

"Go where, Chaya?"

"You know where you are needed. Go."

Gunfire crackled, somewhere not far enough away in Nûrnen. *Holdouts*, Aisha thought. The idea of living again in a house had felt good to her at first, a reminder of the security she'd known as a child—and never since then. Now—

More Saurons revealed themselves every hour, and getting rid of them was not only troublesome but expensive. They knew the alleys and rooftops of the slave city better than the nomads and Bandari who still battled to take complete possession of it . . . and they were *Saurons*, and thus harder than stobor to be rid of completely. Beside her, old Karl her beloved sighed. He'd noted the gunfire, too.

"I thought this stinking place would be ours once we won the big fight," he said. "But the little ones just never seem to end." He sounded tired, dispirited—no wonder, for he went on, "And what happened inside the Citadel— Yeweh! If Hammer-of-God hadn't got out, we might have gone on thinking we had a victory in there. If we'd tried acting on that assumption—" He clicked his tongue between his teeth. "I never have much liked Jackson, but he's got sand, no way around it."

"So many brave men dead," Aisha said, almost in a moan. So many men dead on account of Juchi, on account of her. More and more these days, as pyres flared and bodies were slung into ditches or unceremoniously left where they had fallen, she wondered if Haven wouldn't have been better off had Glorund killed her rather than the other way around. How much guilt could any one pair of shoulders carry?

"Women and children, too, even if they were Saurons, from what Jackson said," Karl answered. His mouth twisted. The idea of killing, especially killing children, didn't come easily to any *mediko*, much less to one whose wife was on the point of giving birth herself. The idea of children killing was even worse. He got the feeling Hammer-of-God wasn't telling everything he'd seen on that score, either. What he had said was quite horrifying enough.

"Allah and the spirits, I wish the *fedaykin* had won!" Aisha said. "The cursed Saurons—their kind"—*my kind, too*, her mind jeered at her—"has no future here without the Citadel." She laughed bitterly. "Cold-blooded, cold-hearted—Allah and the spirits, how I hate them," Aisha said. *How I hate myself.* "In one way, they're like you Bandari—"

"Us Bandari," Karl corrected her. She smiled, warmed by the insistence in his voice.

"Us Bandari," she conceded, and then grew serious once more. "They think in the long term—and may they roast in Eblis' fires for the longest term there is. Now that they've kept the Citadel, they'll be back to where they were before we started this, this"—she didn't know what

to call the great migration the Seven had set in motion—
"in two generations—less. But if they'd lost it, what would
they be? Nothing but a pack of *hotnots*—tougher than
most, yes, but not enough to matter."

"I wouldn't want them after *my* sheep any which way,
but I see what you're saying. How would they ever get off-
planet again, for instance, if they lost the Citadel?"

The *mediko* paused. Aisha's expression was distant,
abstracted; she was listening more to her body than to him.
"Are you all right, love?" he asked.

She didn't answer right away. Her hands were folded
over her belly. Still with that inward look, she finally said,
"Contraction."

Karl set his hand just above hers. Normally, she would
have smiled at his touch. Not now. She was concentrating
on what her womb was doing. He didn't blame her; it had
grown hard and tight. After a few seconds, though, the
contraction eased. He said, "It's probably nothing to think
twice about. Your body's been doing that for a while now,
every now and then, just as it should. It helps you get ready
for giving birth." He moved his hand down so it covered
hers. "And you tighten up there when we make love, if
you'll remember."

Now she did smile, but uncertainty lurked behind the
curve of her lips. She still felt her nomad upbringing; for Karl
to talk so casually about making love, and about what her
body did when they made love, seemed racy almost to the
point of obscenity. But now he needed to know what her
body was doing. She was old for a first pregnancy, and he was
not only her husband, but a *mediko*. She said, "I had another
contraction, about like that one, maybe ten minutes before,
and another one maybe ten minutes before that, and—"

He scowled, thinking hard. "You could be starting labor.
It would be early, Yeweh knows, but not that early. And the
bad news from the Citadel may have stressed you enough
to start things early." The news was worse than bad, especially to Aisha—Barak wasn't just her cousin, he was also,
in a forbidden way, her nephew—and he knew it.

He tried to fight worry with briskness. "How hard are the contractions? Can you walk in the middle of them?" He answered his own question. "Of course you can. Can you talk while they're at their peak?" Again he didn't bother to wait for her reply. "Yes, of course you can. So this may be the foothills of labor, but it's not the mountains. The mountains you'll know when you get to them, I promise."

"You know more about that than I do," Aisha said. That felt strange; the baby was growing inside her, after all, not inside Karl. But it was her first time through the process; everything kept coming as a surprise to her. She remembered how upset she'd been when her navel everted. He'd just laughed and promised her it would go back to normal once the baby came out. He'd helped scores, more likely hundreds, of women in childbed. That a man should put his hand to that—in both the figurative and literal senses of the word—struck her as bordering on the indecent, but she was glad for his experience.

He said, "Do I? With your heritage, who knows but that you could take labor pains that would send another woman screaming?"

"My heritage—" Aisha wanted to spit. Child of incest, exile, accursed . . . try as she would to be free of it, the past kept rising up to smite her.

"That's not what I meant," he said, so briskly she knew he was angry. He didn't care about her past. Absent all else, she could have loved him for that alone. With so much else there—Karl went on, "What I did mean was that I don't know *shaysse* about Sauron obstetrics."

"Who does, that isn't a Sauron?"

Karl rubbed his chin. "Now there's a thought. We've got that frozen-faced Sauron ice queen with us here. . . . If she hasn't given Shulamit the slip by now, we've got her, anyhow. She'll be going into labor somewhere before too long herself. If your blood does cause you any special problems in giving birth, she'll know about them."

He had a special look when he thought he'd been clever, a little smirk that announced he'd put one over on the world. Normally, it made Aisha feel she was invited to share the joke.

Now, though, it just gave her cold chills. "I don't want Sigrid anywhere near me."

"But if she's able to do something or know something that could keep you safe, keep the baby safe—" Karl spread his hands, expecting her to be reasonable. She had no intention of being reasonable. All her experience argued that the world was not a reasonable place, but one where things mostly dreadful happened for reasons mostly capricious. And if it came down to a choice between dying and having Sigrid or any other Sauron save her life, her considered opinion was that she'd rather die. She opened her mouth to tell Karl so, then stopped. The baby . . .

"You don't fight fair," she said.

"Bandari don't, as a general working rule," he answered. "We fight to win."

In that, the folk of the Pale were very much like their enemies who had ruled the Shangri-La Valley for so long. Aisha wondered if they'd brought it out in each other, or whether both Saurons and haBandari had had it from the beginning. The latter, unless she missed her guess. Before she could make the gibe, another contraction clenched in her belly. It felt much the same as the ones before had. After half a minute or so, it went away. She didn't say anything about it, but Karl noticed. "They're coming regularly," he remarked.

"So they are," she said. "Am I in labor?"

"If they lead directly to birth, you're in labor," he answered. "If they go on for a while and peter out, it's false labor. If they go on like this for a long time and then lead to birth, it's premonitory labor. If that's what's happening here, your labor itself is apt to be shorter than it would have been otherwise."

Aisha glared at him. "That's the longest, most complicated way of saying 'I don't know' I've ever heard."

"Then you've never listened to an Edenite preacher once he's all wound up and turned loose," Karl retorted. "I have. You don't know how lucky you are to have escaped that."

"Nice to think I've escaped something," Aisha said musingly. Another spatter of gunfire broke out, this time closer than before. She scowled. "We'll be a long time securing this town. There's more right here than goes into the whole of the Pale."

"More poisonous things, too," Karl said.

"I know," Aisha answered. "If only the Saurons had never come to Haven, this world would be—"

"—A freezing wasteland filled with hungry farmers and hungrier nomads, all of them hating their neighbors for having more than they do when nobody has anything much," Karl interrupted. "Haven was a world at war with itself from the start. The old records say it was planned that way, dumping Russians and Estonians into the Tallinn Valley, planting the New Soviet Men alongside the Sons of Liberty in the west end of the Shangri-La Valley. . . . If they fought among themselves, they wouldn't bother the central authorities. The Saurons just play the game they found when they got here."

He laughed without humor. "So do the Bandari."

Aisha stared at him. "But you've—" She tried again. "But we've—" Everything she'd seen on the trek across the northern steppe, everything she'd heard about what the nomads were doing as they spread joyfully through the Shangri-La Valley, came flooding forward in her mind, as if she were puking up accumulated horror. "We've had our revenge," she said at last.

"That we have," Karl said soberly. "That we have. And how many revenges are being planned against us now? Before, the Saurons slept, only pretended that the Lidless Eye was open. Now it is open in truth."

Another contraction gave Aisha the excuse not to answer. This one, she thought, was a little stronger than those that had gone before. How strong it was in comparison to the ones that would come later, she couldn't guess.

"Here." Karl pointed to the bed. "I don't want you going

anywhere until we're sure what these contractions are doing." She lay down on the bed. The mattress was filled with straw, just as it would have been back in Tallinn Town. It rustled as she lay down on it. Somehow she'd expected the Saurons to have something different, something better—though straw was good enough. The frame underneath creaked; it was of iron, not leather lashings as it would have been elsewhere on Haven. That was different, but she couldn't say with any assurance it was better. Contractions kept coming, every eight or ten minutes. They were stronger, more rhythmic than the ones Aisha had known before, but not strong enough to make her more than mildly uncomfortable. After a while, Karl said, "I'm going out. I may be gone for a little while. Here." He unbuckled the revolver he wore on his hip, held it out to her. "We haven't heard any shooting for a while, but you never can tell."

"Where are you going?" Aisha demanded. "If you're going anywhere far down these streets, you'll need to be armed more than I do."

"I'm going to get Sigrid," he said, and looked defiance at her. She could have stopped him. Even enormously pregnant as she was, she remained stronger and quicker than he. But she admired his *chutzpah*, a Bandari word for something the Bandari had in full measure: unmitigated gall. He was ignoring her wishes for the sake of her safety. His concern touched her enough to let him leave without an argument.

Soon, Aisha would almost have welcomed nearby gunfire as an anodyne for the boredom that rose in a choking cloud. Even the regular contractions of her uterus were not enough to take the edge off that boredom—she'd been having them for quite a while now, and had grown used to them. She tried to find a position where the baby didn't squash her guts against her backbone and where the stretched ligaments that supported her heavy womb didn't sting her at every breath.

Just when she did, just when she was on the point of

dozing off, the door to the house opened. Karl's pistol was in her hand before she consciously realized she'd reached for it: Sauron genes were formidable. Karl was not surprised to see the pistol aimed at him. If anything ever surprised Sigrid, she didn't show it. Without even waiting for the barrel to turn down toward the floor, she told Karl, "This woman is not a piece of glass. Sitting in one place like a hotsprings lichen will do little to advance matters; she needs to be up and moving."

Her Americ was so polished and precise, it made the way the Bandari used the language seem uncouth, as if their dialect belonged only in the mouths of small-time peddlers and grifters. Coupled with Sigrid's belly, which bulged almost as protuberantly as Aisha's, the effect of that elegant language should have been ludicrous. It wasn't. For one thing, Sigrid herself, big-bellied or no, had to be taken seriously. Even if you didn't recognize her for a Sauron—and Aisha hadn't, not right away—you knew she was a person to be reckoned with. For another, the last time Aisha had heard that particular dialect of Americ, it had been in the mouth of Glorund, the Sauron Cyborg Battlemaster. The association sent fear and alarm surging through Aisha. In the hormonal stew of labor, she needed much longer than usual to suppress them.

But Sigrid, no matter what else she might be, was at the moment all business. She beckoned to Aisha. "Get up and walk: around and around in circles inside here will have to do, no matter how dull it is."

Aisha got up and started walking. As Sigrid had said, it was anything but exciting. Karl rummaged in drawers, found a clean sheet, and tucked it on the bed, his hands deft as a tirewoman's. Aisha kept walking. It *was* boring, but being in motion felt good to her.

Karl turned to Sigrid and asked, "Are—women of the Soldiers—liable to vomit during labor like any others, or can I get her water to drink?"

Sigrid must have impressed him a great deal if he used the polite name for her kind rather than calling them *bliddyshayssvol Saurons* the way Bandari usually did.

She answered, "Ice chips would be better, but we've lost refrigeration here. Small sips of water should be tolerated well enough, though." Those chilly gray eyes, like lances made of ice, swung to pierce Aisha. "Small sips." It was an unmistakable order.

"I heard you." Aisha reacted to the arrogant authority in Sigrid's voice the way an unbroken horse would react to a man jumping onto its back: she tried to throw it off. But her gut warned her obeying the Sauron would be wiser. When Karl gave her a cup of water from his canteen she drank sparingly. Around and around and around. Contraction, contraction, contraction. Every so often, the baby would kick her. Of all the things Aisha had imagined labor to be, boring wasn't any of them. When she said that out loud, something sparked in Sigrid's eyes, then faded before Aisha was sure she'd seen it.

Karl laughed at her. "I told you, these are just the foothills," he said. "The mountains are a whole different place." Around and around and around. Something else that hadn't occurred to Aisha was that labor would literally be work. Her Sauron body was a supremely efficient working machine, but it needed fuel, and lots of it. "Can I have something to eat?" she asked.

"No," Karl and Sigrid said in the same breath. She glared at both of them, Sigrid for bringing the word out cold as frozen lump of meat, her husband for not rushing out to get her something she needed. It wasn't like him. Apologetically, he said, "Puking up water is bad enough. You puke up half-digested food and aspirate it into your lungs—" Karl shook his head.

"*Aspirate*? You know that term, do you?" Sigrid drew Karl into a discussion of medical terminology so arcane that Aisha wondered if they'd both stopped speaking Americ. Around and around and around. She'd been doing it for hours. The contractions were a little stronger, a little closer together, than they had been when they started, but not much. She wondered if they'd presently die away. What had Karl called that? False labor, that was it. By the sound of the talk he was having with Sigrid, that was bliddy well near the only comprehensible healing term *medikos* used. Aisha wondered how it had eeled into their jargon.

"You're not as ignorant as I would have supposed," Sigrid told Karl. By the way she said it, she meant it as high praise. If Allah came down to Haven to visit Sigrid—not a likely assumption—she would probably greet Him with something like, "I thought You would be taller."

*Snap!* Aisha heard it rather than felt it, almost as if a slingshot's flexion band had broken. She stopped in her tracks. All at once, the insides of her thighs were wet; her leather trousers clung clammily to her legs. At her feet, almost colorless fluid formed a puddle on the tile floor. Thinking she'd pissed herself, she tried to make the flow stop—and couldn't. That sent real terror through her. Though she was Sauron by birth only and not (Allah and the spirits be praised!) by training, she relied as much as any Soldier on her body's unquestioning obedience.

"What's wrong with me?" she cried, and winced as she listened to her own voice—it was, frankly, a frightened wail.

Karl's head whipped toward her. Though unenhanced, he was quick; he saw the spreading pool of fluid at once. "Your bag of waters has broken," he said. "Nothing to worry about—if anything, it's a good sign. Now your labor ought to get somewhere."

Hardly had he spoken when another contraction took Aisha. This one was different from those that had gone before. They had been distractions, annoyances. Just as she'd realized why labor had its name, now she suddenly understood why contractions were called labor pains. She wasn't as good as a trained Soldier at ignoring such things.

"Oh, my," she said as her womb at last unclenched.

"Yes, indeed. Now we're going as we should." Karl sounded almost indecently pleased with himself. Aisha felt like hitting him. What was this *we* he was talking about?

His body hadn't just tried to tie itself in a knot, with the promise of many more such knottings and unknottings till at last the child came forth. *Bliddy stinking miserable* man, *that's what he is,* she thought. Sigrid's nostrils flared. But for speech, that was the most motion her face had shown since she came into the flat.

"I don't quite like the way the amniotic fluid smells," she said. Karl came over to Aisha. He squatted to peer closely at the little pool on the floor.

"Color's good," he said. "If it were green, I'd be worried."

"What would that mean?" Aisha asked.

"That the baby had emptied its bowels while it was still inside you," he replied. "It's a sign something's wrong in there." He was *mediko* now, not husband; the answer was nothing to do with starting the child that kicked and wiggled even as another contraction started. She was glad of the pang, not just because it meant labor was progressing but also because it distracted her from what Karl had said. She had the measure of war's horrors, but the things *medikos* took for granted could still make her queasy. *You can take the woman off the steppe; taking the steppe out of the woman is harder,* she thought.

"Don't stand there in those soaked pants," Karl told her. "We'll get you on the bed again. This time, you won't get up without your baby. *Our* baby." He let the husband show through for two words. When he turned to Sigrid, though, he was all business once more. "Make sure that door is locked, will you? We can use privacy now."

Maybe he didn't notice, but Aisha saw that she didn't care for orders, even polite ones, from a man of the cattle. Nevertheless, she obeyed without a word. Graceful despite her massive pregnancy, she returned to her seat and waited for what would come.

Karl helped Aisha out of the trousers. She walked over to the bed despite the baby's best efforts to kick her in the sciatic nerve and make her fall. Once there, she hesitated for a moment before she lay down. Exposing herself before Sigrid was almost as disconcerting as doing so before a man would have been. Karl went over to the sink and washed his hands and forearms. He carried soap in his *mediko's* kit; the Bandari had learned filth helped breed illness. Beneath the impassivity Sigrid wore like armor, Aisha thought she detected approval. Maybe Karl sensed it, too: he put the bag by her and said, "If I need anything from here, you'll find it for me faster than I could, I expect."

"Very well," she said, nothing whatever in her voice. Aisha knew a moment of alarm at Sigrid's gaining access to the blades in the *mediko's* kit, then told herself she was being foolish. Sigrid didn't need knives; like any Sauron Soldier, she was her own best weapon. The bed was at an awkward height; Karl had to get down on his knees beside it.

"Now let's see what we have here," he murmured. "Open your legs for me, darling."

How many times he'd touched her there to excite her! Now his fingers probed for a different reason. He withdrew them at once when another contraction took her, then brought them back, exploring deeper.

"Dilated four centimeters already, easily," he said over his shoulder to Sigrid. "Almost halfway there. She'd done a lot of the work before her waters broke."

Sigrid nodded by way of reply. Her nostrils flared again, ever so slightly. Karl's fingers reached deeper still, looking for the baby's head. They didn't find it. Instead, they pierced something soft and slick inside Aisha. For an instant, the pain was a white-hot flare. Then the pieces of Sauron control she possessed brought it back to a level she could bear. But the bed was full of blood, streaming, spurting from her private parts.

"Yeweh!" Karl exclaimed.

"*Placenta previa*," Sigrid said in a voice like a machine's. "The placenta implanted down at the mouth of the womb instead of up behind the baby as it should have. Sometimes there is no clue until—discovery."

"I know what it is," Karl answered grimly. "I also know we're liable to lose her and the baby, too. She's not going to clot fast enough, either, Sauron genes or no. Sauron genes—" His head whipped back toward Aisha's. "Saurons have conscious control over their blood vessels. Can you clamp down on the ones that go to your placenta?"

"But if I do that, what happens to the baby?" Aisha hadn't known she held so much blood. Karl was plainly right; she wasn't clotting fast enough to stop, or even much slow, such a flood. She felt light-headed, woozy. But that thought stayed clear. "The baby will die, won't it?"

Karl let out a long, shuddering breath, as if he'd been kicked in the pit of the stomach and was trying to get his lungs to work again. At last, he said, "Yes."

"Then I won't. Haven't we had enough blood, all of us, all of Haven? Let my blood end it. I won't, I tell you." Aisha was having trouble remembering what she wouldn't, but she wouldn't. She was very sure of that.

"*Shaysse*," Karl muttered. "She's out of her head already."

"Is she?" the midwife asked, looking at him steadily.

He stared down at the blood-soaked bed for another long moment, then turned to Sigrid. "Give me a scalpel."

She reached into the bag and pulled out a sharp, gleaming lancet, but did not put it in Karl's hand. *Had she known what was going to happen?* Aisha wondered, while the cubicle started to go gray around her. *Had she guessed, or just smelled blood when my waters broke?* She had no answers.

Sigrid said, "In your present state, *mediko*, perhaps I would be the more appropriate one to—"

*Take revenge on the line of Juchi*, slid slowly through Aisha's mind. But before she could make the thought pass her lips, Karl screamed, "*Give me the fucking knife!*" Sigrid passed it to him and sat back in the chair to watch.

"I hope you can block some of the pain, darling," Karl said bleakly. "But whether you can or not, this has to be done, and done fast. Yeweh let me be fast enough." He slid the scalpel across Aisha's swollen belly, just above the top-most curls of her pubic hair.

Curiously, the red anguish of a wound was easier for Aisha to turn aside than her labor pains had been. But then, her body seemed very far away from the parts of her that mattered. She knew she was bleeding to death, but somehow it didn't much matter to her. Even with the pain of the incisions in the wall of her belly and then in her womb mostly blocked, she could feel the pressure of what Karl was doing inside her, almost as if he were punching her with thick, soft gloves.

The gray blur she was seeing got darker. She scarcely heard anything, not Karl's jumbled curses and prayers, not the ever-slowing tide of her own breathing. But two things did reach her, there at the very end—a shrill, tiny squall of pure indignation and then Sigrid's voice: "A girl."

Aisha thought Karl leaned over her, but the shadow that might have been his face was swallowed in all the other shadows. Nothing hurt.

# • CHAPTER TWENTY-TWO

*What is taking Sharku so long?* Regiment Leader Ufthak asked himself again. *Didn't I give Chief Assault Leader Valnar orders to have Sharku brought to me the minute he entered the Citadel?*

He, First Citizen Ansel Diettinger, and Gimli the Archivist had watched from Quilland's Tower as Sharku, Regiment Leader Sharku or whatever he called himself these days, had broken through the cattle's earthworks. Special night-vision goggles supplied by Techmaster Thorin from the Vaults had made the entire spectacle visible to even Gimli's failing sight. At least some good had come out of this debacle; he wondered what other delights were hidden in those Vaults? *I'll have to question this Techmaster myself.*

*By Sargun the Mad, what is taking Sharku so long?* Maybe someone had told him about his son? Gizmore or somesuch name, brained by his own grandfather and not expected to live. Would Sharku go to see the brat and its mother? Before coming to me? *I hope not: we don't have time for this nonsense. Sharku has formed an unSauron-like attachment to this cattle woman; maybe I should have thought more about that before putting my votes behind his candidacy.*

His Deputy had put it to words first, "Ufthak, do we really need this Sharku? He lacks discipline."

"Patience, Balzar. Sharku has many followers among the troopers and women, especially the tribute cattle. And he is popular with the veterans."

"Yes, Second Rank, thanks to *our* diligent work on his behalf. Without our efforts, who would have read his discourses? Or cared?" He frowned. "Perhaps we should have thrown our support behind Deathmaster Ghâsh?"

"Ghâsh may be the better tool. However, it was Sharku who predicted the Bandari connection to the Valley revolt." He smiled. "Providing *us* with the first opportunity to pry power out of Cyborg hands in several lifetimes. No, Balzar, like it or not, Sharku is the best counter to Cyborg Rank Bonn we have."

"We cannot forever prevent the Council from appointing a new Battlemaster to act for the First Citizen." He made that latter title a curse. "And it will be Bonn, I think. Who else is there?"

"Bonn did himself no favors by promising amnesty to the cattle in the Keep."

"And gained new popularity when he personally shot them down."

"All true. All the more reason why we must support Sharku. There is no other choice. Bonn and Sharku are here. Ghâsh is not. No, my friend, it is Sharku or Bonn, and we know which we prefer.

"Let Sharku be Battlemaster and send him to spend his seed subduing the cattle. In the Valley, then in the Steppes, and when that is finished he can be sent to the Pale. Work enough for several lifetimes."

"And we rule the Council and the Citadel in his name," Balzar finished. "And here he comes."

Mumak entered first with four rankers with Assault Leader battle tabs and well used weapons. They looked around the room, then the four rankers took places one in each corner. "Clear," Mumak called. "Now, Regiment Leader Ufthak, what's this about work that takes lifetimes?"

Sharku followed his Deputy flanked by two of the largest Soldiers Ufthak had ever seen. Identical twins at that. *Cult of personality*, an inner voice warned. "I was just telling Deputy Balzar that it would take several lifetimes to subdue all the wayward cattle both in the Valley and on the steppes."

"It won't take more than a T-year to break the Valley, not with fifty thousand nomads stirring up trouble. The Valley cattle will submit again to *our* authority soon enough. A task for Regiment Leader Guthril, I think."

The decisiveness in Sharku's voice and manner was new. So was his appearance. His face had changed, planed to slopes and angles, by too little sleep, not enough food, and too many weighty thoughts. Things seen that other men were blind to. His hair had turned steel gray, and he looked a decade older. And dangerous.

"We have been building support for your return," Ufthak said quickly. *Too late to support Bonn. Too late for anything. If you mount a tiger, you ride.* He looked significantly at Balzar. "You have our full support. For anything."

"So we have heard," Mumak answered. "But where are Deathmaster Sharku's supporters?"

"Deathmaster!" Balzar exclaimed. "The Council appointed Ghâsh Deathmaster. Is he not still alive?"

Ufthak looked sternly at his subordinate. *Fool. Land gators have more brain.*

"Deathmaster," Mumak said easily. "Yes, Ghâsh lives. But the Soldiers of the Citadel, not old men and Supply Techs, made Sharku Deathmaster. They raised him then, and can again." Mumak smiled ooldly. "The Soldiers proclaimed him Deathmaster after our great victory over the Klephti."

"Who are they?" Balzar asked.

Mumak looked at Sharku. "Deathmaster, I have just discovered the proper Ranker to tame the Valley. It is time he learned its geography and cattle."

Sharku nodded.

Regiment Leader Ufthak smiled uneasily. "Yes, it appears my Deputy has spent too much time at the Citadel." Balzar started to speak, but Ufthak silenced him with a glare. "You must understand, Deathmaster, matters at the Citadel have been in flux since the death of Battlemaster Carcharoth and the attack on the Inner Keep. Which I must tell you, has come to a most satisfactory conclusion, if you have not heard. All the strange cattle are dead."

"So I've heard. I must thank the Breedmaster for organizing such an effective defense."

Balzar barked in laughter. "A few hundred cattle, against fifteen thousand Sauron breedmates and children. What other outcome could there be?"

"Once again, you underestimate these Bandari barbarians. They are not the usual cattle. They are warriors. The casualties could have been in the thousands instead of the tens had they time to set their bombs."

"Cattle are cattle."

"A T-year in the field will widen your experience, Balzar," Mumak announced. "Deathmaster, why not let the Regiment Leader's Deputy mount a raid on the Pale? A quick training ground for rusty veterans."

"Rusty, my ass!" Balzar shouted. "As a Chief Assault Leader, five years ago I practically exterminated the Red Ch'in when their clan left the upper steppes."

"Yes, a valiant foe. How many effectives did they muster against your battalion; ten thousand, fifteen? We left that many dead in skirmishes against the New Soviet Men."

Balzar's face turned red and he was cut off in mid-shout by Regiment Leader Ufthak. "Silence, Deputy. You forget, these men have just returned from battle. A battle to save your hide. Show them the proper respect. These are our friends and allies."

"It is time to call a meeting of the Council," Sharku said. "There are many things that need to be addressed."

"It may take a T-day or two, maybe more. We no longer have a full roster. Some died as volunteers in Sauron Town and Nûrnen. Others on the Wall and in the Keep. I need to spread word of your victories. Gather support from the uncommitted."

Sharku rubbed his eyes. "Do what is necessary, but do it soon. I am low on patience. This is not a time for politics as usual."

"Yes, Deathmaster. I will call your supporters together and call a meeting. You can speak—"

"Mumak will speak for me. I need to talk to the Breedmaster, see my family, and get some sleep."

"You don't know?" Ufthak asked.

"What?"

Balzar turned his head to hid a grin. "Deathmaster, it is my sorrowful task to inform you that your son, Gimilzor, may be dead. He was seriously injured by one of the cattle during the attack on the Keep. A cattle who called himself Gism or—no matter. He was killed by Battlemaster Carcharoth's pet, a wild Sauron called Dagor."

"Dagor the son of Juchi? The one we brought to the Citadel?"

"Yes. You now have reason to be glad you brought him," Ufthak said. "He saved your son, Deathmaster. And was recognized as a Soldier by the Breedmaster's daughter. The pretty one, not the traitor Sigrid."

"Gasim," Mumak said.

Sharku nodded silently.

The others looked a question.

"Gasim is the boy's grandfather," Mumak said.

Sharku's face was as still as if set in ferro-concrete, like the walls of the Citadel. "I must speak to my wife." He turned and left, flanked by the giant twins.

"I understand, Deathmaster. You have our utmost sympathies," Ufthak said to his back.

"Yes, yes," Deputy Balzar added, no longer bothering to hide the smirk that twisted his lips.

Mumak waved, and the four Assault Leaders followed Sharku. Mumak waited until they left the room then turned to Balzar. "After this Bandari mess is over, I want to see you on the mats."

"And if I don't show?"

"Then I'll hunt you like the cow you are and take your head for my trophy room." Mumak spun and left the room.

"Fool," Ufthak hissed. "You've undone months and months of valuable work. You'll be lucky to keep enough rank to lead an expedition to the Pale. You may end up going as a Trooper. Now get out of my sight before I rip off your impetuous head myself!"

When Balzar left he carried with him the thousand yard stare of the shell shocked or soon-to-be-dead.

❖   ❖   ❖

Chaya waited impatiently. Her son was dead, and Aisha held all her hopes for a new generation. When? The birthing seemed to take an eternity.

But as she waited she sent her orders. This band to the east. Another to guard the great battering ram and take their place when the first crew tired. *Or died.*

Warriors came for orders. And the others, the shamans, mullahs, *imams*, priests, and bishops, even one who called himself *ayohtollah* came to hear of her visions. They demanded them, visions of victory, and she gave them what they wanted, stories of the glorious sack and ruin of the Citadel.

And in her heart nothing remained but ashes.

*The night is endless, and I am frightened.*

Frightened for more than herself, but that was reason enough in itself. She had not been eating, had not been exercising or resting properly; and, at her age, a Sauron was simply a machine clanking and rattling toward its inevitable breakdown, a disastrous breakdown if Sigrid's words were true. Breakdown, the word Sigrid used was *overload*, ruin of judgment, ruined thoughts, disaster for herself and all her children.

She was cold now: *my blood is too thin.* Or perhaps too thick. Does Sauron blood fail as other blood fails? Sigrid would know, but Sigrid was where she must be, at the birthing. Karl knew medicine, but he did not know Sauron women. Only one in this encampment would know how to save Aisha and her child. Of the reasons she had allowed Sigrid to live, that was the most important.

Since leaving the Pale, she had known what it was to prophesy, for her consciousness to split away from her waking self, to see farther, then return and walk alongside herself until she thought, surely, that she must already be mad. Yet no one else thought so—except for Sigrid.

She wished she had the Cyborg here again. Young as Sigrid was, her pale, terrible disapproval would suffice to force Chaya back into self-command. But Sigrid was tending Aisha, and Chaya was afraid.

The curse of blood lay on all her kin. For the first time, she allowed herself to remember: Karl had lost his first wife in childbirth. Her own mother by adoption had miscarried on the steppe and would have had no child at all had she not rescued Chaya from the culling-ground of Angband. Her son Barak's wife had all but died trying to give their house children. And Aisha—Chaya had talked to farmers about livestock, had read the *mediko*'s records, had listened to Sigrid enough to fear what could go wrong. Haven was harsh enough on those of unaugmented background. But the blood, the fearsome Sauron blood . . . even Badri had been part Sauron. What treacheries in the blood had been wrought for her daughters, Chaya and Aisha?

All night long, men and a few women had run in and out of the room, some of them shouting, some of them bearing blood scent. Why, then, did she shudder this time when the outcry rose outside the doors, when the doors slammed open, and the woman in her bloody robe ran in wailing?

Surely, not from surprise.

"Aisha, *khatun*, the *khatun* Aisha!"

Shulamit burst in a moment later.

"Shuli?" Chaya's eyes devoured the girl. "Is my sister still alive?"

"I don't *know!*" Shulamit blurted. "They—Karl and *her*—he screamed at her 'Give me the fucking knife!' And then there was blood all over . . ."

"Aisha's Sauron," Strong-Arm Jackson snapped. "She can control her own bleeding."

"She said she wouldn't!"

"It would kill the child," Chaya said. Aisha had defied Karl to give him this child—and to give Juchi a grandchild. Chaya well knew that she considered it worth her life.

The chair crashed onto the stone floor as Chaya rose.

"Take me to her. Now!"

Shulamit ran as fast as her sturdy legs could pump, but Chaya could run faster. It was torture restraining herself. Let her act as guide to whoever might follow.

"Where?" she threw at the struggling girl.

Shulamit pointed and gasped out sketchy directions. Robes flying, Chaya set herself to run as she had not run since she was a girl. The people whom she passed seemed scarcely to move, except to open their mouths in amazement as the prophet of the Seven raced by them, her long hair escaping her braids to whip at her face and shoulders, her robes flying out like wings. Past a house gutted by fire. Past a square, where five Turks sat devouring an entire sheep. Past a file of Bandari who didn't even have time to shout a greeting. Bandari on their way, praise Yeweh, home.

Like a Sauron—a Cyborg—Chaya tracked Aisha. First, using Shulamit's directions. And then, by sight, by sound, by visions. The reek of blood smelled much like her own. And the wails of the women outside the birthing room . . . Aisha's deathbed, she knew as soon as she heard the mourning chorus rise.

"Stay back!" That was Karl's voice, but almost unrecognizably hoarse. From what? Grief? Even mortal grief could not account for the undertones. Chaya smelled it in the air, under the blood. Fear.

"Stay out!" Sigrid's voice commanded from behind the pathetic barrier of a locked door. A kick slammed it open.

"Yeweh!" What need had they of the Red Room in the Citadel? They had a red room of their own here, blood on the bed, blood on the walls, blood all over everything but the pallor of Aisha's face. A glance confirmed it. Her niece and sister was quite, quite dead. She did not look peaceful, but astonished: they died hard, those of her blood.

Karl looked like a creature from the pits of Hell or the Barad-Dûr of Sauron legends—splashed with his wife's blood, his face ashen where it was not red-smeared, his eyes burning. Clutched against his heart, though, was the child whom Aisha died to bring to life. Naked, still, and still smeared with the fluids of her birth. A healthy girl.

"Keep the Cyborg away," he appealed to Chaya. "She wants to steal the child. I tell you, I will not permit my daughter to be used, I will not—" Karl produced a scalpel from somewhere—please Yeweh, not anywhere it could have harmed the child.

Chaya whirled on Sigrid. "Let him be!" Sigrid was standing nowhere near the child. She indicated that fact with the lift of a brow. She was as bloodied as Karl, Chaya noticed distantly, particularly about the hands. Her face had a peculiar, white, set look.

It looked disturbingly like Aisha's. If anything, Aisha's had more life in it.

"She'll tell you," Karl said rapidly. "Ask her, she'll tell you, the child has Sauron blood—Soldier blood—she'll think she's its logical guardian. Ask her, Chaya. Ask her!"

"It would," Chaya mused, "be logical . . ."

"Oh," said Sigrid with irony that was mildly surprising in a Sauron, even this Sauron, "it would be perfectly logical for me to try to steal this child out of its own father's hands, while he brandishes a scalpel. And logical beyond belief for me to seize it and take it—and where? I can hardly imagine that any of your people would be delighted to see *me* in possession of their prophetess-apparent."

Karl's face had gone livid. Chaya spoke quickly, harshly. "Let be, girl. Let be! Can't you see he's mad with grief?"

"I see," said Sigrid, "that the child needs a nurse, and the father will allow no one near it, even to wash it."

"She means to steal her," Karl said. "She won't have her. I won't let her."

"Then," said Sigrid with as much emotion as Chaya had ever heard in her—something like a wintry ghost of passion—"at least permit someone to look after her."

*Why*, thought Chaya, *the woman cared*. Maybe only for the genes the child carried—but they mattered to her. "Karl—" Chaya said.

Karl's eyes widened and moistened. "It was *placenta previa*," he told Chaya as if excusing himself. "My Aisha could have stopped the blood . . ."

"But the child would have died, and she had made her choice a long while ago? Was that it, Karl?" Chaya asked gently.

She had never seen him look so bad. Not after the worst massacre on the way to Nûrnen. Not even the nightmare hours after he returned to Strang and discovered that his first wife had died giving birth. That time, he blamed himself for abandoning her. This time, Chaya realized, he blamed himself for Aisha's death.

"You are acting like a fool," Sigrid said, cold again. "The child suffers while you indulge yourself, *mediko*."

"Her name is Ruth!" Karl shouted.

"Ruth bat Aisha, fan Haller," Chaya confirmed. She had thought Aisha might have wished to name the child after their mother; best, though, that that name disappear into time and that the girl be called Ruth after the Judge who had been a bridge between two nations.

"Ruth." Sigrid nodded. Her eyes had a look to them; processing the datum, Chaya realized. Entering it in the files.

The safety of an assault rifle clacked as it was snapped down to full automatic.

"Stop right there," Strong Arm Jackson said, long after both women froze. He leaned against the doorpost, his rifle trained on Sigrid's gravid belly. His nostrils flickered at the blood.

Sigrid looked from her belly to the rifle's barrel to the Edenite's face. Her eyes were full of cold laughter. "You, too, Edenite? But then, of you I might logically expect it. The Jackson paranoia is notable even among the Edenites."

Another rifle-clack. Shulamit, at Strong Arm's side. Her hands were careful on the rifle she had won from a Sauron, but her eyes blazed with eagerness.

Sigrid laughed outright. "Oh, now I have all my enemies in one place! A study in paranoia. And you thought," she said to Chaya, as if to the one reasonable person there, "that I could possibly be so stupid as to steal the child *now*?"

Sauron logic, and bitter as gall—bitter as poison. As bitter as the truth that Chaya made herself face. Sigrid's people valued children as highly as any people on Haven. Higher, maybe, since their Race and its continuance was so deeply ingrained in their psychology. Danger to a child might be the one thing a Sauron would avoid at any cost.

And if that was so . . .

"Let me through," she ordered. Chaya stalked past the others to Karl. "Will you let me hold my niece? She is blood of my blood, flesh of my flesh, and you and I are kin." She took up the child Ruth. She was very warm and did not fuss in Chaya's arms. Chaya stepped back out of the path of fire.

"Give me that blanket," she ordered. Chaya washed and swaddled Ruth. Her own tears mingled with the water of the child's first bath. A miracle of newness, this baby, this blend of all their bloods: Sauron, steppe, and Pale.

But she was more than a blend—she was herself. So little, so pretty. *If I were even five years younger, child, I would not yield you up.*

A miracle that the sight and touch of this child could make Chaya wish to go on living.

"Karl," she said, her voice tender. "Come see your daughter."

# • CHAPTER TWENTY-THREE

Chaya gave the baby to Karl. Then she took Sigrid's hand. "Come with me, girl." She led her out of the room.

"Not alone, Grandmother!" Karl shouted. "Not alone with the witch."

"I will go with them," Shulamit, said.

"You will not," Chaya said. "I will choose my own companions. You will stay and care for the child." She looked around the room. "Strong Arm will stay to guard you. I will be guarded by Praise-Be-Given. Now come."

She led the way out of the room of blood and toward the walls. Torches flashed in the truenight darkness, and fires still burned in the wreckage of what had been the most prosperous city on Haven. Around them they could feel rather than see an army assembling. A hundred languages washed around them, as plainsmen, tribes from the High Steppes, Christians in mail armor, Turkomen warriors with curved swords, all assembled for the final jihad against their hated enemy. For a moment Chaya believed: they had taken the greatest city of the world, and only one fortress remained . . .

Far ahead, high above in the distance, the lights of the Citadel blazed brighter than stars, brighter than any torches. "Witch lights," Praise-Be-Given said.

Sigrid snorted.

A dozen torchbearers came to walk with them, but Chaya sent them away after taking a torch from one and giving it to Sigrid. As she handed it to her, she said, "I know what you intend. Be calm, child."

After half an hour they reached the first wall. Chaya ordered a gate opened and they went through.

"There is danger," the gate captain said. A short man, a Ghurka mountaineer of the Central Atlas clans. He fingered his great curved knife. "Corporal Nural crept close to the enemy camp and heard talk that another battalion from the Valley has come."

Chaya swept her hand toward the Pass. "By the time they get here, we'll have the Citadel. Let them break their teeth against *our* walls. Let me through."

She led them on to the final gate, and turned to Praise-Be-Given. "Leave us."

"Judge—"

"I did not request your advice."

The Edenite stifled whatever he was about to say. "I'll be within call," he said. "With a rifle aimed at that one."

"You wanted to talk?" Sigrid asked.

"I want to bargain."

"I assumed as much. What do you offer and what do you want?"

"I offer your life."

"And my horses."

Chaya snorted. "You don't know what I want, yet you ask for more than I offer?"

"Of course, Judge. And I know what you want. You want a friendly voice within the Citadel. You want someone to prevent the doom that faces you and all your people."

*She speaks to me as an equal. Sauron to Sauron. They train them well, for she guesses what I know.* "You already have reason not to wish us all dead," Chaya said.

"I want the horses."

"You are mad."

"No, Judge, only logical. If I have my horses, I will have another reason not to wish all of you dead, and more influence in the Citadel as well. I may be the only one in the Citadel who doesn't want to exterminate you. You do understand that with all the best will in the world it will be impossible to stop—" She waved toward the lights of the Citadel. "You threatened what they hold dearest. Do you think they will ever forget? You're enough like us to know."

"You said 'they'."

"I did, didn't I? I grant that I find you interesting. The Race may need your genes. That you came this close to—harming us—is enough to show that not all the best breeding stock on this world lives in the Citadel. But I still want my horses."

"We may yet win," Chaya said.

Sigrid didn't answer.

"You will warn them of our attack."

"At first light even the tribute maidens can see the forces you've assembled in Nûrnen, and broken or no, the Threat Analysis Computer will know that you have no choice but to attack. The most junior Cadet knows that. You can't feed this horde much longer, and you can't take them home through the waste you've created. You must attack and you must win or you will starve; and the lowest rankers of the Citadel know that. No message I can carry will do them any good in this battle. Why must I tell you this? Has your Sauron blood become so thin you can't think straight?"

Chaya stood rooted for a long moment. "Praise-Be-Given," she called softly.

"Yes, Judge."

"I have an errand for you. I want you back here in an hour with—this woman's horses. And I don't want you to talk about it, not to anyone else, and not to me. Just go and get them!"

Praise-Be-Given handed Sigrid the bridle leads with a sour look. He wouldn't speak to Sigrid. "The dogs followed, Judge," he said. "I wouldn't kill them without orders." The Judge had forbidden him to speak of the horses, so this was his subtle disobedience. His look showed that he valued obedience over good sense, but not much.

Even so, Sigrid nodded her thanks. Dogs and horses seemed well, eager for exercise after their confinement. The two-T-year-old pawed the stony ground in impatience. Sigrid turned to Chaya. "We won't meet again."

"And I won't wish you well. Go, Cyborg."

Sigrid nodded and strode away at a brisk pace. The horses followed contentedly, the foal wobbling unsteadily behind its mother. Sigrid walked steadily, but the back of her neck tingled. Her life depended on the obedience of Praise-Be-Given, and she knew that it would take only a wave of Chaya's hand to end her life.

A line from a school poem came unbidden. *It was only by favor of mine, he cried, that you rode so long alive. . . .*

She was out of sight of the gates, over a low hill, when she heard bells ring in the towers behind her, not the rapid ringing of alarms, but long, slow tolling. The word must be out that Aisha was dead, another of the Seven fallen. Somewhere not too far off, people were firing into the air—not that that had not been a common occurrence since the city fell, but this had a more desperate sound, the concussions closer together and accompanied by shouts and cries.

She picked up speed. Her body felt like a watersack filled to the bursting point. She shut down the awareness. The child at least was quiet. It had dropped some time since. She was beginning to dilate. But she was not yet, not properly, in labor.

There would be time enough. She could control it to a sufficient extent, provided there were no undue delays. This brisk pace was more help than harm: the muscles needed good, steady exercise just before they went to work in earnest.

The wall behind her flashed with torches, but she had no need of light. This was the old road from Nûrnen to Firebase One, a road that the Breedmaster's daughters had traveled a hundred times in childhood. Ahead the road led through an orchard now hacked and burned and full of filth. Human filth lurked amid the rest, drunken flotsam, corpses, and a lone figure with a musket slung on its back, stripping the bodies.

Sigrid paused for a moment, then tied the horses to the

stump of a ruined peach tree. She crept up to the corpse robber. The snap of his breaking neck was oddly pleasant. She took his weapons as spoils of war. The musket was worthless but he had found a good pistol which she kept. Then she turned her back on Nûrnen and its tumult.

The way grew steeper. Sigrid's breath came steady, catching only when she had to haul the foal up the steepest slope.

She hurt all over. A lesser person would have whimpered in misery. The baby's weight dragged at her, and her body, preparing for labor, was slipping her usual degree of control. Processes that should have been automatic, such as breathing and the frequent, sudden urges to piss, became matters of conscious urgency. Besides that, she was in skirts, and hampered when she most needed not to be.

The horses at least were cooperative, and the dogs seemed to comprehend the need for both speed and silence. If her memory was correct—and it might not be, with as much as she had to contend with, challenging even a Cyborg's command of data—there was a high meadow up near the meeting place, with grass sufficient to maintain the horses until they could be collected. A similar place had accommodated them in Cliff Lion Springs, and for similar reasons.

One last steep climb, if memory served—was this what it was like to go senile, this groping at data that should have been there for the asking, this darkening of eye and mind as the body asserted its own imperative demands? She did not remember that she had been so discommoded when her daughter Signy was born, but she had not been climbing mountains then, or fighting a war.

One last climb, no tax on her when she was in condition, grueling now; and yes, there was the level space, the hollow in the mountain's side, paved with rough grass and stones. The grass was half brown with winter, half green with the rains that had been falling off and on through the past few cycles. Sigrid slipped halters and leads and hid them under a stone. The horses went right to the grass. The foal, turned loose, executed a single precise caracole and dived for its mother's teat.

The she-dog understood her duty. She took station on a rock, panting, and with an eye out for a convenient spot of dinner. The he-dog, as always, came to Sigrid's heel.

Her treasure was as safe as it could be. Now, thought Sigrid, for the Citadel.

There were ways into the Citadel other than the route the commandos had taken. There were many such boltholes and escape routes, all of them closer and easier of access than the one called the Cloaca. That one had been built by cattle in an insufficiently paranoiac age. The tunnel Sigrid hunted for was cattle-built on this end, but Soldiers had finished it by turning the adit of a mine into a secret access to their stronghold. In later years it had become a resort of adventurous Soldier children. Sigrid had known it as such, and, like the rest of her agemates, called it Goblin Rock in reference to the outcropping that overshadowed it, of peculiar shape and commanding size. She had had combat exercises there, as all the young Cadets did.

She was certain that the cattle had not discovered it, and nearly certain that its entrance was undamaged by either war or weather. Past the abandoned mineshaft that was its disguise, it should be as solid as it had been when Soldiers carved it out of the rock.

She clambered up the final slope and out onto a brief level. There was the rock with its hunched and looming shape and its gaping mouth. There was the mineshaft's opening within the maw, a black and lightless oblong.

The wind was blowing. Sigrid had barely noticed it— one seldom did, on Haven; it was a constant, like the thin air and the creeping cold. But suddenly it had become the loudest sound in the world: a thin moaning sound as it played around the mineshaft, rustling in the dry grass, hissing over the talus slope.

Sigrid stole through the pitch dark, every sense alert to

what might lie ahead. Then a strange scent, and a restless sound. Someone was sitting in front of the adit, perched on a pile of stones.

Sigrid barely paused, barely hesitated. The he-dog ran ahead of her, but did not bark. He seemed to recognize the scent, although he could not have encountered that precise member of Sigrid's race and personal bloodline before.

"Harad," she said, calm even to coldness.

"Sigrid," said her sister's son, equal calm, equally cold. "Cyborg. I was waiting for you."

"For me?" Sigrid inquired. "Or for some one of the cattle both clever enough and fool enough to try this way into the Citadel?"

"Well," said Harad, his mask of Soldier sternness slipping. "We've got guards on all the boltholes now, in case any more cattle come trampling in. I asked for this one. I thought—I postulated that you might come this way, if you were anywhere near, and if you were going to make a break for it."

"Is it known then?" asked Sigrid. "Do they know where I've been?"

"Breedmaster knows," Harad answered her. "The TAC tells him."

She considered that. Yes, the TAC would know, if there were any way at all for it to gather the data. "Titus is in command in the Inner Keep?"

"You know that Battlemaster Carcharoth is dead?"

"I know that the cattle claim to have killed him," Sigrid said. "And that they claim to have taken the Inner Keep."

"A few came alive past the Battlemaster," Harad said. "He never came out of the tunnels. By then I had been sent to warn the field army. I am told that the Cadets and their mothers had good hunting for a while before they killed all the wild cattle." He paused, and a new note came into his voice. "I reported to the new Deathmaster, and I followed him through the battle as his aide! I am a Soldier now."

"A *new* Deathmaster. Tell me."

"Deathmaster Sharku! Not a Cyborg, but—Aunt Sigrid, he is a Soldier like the old heroes. Like Deathmaster Quilland, or—"

"Or?"

"Or like First Soldier Diettinger, even."

"A rare one indeed, then," Sigrid said.

"Well—but he is a good Soldier. I was just behind him in the battle to Firebase One."

"Where is your officer?"

"At the old guard room inside the tunnel."

"Take me to him. He can send another to watch this portal, and I need you to take me into the Citadel. I'll have errands for some of his Soldiers, too."

Harad nodded. "It is bad, down below?"

"I must report to the Breedmaster."

He stiffened at the implied rebuke, but he was Soldier to the bone. He saluted her crisply. "As you will, Cyborg."

Sigrid returned the salute as if he had been an adult Soldier. She did not compliment him. That would have been redundant. Nor, for the same reason, did she bid him follow.

He fell in behind her in the guard's position. Together, without need of lamp or torch, since they had the light of their own bodies, they walked into the mineshaft.

Shulamit sat cooped up in a stone box of a room, no more window to it than a prison cell, and rocked the cradle with her foot. It was a rich cradle, with plenty of carving and enough gilt to support a family in the Pale for a T-year. One of the *sayerets* had brought it with a bliddy lot of tears and a mumbled something-or-other. Another one had brought nappies for the baby, somebody else a linen shirt, somebody else again a pile of blankets and, much more to the point, a sleepy-eyed cow of a woman with big wet splotches on her blouse. Lost her brat, Shulamit figured, and had milk enough for armies.

Maybe even enough for Ruth, with her Sauron blood.

Shulamit leaned over the cradle. Ruth was asleep. New-borns slept, she was tolerably certain, pretty much nonstop, except when they ate, which was every couple of minutes. The nurse snored on a cot in the next room, ready at the first peep out of the baby to amble in and pop a tit in the waiting mouth.

Surreptitiously, even though there was no one to see, Shulamit rubbed a breast under her shirt. Still there, still dry, and not likely to change, either, till she bred her own brat.

Meanwhile, she was *tantie* and mother-surrogate to this one. "And damn Karl Haller to lower Hell for dumping it on me," she growled, but very quietly so as not to wake the baby. "Why *me* of all the women in the army? He could've picked worse, but damned if I know how."

Ruth had nothing to say to that. Shulamit went back to rocking her. She screwed up her face in her sleep. Shulamit stiffened, but she didn't wake up, or start yelling for another installment of dinner.

"By the Three, they're ugly at that age, aren't they?"

Shulamit started out of her chair. She must have dozed off. No other way Karl fan Reenan could have gotten in on those big feet of his, gotten as far as the cradle and loomed right down over it, poking in with a finger near as big around as the baby's wrist. "Hey!" Shulamit snapped. "Don't wake her up."

Too late. The baby had a healthy set of lungs, and a lot of practice already in expanding them to their full capacity.

Before Shulamit could make a move, Karl scooped the baby up—Yeweh, he knew not to let the head flop, or that was dumb luck—and started rocking her. And she shut up, just like that. Let Shulamit lay a hand on her and she just howled the louder. Let her nurse take her and all she did was yell till the tit was stuffed in her mouth. Five seconds in Karl bloody fan Reenan's hands and she was purring like a kitten.

"You're going to make a wonderful father," Shulamit said sourly.

She could tell when he was blushing, though it wasn't easy, especially in lamplight. It didn't make her feel as much better as she'd thought it would. He ducked his head and stared hard at the baby he was holding, and muttered something that might have been, "Go ahead. Rub it in."

She didn't, for some reason, want to. Seeing him with that baby, considering what she was and all, made Shulamit feel strange. Sauron baby—but *hers*. Aisha's and Old Karl's. And Aisha dead in her birthing chamber. The funeral must be any time now; she had to go and take the baby. Her throat hurt. Her eyes were blurry.

Karl said something. It took a while to register. "The Cyborg is gone."

"What do you mean, gone?" Shulamit asked when she got the words to make sense. "Not—not—" Damn. Say the word. "Not dead?" That was her right and hers alone. She'd promised to kill Sigrid and no one was going to rob her of the pleasure.

"Nobody knows," Karl said. His voice was as thick as Shulamit's felt. He brushed Ruth's head with a finger, ruffling the silky dark hair. She just blinked at him. Couldn't focus yet, Shulamit was fairly sure—though with Saurons you never knew. "There was some sort of meeting the way there always is, and word came in that Aisha was dead, and you went out, didn't you?"

Shulamit nodded, impatient. "I had to take care of the baby. Karl put her in my arms. Chaya went off with that—that thing—and I brought the baby here."

"So you went out, and Strong Arm Jackson had to go somewhere. Chaya brought her back, although the Judge doesn't remember when. . . . Karl said this would happen, especially with all the troubles. She's getting worse, and nothing anyone can do about it

"When everyone came back, Sigrid wasn't there. Nobody can find her. Somebody says they saw her walking through Nûrnen, maybe alone, maybe with one other person. Go-Forward says a gate captain saw her at the walls with Chaya, but people see the Judge everywhere.

Another person, a deserter caught by the Watch, claims he saw a woman-with-child robbing the dead. Since he was caught doing the same, he's not exactly a reliable witness. An old woman scavenging outside Sauron Town says she saw someone walking with some horses—"

"That's got to be her. Unless her horses are still at the stable."

"No, they're gone." Karl shook his head. "The old woman—she's a Nûrnenite so she claims she's part Sauron, of course, they all do . . . or did . . . and can see in the dark—says she was walking into Sauron Town, toward the Citadel."

"She's gone! Blast it! Where's Chaya?"

"She's at the hall, building support for the jihad," Karl said.

"Has Chaya organized a search?"

"The Judge's not concerned. Says we have enough to do as it is. I think she—understands—Sigrid."

"Nonsense. That's not Chaya talking, that's you. She's still got a grip on your balls, hasn't she? With your luck she always will. I'll kill the bitch!"

"You have a one-track mind."

"At least it's a useful track." She reached for her rifle where she'd put it, leaning up against the wall by her chair, and slung it. "Here, take care of the baby for a while, will you?"

"Where are you going?" Karl demanded, as if it wasn't as plain as the nose on his face.

She showed him a flash of fang. "Hunting, up by the Citadel walls."

He shocked the spit right out of her by saying calmly, "No, you're not." And standing, she couldn't help but notice, squarely in her path to the door. With the baby in his arms, sound asleep, so coshing him wasn't an option even if she could have hit that skull hard enough that he'd notice it.

"Shulamit," he said. With his deep voice he actually sounded authoritative, and never mind that he still had the

same foolishly pretty face he'd ever had, on top of that
brick of a body. "You've got your oath and all, and I respect
it, as who doesn't, but this isn't your hunt. Karl bar Edgar
gave you a charge until the jihad is finished. Will you aban-
don it to pursue a private feud?"

"Oh, my," she sneered. "Can't we talk like a book."

He didn't budge. "Go-Forward had an idea you'd try
something like this. He said keep you here, and keep you
penned up if necessary. He doesn't need any renegade
*Ivrit* girl running wild with a hair up her ass, getting in his
way when he's in a hurry."

"Go-Forward Haller never said anything like—"

"He also said," said Karl, and he was enjoying it, she
could see, "that you can rack up trophies enough later
when it's time to do it, but right now you stay put and you
guard that baby. What do you think is the first thing she'll
come for, if she comes back with a troop of Saurons?"

Shulamit's breath caught. He was playing on her paranoia, she knew it as well as she knew the feel of his skin
under her hand, but Yeweh knock him into perdition, he
was *right*.

He nodded, no need for her to say anything. "She wants
Ruth. There's genes in her that the Citadel's hungry for—
not just Sauron and nomad but Pale blood too, fan Haller
blood. That's an outcross they've never seen. And if the
Saurons get Ruth—if they snap you in two the way they
easily can, all it takes is one little shake—Aisha will walk
the nights, you can be sure of it. Aisha died so Ruth could
live. *Not* so she could grow up a Sauron."

"We've broken the Saurons," Shulamit said, but her
defiance had lost its edge. "We've taken the Citadel."

"We have not," Karl said, and his voice was bitter—bitter as gall. "They lied to us, Shuli. General Hammer got
out because only General Hammer was left alive."

"You're lying," Shulamit said, levelly enough considering. But she had the baby to think of, and he knew it, damn
him.

"I wish to Eblis I *were* lying," he said. "But I'm not. The

Judge herself told me. I'm old enough now, Chaya says, and the leaders, with Hammer-of-God gone—they have to know. *We* have to know. So we can get out."

Shulamit shook her head. She was trying to clear it, but he took the gesture for bullheadedness. Which most of the time it would have been, no lie there.

"Where's Hammer then? Isn't he part of the force that's reinforcing the—"

"You see . . . Hammer's buying time for The People, and lives. Chaya ordered him to go into the tunnels under the Citadel, near the Karakul Pass, and wait until the jihad begins—Then he's to lead what's left of our forces back to the Pale."

"How could I be so blind. But Hammer lie—" Shulamit stammered. "I thought I'd see the Citadel fall first. Only the Judge could have made him do it."

"He must have known what his lie would cost. It's a long way down that tunnel," Karl said. "I can see how things are falling apart here. Yeweh, even *you* could if you opened your eyes for a change. Hammer's going to blow Nûrnen up and get out. And we're going with him. With your rifle guarding Ruth, and my warhammer, too, and as many other weapons as we can spare. She's the best thing that came out of this whole bloody war. And you want to give her up so you can go spit in a Sauron's face before she kills you?"

"I might kill her," said Shulamit, low in her throat, meaning every word.

He curled his lip in contempt and stood like a rock, with Ruth for a shield. She couldn't gun him down. Not even as furious as he'd made her, he and his horrible, awful, Yeweh-*verdamt* story of truth and lies; even as easy as it would be to bring up her assault rifle and fire. And not just because of Ruth.

"Ruth—What about Karl? He's going with us?"

"Later. The Judge needs him now. She weakens hour by hour. Aisha's death took something out of her. After Barak . . . Karl's worried she may not survive the night."

She'd happily pound him to a pulp, but not shoot him—no, not kill that great block of balls-for-brains. She loved him almost as much as she hated him, right now, and she needed him, what was worse. She couldn't make it back to the Pale without him, not if the Cyborg got on her trail. And Ruth's.

Ruth, who lay in his arms as if he were her cradle. Ruth, who would be Shulamit's best revenge on that Sauron bitch, a spit in the eye to outdo any other she might have come up with.

Even so, thought Shulamit. She knew whose fault this was, first and foremost and always. "Damn you," she said. "Damn you, Karl fan Reenan."

The Threat Analysis Computer room stood near the end of a blind corridor. Its door had protections, none of them easily apparent even to a Cyborg. There was no label on it but a small plaque engraved with the Lidless Eye. Inside was a chair, a table, a terminal.

There were other rooms like this, other terminals in the Command Center, most of them dead or slaved to the main computer in the Inner Keep. A master strategist might have noticed that these were all on another level. He would also, by the time he came this far, have realized that this was officer country—Cyborg country. The Red Room was near it, about which even Soldiers spoke softly if at all. Whatever the appearances, this was a citadel within the Citadel, secured in ways that no cattle could understand.

Sigrid had passed checkpoints neither manned nor man-trapped. Every Soldier who was not defending the walls must be walled up in the newly secured, trebly guarded Inner Keep. If she had been cursed with imagination, she would have found the stillness eerie. The only sound was the click of the dog's claws on the floor, the clack of her bootheels, the hiss of her breathing. As thick as the walls were, no sound of fighting reached her.

Sigrid stood in front of the door. The Eye was on a level

with her own. She had not allowed herself to think, until now, of where she was.

Home.

Her own quarters had been in the Inner Keep, but she had spent hours—days—years of her life in this wing, some of them in the room she was about to enter. She was not pleased to note that her heart rate had increased by a fraction.

The door was locked as always. She palmed it, and uttered a particular sequence of syllables.

The lock clicked. An infinitesimal degree of tension eased in her neck and back. She was still in the database. She did not exclude the possibility that it was a trap. Nor did she move as the door slid open, but she was hyperalert, poised to spring.

Nothing. The lights were on low, quite bright enough for Cyborg vision. The screen was on, flickering a fraction less steadily than it had when she was here last, almost a Haven-year ago.

The man in front of it did not turn. His ash-fair hair had gone quite gray. His posture was as ramrod-straight as ever, his voice as deep, modulated precisely for the acoustics of the room. "Examine these data, Cyborg. Extrapolate."

Sigrid moved up behind him. She was armed still with the dead-robber's pistol, but she made no move to draw or cock it. She did not feel defenseless, nor did she feel cowed. What she felt . . . gravid, yes. Subtly awkward, with her center of balance so drastically shifted. He would have heard that in her step.

"Breedmaster," she said. It was all the greeting she would give him, or he accept. His control was complete. She detected no sign of emotion, either anger or gladness. His eyes were fixed on the screen.

THREATS TO THE CITADEL, it read in letters that seemed to waver like amber-orange flames against a black sky. RANK ORDER.

Below that was the answer.

THREATS TO THE CITADEL:

1. BREEDMASTER TITUS

2. BATTLEMASTER CARCHAROTH, NOW DECEASED

3. GIMILZOR, SON OF SHARKU AND CHICHEK, CONDITION CRITICAL

4. DEATHMASTER SHARKU'S REGIMENTS

5. THE HORDE ON THE PLAIN

6. THE THREAT ANALYSIS COMPUTER

OTHERS TOO LOW A PROBABILITY TO EVALUATE.

As Sigrid absorbed that, Breedmaster Titus typed in a new query. THREAT ANALYSIS OF THREAT ANALYSIS COMPUTER IF PROVEN DYSFUNCTIONAL.

She had been too long among the Bandari. She was sorely tempted to laugh as they did at flawless absurdity.

The TAC had no sense of humor, misplaced or otherwise. The answer came promptly. PROBABILITY OF MALFUNCTION: NIL.

"So it would say," Sigrid observed.

Titus shook his head. His fingers, long and thin like her own, flashed over the worn keys. ANALYZE PROBABILITY THAT THREAT ANALYSIS COMPUTER HAS REVERSED PRIORITIES.

The cursor blinked. Letters scrolled across the screen. PRIORITIES AS PROGRAMMED.

Sigrid reached past Titus to key in a line. ANALYZE PROBABILITY THAT CITADEL IS THREAT TO CITADEL.

PROBABILITY, the TAC replied, NIL.

She permitted herself the whisper of a sigh. ANALYZE PROBABILITY THAT THE SEVEN ARE KEY TO CITADEL'S PRESERVATION.

The TAC whirred for a long, long moment. At last it replied. PROBABILITY: 67.333% +/- 5.

ANALYSIS OF THREAT TO CITADEL, she typed, OF CYBORG SIGRID.

This response was prompt. PROBABILITY TOO LOW TO EVALUATE.

"How long has it been showing this insanity?" Sigrid demanded.

"Long," said Breedmaster Titus. "It offers little hope.

None, one might say, except that one is arrogant, and Soldier, and therefore unwilling to accept the possibility of defeat."

"That is your analysis?"

At last he turned to face her. Outward expressions of shock were not necessary in a Cyborg, but they were felt.

He was not old for a Soldier, even a Cyborg. Yet he seemed as old as Chaya. His face was a death's head; his eyes had sunk deep in hollow sockets. They glittered as if with fever—and that, too, made her think of Chaya.

As she scanned him, he scanned her, thoroughly. The tilt of his glance indicated her pregnancy. A brow flickered upward: a query. After so long, this subtle communication between Cyborgs was both a pleasure and a pain.

"Bandari," she replied to his implicit question. "A fan Reenan. Nearly pure Frystaat strain."

The Breedmaster of the Citadel did not stoop to admiration. But approval—that, briefly, he would give her. Then he said, "You disobeyed orders."

She bent her head. "I did."

"Was it profitable?"

That was an odd question, even for him. "I have this get of the Bandari founder's line, and I have mares," she said, "who foal on the high steppe."

"And an army of conquest invested against the Citadel."

"It is not my army, and I did not bring it."

"You stink of it."

She resisted the urge to touch her skirt. "One uses what tools one can."

She was quoting one of his own axioms. He did not acknowledge it. "The Citadel is falling," he said. "Three centuries of conquest have been dissipated in unassimilated data, in possibilities we never deigned to consider. We are the last of Sauron. After us there is nothing."

His fingers sought keys, but his eyes remained on Sigrid. She divided her attention between his face and the screen.

ANALYZE THREAT TO HAVEN OF SAURON DOMINATION.

THREAT LEVEL SEVERE. PROBABILITY OF SUCCESS 11.5% +/- 3.

"Even our slaves have turned against us," said Titus.

Sigrid was no stranger to fear. She had been taught to feel it, and to use it, long ago. But this was a stronger fear than she had known since she was a child. "Have you altered the programming?" she asked him.

He laughed harshly. "Would I know how?"

"You might try."

"Perhaps." He turned back to the screen. The initial ranking of threats to the Citadel had scrolled to the top. His name glowed on the screen's boundary like the flames that ringed Nûrnen. "None of us knows what makes this machine work. Some of the younger Soldiers believe it to be an oracle, a soothsayer chained in silicon and steel, immortal and incorruptible. Where it gets its data, how it processes them . . . mysteries as profound as any sha-man's."

Sigrid, who had killed a shaman in Katlinsvale, spoke sharply, in a tone calculated to snap him to his senses. "That is nonsense. The TAC has listening posts all over the Citadel and in Nûrnen, with slave terminals in every base still under our control. You know that as well as I do. You've fallen victim to your own myth-making."

"Don't we all?" His fingertip rested just below his name, underscoring it. "What am I, that I threaten the Citadel above all others?"

"Ask the computer," Sigrid said.

"And be a slave to my own superstition?"

"Are you afraid to learn the answer?"

He knew how she was manipulating him: he had trained her to do it. He chose, or let himself be forced, to yield. He typed slowly, letter by letter: ANALYZE THREAT TO CITADEL OF BREEDMASTER TITUS.

Lights winked. The TAC muttered to itself.

As soon as the image occurred to Sigrid, she discarded it. She was letting the situation, and its imagined ramifications, affect her more strongly than the actual data warranted. Hormones, she thought. Pregnancy laboring to terminate itself in spite of her control.

REFERENCE IN ARCHIVES, the TAC informed them. FILENAME DENETHOR.

Titus sat absolutely still. When he spoke, his voice was perfectly calm. "What utter nonsense."

"Isn't it?" Sigrid's legs had had enough. She lowered herself to the floor, knowing perfectly well how vulnerable that made her—but certain of one thing in a rapidly shifting universe. The Breedmaster of the Citadel would do no harm to a woman pregnant with so interesting a combination of genes. She made herself as comfortable as she could, never taking her eyes from Titus.

He stared at the screen, and at the name of the file. "So the TAC imagines that I despair. Does the TAC forget that I am a Cyborg?"

"I doubt it," said Sigrid. "It very probably remembers the latest, and late, Battlemaster."

"Two Cyborgs gone senile in one cycle is highly improbable."

"Not by the laws of coincidence. The Judge of the Seven, Sauron stock, has fallen victim to age and stress as well. She's taken another route. She has her jihad. We can ask the TAC—"

"And I should make a third gone senile?" Titus turned away from the screen, flexing his shoulders. As worn and haggard as his face was, his eyes were clear, if bleak. "Yes, I spend my hours shut up here with my *palantir*, scrying out what future I can for the Race. No, I'm not blind to the advantages as well as the disadvantages of our position. Nûrnen has fallen. A significant proportion of the population of the steppe rampages around our walls. A sortie tried but failed to seize our inner citadel.

"Against which we can place the failure of that attempt, the strength of the Citadel to withstand siege at the low level of technology the cattle can bring to bear—"

"Not so low," Sigrid said. It was no light thing to interrupt a senior Cyborg in midspeech, but this was no light occasion. "They have captured assault rifles, plus the munitions stores in Nûrnen. Whose brilliant idea was it to scatter them through a city so vulnerable to attack?"

"It was a Council decision of the fifth generation on Haven," Titus answered coldly. "Yes, I comprehend our folly. All of it, with quite distressing clarity. We committed the sin of hubris, as our ancestors would observe."

"Not, I hope, to the point of total destruction," said Sigrid.

"As Old Sauron did?" He went on in her silence. "The Race is prone to arrogance. We never have disciplined ourselves sufficiently to breed it out. For which now, as before, we pay. Still, we have advantages. We have the Citadel. We have our forces in the Valley, Sharku's reinforcements have come, Ghâsh's force is coming as well. We can eliminate the horde between us, make a lesson of it that will resonate as strongly in the myths of Haven as the Wasting itself."

"That's arrogance still," Sigrid said, "and as blind as thinking that the cattle would never dare to throw an army against the Citadel."

His brows went up. If he was angered, he chose not to show it. "You believe so, Cyborg? Explain."

"You're not considering the Bandari," Sigrid said. "The nomads, yes—they have no more sense than four-footed cattle, and no more thought for the future. Their only coherent impulse is greed—for food, for loot, for rutting. The Bandari are different. Too many of them are Soldiers by blood, gathered from the culling grounds of the Bases and raised as warriors in a warrior culture, if not quite up to the standard of ours. But close, Breedmaster. Chillingly close."

"I am aware," the Breedmaster said, "of the Bandari and their experiment with the question of nature over nurture. Granted that they can field formidable forces—their numbers can hardly be greater than ours, cattle and cannon fodder aside."

"True," said Sigrid. "What you don't know is their hard

common sense. They've perpetrated a substantial deception among their *hotnots*: that the inner Citadel is theirs, and that the horde has only to mount an assault and the rest of the Citadel will fall. Under cover of that, they're getting out—taking all the machines and weapons and munitions they can gather, and heading for the Pale."

Titus' eyes narrowed. He almost—almost—smiled. "Oh, are they? Wise people."

"Will you allow it? Assault rifles, explosives, even such trivialities as light fixtures and the principle of central heating, in the hands of the *Ivrit*?"

"Have you made any effort to stop them?"

Sigrid stiffened. Part of that, to be sure, was a tightening of her abdomen that was too evidently a contraction. "I am here. I came in through the adit, with Harad for escort."

He typed ANALYZE THREAT TO CITADEL FROM BANDARI.

ALREADY DONE. FILENAME GIBBON.

"Gibbon?" Sigrid asked.

"I know the reference," Titus said. "You came with Harad, and sent him to his mother, who is approaching the door with her customary unhurried haste."

So she was. Sigrid should have heard her, but it was difficult to concentrate when so much of her control was focused on keeping the baby from arriving in the middle of this battle of wills.

# • CHAPTER TWENTY-FOUR

Sieglinde, unlike the Breedmaster, had changed minimally, if at all. Her face was as long and pale as Sigrid's own, but where Sigrid's was all planes and angles, Sieglinde's was rounded, her eyes dark blue to Sigrid's colorless gray, her hair pale gold and worn in plaits like a tribeswoman's. The rest of her was curved as Soldier women seldom were, with hips designed for bearing children, and breasts made to be heavy with milk. Sieglinde was beautiful, in short, and serenely conscious of it.

"Sigrid," she said, standing in the doorway, apparently oblivious to the Breedmaster's presence, "I'll never understand why you keep chopping your hair off like that. It makes you look perfectly awful."

One tended to forget the exact and inimitable experience that was Sieglinde. Sigrid took a moment to shift her mind to the necessary level, then said, "You omitted to mention my arrival to Cyborg Rank Bonn, I see."

"Oh," said Sieglinde. "Well. He was busy, you know. And since he isn't family . . ." She shrugged her magnificent shoulders. "I've had another baby since you left. Cyborg this time. His name is Rhun. He's very good stock. Excellent potential."

"Indeed," said Sigrid. Titus said nothing. He was amused, Sigrid suspected. Or bemused. Neither of his daughters was exactly standard Soldier issue.

Sieglinde was studying Sigrid with a peculiar intensity. "How fast are the contractions coming?"

Sigrid sensed rather than saw Titus' stiffening to attention. Breedmaster or no, he was no match for Sieglinde in detecting the exact progression of a woman's pregnancy. It made Sieglinde a useful assistant, although Sigrid was better in the actual process of assisting a birth.

"It's early yet," Sigrid said to her sister. "Contractions every quarter-hour or so. I have at least twelve hours before I'll be needing the delivery room."

"Less than that," said Sieglinde, "with all the climbing and scrambling you had to do to get here. It was good for you, really, but strenuous, and the altitude you had to go to was not very safe. You ought to be lying down."

"Soon," said Sigrid. She turned to Titus. "Breedmaster, consider. The Bandari must be stopped. I admit my fault in letting them get as far as they did. My being under guard, and under oath to one of them who was of Soldier blood, does not excuse the delay."

"You swore oath to a Bandari?"

Sigrid bore the Breedmaster's icy glare with as much equanimity as she could muster. "I allowed myself to be trapped into it. I further allowed myself to break it when it suited my purposes."

"Ah," said the Breedmaster. "Tell me, then. How would you stop the Bandari?"

"Bring out a Hellburner," Sigrid said.

Neither of them failed to comprehend, which spoke well of them as Soldiers. Sieglinde even nodded, slowly, as if she had been reminded of something that she had been trying to remember.

Titus did not change expression at all. "Granted that we keep that last relic of Old Sauron in vaults so deep and so well guarded that even Cyborgs are never told of them. Granted that you found those Vaults as a child, and extracted the secret of what they held from those whose discretion should have been less susceptible to young ferocity. Granted, even, that we have in Cyborg Rank Bonn both the commander of troops in the Citadel and the holder of the keys to the Vault. Granted all that, and supposing that the bombs have not deteriorated into uselessness in the three and a half centuries since they were laid down—does this crisis merit so extreme a solution?"

"Our technology," said Sigrid, "is about to disperse into the Pale. Our Citadel is about to be attacked by a horde of cattle—and even if we drive them off, the fact remains. Our myth has been breached. Our commanders can be deluded into wild drillbit chases across the length of the Valley. Our innermost stronghold can be invaded by determined, if suicidal, commandos. The cattle have made fools of us, Breedmaster, and shown our every weakness. Haven will never forget it. Unless," she said, "we prove to them that, like gods, we slept, and let mere mortals have their will with us. Now we wake. Now we loose the lightnings."

"Prettily phrased," Titus said, "as befits a sojourner among the cattle."

Sigrid refused to be baited. "Bonn has the key to the Vault. He also has as much knowledge of the Vault's contents and its uses as any Soldier on Haven. If even one of the bombs is still usable, if he can see it armed and placed—"

"Nuclear weapons are filthy," Sieglinde pointed out. "We'll slag this whole end of the valley, and the fallout will take care of the rest. Including us."

"I don't think so. I was told there were smaller weapons. Breedmaster, I don't know, but the Archive Caste will know. Archivist Gimli has a son who knows, even if he wouldn't tell me," Sigrid said. "And isn't it about time we found out?"

"Find out. Yes, we should know. Still," Sieglinde fretted. "It's so dangerous. What if it doesn't work?"

"We find alternatives," said Titus before Sigrid could speak. "Yes, I have thought of this solution. It's final, there's that to be said for it—if it works."

"I don't think we have much choice but to try it," Sigrid said. "Get the Bandari out of here, loaded with our machines and armed with weapons they found in Nûrnen—the machines, too; they were already using them to make arrows and bullets and it won't be long before they can make other things too. Give them time, and you can be sure that the next War of the Seven won't take so long to settle."

Titus nodded. He was looking less gray, she noted. More like his old, cold self. He turned back toward the TAC. Its screen, ignored, had reverted to default: a blank and featureless square. He slapped a button on a pad next to it. "Cyborg Rank Bonn."

The Cyborg's voice sounded out of the keyboard, no more mechanical from that source than from his actual throat. "Breedmaster."

"The TAC Room," said Titus. "At your earliest convenience."

"Noted," said Cyborg Rank Bonn. "On my way."

Bonn was, if anything, more conscientiously perfect a Cyborg than Titus. He greeted Sigrid with minimal surprise and no evident censure. Sieglinde received the inclination of the head due a woman of the Race; Titus, a glance that determined his mental and physical condition, his relation to the two women, and his degree of emotional investment in this meeting. Sigrid assessed Bonn in the same way. Mental condition good, physical condition excellent, relation warily respectful, emotional investment neutral, but potentially strong considering the principals of this meeting and their location next to the TAC. Something, he could not help but know, was up.

Titus wasted no time in preliminaries. "How soon can you open the deep Vault and arm one of the bombs there?"

Bonn's brows went up toward his hairline—absolute astonishment. He was, as a trooper might say, floored.

Foolish of him, Sigrid thought. The expedient had occurred to Titus as it had to Sigrid. Bonn, keeper of the key and the Vault, should have considered its use long since.

He was of course aware of this. "I . . . had given the matter some thought," he said. "As extreme as the measure would be, however—"

"Extreme measures are necessary," Sigrid said crisply. The tone of command in a woman's voice brought him around to face her, drawn instinctively to attention. "How soon can you do it?"

"I would have to run tests," Bonn said. "Several hours at least. A day, two . . ."

"T-day or Haven day?"

His mouth, which was open, snapped shut. "Several hours, Cyborg. Ten to twelve, by best estimate."

"Make it six," she said.

He blinked once. "May one ask the reason for the urgency?"

"Assault rifles in the Pale," Sigrid answered. "Caravans of our machines and our munitions, leaving Nûrnen continually since the commandos failed to take the inner Citadel."

Bonn was a soldier-Cyborg. He needed no more than that to salute her, nod to Titus, incline his head to Sieglinde, and disappear.

As soon as he was gone, Sieglinde applauded. "Oh, that was wonderful! He dotes on you, you know. He'd do anything if you asked."

"Nonsense," said Sigrid. "He understands military necessity."

"He understands that you asked, and he could answer." Sieglinde smiled. "He could sire your next son. Don't you think?"

"I think that we should get a move on," said Sigrid. "Breedmaster, by your leave?"

Titus nodded. His eyes had a cold glint of what might have been humor. "By all means. The larger labor room has a communications installation concealed behind the west wall."

Sigrid had not known that. "That will do well," she said.

The labor room was a familiar place—too familiar, and yet perfectly strange after so long in the wilds of Haven and among the horde. As the door of its airlock sighed shut, Sigrid caught herself sighing with it, and gravitating toward the surprising comfort of the hard flat cot. The chair that she would be using later was waiting, covered with a sterile sheet. The instruments were laid out, also covered to signify that they were sterilized.

It was—yes, it was comforting. She would be safe here.

Her son would be born as a Soldier should, in a sterile, pressurized environment, assisted by those of Soldier blood.

At the moment that was only Sieglinde. Breedmaster Titus would come later, or so she surmised. He would be curious to see the outcome of her experiment with the Bandari genepool.

Sieglinde was highly efficient and very skilled. She ascertained in a glance but little slower than Sigrid's that everything was in order. That done, she went to the west wall, which supported a row of shelves and a cabinet, and pressed a corner of the cabinet. The whole wall sank in to a precise centimeter deeper than the cabinet's depth, and slid aside.

There was a room beyond. Sigrid had never suspected its existence in this precise place, although she had postulated one like it somewhere in the stronghold, a secret reserved for senior Cyborgs and First Citizens since the founding of the Citadel. She forbore for the moment to inquire as to how Sieglinde knew of it. Titus had told her, of course, most probably after Sigrid went AWOL, when he had no other of his blood to whom to entrust the secret.

She also forbore, with an effort, to resent both Sieglinde's knowledge and her own ignorance. She moved away from the labor couch toward the hidden room. It was lit, if dimly—the light here was set for Cyborg sensitivity. To some degree the place resembled the TAC room: it had a desk, a chair, a computer, and a monitor. It also held a row of blank screens set in the wall, a set of unlabeled cabinets, and a glass case. In the case lay three objects: a gray eyepatch, a hand blaster with a green light glimmering miraculously on its charge plate, and a bound printout from a ship's library computer, opened to a random page. Her glance caught a line: "'Towers fell and mountains slid; walls crumbled and melted, crashing down. . . .'"

"Not if I can help it," she said aloud, in silence that had not been broken, possibly, in years. Sieglinde, behind her, said nothing, simply waited—like, Sigrid found herself thinking, an acolyte at an ancient Terran rite.

Well, and it was ritual enough—ritual of destruction. The rite of war in the Soldier sect.

She spared the cabinets and the case a glance, but no more than that. They were relics, both of them, and as close to sentimentality as Soldiers could ever come. Closer, she might have said before she saw them.

She went past them to the desk, moving heavily. The baby had dropped, and solidly. Not long now before it insisted on being born.

The box next to the computer terminal was a power source, the most reliable in the Citadel according to the Archivist Caste. It was independent from the rest of the Citadel. The birthing room computer, she suspected, was like it, an independent system, linkable with but not slaved to the TAC. *And some day these will cease to work, because they will be myths. Titus is correct; we regard the TAC as the cattle regard their shamans.*

She took a breath, which caught on a stronger contraction than heretofore, and sat in front of the monitor. After a brief pause, she flipped the power switch.

All screens, monitor included, came to life at once. Those on the wall were surveillance screens—part of the TAC, she realized. No wonder this room was a secret. The TAC room would be only its outer manifestation, and a much lesser one at that. This must be its heart—the central headquarters for its gathering of intelligence. Some of the screens showed nothing but a gray blankness. Most, however, were still functioning. They showed barracks—most empty, a few occupied by old men or young boys—and mess halls, empty at this hour. There were the women's quarters, rooms full of silent, grim-faced women and tired children, some of them wounded, some clearly under restraint—those would have been trying to escape.

There was the TAC room itself, and the Breedmaster in it, a gray and motionless figure. Only his eyes seemed alive, glittering as they fixed on the screen. He must know that he was being observed: he had told Sigrid where to go, if not what she would find there. He showed no sign of awareness that she watched. She would have been startled if he had.

Sieglinde reached past her, touched a key. "This sets a scan," she said. "I'll spell you when the baby starts to come. You won't be wanting to concentrate very hard then."

"Bet on it," said Sigrid.

Sieglinde laughed. "Oh, brave Cyborg! You'll have your baby in this chair, you think? *I* think not."

"I will if it's convenient," Sigrid said. While she spoke, she scanned the screens, which scanned the Citadel. There was a pattern, she observed: top to bottom, bottom to top, uppermost Keep to lowermost corridor and back again. There were blank spots, cameras out of order or blocked. There was a pattern in that. A hint—a suggestion . . .

She tensed. A contraction had caught her just then, but that was allowed for, and therefore ignorable. Something . . .

Sieglinde touched a second key and tapped out a brief code sequence. Sigrid noted its format. The screen she had been staring at stopped scanning and stilled.

There, again. Movement. Bodies in dimness, a glow of light that would have blinded Cyborg eyes, but must have seemed faint to the cattle who crept through the passage. From its timing and placement, and the rough look of its walls, it was deep down, probably at or near the bottom. The ones lower were not tracking. That was the pattern.

Someone was knocking out camera eyes. That took knowledge or damned sharp intuition, or maybe just good eyesight. Somehow they'd missed this one. There was a bend in the corridor, a sudden ascent up a crumbling stair. A room opened beyond. It seemed to be a storage room of

some kind, empty now except for a few dusty objects—
mess-hall gear, Sigrid thought, as her eyes made sense of
the shapes. A couple of tables, a broken bench, a counter
in front of a latched door. Either some optimist had
thought the population of the Citadel would grow till it
even filled the bowels of the stronghold, or a pessimist had
figured on a retreat this deep, possibly from fallout;
though she might be projecting that from her meeting
with the Breedmaster.

Whatever the place was, it had seen the passage of feet:
the dust was scuffed and in places polished clean, and the
door at the end was ajar. The few furtive figures crept
through in file, hunched and misshapen—carrying packs,
she saw, and doing something along the wall: laying cable,
from the look of them.

They were not moving like Soldiers. They were too
slow, and too heavy on their feet.

Cattle. What were cattle doing in the deeps of the Citadel? Why would they be laying cable?

The answer came in a flash. The solution was equally
swift. The computer's screen gave it to her. It was not the
TAC, that computer. If the TAC was a Cyborg of computers, this was an aging nomad, arthritic and somewhat
feebleminded, with an imperfect command of Americ.

It was, however, a computer, and adequate for what she
meant to do. Its keys were peculiarly crisp to the touch,
and much less worn than the TAC's. This machine had had
little use, as if it were intended more for backup than for
actual and continual function.

It was also on a battery that could fizzle and die without
warning. If she had been a Bandari she would have cursed,
then prayed, to cover all eventualities. She, Soldier and
Cyborg, simply keyed in the first command as the screen
prompted.

A file appeared. Its label was MT DOOM.

The computer bumped and ground like a tavern whore.
Sigrid herself could process data faster—but these data
she did not have, nor the capacity to execute them.

Abruptly the computer stopped. A message pursued the cursor across the screen.

FILE LOADED. EXECUTE? Y/N

Y, typed Sigrid. And sat back, and waited.

Sapper knew quite well that he had let himself be separated from the rest of his party. It bothered him, but he was much more interested in what he was finding, what he couldn't stop to examine because it was time to blow it all to Hell and gone, but surely he could look at *one* more heating duct, *one* more loudspeaker. Technology that the Pale only dreamed of, so common here that the Saurons had indulged in double and even triple redundancy in even minor installations, like water heaters in private baths and shower cubicles that didn't seem ever to have been used, just kept in reserve for emergency.

His power torch was dimming. Suddenly he was very uneasy. He'd better catch up with the others before it actually went out—or before somebody caught on and sent a Soldier down here to investigate.

He made his way back to the corridor and paused to orient himself. That wasn't easy: Saurons built with a numbing uniformity, and seemed to think that posting signs was, unlike doubled water heaters, a needless redundancy. After some reflecting, he decided to turn left. He was bliddy late—the others would all be at the rendezvous, cursing him out. And with reason. The timed charges that they'd laid in the Inner Keep of the Citadel would go off soon. Too bad there hadn't been time to do more. Much more.

The passage divided without warning. He didn't remember any such thing from the charts he'd found in Nûrnen. He chose at random again, right this time, and found a stair. It led down to where he would meet the others.

Sapper's assistants were having a grand time of it working their way through the bowels of the Citadel. The sounds of distant gunfire, up in the Keep, had stopped long ago. *How long have we wandered in this accursed warren?* Rich-in-Virtue Beagle asked himself. From the lack of battle noise in the Keep it was obvious that the raid on the Citadel had come to disaster. Soon the Saurons would sniff them out.

*Let Sapper's surprise be finished in time, Oh Lord!*

Rich-in-Virtue gnawed at a piece of muskylope jerky—last piece. His canteen was empty, too. They were too close to their bolt hole to lay any more charges.

He caught up with the rest of the party. *Where was Sapper?* So few commandos! Fewer than twenty. *Are we the Chosen, or the Abandoned?*

He followed them into a large bare room, long abandoned, that must once have served as a mess hall. It still had a long table set up, and two more folded in a corner, and a couple of benches. Some wag had drawn a rough outline of a man on the wall, given him a single lidless eye, and stuck an arrow into it.

The looked around at one another in the light of Sauron lamps—magic lamps, the *hotnots* said; they were battery torches, actually—and took stock.

"Where's Sapper?" asked Shlomo.

"Please God," said Rich-in-Virtue Beagle. "He had a last thing he wanted to do. He sent us ahead."

*"Nudnik!"* spat the Bandari. *"Schmuch! Shlymel!* You left him *alone?"*

"There wasn't anybody there," the Edenite defended himself.

"There, now," said the woman in command. "That's enough, boys."

*Where were the Saurons?* Rich-in-Virtue asked himself.

"Here comes Sapper," Shlomo said.

Something changed in the air around them. The room rocked.

"My babies!" Sapper shouted. The room rocked again and dust began to fill the air, as Sapper danced a jig. "A fig for you, Saurons!"

*He's mad!* thought Rich-in-Virtue. *Delightfully mad.*

Suddenly the doors that slid, slid shut. Those that were on hinges were closing even as one of the engineers, quicker on the uptake that the others, bolted for the nearest. He made it—caught hold of it to muscle it back again—and grunted as it resisted him. The grunt turned into a howl: the door, closing inexorably, had crushed his fingers.

One of the women had better luck and more sense. She reached the door that they had meant to leave by, and thrust her rifle barrel in between door and jamb. The door groaned to a stop. She put her back into it, using it for a prybar. Her fellow survivors ran to give her a hand.

The door stayed stubbornly where it was, and the rifle's barrel was bending slowly but surely out of shape. The knot of commandos in the middle of the mess hall unraveled suddenly in a kind of controlled panic, some heading for doors, to beat on them or dash against them, some scrambling up to see if the recesses in the walls were windows, still others—those were engineers—examining the walls for panels, partitions, or any possible way out. All they found was solid wall and no exit, not even to the mess kitchen.

The room rocked again as another round of charges went off. Rich-in-Virtue noticed that Sapper was no longer dancing. He stood frozen in thought, his brows furrowed.

Rich-in-Virtue studied the walls to see how they might escape. The recesses were full of nothing but dust. "They slide, don't they? Open, I mean."

"They don't—" Shlomol cried.

Rich-in-Virtue was too busy watching the recesses become slots, and the slots extrude what looked like, what were, long narrow tubes to answer. *Gun barrels?*

Something hissed. It was faint at first, especially under the hammering and banging and cursing of the people trying to get out of the room which had become a trap.

Shlomo bar Meshulam gestured, and two of his cousins boosted him to their shoulders. He was fan Gimbutas, an

engineer born and bred. If he could just see a way past the
metal barrels or even just figure out what they were, he
being a Gimbutas and all, maybe he could do something
about them.

He leaned closer to the pipes. "Gas!" he cried.

Rich-in-Virtue Beagle could hear a faint hiss.

*Gas.* The word was as soft as the hiss through the tubes.
A word from childhood stories.

"The Saurons are gassing us!" Shlomo shouted, flinging
himself at the pipes, trying to bend them into shutdown.
But the metal was ancient, stronger than steel; he dropped
like a stone and lay gasping. Instants later, he convulsed
and died. Others followed.

*Hell will be like this for the Unvirtuous*, thought Rich-
in-Virtue Beagle.

Commandos were screaming, clawing at the walls,
doors, anything that might let them out. Here and there,
people were quiet. Some had already fallen and were not
in convulsions because they had already died. Others withdrew into some fastness of the spirit, their eyes shut, their
lips moving, their faces suddenly old.

The mist from the pipes poured down like water.

With a swift flash of decision that even to Rich-in-
Virtue's dimming eyes held rage, some of the Bandari shot
themselves rather than wait . . . *rather than wait again.*
Some shred of memory teased at his fading consciousness,
then was replaced by the figure of the Bandari commander.

He hadn't been sure of this Sapper, less sure than he
was of any of the clever, wicked Bandari because of the
man's idolatrous love for gears and fires and stinks. Let
alone this harrowing of the Citadel, which surely must be
blasphemy: Christ harrowed Hell, and suffering humanity
was not so pure that it dared follow in His footsteps.

*The Elders in Strang would never approve of this.* And
they'd be right. It wasn't much consolation that he'd never
live to hear them thunder retribution against them.

Sapper was closer at hand, comforting as he stood

before his people, straight as the very Eldest of them all. And he spoke in a tone that was soft and yet so eerily distinct that Rich-in-Virtue knew he was going to take it into the dark with him.

*"Never again! Never again, our ancestors swore."*

Sapper raised those skillful hands of his, bleeding now from the fight with one of the metal doors, the first and only time he'd ever lost such a battle. His voice rose in a battlefield bellow. "Yeweh's curse be on you and all your blood, Saurons!"

Then, more gently, "No, my little ones. Not, like Saul, with your own blood on your heads."

Those of the Bandari who still lived had dragged themselves near him. His rifle was automatic, a prize from the Saurons, and as tears streamed down his face, he used it to protect his followers from one last sin.

"My followers, my children. Never again."

As gunshots still echoed in the mess hall Sapper swayed and staggered.

*I don't want to be the last one!* Rich-in-Virtue thought. It didn't hurt as much to breathe if he lay as flat as he could. He was Elect, he knew that, but there were words a man ought to say at a time like this.

*The Lord gives, the Lord takes, blessed be the name of the Lord.* He watched Sapper as he might have watched an Elder—

The engineer cast one look around the chamber, his eyes lingering on the mechanisms killing them. Then he braced himself against the wall and drew a breath that should have killed him. *For another curse?* Rich-in-Virtue didn't think so.

"Sh'ma Yisroel, Adonoi Elohenu, Adonoi Echad!" He ran out of air on the last word and fell as a tree falls, not bending, giving away only his life.

# • CHAPTER TWENTY-FIVE

They felt the explosions in the hidden room, even through the stone walls of the Citadel.

Sieglinde left the birthing computer for another screen and activated it.

REPORT

The TAC blanked momentarily.

HEAVY DAMAGE TO INNER KEEP

CASUALTIES?

ESTIMATED 20% +/- 3%. REVISED ESTIMATE IN TEN MINUTES

"We could have been there," Sieglinde said coldly. "Twenty percent. A thousand women and children your Bandari have killed." She turned back to the screens. "At least you've put a stop to them before they could do any more damage."

"Yes, we are cursed," said Sigrid in front of the screen that showed the mess hall in the Citadel's deeps. "So have we always been."

She levered herself up from the chair. The camera was focused on Sapper. He stood tall and proud, then fell. A boy near him crumpled to the floor. There were still others alive, climbing over one another to get at the lone centimeter of opening sustained by the Bandari woman's rifle barrel. It would do them no good. They were fighting, struggling like animals, using up what oxygen was left. What little came in would never be enough.

"Vengeance is mine, saith the Lord," said Sigrid, who had read the scriptures of the Pale, and found them to be arrant, but occasionally compelling nonsense. She powered down the computer, shut off the screens, disconnected the precious battery. Sieglinde was still behind her, silent and watchful.

"I think," said Sigrid, rising with great care, "that it's time I used the couch out there."

"Past time, I'd say," Sieglinde responded, with a glance at the chair in which Sigrid had been sitting. Its seat was damp.

Her skirts were worse, clinging to her legs and rump.

She had not even noticed when the waters broke. *Concentration,* she thought wryly, *indeed.*

Mumak hurried down the corridor toward the central elevator of the Command Center. Sharku had spent the past eight hours in the Infirmary waiting with Chichek by Gimilzor's bed. There were those Soldiers who thought such a display of concern for even a son near death showed a lack of discipline. Mumak was not one of them.

He had known Gimilzor ever since the Breedmaster had declared him *birthed.* On more than one occasion, watching the Deathmaster and his son, he had wished for a little Soldier of his own. Instead he had been *blessed*— that's what Breedmaster Titus and his own wife called it—with three daughters. Not a Soldier in the lot.

As he waited for the elevator to open, his fingers absently traced his new collar tabs. Senior Regiment Leader Mumak. Who would have ever thought he would rise so far? *Not me,* he thought. And none of it would have ever happened without Sharku.

They had been Cadets in the same barracks. Even as a young Cadet, it was clear that Sharku would go far. He had an analytical mind like a Cyborg, without the rigid mindset and inability to accept random data that characterized most Cyborgs. Sharku was insightful as well as analytical: an unusual combination of traits for a Soldiers.

Maybe it was all the reading Sharku had done as a Cadet. It was impossible to recall a time when he had not had his nose stuck in a history or was talking about Sauron

Role Models, such as Machiavelli or Alexander. Sharku had put up with a fair amount of hazing for it too, until he'd taken a few of the youngsters to the mat. After that, most of them had begun to listen to this peculiar Cadet with the odd notions and the propensity of quoting from the Founder's journals.

As Mumak stepped onto the elevator, he recognized Councilor Smaug. He wasn't surprised at his respectful congratulations. "Fine soldiering, Deputy. Tell Deathmaster Sharku that he has my support. I have supported him from the beginning; too bad Cyborg Carcharoth went dysfunctional. Overbreeding: it's probably infected the entire line. Look at Cyborg Rank Zold, the leader of the Revolt against the First Diettinger, or even Mad Sargun; all Cyborgs. They've been disordered since the Founding. It's time for a Battlemaster from the ranks."

"Exactly," Mumak said. *Where were you, Smaug, when Sharku faced the Council and only Gimli the Archivist rose in his support? Carcharoth may have been mad, but at least he had the strength of his own convictions.*

"Remember to tell him," Smaug called after Mumak exited the elevator.

"I will, Regiment Leader," Mumak said, wringing the contempt out of each word before it left his lips. *Another parade Regiment Leader, like Regiment Leader Ufthak: the Citadel is full of them. None of you have ever commanded any unit larger than a company. At least until now—the first Grand Muster in two hundred years.*

Mumak reached the Infirmary. Outside the door the twin giants stood as still as statues, assault rifles cradled in arms. Their eyes followed Mumak as he entered.

Sharku looked bad. He stood next to the bed, his eyes staring at the stricken boy, willing him to wake up and take command of his body. *And how long has he been standing there? I bet he hasn't slept since truenight began, and I know he's only gotten two hours' sleep since we reached the Bandari earthworks.* Soldiers didn't need a lot of sleep, unlike food, which they consumed in great quantities as fuel for their accelerated metabolism. But they did need *some*. Especially now, with so much work yet to be done.

Chichek, her head fallen to her breast, was asleep on the room's only chair.

Sharku greeted him with a nod.

Gimilzor, his head swathed in bandages, lay motionless on the bed. In one corner, sitting up against the wall, resting on his haunches nomad style, was Dagor; Juchi the Accursed's son, the wild Soldier who had first given Sharku evidence of the Bandari conspiracy. Sharku nodded to him; he had saved the Deathmaster's son. He couldn't think of a better bodyguard for his wife and heir.

Mumak signaled Sharku to follow him. Reluctantly, and with a shrug that showed he knew that watching his son would not heal his wounds, Sharku joined him in the corridor.

"How is the little Soldier?"

"No change."

"Sorry to hear that, sir. But you have to come. We've got support here: high ranks. Most of the rank and file are with us."

Sharku stood as if he hadn't heard.

"Sir, you've got to come take charge. The Councilors sing your praises, even more than they do for the Breedmaster's daughter. Chief Assault Leader Ufthak will keep an eye on his father. In the elevator, I was accompanied by old Smaug, and he promised his support. Not that we need it. Yet, Smaug is a good weather vane; he turns with the wind. Dammit, Sharku, you've got to listen!"

Sharku's look was cold, but Mumak didn't flinch. "Your orders, sir?"

"Did our courier return safely?" Sharku asked.

"Yes, sir. Assault Leader Vizgor just returned from the encampment. He had no trouble getting across their lines. The cattle are preoccupied it appears. Another of their great *khans* had died: Juchi's daughter, I believe. There is great wailing and lamenting in Nûrnen. I suspect Sigrid's disappearance has riled up the chieftains, too. Bad omens, or some such cattle superstition."

"How are our allies?"

"Deathmaster Ghâsh has finally arrived with the remainder of our force."

Sharku's eyebrows raised. "Will Ghâsh's return present a complication?"

"No. Once Ghâsh saw the ringwall, he couldn't stop damning Carcharoth and the Council. Guthril briefed him on the situation here."

"Good."

"Ghâsh agrees. Also, Guthril reports that Lagduf will move as you direct."

"Good. Once the barbarians begin their great assault, jihad, Cyborg Sigrid calls it, Ghâsh and Guthril can push them from behind. Past time for a final reckoning."

The controlled force of Sharku's words sent a chill down Mumak's spine. Were he one of the cattle chieftains, he would have crossed himself or fallen to his knees. Instead he wondered what new world they were about to bring forth.

Then they felt the blasts.

The explosions had come from the Inner Keep. They ran through the corridors toward that part of the Citadel, Sharku leading, with Mumak and the giant twins behind him. A tiny figure, a blond miniature of Sigrid, ran from the stairwell to tug at his sleeve.

"Mother says to come this way," she said.

Sharku frowned. "Signy, what are you doing here?"

"Sir, she said if you wouldn't come to say that Breedmaster Titus demands your attention," the little Cyborg said formally. "Please come."

"You'd better go, Deathmaster," Mumak said. "We'll investigate. I'll send someone if you're needed."

The Cyborg child led Sharku, not to the labor rooms as he'd expected, but to the segment of the women's quarters just past that, a sort of half-barracks, half-maternity ward where the new mothers and their offspring could rest and get used to one another before they got down to the serious business of living. Not that the Breedmaster's daughter was using it as such. When Sharku came in, she had a computer terminal going and was sitting at it with the Breedmaster behind her, frowning and saying, "Nothing here, either. We're going to have to manufacture it."

Sharku looked around for sign of a baby. There was a cradle in the corner of the small, cell-like room, next to the hard spare bed—that wasn't standard issue, he knew. Chichek had been in one of these rooms when she had Gimilzor. Her bed had been decadent by Soldier standards, big and soft and piled with blankets.

He had to stop for a few seconds. He told himself it was to let the two Cyborgs become aware of his presence, but he knew better than that. They'd heard him coming from half the Citadel away.

What he really needed was to deal with memories. Soldiers died. That was the law of war. The law of life, for the matter of that. But a Soldier as young as Gimilzor—

Something stirred in the cradle and started to squawk. The Breedmaster's second, non-Cyborg daughter came hurrying in from the door just beyond. She ignored Sharku completely and bent to scoop up the baby.

Sharku caught himself staring. He'd expected your normal Soldier baby: red, wrinkled, and tiny. The one wriggling and fussing in the tall blond woman's arms had a reddish cast to its skin, but that skin was a good deal darker than most Soldiers'. *Cafe au lait,* he thought, *whatever that originally meant.* He'd read it in an archive somewhere. In contrast to the dark skin, the fuzz of hair on the solid round skull was brassy fair. It was a big baby, too, for its age, solid and compact.

"Frystaat genes," said Sigrid next to him. He just managed not to jump like a cat.

She saw it anyway, of course. Her eyes held a glint of amusement. It wasn't cold, which startled him. Not for a Soldier, at least—and for a Cyborg it was downright warm. "I . . . heard about your experiment," he managed to say.

"Oh, yes," she said. "Everyone's heard of the fan Reenan in the Citadel. That will continue, you can be sure."

"He's a good, strong baby," said Sharku.

"Yes," said the Breedmaster, still at the terminal. "He won't be set out for the stobor."

There was irony in that, and a dangerous edge. Sigrid raised a brow at Titus, but addressed Sharku. "We've decided, pending Council approval"—which would be a rubber stamp, Sharku knew perfectly well—"that the age of infant exposure is over. This whole bloody war was the result of it. The Bandari have been adopting and raising our castoffs wholesale. Hereafter, if a child fails to meet standard, we have two choices. Keep it and raise it as a kind of sub-Soldier, or kill it. There will be no more Soldier-bred Bandari."

"No more Juchis," said Sieglinde from where she sat rocking the baby. "No more Chayas."

The Cyborgs nodded. Sharku kept his tongue between his teeth.

"What the Hell's going on down in the Inner Keep?"

"Bombs," Sieglinde said. "Sigrid's precious Bandari friends set them. The TAC says about 20% casualties."

Sharku stood rigidly still.

"Yes," said Sigrid as if she could read his thoughts. "The world is changing. It almost changed us right out of existence. We pulled this one out of the fire in a very literal sense. The next one might not be as easy."

"There won't be a 'next one,'" Sharku said.

They were all staring at him, a row of near-identical faces, identical expressions: pale brows raised, pale eyes level.

"It seems," said Titus after a stretching moment, "that the Citadel has a new Battlemaster. What is it the old Terrans called a man hailed by his troops as commander in the field? Imperator?"

"A victim of necessity, maybe," said Sharku, and added carefully, "Breedmaster. But I was elected Deathmaster."

"Battlemaster," said the Breedmaster with equal care. "It seems you've acquired the office by default."

"Temporarily," said Sharku, "and with all due regard to the prerogatives of the Cyborgs in the Citadel."

"Of which we, and Sieglinde's son in the nursery, are the sole remaining representatives," Sigrid said.

"There is Cyborg Rank Bonn," Sharku said.

"So there is," Titus said. "So there is. Would your Soldiers accept him?" He smiled thinly. "A non-Cyborg Battlemaster is hardly traditional, but then neither am I. Or my children. And I am Breedmaster of the Citadel."

Sharku found that his heart was beating a fraction faster than normal, in spite of the controls he had on it. He didn't want the bloody job, but damn it, who else was there?

"We have been trying," said Titus, "to trace your bloodlines. Are you aware of the gap in the records along about the time of the Cyborg Rebellion?"

Sharku stiffened. "I am aware of that, yes, Breedmaster. Is there some reason why it's important?"

"Perhaps," the Breedmaster said. "You are undoubtedly descended from First Citizen Galen Diettinger. One of your lines descends from the Lady Althene, yes?"

"I hadn't been aware—" Sharku caught Sigrid's eye and shut his mouth. He started again. "It does?"

"Yes," said Sigrid, "it does. And that is a very convenient fact."

That was so blunt it was almost subtle. Sharku blinked twice as his brain clicked through the data. Cyborg he wasn't, but he wasn't stupid, either. Unless stupid meant letting his troops hail him Deathmaster without any input from the Council.

"At the moment," Sigrid said, "the Citadel is as close to anarchy as it's come in centuries. There's bloody carnage in the Inner Keep. Nûrnen has been sacked, and outside the walls is a reeking slaughterhouse and a howling pack of barbarian cattle. Inside is a population severely depleted by war and attrition, and we don't know the full extent of the genetic losses in the Inner Keep. We have no firm leadership. The Council has been little more than a ceremonial body for generations. The Cyborgs are gone, except for us.

"All we have are ourselves—and you."

Titus' deep, gravelly voice brought Sharku's eyes to him. Strange to realize that that particular quality and timbre wouldn't be heard again until Sieglinde's son Rhun grew up. Titus was the last adult male Cyborg, aside from Bonn, and he was hardly a candidate. There weren't any more of his generation, or of any generation but the very latest.

"Battlemaster," said Titus, "we believe we have found a solution to the problem of how to organize and focus the race. This war found us with our pants down—there's no other way to put it. We were arrogant, poorly prepared, and as close to easy prey for the cattle as we've ever been. We almost lost this war. We cannot afford to repeat the experience, even as a lesson to our young Soldiers in the perils of arrogance."

"Therefore," said Sigrid, as smoothly as if they'd rehearsed it, "we propose to return the race to its original strength, under strong and consistent leadership."

"Yours," said Titus.

"Not yours? You're the Breedmaster," Sharku said. "You"—he slid a glance at Sigrid—"are the Breedmaster to be. Wouldn't it be logical—"

"Logical, perhaps, but not *possible*," said Sigrid. "The troops are highly resistant to the prospect of further Cyborg leadership. They would rebel."

Since that was exactly what all his Soldiers were saying, Sharku could hardly argue with her. He didn't need to wonder where she'd found it out. Her father manned the TAC. The TAC knew everything.

"So why me?" he asked, probing further. "Why me in particular? If you're just looking for a figurehead, anyone on the Council would do a whole lot better than an officer promoted from the ranks."

"I doubt that," Sigrid said. "No one on the Council has led troops in battle and won their loyalty by it. Nor can any of them claim descent from the Lady Althene."

"Can I, really?" Sharku asked pointedly.

"That," said Breedmaster Titus, "can be taken care of."

"Sometimes, necessary symbols are not lies," said

Sigrid, "even when they are not strictly factual. The Race needs a leader who can be symbol as well as administrator. We forgot that. The Seven didn't. Their whole war ran on symbols. Now we'll destroy them using Hellfire, the most symbolic and most terrible weapon of all."

"So you approve of using Gimli's old weapons?"

"They are needed. All Haven will remember. So will the Race—and the Soldiers are ready for a leader who will make the changes needed."

"I've long said we should restore what Galen Diettinger built," Sharku muttered. He frowned. "But I don't think—"

"Then don't," she said, so crisp she crackled. "Just take orders. You will be First Citizen of the Citadel. No one else is suitable."

"If I am First Citizen, why should I listen to your orders?"

Sigrid smiled. "You are not First Citizen until you obey that last command."

"No one else is suitably manipulable?"

Their answer was silence. He could feel their calm conviction that he'd give in.

The trouble was, he could see what they were getting at. It made sense. If they'd had a better candidate, he'd be right behind them pushing the man to come around.

But—

"Exactly how tight a leash do you expect to keep me on, once I'm officially in charge of the Citadel and all its goods and chattels?"

"You will do as you see fit," Sigrid answered, "after giving, or so we hope, due consideration to the advice of the Council and the Breedmaster."

"And the Breedmaster's daughter?"

She lifted her chin slightly. She wasn't pretty; a Cyborg wasn't, and this one had just given birth. She wasn't softly beautiful as her sister was. But there was something compelling about her, about the juxtaposition of her clear and apparent femaleness and her Cyborg strength.

A woman like no other—not on Haven, and maybe not

anywhere in the lost worlds. Maybe not like anyone since the Lady Althene. "The Breedmaster's daughter," she said, "has a duty of her own to perform."

"As Breedmaster in training, yes," he said. "But for the rest of it—"

She cut him off. "The First Citizen has never been a solo office. There has always been a separate advisor and virtual coruler."

"Consort," said Titus. "Queen, if you will, since the cattle have a distressing propensity to look on our First Citizen as a king."

Sharku couldn't speak. Couldn't say anything at all. The only word in his mind was a name. Chichek.

Chichek, his flower of the steppe. Chichek, the mother of his dying son, by whom he'd hoped to get another son, and the sooner the better. Chichek who was cattle, no Soldier blood at all, and completely unsuited to be queen in the Citadel.

"There would have to be children," Sigrid said, "in order to continue the line, and to provide a new generation of rulers. I am prepared to do that duty. Your genetic material is good. You've proved yourself on the battlefield as both soldier and commander. Your fertility is likewise proven. Ideally, I would be paired with a Cyborg, but since that's no longer an option—"

"Unless you paired with the Breedmaster," Sharku was rattled enough to interrupt, "and concentrated the genes."

"No," she said without perceptible offense. "We're already skirting the limit—as witness my brother's succumbing to lethal recessives. An outcross is essential. Our files indicate that we two will cross well."

"But—" said Sharku.

Her eyes on him were clear, hard, and yet somehow, in a cold way, sympathetic. "I won't require strict monogamy. Except legally, of course. What we do is symbolic. It's duty. We do what we must. If you want to keep a harem of tribute maidens, you may. I may choose to do the same with suitable males, whether of our race or of the cattle."

"That—" Sharku's throat closed. He forced it open. "That sounds reasonable enough."

"I knew you'd think so," she said.

He looked at her. No, she wasn't hard to look at. To think of her in his bed instead of warm, lissome Chichek, her lean whipcord Cyborg strength that meant he'd have to work to keep her pleasured instead of holding back as he always had to do with unaugmented women . . .

Duty, he told himself. Hard or soft, a Soldier did his duty. Good for him if it could be pleasure, too.

But Chichek—God, Chichek . . . would learn to accept her somewhat lessened status. She, after all, had no more choice in it than he.

He drew himself up. "Lady," he said. "Duty commands, necessity dictates—I won't deny either of them. But for me, for the man I am . . . I'd be honored to be your consort."

She bent her head. She had the manner, no question. She didn't even have to think about it. It was bred in.

"Good, then," said the Breedmaster. He sounded relieved, which might be a failure of control, and might not. He looked old—and that was disturbing. How long before he went Carcharoth's way and dreamed dreams and saw visions born of a senile brain?

Not now, Sharku thought. Not yet. Not till he could afford to indulge a fine madness. That much Sharku knew of the Breedmaster. But that it would be soon, he also knew. Otherwise Titus would have taken control himself, Cyborg or no Cyborg.

It took a great deal of courage for a man who held that much power to admit that he couldn't handle more. He'd never say it, nor would he thank Sharku for saying it for him. Best simply to know it, accept it, deal with it. The man who could have been king of the Citadel had abdicated before anyone knew there was such an office.

The man he'd chosen for the burden saluted him as officer to officer. "Breedmaster," he said.

"Battlemaster," said Titus. "First Citizen. Come now and claim your own."

❖    ❖    ❖

The Council seats in the great chamber looked half-empty. The battles for the outer works, the Pass, and especially the battle of Firebase One had taken their toll among the older men who made up its membership, but the Soldiers' tiers behind him were packed—all the way up to the roof-level. Company guidon banners of First Regiment were massed in the first row. Above them much of the expeditionary force and the Citadel garrison were there, all but those with essential duties. The holo of Galen Diettinger behind the First Citizen's chair was cracked and scarred, and the banner above it was awry. There was dust everywhere, and cracks in the walls—but the Soldiers held Council here once again. And Sharku's First Regiment companies had brought their assault rifles. The weapons were grounded, but they were there.

Sharku concluded his report. "I request that Gimli arm one of the weapons known as—" he hesitated at the unfamiliar term—"*a neutron bomb*. I am told that four remain in the Vaults, with five of the class known as Hellburners."

The surviving Councilors looked at each other. "Nuclear weapons?" Ansel Diettinger said doubtfully. "Is that required?"—a long hesitation, then grudgingly—"Deathmaster?"

Sharku nodded crisply. "It is needed. We could defeat this attack without it, but it would cost time we no longer have. We will face famine this winter, no matter what we do. I will not sacrifice good Soldiers when we don't have to."

A low mutter of approval came from the ranks of Soldiers around them.

"Casualties among our subject populations have been even heavier than among the Soldiers. We cannot increase our exactions from the surviving peasantry of the Administered Zone, because they'd starve. We need order *soon*, and we will need every remaining Soldier to provide it.

"The western Shangri-La is still in revolt; but it is the only large food-surplus zone within our reach. We must pacify it *immediately*, if necessary by driving the nomads loose in the Valley west into the rebel areas, and all our spare military capacity must be devoted to this."

"In short," he concluded, "we either destroy the horde before our walls immediately, or civilization—and the Race—in this part of Haven will pay a price I don't intend to pay."

A heavy silence fell over the Council, but everyone present remembered Sharku's last speech—the advice unheeded, that might have spared Sauron-on-Haven its brush with extinction.

"I call for a vote."

A heavy crashing came from the tiers above, as Sharku's men slammed their rifle-butts down in earthquake unison. The Battlemaster's face was as impassive as chiseled stone, but he felt a grim smile behind it. This too was not without precedent in the long history of the Race.

"By acclamation," Gimli the Archivist said. "Battlemaster Sharku is authorized to take all necessary measures." Nods of approval. "You do not rate our prospects highly," Gimli went on.

Sharku gave him a considering look; Gimli had been the only Council member to back him against Carcharoth at the last meeting, half a T-year ago.

"On the contrary. The last time I spoke to the Council, I did more than recommend that we resist the temptation to strip the Citadel for operations in the west. I said that the great Plan to turn Haven into a new Sauron Homeworld had faded. I said then and I say now that we have become decadent, static, that we are sliding into barbarism more slowly than the cattle after the *Dol Guldur* bombed them. More slowly, but just as surely.

"*Armies learn from defeat.*" He waved at the evident signs of disaster that had reached even this chamber. In the stillness they could hear faintly the keening of the tribute maidens in the Inner Keep as they mourned their dead children.

"This catastrophe is our opportunity. We cannot endure as a fragment of high technology squatting on a subsistence-peasant base. We will never re-create

Homeworld with animal transport and wooden plows! The Sauron ideal requires a unified world, and only an industrialized world can sustain a universal State. We must develop technologies suitable to this planet and its resources; we must increase the productivity of our subject peoples until they can support a true planetwide empire.

"The Sauron Unified State had more castes than just Soldiers. We must bring back those castes: scholars, administrators. Let the Archivists become what they once were—Technicians. And we must bring back the Teachers and Engineers."

"And Scientists," a soft voice said from beside him.

He nodded approval at Sigrid. "And Scientists."

"Above all, we must recognize that our presence has presented a massive challenge to the human norms of Haven. Environmental challenge accelerates evolution—and we have spread our genes well beyond the area of our control, as well. Now *Haven* presents a challenge to *us*. We must master that challenge, master this world, and be ready to face the greater challenges that will—inevitably—arise when we make contact with other worlds again . . . or they make contact with *us*."

"You'll bring the Empire down on us," Ansel Diettinger said. He was, for a little while yet, First Citizen, and Sharku answered him.

"We don't know if the Empire still exists. It may have dissolved in war and chaos. If—no, *when* we go back to the stars, we are as likely to find allies as enemies. But whatever we find, it will be better than this! Than cowering in caves, bleating like cattle! This was never Galen Diettinger's dream, that we hide here until we lose all knowledge of our destiny! It is time to go back. It is time to build a new Homeworld. It is time to realize our destiny."

A sound grew; for a moment Sharku did not recognize it. It was cheering, but from the lungs and mouths of Soldiers. Rank upon rank of them in the tiers behind him, roaring out his name to the pounding beat of their rifles on the concrete floor.

"Sharku! Sharku!"

It shook him for a moment, before Soldier logic reasserted itself. *Carcharoth led them to near disaster. I retrieved the situation.*

The irony of it did not escape him. Galen Diettinger had led one shipload of fugitives from the wreck of Old Sauron, and the Race on Haven would have worshipped him as a god, if their severe rationalism had allowed such indulgence. Sharku had managed to pull the Citadel back from the brink of destruction, and now he was receiving the same adulation. *It is time*, he thought, *that the Race produced great leaders who are* not *confined to retrieving something from the edge of extinction.*

The cheering died; Soldiers felt self-conscious in such displays. Breedmaster Sigrid's precisely controlled Cyborg tones dropped into the silence.

"Battlemaster Sharku is correct. Drastic restructuring of our system, in line with the original plans of First Citizen Diettinger and Lady Althene, is in order." She paused, staring at Sharku. "Battlemaster Sharku has shown himself fit to assume command. He is of Diettinger's direct line. I am of Lady Althene's line, and I am now his consort. I believe the implications are obvious."

The Council stood. "Moved, before the Council and the Soldiers-in-Arms," Gimli said, an almost imperceptible glee in his voice, "that Battlemaster Sharku assume the Rank of First Citizen. That this Council dissolve itself, and a new Council be summoned at the pleasure of First Citizen Sharku, to advise him."

"*Ave! Ave Sharku! FIRST SOLDIER SHARKU!*" The rifle butts pounded against the floor, the drumming rhythm overpowering. Dust flew through the chamber. "First Soldier. First Soldier!"

Feeling a weight heavier than worlds, Sharku walked up the steps to the dais and sat, in the chair that had been Galen Diettenger's. The Councilors stood and saluted, then filed down to take their seats among the ordinary Soldiers. Ansel Diettinger hesitated, then saluted and joined the other former Councilors. Sharku met Gimli's eye and nodded imperceptibly.

*Perhaps I should refuse the crown thrice,* Sharku thought mordantly. But no: Soldiers did not use such tricks of rhetoric; besides, only Sigrid and Gimli would understand the reference.

*"Ave! Ave Sharku! FIRST SOLDIER SHARKU!"*

# • CHAPTER TWENTY-SIX

Chaya's voice rose to a hawk's scream as she swept forward. The hill had been incorporated into the great inner ring facing the Citadel, and her augmented voice was powerful enough to reach two score thousand of the warriors crowded below. Their waiting was patient, but tense, leashed eagerness crackling in the dim chill air. They had sweated and dug until their palms were flayed meat, moved in unaccustomed obedience to the orders of the Seven with a discipline only the strongest of their own *khans* could command. Now they scented the purpose for which they had gathered from half a planet: to kill. And kill and kill, until nothing of Sauron-on-Haven lived.

"The Lord God of Hosts has delivered them into our hands," she cried. The sound of it was like nothing human. "Warriors of Haven, warriors of humanity—slay them all, slay them with the edge of the sword, leaving not one Sauron alive to breathe. Now for wrath, ruin, and a red nightfall! Death to the Saurons!"

A roar surged across the mass of them, dun-black under the light of Cat's Eye and tinged with red on their blades. It built like surf on the sea none of them had ever seen, like the beating heart of a giant taller than the stars. It seemed inconceivable that it could grow, but it did as the main gate of the Citadel swung open and the distance-tiny figures of the garrison filed out, flowing smoothly into extended battle-formation and moving forward.

A balefire flickered beside Chaya. Bandari threw armfuls of heartlog on it, the resin-soaked wood blazing up in white-hot tongues of flame. The Judge stood oblivious to it, her fists clenched over her head, the long sleeves of her robe falling back from the weathered, corded skin of her arms. Her eyes showed white all around the rims, and there was foam on the lips drawn back in a rictus from her teeth. Now there would be vengeance for Barak, for Juchi, for all the unnumbered dead. Her son fell in flames before her eyes.

"*Death!*" she screamed. "*Death! Death!*"

The horde took it up. No chant could be unified in a mass so large, but it rolled over them in long waves, like the slurred voice of a stricken god.

"*DEATH!*" it boomed. Echoes thundered back from the walls and the mountains, until it seemed stone would shiver and break. The sound woke things older than thought and speech, until every brain in the host vibrated with it. "*DEATH! DEATH!*"

Chaya stood and howled; the men of the jihad howled with her as they flowed past, over the fortifications and down into the plain, parting around her hilltop perch as water might at a rock in a waterfall. Shrieking, sheerly mad, two hundred thousand men cataracted past her and onto the plain. Cat's Eye stood baleful behind the Citadel across the arc of the sky, its light a path of blood beneath their feet.

"GO FORTH TO CONQUER!" she screamed.

Karl Haller, the last of the Seven able to ride, led the charge. Chaya watched until he was out of sight. *We are the kings who die for the People.* Or wander through their legends for a thousand years.

As the hordes swept forward, Chaya, twin to Juchi, the Accursed, Judge of the haBandari, walked slowly back down the hill, away from the battle, and walked alone into the growing light of the Cat's Eye.

"So much for strategy," Tameetha bat Irene croaked, and tried to raise her voice. It failed, and she put a hand to the bandages that wrapped her throat.

She was sitting on the firing step on the inner ring of the

fortifications, still too weak to stand for long. Frustration burned in her, and even now the Bandari watching could sympathize. To come so far, and miss the in-taking of the Citadel!

"Shut up," Raisa said beside her. The Russki girl from the Sozzled Stobor looked paler than usual; the horde's chant of *Death!* was echoing all around, and there was no mind behind the eyes of the fur-clad warriors who swarmed forward over the slope of the earthworks. Toward the Saurons and their waiting guns.

"I can talk, *shiks*, I just can't shout," Tameetha choked out.

"So don't try, or you'll be dumb as a fish again!" She stayed very close to the Bandari. That she was blond as a Sauron was coincidence—she was pure unaugmented human stock, simply someone from a Valley community with a great deal of Russki and Finn in its background— but a passing tribesman might not pause to think when he saw the yellow hair.

Tameetha snarled and signaled to Karl fan Reenan. He cleared his throat and relayed the whispered orders to the Bandari who waited below.

"Remember the dispositions," he called in a megaphone bellow. "The *aluf* says, let the *hotnots* finish the Saurons." A growl of unhappiness. The folk of the Pale had a feud old as the Citadel with its masters; that hatred was deep and black. "The second regiment is backing them up. We pull out and guard the upper pass section—Hammer says that's the point of maximum danger during the assault.

"We have our orders; what are we, a bunch of furry-arsed nomad *shlymels*?" That was not tactful, but very few of the wandering tribes understood Bandarit, and they were all charging past like a herd of muskylope in *musth* anyway. "*Trek!*"

There were a thousand or so of the Pale's warriors here; the remainder were with the jihad or on the outer fortifications keeping the Sauron field army at bay. The ones here gave a single deep shout, almost lost in the screaming of the horde, and swung into the saddle.

✧      ✧      ✧

Cyborg Rank Bonn made his dispositions in a few crisp sentences. "Full automatic," he concluded. "Open fire at four hundred meters."

*It is necessary to redirect the enemy,* he thought dispassionately. The maximum number had to be steered into the killing radius—a task involving careful timing.

The cattle were reacting with typical mindlessness, swarming over their inner ring of fortifications—quite good earthworks, though—with no fire preparation, no maneuver, no provision for mutual support. Their numbers were stunning: eighty to a hundred thousand, he estimated, filling his sight from left to right across the kilometer or so of bare space. As many more in the second wave, and a third rushing in on their heels; his position on the high ground of the Citadel's outer rim showed it in panoramic sight, like huge moving carpets spilling down out of the enemy fortifications and flowing up toward him.

Outnumbering his force of four hundred or so by nearly two hundred to one. Still, his were all Soldiers and equipped with automatic weapons. Military history showed clearly the psychological effect of massed automatic weapons fire could not be countered by any advantage of mass. His men didn't carry enough ammunition actually to kill all the cattle approaching, but they had more than enough to stall the horde in place and then retreat smartly inside the walls. Dealing with the survivors . . .

His lips thinned. He did not intend that many survive.

The open space between him and the horde was a shrinking semicircle, shrinking back toward the inner semicircle his men made about the main gate. From behind them, along the Bandari-designed earthworks, came massive *thumps*. Spigot-mortars firing; of course, they would have this area zeroed in. The Soldiers took cover as the massive shells landed. *Not too bad*, he decided, picking himself back up and shaking his head to free it of the dirt. *And they won't have time for more than one more* stonk.

Very close now.

Four hundred meters. No need for further orders. The early morning darkness made the muzzle-flashes of the assault rifles bright red knives stabbing into the horde. Men fell in swathes, scarcely a shot wasted, many striking multiple targets. His own weapon was on semiauto; Cyborg speed made it possible to fire just as rapidly as automatic, and to pick individual targets for each shot. He concentrated on the mounted nobles and *khans* grouped around their horse-tail banners, conspicuous among the dismounted majority.

Cyborg Rank Bonn frowned slightly as he switched magazines with blurring speed, firing again before the empty struck the ground. More than five thousand nomads had died in the last thirty seconds, but no slackening came in the pressure from behind. Even among the ranks running forward over the heaped, writhing dead and wounded, like spray breaking over rock—but the rock here slid and screamed and writhed. The smell of blood was overpowering, but the ear-numbing roar of the horde had not altered into the expected shrieks of fear. Three hundred meters to the outermost, then two hundred. The rifle barrels were shining bars of light to his IR-sensitive eyes, nearing the point at which the chambers would cook off the rounds before the bolts closed.

Another sound struck his ears, which were capable of sorting components from the high-decibel chaos of two hundred thousand men shrieking at the top of their lungs. A long bass note, like thousands of out-of-tune guitars. Then a keening whistle, loud even when compared to the shouting.

A hundred thousand arrows lifted from the horde and rose into the light of Cat's Eye, crimson blinks as they turned and fell toward the Saurons. *Ah. They were capable of more coordination than I anticipated.*

"Retreat!" he bellowed. Any longer, and too many would be caught among the enemy—who were, however, now nicely concentrated. The files of Soldiers turned and ran for the postern gates in the high wall behind them.

Another of the huge mortar shells landed. This one was not quite six meters from Bonn's position. He did not precisely lose consciousness—it was very difficult to knock a Cyborg out—but for sixty crucial seconds, he was unable to do more than stagger slowly.

*I am cut off.* The feeling did not bring fear, but more a sensation of intense annoyance. Another huge whine of arrows.

Bonn was a Cyborg. He could dodge; he could even keep firing one-handed as he batted arrows out of the air above him and twisted free of the paths of others. The rocky ground sang and sparked as the iron heads landed, and the earth grew a carpet of feathered bristles close-set as a drillbit's hairs. A third whistling volley rose from the plainsmen; they screamed their joy to see the Saurons retreat. Thousands more levelled smoothbores loaded with double charges and four or five balls each at the scattering of men around Bonn. The front of the horde belched fire and black-powder smoke. Those lead balls he could *not* dodge. Three tore into him, one into his groin, another into the inner thigh, one into his ribs.

Pain was merely a datum, incapable of affecting his behavior. None of the damage was immediately crippling to an organism capable of shutting down arteries and rerouting the blood flow. He kept firing and noted calmly that about half his men were doing likewise. Then less than half.

He was still functioning at what he estimated was approximately ninety-one percent of optimum combat capacity when the first of the tribesmen reached him. He threw the bayonetted rifle through the man's chest like a spear. Long-bladed knives appeared in both his hands, and he moved in a flickering stroboscopic blur of motion into the mass of the horde, where their own numbers would hamper them. He kept moving for nearly a hundred meters, killing or crippling with metronomic regularity, twice every .75 seconds on average. It was the bulk of his own kills, many still thrashing, that stopped him. One leg was crushing in a nomad's rib cage, both hands were slicing through flesh—a throat and a stomach—and his head was butting forward to smash in the frontal bones of a fourth enemy when the clubbed musket chanced to strike full on his spine in the small of his back.

Not even a Cyborg could command legs severed from the brain's nerve impulses. Bonn used the leverage of his shoulders to turn as he fell, and the knives cut the man who'd killed him nearly in half as he slumped backwards on the mound of corpses he'd made. Another man rushed in with a curved shamsir raised over his head, and catapulted backward with a bone-deep slash across the front of his thighs. Another nomad chopped into Bonn's legs with an axe—costing him not even pain—and died with a knife-point through the top of his skull. Bonn flipped the weapon out and through the eye of another taking aim at him with a musket from three meters away.

The arrow went through his throat from left to right just behind the jaw. It had a four-bladed head, two triangles. The carotids were both sliced through, and blood began to pour down his severed windpipe. Bonn clamped control down on the arteries, keeping consciousness just long enough to fling the other knife into the archer's stomach.

A slamming *thump* sounded from behind the Citadel's walls. Black against the reddish sky, a dot hurtled skyward and out, aiming for the horde's center of mass a kilometer from the Citadel. Less than five hundred meters from Bonn's position.

He was dying. He allowed himself a smile at the nomad who poised above him with sword raised. *Sharku may have calculated the probability of this*, he thought. It was reassuring; such a Soldier was fit to rule. His kind had not performed optimally of late.

There was a single instant of intense light.

Blackness.

*"Trek! Trek! Trek!"*

*Music to soothe the savage ears*, thought Hammer-of-God. The army of the Pale, all that was left of it, was marching out of Nûrnen. There had been six thousand a few T-months ago; a third had gone ahead, another third was still in the fight, or spreading Sapper's little going-away presents through Nûrnen. Much joy the Saurons—or the nomads, in the unlikely event they won—might have of it. The rest of the People were mustered and moving, cavalry and foot, wagons and muskies, to the immemorial music of the Bandari caravan.

They *looked* like a caravan, an extraordinarily well-armed, well-provisioned, well-stocked caravan. Any of them who didn't know exactly how tempting they'd be to raiders on the way back to the Pale, probably deserved to get an arrow in the gullet for his stupidity. On the other hand, while some raiders might have managed to steal assault rifles from the wreck of Nûrnen, many of the riders in this caravan had one, and ammunition if not to burn then by the Three to shoot Hell out of any number of *hot-nots*. Plus they'd be meeting the Pale's screening force, and falling back with it past the Bases. Dyar would be sticky, if the Saurons got reckless—but reckless overconfidence was something he was reasonably sure had been well and truly knocked out of the Saurons for the present.

He sat his big brown gelding on top of a pile of rubble, ignored the black-red throb of pain in his leg, and watched them swing past. As always happened with Bandari, once they got going they started to sing. The lot in front of him had a round going:

*Seven they fought the battle of Nûrnen town,*
*Battle of Nûrnen town, battle of Nûrnen town,*
*Seven they fought the battle of Nûrnen town,*
*Oh, lordy, they fought!*

Farther down, it was a bawdy song that would have made a land gator blush, and past that, good solid Psalm-singing such as even an Edenite could approve of.

*O clap your hands, ye people;*
*Shout unto God with the voice of triumph!*

And for punctuation throughout, the clap of explosions in the city behind them. One, two, three—pause. Had one missed fire? No, there went the next, and the one after that.

Hammer found that he was grinning. He must have looked like a tamerlane. There went a line of storehouses, right up in flames that clawed the sky. And there went half the armorers' quarter with a wondrous whoosh and roar. And away past the city, up around the mountain, the deeper *crump* of a mine collapsing. A great pity they hadn't been able to do the same with the Citadel.

Sword-of-Righteous-Wrath sat beside him; a young cousin pale with loss of blood. "War is waste," he said unexpectedly.

"Of many things," Hammer-of-God nodded. "We're destroying what it took generations of sweat to build. War is always expensive, though—and our enemies will be much poorer for a few generations."

Glorious, glorious destruction. " 'The hills melted like wax,' " he said to no one in particular, " 'at the presence of the Lord, at the presence of the Lord of the whole earth.' "

" 'The heavens declare his righteousness, and all the people see his glory.' " Ilderim *Khan* inclined his turbaned, infidel head. While his eyes were laughing, his face was as sober as an Elder's. "We too are people of the Book."

"God is not mocked," said Hammer, but with less outrage than he might have mustered, if he had been less busy counting explosions. Marija bat Yentle fan Gimbutas, Sapper's only surviving protege, had been given a free hand with captured Sauron and Nûrnenite ordnance. She had mined or boobytrapped or slow-matched every important installation in or near Nûrnen, set it all to go off on a schedule too complicated for ordinary mortals to understand, and assured Hammer-of-God that yes, it would happen exactly as Hammer wanted it.

And so it was doing. Except for the Citadel. Well, it was not given to any man to accomplish everything.

"We disabled them," Hammer said.

"As far as you knew," said Ilderim *Khan*. His mare, a slab-sided, ewe-necked, hammer-headed nag the color of beaten gold, took a sudden dislike to Hammer's gelding, who had done nothing whatsoever to earn it. She squealed shrilly and struck at him with her forefeet.

Hammer's horse, being a sensible beast and well aware of his position in the universe—far on the periphery, with the mare in the center—backed up and started to slide down the slope. Just as he got the gelding back to solid ground, the ground itself rocked, flinging them both down. More of Marija's destruction.

He had time, while he fell, to think, *Hellfire! My leg!* And time in landing to twist, and to feel the wrench as muscles gave way. But not the leg—not, by the Three, the bloody leg.

Then Ilderim *Khan* was there, pulling him to his feet—one foot, anyway, and the other would damned well carry him regardless—and saying something, but what it was, he couldn't hear. The whole world was mumbling in the wake of the explosion. Munitions dump, he thought.

That had to have been a mistake, or a chain reaction. All munitions should be on Bandari wagons, making their way back to the Pale.

He took the reins of his humbly apologetic horse, rubbed the long nose in acceptance of the apology, and took stock. The column was still moving, if slower than before, and with some runaways among the animals. For the most part it was in decent order.

"Sauron's revenge," he said, though he could barely hear himself. He turned to bare his teeth at the Citadel.

Nothing, still, from up there. Uneasiness, that had been niggling at the back of his mind, moved to the fore. He flipped the reins back over the horse's neck and contemplated sixteen hands of Shangri-La Valley thoroughbred, his bloody miserable excuse for a left leg, and a rock that might do for a mounting block. *Vanity of vanities*, his inner voice rebuked him. *All is vanity.*

He'd made it his job to see the army of the Pale out of

Nûrnen. Another regiment led by Karl had passed the Citadel and was riding fast toward where he waited at the Gates of Paradise. There were flames behind, in a pall of foul smoke. It looked like Hell, and Hell too all about them, blasted and ruined fields, mines blown up and flooded, bridges burned or blown to smithereens, the orchards ringbarked, the forests torched. Raiders still rode through the desolation, and would ride, for all Hammer knew or cared, till Judgment Day.

"Such a judgment," he said. His hearing was coming back: his voice sounded dim still and tinny, but better than before. "'Happy shall he be, that rewardeth thee as thou hast served us. Happy shall he be, that taketh and dasheth thy little ones against the stones.'"

The caravan was past his vantage point, the head of it well on up the road, heading for the earthworks, and from there to the pass. He shot another glance back at the Citadel.

"*Selah*," he said harshly. "Thy will be done." He pulled and heaved himself into the saddle, glaring away Ilderim *Khan*'s offer of help.

It took him a moment to see again through the red fog of pain from his leg. Once that faded to a ruddy haze, he half-turned the gelding on the hill, and took one last look at the battlefield at the gates of the Citadel.

The saddle was no more comfortable for Hammer-of-God's leg than the ground, but morning's infusion had dulled the pain a bit. Nothing but a hot bath and a day's sleep could really help, and Hellmouth alone knew when he'd get *that*. The last of the blockforce were clattering by him, over the crest and down the other side of the pass to deploy. Tumbled stone lay about them, the wreckage of the great Wall, more recent debris from the mortar bombs that had sledgehammered through the Sauron blockhouses a few cycles ago.

"Call it a precaution," he said to the other commanders. "Call it a message from God. But we'll stay here until we see what happens."

Down below the hill, a gaggle of *hotnots* had gathered,

Mongols, Christian Ironmen, Turks, a couple of Tartars, some of the Cossack chiefs. They looked from him to the retreating column, broad-cheeked faces flat, empty of expression. The ones who wanted to avoid the assault on the Citadel, the better to stake out claims around it. He gave them his widest, whitest grin, and swept his arm wide, encompassing the whole vast field of desolation. "It's all yours," he said in steppe Turki. "Every last blood-dripping bit of it. God give you joy of it."

He waved them on. Karl's regiment was well into the Pass now. Up ahead, the Bandari were singing a song he knew well, one of his favorites of them all.

> Turn around and go back down,
>    Back the way you came —
> See Babylon, the mighty city,
>    Rich in treasure, wide in fame:
> We have brought her towers down,
>    Made of her a pyre of flame.
> and—
>    Oh, Lord, the pride of man,
>    broken in the dust again!

Sharku saw Cyborg Bonn die. He turned tight-lipped to Sigrid. "That's another we couldn't afford to lose."

"It may make our jobs simpler, though," she said.

"You're a cold one."

"I might say the same of you. By the way, what will you do about your—former wife?"

"I haven't decided. Have you?"

"Not entirely."

"I won't have her harmed. Or humiliated."

"I had no intent to do that," Sigrid said. She turned motionless as she examined the battle below, Cyborg senses and Cyborg analysis in full play. Then she turned to Sharku. "Bonn did well. It's time. Mumak."

"Yes, Lady Sigrid?"

"Tell Gimli it's time to use the Sundevil."

Mumak looked from her to Sharku, unsure. "First Soldier?"

"Do it."

When Mumak had left to find Gimli, Sigrid spoke quietly. "I was with those" —she pointed out to the battlefield— "too long. I should have recalled the ways of the Soldiers. Of course he was right: the First Soldier ranks even a Cyborg Breedmaster. I won't make that mistake again. Sharku, do you think we will ever be—friends?"

"I don't know."

Then it was too late for talk, as the great doors behind them opened and Soldiers rolled a long thin tube on wheels out onto the upper parapet. Old Gimli, his robes discarded for a coverall with green and gold epaulettes, directed. "Mastertech Thorin, do we have steam?"

"Three hundred pounds, Techmaster."

"I see you started early reviving the old ranks," Sigrid said quietly.

"I saw no reason to wait."

"Load," Gimli said.

Sharku watched with interest. Nothing like this had happened for three hundred years, and every senior ranker he could spare was up on the parapet, along with a hundred picked Cadets.

Behind the Cadets a company of the First Regiment under Vizgor stood guard. No one would interfere.

A section of the First escorted a group of techs, who brought out a shiny steel cylinder rounded at the ends. It was a meter in diameter and half again that long. They inserted it into the tube of the steam catapult. Gimli bent over it. Sharku could see that he opened a panel on the cylinder and made adjustments with some kind of control. "I'll never understand that sort of thing," he said quietly.

"You don't have to," Sigrid said. "You command. But our children will understand it."

Sharku turned to look out over the parapet into brightening daylight. The hordes were riding hard toward the gates. They had regrouped after recoiling from Bonn's sally. When they reached extreme arrow range the leaders halted them and set up groups to begin a continuous hail of arrows against the lower battlements. None reached as high as the parapet where Sharku stood, but he heard the *zing!* of a rifled slug over his head. Even the high parapet wouldn't be safe for long now.

Then they heard the chug of the Bandari mortars. Something exploded behind the main gate.

There was a cheer from below, and barbarians in baggy pants ran forward carrying an enormous battering ram. Sharku counted twenty companies, well disciplined, carrying ladders.Other groups came forward with muskets and Bandari rifles to fire at the Soldiers protecting the walls. Hundreds fell, but when one dropped another came up to take his place.

"Notice how the Bandari direct them," Sigrid said. "I can almost feel sorry for them."

"Do you think the Bandari officers know there won't be any help from the Inner Keep?" Sharku asked.

"No, but it probably wouldn't make any difference. Not to them," she said.

"Interesting. I see why you're interested in their genes."

"We'll have to decide what to do about them when this is over," Sigrid said.

"I'd have thought that obvious. There'll be work for a dozen Deathmasters next month."

"I wouldn't be too hasty about killing them all," Sigrid said. "They aren't the enemy." She pointed up to the sky. "There's the real enemy of the Race. We may need allies." When he frowned she said "You've read history. What did Alexander do with the Persians? And Rome with the Franks . . ."

"Techmaster Gimli reports all is ready."

Sharku looked down at Harad. "Thank you. Mumak."

"Sir."

"Sound the warning. Gimli, aim for the center of that group."

Mumak raised his hand high, then dropped it. Trumpets sounded, deep tones, then came a sound that no one alive had ever heard: the old air raid warnings of the Citadel began their keening wails.

Down below the barbarians paused in their headlong rush. The Bandari leaders shouted them on. "*Am Bandari Hai!*" The cry came faintly up to the battlements. "*Allahu Akbar!*" ten thousand throats roared in answer.

And still the sirens wailed.

"Take cover, First Soldier," Mumak shouted. "Clear the battlements! My Lady, inside!" There was fear in Mumak's voice, but he didn't go inside until everyone else had left the parapet. When he had seen to the closing of the great bronze doors, he sidled up to Sharku. "Thought I'd shit in my pants when I heard those damn things," he muttered.

"Down," Gimli said. "Behind the stone walls. Away from the windows. Don't look out. First Deputy Mumak, are the battlements clear?"

"Clear, Techmaster."

"Fire."

The whoosh of the catapult was astonishingly soft, almost an anti-climax after all the shouting. A hush fell over the Citadel, and the only sound was the wailing sirens.

The attack pouring over the plain before the Citadel was the most impressive thing Hammer-of-God had ever seen. Even across kilometers there was a sense of majesty to the sheer *size* of the horde; shapeless, though, except for the fringe of Bandari order along its rear, where the siege mortars were being levered forward. There were still fires across an arc of horizon behind *them,* showing that the first two-score thousand nomads down into the Valley were busily at work, converting it into the sort of desert they felt comfortable in.

Hammer blinked red-rimmed eyes and kept his spine ramrod-straight; his armor itched underneath, and he felt like something the cat dragged in . . . but he was the victor here.

"They'll run out of men before we do," Hammer-of-God said, looking down on the slaughter with a face that might have been carved from stone. The tiny Sauron force was hardly a dot before the advancing thousands. "Not like the *soldati* to make a gesture like that. I'd have expected them to wait on the walls."

"What's that on the high parapet?" Sword-of-Righteous-Wrath asked.

Hammer-of-God turned his telescope to the highest level of the Citadel. There were a lot of Saurons up there, and they'd brought out one of their steam catapults. As he watched, the Saurons loaded it, then—

"They're going inside," Sword-of-Righteous-Wrath said. "All of them, General?"

"All," Hammer-of-God said. A horror came over him. "As if it's something they don't want to watch—"

He saw a puff from the catapult, and a dot arced out high over the plain, shooting far past the advance and into the main battle of the hordes. Then it blossomed into— something, like a dandelion seed, so that it *floated* down toward the battlefield.

Later, he said he had heard the voice of God. All he knew was that he was shouting to the Bandari. "Look away! Don't look at that Hellish thing! Turn your heads, hide your eyes!" he screamed.

A moment, and some of the others around him took up the cry, although they couldn't know why, only that their General was—frightened? Hammer-of-God? Whatever they heard in his voice made them believe.

Even with eyes closed and heads turned away the light was nearly blinding. A flash, and more than a flash, because it was already brighter than the sun and it grew brighter still, brighter than any light seen on Haven in three centuries and more.

Light. For an instant he could *see* the bones of his hand, and then there was nothing—nothing but red-shot darkness, and pain. Hands bore him up; others were shouting, screaming, a horse was screaming in pain until a pistol-shot silenced it. All that was muffled, below a roaring that echoed back and forth from the stony walls around him until his head rang like a bell in some heathen temple.

"General!" Someone was shouting in his ear. "What shall we do?" Felt like young Sword-of-Righteous-Wrath from the strength. "They're blind! All the horde, they're blind! And—*Jesus wept*, General, they're falling, they're falling, the whole horde, blind and dying, General, what shall we do?"

He forced his brain to function. Pain was nothing new to him, even if this time it lanced from his eyes into his head.

"Which direction does the wind blow?"

"Down into the Shangri-La."

"Get everyone moving out to the steppes—everyone who can. *Fast*."

"But what happened?" Shulamit whimpered. "What happened?"

"The pride of man, broken in the dust again," Hammer-of-God said. "We presumed too much. We have gone into the lair and awakened the lioness."

He could barely see shapes and outlines, so he knew he wasn't blind. He almost regretted that, because it meant he'd have to live to serve out Chaya's judgment. *Take my children home.* "Aye, Judge." he said aloud.

Aisha's baby was crying loudly now. He could hear her above the wails and screams of the people. And from far below in the pass, too far to hear any distinct sounds, there was a high pitched moaning.

From the wagon behind him someone keened, "In Rama was there a voice heard, lamentation and weeping, and great mourning, Rachel weeping for her children, and would not be comforted, because they are not."

*O God, the pride of man, broken in the dust again.* "Trek, trek," he shouted. "Move, you bliddy bastards."

He turned for one last look into the Pass. His vision was still red, and he couldn't see the plateau below the Citadel. "What do you see, Sword-of-Righteous-Wrath?"

"I see the people dying."

Hammer-of-God turned away. "The Wasting. The Wasting has come again to Haven."

❖     ❖     ❖

Mumak wouldn't let Sharku be the first out on the battlements. He stood in his way until Gimli and his Technician Caste rankers reported that it was safe.

Sharku waited impatiently. Mumak had been given responsibility for his safety and Lady Sigrid's, and, in the old order Sharku intended to bring back, a taskmaster was supreme in his own domain, no matter whom that might inconvenience. It was time to set new examples, but that didn't make the waiting easier.

Finally, he was able to examine the *strike zone*.

It was a scene he had only heard of from schoolbooks. Thousands, tens of thousands dead, but worse were the dying, who lay in heaps, still twitching and writhing in what must have been the agony of the damned.

He felt Sigrid's hand on his shoulder. They looked into each other's eyes briefly, then back to the killing ground. There was nothing to say.

"Semaphore from Deathmaster Ghâsh," Harad reported. "The cattle are broken. He requests permission to storm their earthworks."

"Denied. Have him wait until the cattle are thinned. Mumak."

"Sir."

"Tell the gunners to let all through the Pass who want to go through. Let them harry the steppes. They can carry the tale of what happens to those who earn the wrath of the Citadel."

"Yes, First Soldier."

"You said I was a cold one," Sigrid said quietly.

"Techmaster."

"Aye, First Soldier."

"Tell me what has happened out there."

"I estimate the weapon to have a yield of eight *kilotons*, First Soldier. Shall I explain?"

"Briefly."

"It is a measure of weapon power. Eight *kilotons* is small. We have one Hellfire weapon that should yield nine hundred *kilotons*, if the descriptions are accurate."

"What will happen now?"

"Those behind stone walls, or in mines, will not be harmed at all," Gimli said. "You understand I report what the Archive Computers tell me. No one living has seen anything like this."

"Continue."

"Of those within three hundred meters of *ground zero* all were dead instantly or within seconds. To five hundred meters, ninety-five percent will die within the day, and virtually all will be dead within the week. At two kilometers half will die. Beyond that, increasing numbers will live, with various degrees of injury."

"Describe the injuries." Sharku watched the scene below. Many of those who had been moving now lay still, but there were many others wandering blindly on the battlefield.

"Their hair and beards will fall out. They will bleed at the gums, and, in the worst cases, teeth will fall out. Cuts and bruises will take long healing if they ever heal. Of those who recover, many will be sterile."

"The women behind the earthworks? Will they bear healthy children?" Sigrid asked.

"Those behind two meters of earth at that distance will be as safe as you and I," Gimli said.

Sigrid nodded in satisfaction. "There's our labor force. And the tribute maidens we'll need to replace what we lost to Sapper's bombs."

Sharku stood rigidly, looking at the battlefield, but seeing more than that, seeing the vast wastelands the Bandari had created. To the southeast smoke still curled from the ruins of Nûrnen. Behind him, work crews were clearing the Inner Keep of wreckage. A banner unfurled from the battlement; as he watched, the Lidless Eye—opened.

"Never closed again," he said quietly. He looked back at the field of slaughter. "Never closed again. We cower behind walls. We hide from the Empire, and for what? So that the cattle can breed warriors who may one day kill us?

No. It is time and past time to look the Empire in the face."

He looked down at Harad, and pointed up, out beyond Cat's Eye to the stars beyond. "That's your destiny." Then he turned back to face the Soldiers along the battlements, and shouted. "Never closed again."

"Never closed again," Sigrid answered.

A moment's hesitation, then a Soldier shouted it. "Never closed again!" The cry was taken up by the Soldiers of the First Regiment who stood guard over their First Soldier. "Never closed again!" Others joined the cry, until it resounded through the Citadel, ringing from the stones, echoing through corridors from the Inner Keep to the outer gates, until every voice in that vast fortress was shouting.

"NEVER CLOSED AGAIN!"

# THE END

# FALLEN ANGELS

Two refugees from one of the last remaining orbital space stations are trapped on the North American icecap, and only science fiction fans can rescue them! Here's an excerpt from *Fallen Angels*, the bestselling new novel by Larry Niven, Jerry Pournelle, and Michael Flynn.

\*　　\*　　\*

She opened the door on the first knock and stood out of the way. The wind was whipping the ground snow in swirling circles. Some of it blew in the door as Bob entered. She slammed the door behind him. The snow on the floor decided to wait a while before melting. "Okay. You're here," she snapped. "There's no fire and no place to sit. The bed's the only warm place and you know it. I didn't know you were this hard up. And, by the way, I don't have any company, thanks for asking." If Bob couldn't figure out from that speech that she was pissed, he'd never win the prize as Mr. Perception.

"I am that hard up," he said, moving closer. "Let's get it on."

"Say what?" Bob had never been one for subtle technique, but this was pushing it. She tried to step back but his hands gripped her arms. They were cold as ice, even through the housecoat. "Bob!" He pulled her to him and buried his face in her hair.

"It's not what you think," he whispered. "We don't have time for this, worse luck."

"Bob!"

"No, just bear with me. Let's go to your bedroom. I don't want you to freeze."

He led her to the back of the house and she slid under the covers without inviting him in. He lay on top, still wearing his thick leather coat. Whatever he had in mind, she realized, it wasn't sex. Not with her housecoat, the comforter and his greatcoat playing chaperone.

He kissed her hard and was whispering hoarsely in her ear before she had a chance to react. "Angels down. A scoopship. It crashed."

"Angels?" Was he crazy?

He kissed her neck. "Not so loud. I don't think the 'danes are listening, but why take chances? Angels. Spacemen. *Peace* and *Freedom.*"

She'd been away too long. She'd never heard spacemen called *Angels.* And— "Crashed?" She kept it to a whisper. "Where?"

"Just over the border in North Dakota. Near Mapleton."

"Great Ghu, Bob. That's on the Ice!"

He whispered, "Yeah. But they're not too far in."

"How do you know about it?"

He snuggled closer and kissed her on the neck again. Maybe sex made a great cover for his visit, but she didn't think he had to lay it on so thick. "We know."

"We?"

"The Worldcon's in Minneapolis-St. Paul this year—"

The World Science Fiction Convention. "I got the invitation, but I didn't dare go. If anyone saw me—"

"—And it was just getting started when the call came down from *Freedom.* Sherrine, they couldn't have picked a better time or place to crash their scoopship. That's why I came to you. Your grandparents live near the crash site."

She wondered if there was a good time for crashing scoopships. "So?"

"We're going to rescue them."

"We? Who's we?"

"The Con Committee, some of the fans—"

"But why tell me, Bob? I'm fafiated. It's been years since I've dared associate with fen."

Too many years, she thought. She had discovered science fiction in childhood, at her neighborhood branch library. She still remembered that first book: *Star Man's Son,* by Andre Norton. Fors had been persecuted because he was different; but he nurtured a secret, a mutant power. Just the sort of hero to appeal to an ugly-duckling little girl who would not act like other little girls.

SF had opened a whole new world to her. A galaxy, a

universe of new worlds. While the other little girls had played with Barbie dolls, Sherrine played with Lummox and Poddy and Arkady and Susan Calvin. While they went to the malls, she went to Trantor and the Witch World. While they wondered what Look was In, she wondered about resource depletion and nuclear war and genetic engineering. Escape literature, they called it. She missed it terribly.

"There is always one moment in childhood," Graham Greene had written in *The Power and the Glory*, "when the door opens and lets the future in." For some people, that door never closed. She thought that Peter Pan had had the right idea all along.

"Why tell *you*? Sherrine, we want you with us. Your grandparents live near the crash site. They've got all sorts of gear we can borrow for the rescue."

"Me?" A tiny trickle of electric current ran up her spine. But . . . *Nah*. "Bob, I don't dare. If my bosses thought I was associating with fen, I'd lose my job."

He grinned. "Yeah. Me, too." And she saw that he had never considered that she might not go.

*'Tis a Proud and Lonely Thing to Be a Fan*, they used to say, laughing. It had become a *very* lonely thing. The Establishment had always been hard on science fiction. The government-funded Arts Councils would pass out tax money to write obscure poetry for "little" magazines, but not to write speculative fiction. "Sci-fi isn't literature." *That* wasn't censorship.

Perversely, people went on buying science fiction without grants. Writers even got rich without government funding. *They couldn't kill us that way!*

Then the Luddites and the Greens had come to power. She had watched science fiction books slowly disappear from the library shelves, beginning with the children's departments. (That wasn't censorship either. Libraries couldn't buy *every* book, now could they? So they bought "realistic" children's books funded by the National Endowment for the Arts, books about death and divorce, and really important things like being overweight or fitting in with the right school crowd.)

Then came paper shortages, and paper allocations. The science fiction sections in the chain stores grew smaller. ("You can't expect us to stock books that aren't selling." And they can't sell if you don't stock them.)

Fantasy wasn't hurt so bad. Fantasy was about wizards

and elves, and being kind to the Earth, and harmony with nature, all things the Greens loved. But science fiction was about science.

Science fiction wasn't exactly outlawed. There was still Freedom of Speech; still a Bill of Rights, even if it wasn't taught much in the schools—even if most kids graduated unable to read well enough to understand it. But a person could get into a lot of unofficial trouble for reading SF or for associating with known fen. She could lose her job, say. Not through government persecution—of course not—but because of "reduction in work force" or "poor job performance" or "uncooperative attitude" or "politically incorrect" or a hundred other phrases. And if the neighbors shunned her, and tradesmen wouldn't deal with her, and stores wouldn't give her credit, who could blame them? Science fiction involved science; and science was a conspiracy to pollute the environment, "to bring back technology."

Damn right! she thought savagely. We do conspire to bring back technology. Some of us are crazy enough to think that there are alternatives to freezing in the dark. *And some of us are even crazy enough to try to rescue marooned spacemen before they freeze, or disappear into protective custody.*

Which could be dangerous. The government might declare you mentally ill, and help you.

She shuddered at that thought. She pushed and rolled Bob aside. She sat up and pulled the comforter up tight around herself. "Do you know what it was that attracted me to science fiction?"

He raised himself on one elbow, blinked at her change of subject, and looked quickly around the room, as if suspecting bugs. "No, what?"

"Not Fandom. I was reading the true quill long before I knew about Fandom and cons and such. No, it was the feeling of hope."

"Hope?"

"Even in the most depressing dystopia, there's still the notion that the future is something we build. It doesn't just happen. You can't predict the future, but you can invent it. Build it. That is a hopeful idea, even when the building collapses."

Bob was silent for a moment. Then he nodded. "Yeah. Nobody's building the future anymore. 'We live in an Age of Limited Choices.'" He quoted the government line without cracking a smile. "Hell, you don't *take* choices off a list. You *make* choices and *add* them to the list. Speaking of which, have you made your choice?"

That electric tickle . . . "Are they even alive?"

"So far. I understand it was some kind of miracle that they landed at all. They're unconscious, but not hurt bad. They're hooked up to some sort of magical medical widgets and the Angels overhead are monitoring. But if we don't get them out soon, they'll freeze to death."

She bit her lip. "And you think we can reach them in time?"

Bob shrugged.

"You want me to risk my life on the Ice, defy the government and probably lose my job in a crazy, amateur effort to rescue two spacemen who might easily be dead by the time we reach them."

He scratched his beard. "Is that quixotic, or what?"

"Quixotic. Give me four minutes."

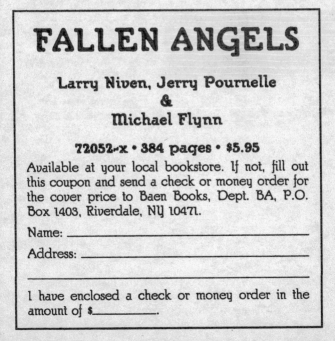